Without a Doubt

SERIES

Irish Born Trilogy
Born in Fire • Born in Ice • Born in Shame

Dream Trilogy
Daring to Dream • Holding the Dream • Finding the Dream

Chesapeake Bay Saga
Sea Swept • Rising Tides • Inner Harbor • Chesapeake Blue

Gallaghers of Ardmore Trilogy
Jewels of the Sun • Tears of the Moon • Heart of the Sea

Three Sisters Island Trilogy
Dance Upon the Air • Heaven and Earth • Face the Fire

Key Trilogy
Key of Light • Key of Knowledge • Key of Valor

In the Garden Trilogy
Blue Dahlia • Black Rose • Red Lily

Circle Trilogy
Morrigan's Cross • Dance of the Gods • Valley of Silence

Sign of Seven Trilogy
Blood Brothers • The Hollow • The Pagan Stone

Bride Quartet
Vision in White • Bed of Roses • Savor the Moment • Happy Ever After

The Inn Boonsboro Trilogy
The Next Always • The Last Boyfriend • The Perfect Hope

The Cousins O'Dwyer Trilogy
Dark Witch • Shadow Spell • Blood Magick

The Guardians Trilogy
Stars of Fortune • Bay of Sighs • Island of Glass

Chronicles of The One
Year One • Of Blood and Bone • The Rise of Magicks

The Dragon Heart Legacy
The Awakening • The Becoming

eBooks by Nora Roberts

Cordina's Royal Family
Affaire Royale • *Command Performance* • *The Playboy Prince* • *Cordina's Crown Jewel*

The Donovan Legacy
Captivated • *Entranced* • *Charmed* • *Enchanted*

The O'Hurleys
The Last Honest Woman • *Dance to the Piper* • *Skin Deep* • *Without a Trace*

Night Tales
Night Shift • *Night Shadow* • *Nightshade* • *Night Smoke* • *Night Shield*

The MacGregors
The Winning Hand • *The Perfect Neighbor* • *All the Possibilities* • *One Man's Art* • *Tempting Fate* • *Playing the Odds* • *The MacGregor Brides* • *The MacGregor Grooms* • *Rebellion/In from the Cold* • *For Now, Forever*

The Calhouns
Suzanna's Surrender • *Megan's Mate* • *Courting Catherine* • *A Man for Amanda* • *For the Love of Lilah*

Irish Legacy
Irish Rose • *Irish Rebel* • *Irish Thoroughbred*

Jack's Stories
Best Laid Plans • *Loving Jack* • *Lawless*

Summer Love • *Boundary Lines* • *Dual Image* • *First Impressions* • *The Law Is a Lady* • *Local Hero* • *This Magic Moment* • *The Name of the Game* • *Partners* • *Temptation* • *The Welcoming* • *Opposites Attract* • *Time Was* • *Times Change* • *Gabriel's Angel* • *Holiday Wishes* • *The Heart's Victory* • *The Right Path* • *Rules of the Game* • *Search for Love* • *Blithe Images* • *From This Day* • *Song of the West* • *Island of Flowers* • *Her Mother's Keeper* • *Untamed* • *Sullivan's Woman* • *Less of a Stranger* • *Reflections* • *Dance of Dreams* • *Storm Warning* • *Once More with Feeling* • *Endings and Beginnings* • *A Matter of Choice* • *Summer Desserts* • *Lessons Learned* • *One Summer* • *The Art of Deception* • *Second Nature* • *Treasures Lost, Treasures Found*

Nora Roberts & J. D. Robb

Remember When

J. D. Robb

ANTHOLOGIES

From the Heart • *A Little Magic* • *A Little Fate*

Moon Shadows
(with Jill Gregory, Ruth Ryan Langan, and Marianne Willman)

The Once Upon Series
(with Jill Gregory, Ruth Ryan Langan, and Marianne Willman)
Once Upon a Castle • *Once Upon a Star* • *Once Upon a Dream* •
Once Upon a Rose • *Once Upon a Kiss* • *Once Upon a Midnight*

Silent Night
(with Susan Plunkett, Dee Holmes, and Claire Cross)

Out of This World
(with Laurell K. Hamilton, Susan Krinard, and Maggie Shayne)

Bump in the Night
(with Mary Blayney, Ruth Ryan Langan, and Mary Kay McComas)

Dead of Night
(with Mary Blayney, Ruth Ryan Langan, and Mary Kay McComas)

Three in Death
Suite 606
(with Mary Blayney, Ruth Ryan Langan, and Mary Kay McComas)

In Death
The Lost
(with Patricia Gaffney, Ruth Ryan Langan, and Mary Blayney)

The Other Side
(with Mary Blayney, Patricia Gaffney, Ruth Ryan Langan,
and Mary Kay McComas)

Time of Death
The Unquiet
(with Mary Blayney, Patricia Gaffney, Ruth Ryan Langan,
and Mary Kay McComas)

Mirror, Mirror
(with Mary Blayney, Elaine Fox, Mary Kay McComas, and R. C. Ryan)

Down the Rabbit Hole
(with Mary Blayney, Elaine Fox, Mary Kay McComas, and R. C. Ryan)

ALSO AVAILABLE . . .
The Official Nora Roberts Companion
(edited by Denise Little and Laura Hayden)

Without a Doubt

Nora Roberts

ST. MARTIN'S GRIFFIN
NEW YORK

Published in the United States by St. Martin's Griffin, an imprint of St. Martin's Publishing Group

www.stmartins.com

Library of Congress Control Number: 2021948872

ISBN 978-1-250-83178-1 (trade paperback)

Our books may be purchased in bulk for promotional, educational, or business use. Please contact your local bookseller or the Macmillan Corporate and Premium Sales Department at 1-800-221-7945, extension 5442, or by email at MacmillanSpecialMarkets@macmillan.com.

Night Moves first published by St. Martin's Paperbacks

This Magic Moment first published by St. Martin's Paperbacks

First St. Martin's Griffin Edition: 2021

10 9 8 7 6 5 4 3 2 1

Night Moves

Chapter 1

"What the hell are you doing in a place like this?"

Maggie, on her hands and knees, didn't look up. "C.J., you're playing the same old song."

C.J. pulled down the hem of his cashmere sweater. He was a man who made worry an art, and he worried about Maggie. Someone had to. Frustrated, he looked down at the sable-brown hair twisted untidily into a knot on top of her head. Her neck was slender, pale, her shoulders curved slightly forward as she rested her weight on her forearms. She had a delicate build, with the kind of fragility C.J. had always associated with nineteenth-century English aristocratic ladies. Though perhaps they, too, had possessed endless stores of strength and endurance under frail bones and porcelain skin.

She wore a T-shirt and jeans that were both faded and slightly damp from perspiration. When he looked at her hands, fine-boned, elegant hands, and saw they were grimy, he shuddered. He knew the magic they were capable of.

A phase, he thought. She was just going through a phase. After two marriages and a few affairs, C.J. understood that women went through odd moods from time to time. He brushed at his trim, sandy mustache with one finger. It was up to him to guide her back, gently, to the real world.

As he glanced around at nothing but trees and rocks and isolation, he wondered, fleetingly, if there were bears in the woods. In the real world, such things were kept in zoos. Keeping a nervous lookout for suspicious movements, he tried again.

"Maggie, just how long are you going to go on this way?"

"What way is that, C.J.?" Her voice was low, husky, as if she'd just been awakened. It was a voice that made most men wish they'd awakened her.

The woman was infuriating. C.J. tugged a hand through his carefully styled, blow-dried hair. What was she doing three thousand miles from L.A., wasting herself on this dirty work? He had a responsibility to her and, damn it, to himself. C.J. blew out a long breath, an old habit he had whenever he met with opposition. Negotiations were, after all, his business. It was up to him to talk some sense into her. He shifted his feet, careful to keep his polished loafers out of the dirt. "Babe, I love you. You know I do. Come home."

This time Maggie turned her head, looking up with a flash of a smile that involved every inch of her face—the mouth that stopped just short of being too wide, the chin a bit pointed, the sweep of cheekbones that gave her face a diamond shape. Her eyes, big, round and shades darker than her hair, added that final spark of animation. It wasn't a stunning face. You'd tell yourself that while you tried to focus in on the reason you were stunned. Even now, without makeup, with a long streak of topsoil across one cheek, the face involved you. Maggie Fitzgerald involved you because she was exactly what she seemed. Interesting. Interested.

Now she sat back on her haunches, blowing a wisp of hair out of her eyes as she looked up at the man who was frowning at her. She felt a tug of affection, a tug of amusement. Both had always come easily to her. "C.J., I love you, too. Now stop acting like an old woman."

"You don't belong here," he began, more exasperated than insulted. "You shouldn't be grubbing around on your hands and knees—"

"I like it," she said simply.

It was the very simplicity of the tone that told him he had a real problem. If she'd shouted, argued, his chances of turning her around would've been all but secured. But when she was like this, calmly stubborn, changing her mind would be like climbing Mount Everest. Treacherous and exhausting. Because he was a clever man, C.J. changed tactics.

"Maggie, I can certainly understand why you might like to get away for a while, rest a bit. No one deserves it more." That was a nice touch, he thought, because it was true. "Why don't you take a couple weeks in Cancún, or go on a shopping spree in Paris?"

"Mmm." Maggie shifted on her knees and fluffed up the petals of the pansies she was planting. They looked, she decided, a bit sick. "Hand me that watering can, will you?"

"You're not listening."

"Yes, I am." Stretching over, she retrieved the can herself. "I've been to Cancún, and I have so many clothes now I left half of them in storage in L.A."

Without breaking stride, C.J. tried a different turn. "It's not just me," he began again, watching as she drenched the pansies. "Everyone who knows you, who knows about this, thinks you've—"

"Slipped a gear?" Maggie supplied. Overdid the water, she decided as the saturated blossoms drooped. She had a lot to learn about the basics of country life. "C.J., instead of nagging me and trying to talk me into doing something I've no intention of doing, why don't you come down here and give me a hand?"

"A hand?" His voice held the slightly appalled note it might have if she'd suggested he dilute prime scotch with tap water. Maggie chuckled.

"Pass me that flat of petunias." She stuck the small spade in the ground again, fighting the rocky soil. "Gardening's good for you. It gets you back in touch with nature."

"I've no desire to touch nature."

This time she laughed and lifted her face to the sky. No, the closest C.J. would come to nature would be a chlorinated pool—solar-heated. Up to a few months ago she'd barely gotten much closer herself. She'd certainly never attempted to. But now she'd found something—something she hadn't even been looking for. If she hadn't come to the East Coast to collaborate on the score for a new musical, if she hadn't taken an impulsive drive south after the long, grueling sessions had ended, she never would've happened on the sleepy little town tucked into the Blue Ridge.

Do we ever know where we belong, Maggie wondered, unless we're lucky enough to stumble onto our own personal space? She only knew that she'd been heading nowhere in particular and she'd come home.

Maybe it had been fate that had led her into Morganville, a cluster of houses cupped in the foothills that boasted a population of 142. From the town proper, it spread out into farms and isolated mountain homes. If fate had taken her to Morganville, it had again taken her past the sign that listed the sale of a house and twelve acres. There'd been no moment of indecision, no quibbling over the price, no last-minute doubts. Maggie had met the terms and had had the deed in her hand within thirty days.

Looking up at the three-story frame house, with shutters still hanging crooked, Maggie could well imagine her friends and colleagues wondering about her mental state. She'd left her Italian-marble entrance hall and mosaic-tiled pool for rusty hinges and rocks. She'd done it without a backward glance.

Maggie patted the dirt around the petunias, then sat back. They looked a bit more spritely than her pansies. Maybe she was beginning to get the hang of it. "What do you think?"

"I think you should come back to L.A. and finish the score."

"I meant the flowers." She brushed off her jeans as she rose. "In any case, I am finishing the score—right here."

"Maggie, how can you work here?" C.J. exploded. He tossed out both arms in a gesture she'd always admired for its unapologetic theatrics. "How can you live here? This place isn't even civilized."

"Why? Because there's no health club and boutique on every other corner?" Wanting to temper the words, she tucked a hand through C.J.'s arm. "Go ahead, take a deep breath. The clean air won't hurt you."

"Smog's underrated," he mumbled as he shifted his feet again. Professionally he was her agent, but personally C.J. considered himself her friend, perhaps her best friend since Jerry had died. Thinking of that, he changed his tone again. This time it was gentle. "Look, Maggie, I know you've been through some rough times. Maybe L.A. has too many memories for you to deal with right now. But you can't bury yourself."

"I'm not burying myself." She put her hands on his forearms, squeezing for both emphasis and support. "And I buried Jerry nearly two years ago. That was another part of my life, C.J., and has nothing to do with this. This is home. I don't know how else to explain it." She slid her hands down to his, forgetting hers were smeared with earth. "This is my mountain now, and I'm happier here, more settled, than I ever was in Los Angeles."

He knew he was beating his head against a wall, but opted to give it one more shot. "Maggie." He slipped an arm around her shoulder, as if, she thought ruefully, she was a small child needing guidance. "Look at that place." He let the silence hang a moment while they both studied the house on the rise above. He noticed that the porch was missing several boards and that the paint on the trim was peeling badly. Maggie saw the sun reflecting off the window glass in rainbows. "You can't possibly be serious about living there."

"A little paint, a few nails." She shrugged it away. Long ago she'd learned that surface problems were best ignored. It was the problem simmering under the surface, not quite visible, that had to be dealt with. "It has such possibilities, C.J."

"The biggest one is that it'll fall down on your head."

"I had the roof fixed last week—a local man."

"Maggie, I'm not at all convinced there are any local men, or women, within ten miles. This place doesn't look fit for anything but elves and gnomes."

"Well, he might've been a gnome." Her sense of fun spurred her on as she stretched her back muscles. "He was about five foot five, stocky as a bull and somewhere around a hundred and two. His name was Bog."

"Maggie—"

"He was very helpful," she went on. "He and his boy are coming back to deal with the porch and some of the other major repairs."

"All right, so you've got a gnome to do some hammering and sawing. What about this?" He swept his hand around to take in the surrounding land. It was rocky, uneven and overgrown with weeds and thickets. Not even a dedicated optimist could've considered any part of it a lawn. A burly tree slanted dangerously toward the house itself, while thorny vines and wildflowers scrambled for space. There was a pervading smell of earth and green.

"Like Sleeping Beauty's castle," Maggie murmured. "I'll be sorry in a way to hack it down, but Mr. Bog has that under control, too."

"He does excavation work, too?"

Maggie tilted her head and arched her brows. It was a look that made anyone over forty remember her mother. "He recommended a landscaper. Mr. Bog assures me that Cliff Delaney is the best man in the county. He's coming by this afternoon to take a look at the place."

"If he's a smart man, he'll take one look at that gully you call a road leading up here and keep on going."

"But you brought your rented Mercedes all the way up." Turning, she threw her arms around his neck and kissed him. "Don't think I don't appreciate that or the fact that you flew in from the Coast or that you care enough to be concerned. I appreciate all of it. I appreciate you." She ruffled his hair, something no one else would've gotten away with. "Trust my judgment on this, C.J. I really do know what I'm doing. Professionally, my work can't do anything but improve here."

"That's yet to be seen," he muttered, but lifted a hand to touch her cheek. She was still young enough to have foolish dreams, he thought. Still sweet enough to believe in them. "You know it's not your work I'm worried about."

"I know." Her voice softened, and with it her eyes, her mouth. She was not a woman who guided her emotions, but one who was guided by them. "I need the peace here. Do you know, this is the first time in my life I've gotten off the merry-go-round? I'm enjoying the solid ground, C.J."

He knew her well and understood that there was no moving her, for the moment, from the position she'd taken. He understood, too, that from birth her life had been ribboned with the stuff of fantasies—and of nightmares. Perhaps she did need to compensate, for a time.

"I've got a plane to catch," he grumbled. "As long as you insist on staying here, I want you to call me every day."

Maggie kissed him again. "Once a week," she countered. "You'll have the completed score for *Heat Dance* in ten days." With her arm around his waist, she led him to the end of the uneven, overgrown path where his Mercedes sat in incongruous splendor. "I love the film, C.J. It's even better than I thought it would be when I first read the script. The music's all but writing itself."

He only grunted and cast one look behind him at the house. "If you get lonely—"

"I won't." With a quick laugh, Maggie nudged him into the car. "It's been enlightening discovering how self-sufficient I can be. Now, have a nice trip back and stop worrying about me."

Fat chance, he thought, automatically reaching in his briefcase to make certain his Dramamine was there. "Send me the score, and if it's sensational, I might stop worrying . . . a little."

"It is sensational." She backed off from the car to give him room to turn around. "*I'm* sensational!" she shouted as the Mercedes began to inch around. "Tell everyone back on the Coast that I've decided to buy some goats and chickens."

The Mercedes stopped dead. "Maggie . . ."

Laughing, she waved at him and backed down the path. "Not yet . . . but maybe in the fall." She decided it was best to reassure him, or else he might get out and start again. "Oh, and send me some Godiva chocolates."

That was more like it, C.J. thought, and put the car in gear again. She'd be back in L.A. in six weeks. He glanced in his rearview mirror as he started to drive away. He could see her, small and slender, still laughing, against the backdrop of the overgrown land, greening trees and dilapidated house. Once again he shuddered, but this time it wasn't from an offense of his sensibilities. This time it was from something like fear. He had a sudden flash of certainty that she wasn't safe there.

Shaking his head, C.J. reached in his pocket for his antacids as the car bumped noisily over a rock. Everyone told him he worried too much.

Lonely, Maggie thought as she watched the Mercedes bump and wind its way down her excuse for a lane. No, she wasn't lonely. She was as certain as she'd ever been about anything that she'd never be lonely here. She felt an unexpected sense of foreboding that she shrugged off as ridiculous.

Wrapping her arms around herself, she turned in two slow circles. Trees rose up out of the rocky hillside. The leaves were hardly more than buds now, but in a few weeks they would grow and spread, turning the woods into a lush cover of green. She liked to imagine it that way and to try to picture it in the dead of winter— white, all white and black with ice clinging to the branches and shimmering on the rocks. In the fall there'd be a tapestry outside every window. She was far from lonely.

For the first time in her life, she had a chance to put her own stamp on a place. It wouldn't be a copy of anything she'd had before or anything that'd been given to her. It was hers, absolutely, and so were any mistakes she made here, any triumphs. There'd be no press to compare this isolated spot in western Maryland with her mother's mansion in Beverly Hills or her father's villa in the south of France. If she was lucky, very, very lucky, Maggie thought with a satisfied sigh, there'd be no press at all. She could make her music and live her life in peace and solitude.

If she stood very still, if she closed her eyes and didn't move, she could hear the music all around her. Not birdsong but the ruffle of air through branches and tiny leaves. If she concentrated, she could hear the faint trickle of the narrow creek that ran along the other side of the lane. The quality of silence was rich, flowing over her like a symphony.

There was a place for glitz, she mused, and for glamour. She simply didn't want that place any longer. The truth was she hadn't wanted that place for a very long time but hadn't known the way out. When your birth had been celebrated by the international press, your first step, your first words, cataloged for the public, it was natural to forget there was another way of life.

Her mother had been one of the greatest blues and ballad singers in America, her father a child actor turned successful film director. Their courtship and marriage had been followed religiously by fans around the world. The birth of their daughter had been an event treated like the birth of royalty. And Maggie had lived the life of a pampered princess. Gold carousels and white fur coats. She'd been lucky because her parents had adored her, and each other. That had compensated for the make-believe, often hard-edged world of show business, with all its demands and inconstancy. Her world had been cushioned by wealth and love, rippled continually with publicity.

The paparazzi haunted her on dates through her teenage years—to her amusement but often to the boys' frustration. Maggie had accepted the fact that her life was public domain. It had never been otherwise.

And when her parents' private plane had crashed into the Swiss Alps, the press had frozen her grief in glossies and newsprint. She hadn't tried to stop it; she'd realized that the world had mourned with her. She'd been eighteen when the fabric of her world had torn.

Then there had been Jerry. First friend, then lover, then husband. With him, her life had drifted into more fantasy, and more tragedy.

She wouldn't think of any of that now, Maggie told herself as she picked up her spade and began to fight the tough soil again. All that was really left of that portion of her life was her music. That she would never give up. She couldn't have if she'd tried. It was part of her the way her eyes and ears were part of her. She composed words and music and twined them together, not effortlessly, as it sometimes seemed from the fluid finished result, but obsessively, wonderingly, constantly. Unlike her mother, she didn't perform but fed other performers with her gift.

At twenty-eight, she had two Oscars, five Grammys and a Tony. She could sit at the piano and play any song she'd ever written from memory. The awards were still in the packing boxes that had been shipped from L.A.

The little flower plot she was planting in a spot perhaps no one would see but herself was a labor of love with no guarantee of success. It was enough that it gave her pleasure to add her own peculiar spot of color to the land she'd claimed as hers. Maggie began to sing as she worked. She'd completely forgotten her former feeling of apprehension.

Normally he didn't do the estimating and initial planning on a job himself. Not anymore. For the past six years Cliff Delaney had been in the position of being able to send one or two of his best men out on the first stage of a project; then he would fine-tune. If the job was interesting enough, he would visit the site while work was in progress, perhaps handle some of the grading and planting himself. He was making an exception.

He knew the old Morgan place. It had been built by a Morgan, even as the tiny community a few miles away had been named after one. For ten years, since William Morgan's car had crashed into the Potomac, the house had stood empty. The house had always been stern, the land formidable. But with the right touch, the right insight, Cliff knew, it could be magnificent. He had his doubts that the lady from L.A. had the right insight.

He knew of her. Naturally he knew of her. Anyone who hadn't

spent the last twenty-eight years in a cave knew Maggie Fitzgerald. At the moment, she was the biggest news in Morganville—all but eclipsing the hot gossip of Lloyd Messner's wife running off with the bank manager.

It was a simple town, the kind that moved slowly. The kind of town where everyone took pride in the acquisition of a new fire engine and the yearly Founder's Day parade. That's why Cliff chose to live there after he'd reached a point where he could live anywhere he chose. He'd grown up there and understood the people, their unity and their possessiveness. He understood their failings. More, perhaps much more, than that, he understood the land. He had serious doubts that the glamorous songwriter from California would understand either.

C.J. had estimated six weeks before she flew back. Cliff, without ever setting eyes on her, cut that in half. But perhaps before Maggie Fitzgerald grew bored with her shot at rural living, he could put his own mark on the land.

He turned off the paved road onto the quarter-mile lane that cut through the Morgan property. It had been years since he'd been on it, and it was worse than he remembered. Rain and neglect had worn ruts in the dirt. From both sides of the lane, branches reached out to whip at the truck. The first order of business would be the lane itself, Cliff thought as his small pickup bounced over ruts. It would be graded, leveled, filled. Drainage ditches would have to be dug, gravel spread.

He went slowly, not for the truck's sake but because the land on either side of the lane appealed to him. It was wild and primitive, timeless. He'd want to work with that, incorporate his own talents with the genius of nature. If Maggie Fitzgerald wanted blacktop and hothouse plants, she'd come to the wrong place. He'd be the first one to let her know.

If he had a distrust of outsiders, Cliff considered he'd come by it honestly. They came, often from the rich suburbs of D.C., and wanted their lawns flat and free of the poplar and oak that had first claim. They wanted neat little flowers in orderly rows. Lawns should be even, so that their mowers could handle the weekly cutting effortlessly. What they wanted, Cliff thought derisively, was to say they lived *in the country* while they brought city attitudes and city tastes with them. By the time he rounded the last bend, he was already out of patience with Maggie Fitzgerald.

Maggie heard the truck coming before it was in sight. That was something else she liked about her new home. It was quiet—so quiet that the sound of a truck, which would have been ignored in the city, brought her to attention. Halfheartedly brushing her hands on the seat of her pants, she rose from her planting, then shielded her eyes against the sun.

While she watched, the truck rounded the curve and parked where the Mercedes had been only an hour before. A bit dusty from the road, with its chrome dull rather than gleaming, the truck looked much more comfortable than the luxury car had. Though she couldn't yet see the driver through the glare of sun on windshield, Maggie smiled and lifted a hand in greeting.

The first thing Cliff thought was that she was smaller than he'd expected, more delicate in build. The Fitzgeralds had always been larger than life. He wondered, with a quick grunt, if she'd want to raise orchids to match her style. He got out of the truck, convinced she was going to annoy him.

Perhaps it was because she'd been expecting another Mr. Bog that Maggie felt a flutter of surprise when Cliff stepped out of the truck. Or perhaps, she thought with her usual penchant for honesty, it was because he was quite simply a magnificent example of manhood. Six-two, Maggie decided, with an impressive breadth of shoulders. Black hair that had been ruffled by the wind through the open truck windows fell over his forehead and ears in loose waves. He didn't smile, but his mouth was sculpted, sensual. She had a fleeting regret that he wore dark glasses so that his eyes were hidden. She judged people from their eyes.

Instead, Maggie summed him up from the way he moved— loosely, confidently. Athletic, she concluded, as he strode over the uneven ground. Definitely self-assured. He was still a yard away when she got the unmistakable impression that he wasn't particularly friendly.

"Miss Fitzgerald?"

"Yes." Giving him a neutral smile, Maggie held out a hand. "You're from Delaney's?"

"That's right." Their hands met, briefly, hers soft, his hard, both of them capable. Without bothering to identify himself, Cliff scanned the grounds. "You wanted an estimate on some landscaping."

Maggie followed his gaze, and this time her smile held amusement. "Obviously I need something. Does your company perform miracles?"

"We do the job." He glanced down at the splash of color behind her, wilted pansies and soggy petunias. Her effort touched something in him that he ignored, telling himself she'd be bored long before it was time to pull the first weeds. "Why don't you tell me what you have in mind?"

"A glass of iced tea at the moment. Look around while I get some—then we'll talk about it." She'd been giving orders without a second thought all her life. After giving this one, Maggie turned and climbed the rickety steps to the porch. Behind the tinted glasses, Cliff's eyes narrowed.

Designer jeans, he thought with a smirk as he watched the graceful sway of hips before the screen door banged shut at her back. And the solitaire on the thin chain around her neck had been no less than a carat. Just what game was little Miss Hollywood playing? She'd left a trace of her scent behind, something soft and subtle that would nag at a man's senses. Shrugging, he turned his back on the house and looked at the land.

It could be shaped and structured without being tamed. It should never lose its basic unruly sense by being manicured, though he admitted the years of neglect had given the rougher side of nature too much of an advantage. Still, he wouldn't level it for her. Cliff had turned down more than one job because the client had insisted on altering the land's personality. Even with that, he wouldn't have called himself an artist. He was a businessman. His business was the land.

He walked farther away from the house, toward a grove of trees overrun with tangling vines, greedy saplings and thistles. Without effort he could see it cleared of undergrowth, richly mulched, naturalized perhaps with jonquils. That one section would personify peace, as he saw it. Hitching his thumbs in his back pockets, Cliff reflected that from the reams that had been written about Maggie Fitzgerald over the years, she didn't go in much for peace.

Jet-setting, the fast lane, glitter and glitz. What the hell had she moved out here for?

Before he heard her, Cliff caught a fresh whiff of her perfume. When he turned, she was a few paces behind him, two glasses in her hand. She watched him steadily with a curiosity she didn't bother to hide. He learned something more about her then as she stood with her eyes on his face and the sun at her back. She was the most alluring woman he'd ever met, though he'd be damned if he knew why.

Maggie approached him and offered a glass of frosty tea. "Want to hear my ideas?"

The voice had something to do with it, Cliff decided. An innocent question, phrased in that sultry voice, conjured up a dozen dark pleasures. He took a slow sip. "That's what I'm here for," he told her with a curtness he'd never shown any potential client.

Her brow lifted at the tone, the only sign that she'd noticed his rudeness. With that attitude, she thought, he wouldn't have the job for long. Then again, he didn't strike her as a man who'd work for someone else. "Indeed you are, Mr. . . . ?"

"Delaney."

"Ah, the man himself." That made more sense, she decided, if his attitude didn't. "Well, Mr. Delaney, I'm told you're the best. I believe in having the best, so . . ." Thoughtfully, she ran a fingertip down the length of her glass, streaking the film of moisture. "I'll tell you what I want, and you tell me if you can deliver."

"Fair enough." He didn't know why her simple statement should annoy him any more than he could understand why he was just noticing how smooth her skin was and how compelling were those large velvet eyes. Like a doe's, Cliff realized. He wasn't a man who hunted but a man who watched. "I'll tell you up front that my company has a policy against destroying the natural terrain in order to make the land into something it's not. This is rough country, Miss Fitzgerald. It's supposed to be. If you want an acre or two of manicured lawn, you've bought the wrong land and called the wrong landscaper."

It took a great deal to fire up her temper. Maggie had worked long and hard to control a natural tendency toward quick fury in order to block the label of temperamental daughter of temperamental artists. "Decent of you to point it out," she managed after three long, quiet breaths.

"I don't know why you bought the place," he began.

"I don't believe I've offered that information."

"And it's none of my business," Cliff finished with an acknowledging nod. "But this—" he indicated the property with a gesture of his hand "—is my business."

"You're a bit premature in condemning me, aren't you, Mr. Delaney?" To keep herself in check, Maggie took a sip of tea. It was cold, with a faint bite of lemon. "I've yet to ask you to bring on the bulldozers and chain saws." She ought to tell him to haul his buns into his truck and take off. Almost before she could wonder why she didn't, the answer came. Instinct. Instinct had brought her to Morganville and to the property she now stood on. It was instinct that told her he was indeed the best. Nothing else would do for her land. To give herself a moment to be sure she didn't do anything rash, Maggie took another sip from her glass.

"That grove there," she began briskly. "I want it cleared of undergrowth. It can't be enjoyed if you have to fight your way through thorns and thickets to walk in it." She shot him a look. "Don't you want to take notes?"

He watched her, consideringly. "No. Go on."

"All right. This stretch right here, in front of the porch—I imagine that was a lawn of sorts at one time." She turned, looking at the knee-high weeds. "It should be again, but I want enough room to plant, I don't know, some pines, maybe, to keep the line between lawn and woods from being too marked. Then there's the way the whole thing just sort of falls away until it reaches the lane below."

Forgetting her annoyance for the moment, Maggie made her way across the relatively flat land to where it sloped steeply down. Weeds, some of them as tall as she, grew in abundance wherever the rocks would permit. "It's certainly too steep for grass to be practical," she said half to herself. "But I can't just let all these weeds have their way. I'd like some color, but I don't want uniformity."

"You'll want some evergreens," he said from behind her. "Some spreading junipers along the bottom edge of the whole slope, a few coming farther up over there, with some forsythia mixed in. Here, where the grade's not so dramatic, you'd want some low ground cover." He could see phlox spilling and bumping over the rocks. "That tree's got to come down," he went on, frowning at the one that leaned precariously toward her roof. "And there's two, maybe three, on the rise behind the house that've got to be taken down before they fall down."

She was frowning now, but she'd always believed in letting an expert set the plan. "Okay, but I don't want you to cut down anything that doesn't have to be cleared."

Maggie could only see her own reflection in his glasses when he faced her. "I never do." He turned and began to walk around the side of the house. "That's another problem," Cliff continued without checking to see if she was following. "The way that dirt wall's eroding down from the cliff here. You're going to end up with a tree or a boulder in your kitchen when you least expect it."

"So?" Maggie tilted her head so she could scan the ridge behind her house. "You're the expert."

"It'll need to be recut, tapered back some. Then I'd put up a retaining wall, three, maybe four, feet high. Crown vetch'd hold the dirt above that. Plant it along the entire slope. It's hardy and fast."

"All right." It sounded reasonable. He sounded more reasonable,

Maggie decided, when he was talking about his business. A man of the land, she mused, and wished again she could see beyond the tinted glass to his eyes. "This part behind the house has to be cleared." She began to fight her way through the weeds and briars as she talked. "I think if I had a walkway of some kind from here to the lane, I could have a rockery . . . here." A vague gesture of her hands indicated the spot she had in mind. "There're plenty of rocks," she muttered, nearly stumbling over one. "Then down here—"

Cliff took her arm before she could start down the slope on the far side of the house. The contact jolted both of them. More surprised than alarmed, Maggie turned her head.

"I wouldn't," Cliff said softly, and she felt a tiny trickle, an odd excitement, sprint up her spine.

"Wouldn't what?" Her chin automatically tilted, her eyes challenged.

"Walk down there." Her skin was soft, Cliff discovered. With his hand wrapped around her arm, he could touch his fingertips to his thumb. Small and soft, he mused, enjoying the feel of his flesh against hers. Too small and soft for land that would fight back at you.

Maggie glanced down to where he held her. She noticed the tan on the back of his hand; she noticed the size and the strength of it. When she noticed her pulse wasn't quite steady, she lifted her gaze again. "Mr. Delaney—"

"Snakes," he said simply, and had the satisfaction of seeing her take two quick steps back. "You're almost sure to have some down in a spot like that. In fact, with the way this place is overgrown, you're likely to have them everywhere."

"Well, then—" Maggie swallowed and made a Herculean effort not to shudder "—maybe you can start the job right away."

For the first time, he smiled, a very slight, very cautious, curving of lips. They'd both forgotten he still held her, but they were standing much closer now, within a hand span of touching. She certainly hadn't reacted the way he'd expected. He wouldn't have been surprised if she'd screeched at the mention of snakes, then had dashed into the house, slamming and locking the door. Her skin was soft, Cliff mused, unconsciously moving his thumb over it. But apparently she wasn't.

"I might be able to send a crew out next week, but the first thing that has to be dealt with is your road."

Maggie dismissed this with a shrug. "Do whatever you think best there, excluding asphalt. It's only a means of getting in and out to me. I want to concentrate on the house and grounds."

"The road's going to run you twelve, maybe fifteen, hundred," he began, but she cut him off again.

"Do what you have to," she told him with the unconscious arrogance of someone who'd never worried about money. "This section here—" She pointed to the steep drop in front of them, making no move this time to go down it. At the base it spread twenty feet wide, perhaps thirty in length, in a wicked maze of thorny vines and weeds as thick at the stem as her thumb. "I want a pond."

Cliff brought his attention back to her. "A pond?"

She gave him a level look and stood her ground. "Allow me one eccentricity, Mr. Delaney. A small one," she continued before he could comment. "There's certainly enough room, and it seems to me that this section here's the worst. It's hardly more than a hole in the ground in a very awkward place. Do you have an objection to water?"

Instead of answering, he studied the ground below them, running through the possibilities. The truth was, she couldn't have picked a better spot as far as the lay of the land and the angle to the house. It could be done, he mused. It wouldn't be an easy job, but it could be done. And it would be very effective.

"It's going to cost you," he said at length. "You're going to be sinking a lot of cash into this place. If you're weighing that against resale value, I can tell you, this property won't be easy to sell."

It snapped her patience. She was tired, very tired, of having people suggest she didn't know what she was doing. "Mr. Delaney, I'm hiring you to do a job, not to advise me on real estate or my finances. If you can't handle it, just say so and I'll get someone else."

His eyes narrowed. The fingers on her arm tightened fractionally. "I can handle it, Miss Fitzgerald. I'll draw up an estimate and a contract. They'll be in the mail tomorrow. If you still want the job done after you've looked them over, call my office." Slowly, he released her arm, then handed her back the glass of tea. He left her there, near the edge where the slope gave way to gully as he headed back toward his truck. "By the way," he said without turning around, "you overwatered your pansies."

Maggie let out one long, simmering breath and dumped the tepid tea on the ground at her feet.

Chapter 2

When she was alone, Maggie went back inside, through the back door, which creaked ominously on its hinges. She wasn't going to think about Cliff Delaney. In fact, she doubted if she'd see him again. He'd send crews out to deal with the actual work, and whatever they had to discuss would be done via phone or letter. Better that way, Maggie decided. He'd been unfriendly, abrupt and annoying, though his mouth had been attractive, she reflected, even kind.

She was halfway through the kitchen when she remembered the glasses in her hand. Turning back, she crossed the scarred linoleum to set them both in the sink, then leaned on the windowsill to look out at the rise behind her house. Even as she watched, a few loose stones and dirt slid down the wall. A couple of hard rains, she mused, and half that bank would be at her back door. A retaining wall. Maggie nodded. Cliff Delaney obviously knew his business.

There was just enough breeze to carry a hint of spring to her. Far back in the woods a bird she couldn't see sang out as though it would never stop. Listening, she forgot the eroding wall and the exposed roots of trees that were much too close to its edge. She forgot the rudeness, and the attraction, of a stranger. If she looked up, far up, she could see where the tops of the trees met the sky.

She wondered how this view would change with the seasons and found herself impatient to experience them all. Perhaps she'd never realized how badly she'd needed a place to herself, time to herself, until she'd found it.

With a sigh, Maggie moved away from the window. It was time to get down to work if she was to deliver the finished score as promised. She walked down the hall, where the wallpaper was peeling and curled, and turned into what had once been the back parlor. It was now her music room.

Boxes she hadn't even thought of unpacking stood in a pile against one wall. A few odd pieces of furniture that had come with the house sat hidden under dustcovers. The windows were uncurtained, the floor was uncarpeted. There were pale squares intermittently on the walls where pictures had once hung. In the center of the room, glossy and elegant, stood her baby grand. A single box lay open beside it, and from this Maggie took a sheet of staff paper. Tucking a pencil behind her ear, she sat.

For a moment she did nothing else, just sat in the silence while she let the music come and play in her head. She knew what she wanted for this segment—something dramatic, something strong and full of power. Behind her closed eyelids she could see the scene from the film sweep by. It was up to her to underscore, to accentuate, to take the mood and make it music.

Reaching out, she switched on the cassette tape and began.

She let the notes build in strength as she continued to visualize the scene her music would amplify. She only worked on films she had a feeling for. Though the Oscars told her she excelled in this area of work, Maggie's true affection was for the single song— words and music.

Maggie had always compared the composing of a score to the building of a bridge. First came the blueprint, the overall plan. Then the construction had to be done, slowly, meticulously, until each end fit snugly on solid ground, a flawless arch in between. It was a labor of precision.

The single song was a painting, to be created as the mood dictated. The single song could be written from nothing more than a phrasing of words or notes. It could encapsulate mood, emotion or a story in a matter of minutes. It was a labor of love.

When she worked, she forgot the time, forgot everything but the careful structuring of notes to mood. Her fingers moved over the piano keys as she repeated the same segment again and again, changing perhaps no more than one note until her instincts told her it was right. An hour passed, then two. She didn't grow weary or bored or impatient with the constant repetition. Music was her business, but it was also her lover.

She might not have heard the knock if she hadn't paused to rewind the tape. Disoriented, she ignored it, waiting for the maid to answer before she recalled where she was.

No maids, Maggie, she reminded herself. *No gardener, no cook. It's all up to you now.* The thought pleased her. If there was no one to answer to her, she had no one to answer to.

Rising, she went back into the hall and down to the big front door. She didn't have to develop the country habit of leaving the doors unlocked. In L.A., there'd been servants to deal with bolts and chains and security systems. Maggie never gave them a thought. Taking the knob in both hands, she twisted and tugged. She reminded herself to tell Mr. Bog about the sticking problem as the door swung open.

On the porch stood a tall, prim-looking woman in her early fifties. Her hair was a soft, uniform gray worn with more tidiness than style. Faded blue eyes studied Maggie from behind rose-framed glasses. If this was the welcome wagon lady, Maggie thought after a glance at the unhappy line of the woman's mouth, she didn't seem thrilled with the job. Much too used to strangers' approaches to be reserved, Maggie tilted her head and smiled.

"Hello, can I help you?"

"You are Miss Fitzgerald?" The voice was low and even, as subdued and inoffensive as her plain, pale coatdress.

"Yes, I am."

"I'm Louella Morgan."

It took Maggie a moment; then the name clicked. Louella Morgan, widow of William Morgan, former owner of the house that was now hers. For an instant Maggie felt like an intruder; then she shook the feeling away and extended her hand. "Hello, Mrs. Morgan. Won't you come in?"

"I don't want to disturb you."

"No, please." As she spoke, she opened the door a bit wider. "I met your daughter when we settled on the house."

"Yes, Joyce told me." Louella's gaze darted around and behind Maggie as she stepped over the threshold. "She never expected to sell so quickly. The property had only been on the market a week."

"I like to think it was fate." Maggie put her weight against the door and pushed until she managed to close it. Definitely a job for Bog, she decided.

"Fate?" Louella turned back from her study of the long, empty hall.

"It just seemed to be waiting for me." Though she found the woman's direct, unsmiling stare odd, Maggie gestured toward the living room. "Come in and sit down," she invited. "Would you like some coffee? Something cold?"

"No, thank you. I'll stay only a minute." Louella did wander into the living room, and though there was a single sofa piled with soft, inviting pillows, she didn't accept Maggie's invitation to sit. She looked at the crumbling wallpaper, the cracked paint and the windows that glistened from Maggie's diligence with ammonia. "I suppose I wanted to see the house again with someone living in it."

Maggie took a look at the almost-empty room. Maybe she'd start stripping off the wallpaper next week. "I guess it'll be a few weeks more before it looks as though someone is."

Louella didn't seem to hear. "I came here as a newlywed." She smiled then, but Maggie didn't see anything happy in it. The eyes, she thought, looked lost, as if the woman had been lost for years. "But then, my husband wanted something more modern, more convenient to town and his business. So we moved, and he rented it out."

Louella focused on Maggie again. "Such a lovely, quiet spot," she murmured. "A pity it's been so neglected over the years."

"It is a lovely spot," Maggie agreed, struggling not to sound as uncomfortable as she felt. "I'm having some work done on both the house and the land . . ." Her voice trailed off when Louella wandered to the front window and stared out. *Heavens*, Maggie thought, searching for something more to say, *what have I got here?* "Ah, of course I plan to do a lot of the painting and papering and such myself."

"The weeds have taken over," Louella said with her back to the room.

Maggie's brows lifted and fell as she wondered what to do next. "Yes, well, Cliff Delaney was out this afternoon to take a look around."

"Cliff." Louella's attention seemed to focus again as she turned back. The light coming through the uncurtained windows made her seem more pale, more insubstantial. "An interesting young man, rather rough-and-ready, but very clever. He'll do well for you here, for the land. He's a cousin of the Morgans, you know." She paused and seemed to laugh, but very softly. "Then, you'll find many Morgans and their kin scattered throughout the county."

A cousin, Maggie mused. Perhaps he'd been unfriendly because he didn't think the property should've been sold to an outsider. Resolutely, she tried to push Cliff Delaney aside. He didn't have to approve. The land was hers.

"The front lawn was lovely once," Louella murmured.

Maggie felt a stirring of pity. "It will be again. The front's going to be cleared and planted. The back, too." Wanting to reassure her, Maggie stepped closer. Both women stood by the window now. "I'm going to have a rock garden, and there'll be a pond where the gully is on the side."

"A pond?" Louella turned and fixed her with another long stare. "You're going to clear out the gully?"

"Yes." Uncomfortable again, Maggie shifted. "It's the perfect place."

Louella ran a hand over the front of her purse as if she were wiping something away. "I used to have a rock garden. Sweet william and azure Adams. There was wisteria beneath my bedroom window, and roses, red roses, climbing on a trellis."

"I'd like to have seen it," Maggie said gently. "It must've been beautiful."

"I have pictures."

"Do you?" Struck with an idea, Maggie forgot her discomfort. "Perhaps I could see them. They'd help me decide just what to plant."

"I'll see that you get them. You're very kind to let me come in this way." Louella took one last scan of the room. "The house holds memories." When she walked out into the hall, Maggie went with her to tug open the front door again. "Goodbye, Miss Fitzgerald."

"Goodbye, Mrs. Morgan." Her pity stirred again, and Maggie reached out to touch the woman's shoulder. "Please, come again."

Louella looked back, her smile very slight, her eyes very tired. "Thank you."

While Maggie watched, she walked to an old, well-preserved Lincoln, then drove slowly down the hill. Vaguely disturbed, Maggie went back into the music room. She hadn't met many residents of Morganville yet, she mused, but they were certainly an interesting bunch.

The noise brought Maggie out of a sound sleep into a drowsy, cranky state. For a moment, as she tried to bury her head under the pillow, she thought she was in New York. The groan and roar sounded like a big, nasty garbage truck. But she wasn't in New York, she thought as she surfaced, rubbing her hands over her eyes. She was in Morganville, and there weren't any garbage trucks. Here you piled your trash into the back of your car or pickup and hauled it to the county dump. Maggie had considered this the height of self-sufficiency.

Still, something was out there.

She lay on her back for a full minute, staring up at the ceiling. The sunlight slanted, low and thin, across her newly purchased quilt. She'd never been a morning person, nor did she intend to have country life change that intimate part of her nature. Warily, she turned her head to look at the clock: 7:05 a.m. Good heavens.

It was a struggle, but she pushed herself into a sitting position and stared blankly around the room. Here, too, boxes were piled, unopened. There was a precariously stacked pile of books and magazines on decorating and landscaping beside the bed. On the wall were three fresh strips of wallpaper, an ivory background with tiny violets, that she'd hung herself. More rolls and paste were pushed into a corner. The noise outside was a constant, irritating roar.

Resigned, Maggie got out of bed. She stumbled over a pair of shoes, swore, then went to the window. She'd chosen that room as her own because she could see out over the rolling pitch of what would be her front yard, over the tops of the trees on her own property to the valley beyond.

There was a farmhouse in the distance with a red roof and a smoking chimney. Beside it was a long, wide field that had just been plowed and planted. If she looked farther still, she could see the peaks of mountains faintly blue and indistinct in the morning mist. The window on the connecting wall would give her a view of the intended pond and the line of pines that would eventually be planted.

Maggie pushed the window up the rest of the way, struggling as it stuck a bit. The early-spring air had a pleasant chill. She could still hear the constant low sound of a running engine. Curious, she pressed her face against the screen, only to have it topple out of the window frame and fall to the porch below. One more thing for Mr. Bog to see to, Maggie thought with a sigh as she leaned through the opening. Just then the yellow bulk of a bulldozer rounded the bend in her lane and broke into view.

So, she thought, watching it inch its way along, leveling and pushing at rock and dirt, Cliff Delaney was a man of his word. She'd received the promised estimate and contract two days after his visit. When she'd called his office, Maggie had spoken to an efficient-sounding woman who'd told her the work would begin the first of the week.

And it's Monday, she reflected, leaning her elbows on the sill. Very prompt. Narrowing her eyes, she looked more closely at the man on top of the bulldozer. His build was too slight, she decided, his hair not quite dark enough. She didn't have to see his face to know it wasn't Cliff. Shrugging, she turned away from the window. Why should she have thought Cliff Delaney would work his own machines? And why should she have wanted it to be him? Hadn't she already decided she wouldn't see him again? She'd hired his company to do a job; the job would be done, and she'd write out a check. That was all there was to it.

Maggie attributed her crankiness to the early awakening as she snatched up her robe and headed for the shower.

Two hours later, fortified with the coffee she'd made for herself and the bulldozer operator, Maggie was on her knees on the kitchen floor. Since she was up at a barbaric hour, she thought it best to do something physical. On the counter above her sat her cassette tape player. The sound of her score, nearly completed, all but drowned out the whine of machinery. She let herself flow with it while words to the title song she'd yet to compose flitted in and out of her mind.

While she let her thoughts flow with the music she'd created, Maggie chipped away at the worn tile on the kitchen floor. True, her bedroom had only one wall partially papered, and only the ceiling in the upstairs bath was painted, *and* there were two more steps to be stripped and lacquered before the main stairway was finished, but she worked in her own way, at her own speed. She found herself jumping from project to project, leaving one partially done and leaping headlong into the next. This way, she reasoned, she could watch the house come together piece by piece rather than have one completed, out-of-place room.

Besides, she'd gotten a peek at the flooring beneath the tile when she'd inadvertently knocked an edge off a corner. Curiosity had done the rest.

When Cliff walked to the back door, he was already annoyed. It was ridiculous for him to be wasting time here, with all the other jobs his firm had in progress. Yet he was here. He'd knocked at the front door for almost five minutes. He knew Maggie was inside, her car was in the driveway, and the bulldozer operator had told him she'd brought out coffee an hour or so before. Didn't it occur to her that someone usually knocked when they wanted something?

The music coming through the open windows caught his attention, and his imagination. He'd never heard the melody before. It was compelling, sexy, moody. A lone piano, no backdrop of strings or brass, but it had the power of making the listener want to stop and hear every note. For a moment he did stop, both disturbed and moved.

Shifting the screen he'd found into his other hand, Cliff started to knock. Then he saw her.

She was on her hands and knees, prying up pieces of linoleum with what looked like a putty knife. Her hair was loose, falling over one shoulder so that her face was hidden behind it. The deep, rich sable brown picked up hints of gold from the sunlight that streamed through the open door and window.

Gray corduroys fit snugly over her hips, tapering down to bare ankles and feet. A vivid red suede shirt was tucked into the waist. He recognized the shirt as one sold in exclusive shops for very exclusive prices. Her wrists and hands looked impossibly delicate against it. Cliff was scowling at them when Maggie got too enthusiastic with the putty knife and scraped her knuckle against a corner of the tile.

"What the hell are you doing?" he demanded, swinging the door open and striding in before Maggie had a chance to react. She'd barely put the knuckle to her mouth in an instinctive move when he was crouched beside her and grabbing her hand.

"It's nothing," she said automatically. "Just a scratch."

"You're lucky you didn't slice it, the way you're hacking at that tile." Though his voice was rough and impatient, his hand was gentle. She left hers in it.

Yes, his hand was gentle, though rough-edged, like his voice, but this time she could see his eyes. They were gray; smoky, secret. Evening mists came to her mind. Mists that were sometimes dangerous but always compelling. That was the sort of mist she'd always believed had cloaked Brigadoon for a hundred years at a time. Maggie decided she could like him, in a cautious sort of way.

"Who'd be stupid enough to put linoleum over this?" With the fingers of her free hand, she skimmed over the hardwood she'd exposed. "Lovely, isn't it? Or it will be when it's sanded and sealed."

"Get Bog to deal with it," Cliff ordered. "You don't know what you're doing."

So everyone said. Maggie withdrew a bit, annoyed by the phrase. "Why should he have all the fun? Besides, I'm being careful."

"I can see that." He turned her hand over so that she saw the scrape over her thumb. It infuriated him to see the delicacy marred. "Doesn't someone in your profession have to be careful with their hands?"

"They're insured," she tossed back. "I think I can probably hit a few chords, even with a wound as serious as this." She pulled her hand out of his. "Did you come here to criticize me, Mr. Delaney, or did you have something else in mind?"

"I came to check on the job." Which wasn't necessary, he admitted. In any case, why should it matter to him if she was careless enough to hurt her hand? She was just a woman who had touched down in his territory and would be gone again before the leaves were full-blown with summer. He was going to have to remember that, and the fact that she didn't interest him personally. Shifting, he picked up the screen he'd dropped when he'd taken her hand. "I found this outside."

It wasn't often her voice took on that regal tone. He seemed to nudge it out of her. "Thank you." She took the screen and leaned it against the stove.

"Your road'll be blocked most of the day. I hope you weren't planning on going anywhere."

Maggie gave him a level look that held a hint of challenge. "I'm not going anywhere, Mr. Delaney."

He inclined his head. "Fine." The music on the tape player changed tempo. It was more hard-driving, more primitive. It seemed something to be played on hot, moonless nights. It drew him, pulled at him. "What is that?" Cliff demanded. "I've never heard it before."

Maggie glanced up at the recorder. "It's a movie score I'm composing. That's the melody for the title song." Because it had given her a great deal of trouble, she frowned at the revolving tape. "Do you like it?"

"Yes."

It was the most simple and most direct answer he'd given her thus far. It wasn't enough for Maggie.

"Why?"

He paused a moment, still listening, hardly aware that they were both still on the floor, close enough to touch. "It goes straight to the blood, straight to the imagination. Isn't that what a song's supposed to do?"

He could have said nothing more perfect. Her smile flashed, a quick, stunning smile that left him staring at her as though he'd been struck by lightning. "Yes. Yes, that's exactly what it's supposed to do." In her enthusiasm she shifted. Their knees brushed. "I'm trying for something very basic with this. It has to set the mood for a film about a passionate relationship—an intensely passionate relationship between two people who seem to have nothing in common but an uncontrollable desire for each other. One of them will kill because of it."

She trailed off, lost in the music and the mood. She could see it in vivid colors—scarlets, purples. She could feel it, like the close, sultry air on a hot summer night. Then she frowned, and as if on cue, the music stopped. From the tape came a sharp, pungent curse, then silence.

"I lost something in those last two bars," she muttered. "It was like—" she gestured with both hands, bringing them up, turning them over, then dropping them again "—something came unmeshed. It has to build to desperation, but it has to be more subtle than that. Passion at the very edge of control."

"Do you always write like that?" Cliff was studying her when she focused on him again, studying her as he had her land—thoroughly, with an eye both for detail and an overview.

She sat back on her haunches, comfortable now with a conversation on her own turf. He could hardly frustrate her in a discussion of music. She'd lived with it, in it, all her life. "Like what?" she countered.

"With the emphasis on mood and emotions rather than notes and timing."

Her brows lifted. With one hand, she pushed back the hair that swept across her cheek. She wore an amethyst on her finger, wine-colored, square. It caught the light, holding it until she dropped her hand again. As she thought it over, it occurred to her that no one, not even her closest associates, had ever defined her style so cleanly. It pleased her, though she didn't know why, that he had done so. "Yes," she said simply.

He didn't like what those big, soft eyes could do to him. Cliff rose. "That's why your music is good."

Maggie gave a quick laugh, not at the compliment, but at the grudging tone with which he delivered it. "So, you can say something nice, after all."

"When it's appropriate." He watched her stand, noting that she moved with the sort of fluidity he'd always associated with tall, willowy women. "I admire your music."

Again, it was the tone, rather than the words, that spoke to her. This time it touched off annoyance, rather than humor. "And little else that has to do with me."

"I don't know you," Cliff countered.

"You didn't like me when you drove up that hill the other day." With her temper rising, Maggie put her hands on her hips and faced him squarely. "I get the impression you didn't like me years before we met."

That was direct, Cliff decided. Maggie Fitzgerald, glamour girl from the Coast, didn't believe in evasions. Neither did he. "I have a problem with people who live their lives on silver platters. I've too much respect for reality."

"Silver platters," Maggie repeated in a voice that was much, much too quiet. "In other words, I was born into affluence, therefore, I can't understand the real world."

He didn't know why he wanted to smile. Perhaps it was the way color flooded her face. Perhaps it was because she stood nearly a foot beneath him but gave every appearance of being ready to Indian-wrestle and win. Yet he didn't smile. Cliff had the impression that if you gave an inch to this lady, you'd soon be begging to give a mile. "That about sums it up. The gravel for the lane'll be delivered and spread by five."

"Sums it up?" Accustomed to ending a conversation when she chose, Maggie grabbed his arm as he started to turn for the door. "You're a narrow-minded snob, and you know nothing about my life."

Cliff looked down at the delicate hand against his tanned muscled arm. The amethyst glowed up at him. "Miss Fitzgerald, everyone in the country knows about your life."

"That is one of the most unintelligent statements I've ever heard." She made one final attempt to control her temper, then forgot it. "Let me tell you something, Mr. Delaney—" The phone interrupted what would have been a stream of impassioned abuse. Maggie ended up swearing. "You stay there," she ordered as she turned to the wall phone.

Cliff's brows lifted at the command. Slowly, he leaned against the kitchen counter. He'd stay, he decided. Not because she'd told him to, but because he'd discovered he wanted to hear what she had to say.

Maggie yanked the receiver from the wall and barked into it. "Hello."

"Well, it's nice to hear that country life's agreeing with you."

"C.J." She struggled to hold down her temper. She wanted neither questions nor I-told-you-sos. "Sorry, you caught me in the middle of a philosophical discussion." Though she heard Cliff's quick snort of laughter, she ignored it. "Something up, C.J.?"

"Well, I hadn't heard from you in a couple of days—"

"I told you I'd call once a week. Will you stop worrying?"

"You know I can't."

She had to laugh. "No, I know you can't. If it relieves your mind, I'm having the lane fixed even as we speak. The next time you visit, you won't have to worry about your muffler falling off."

"It doesn't relieve my mind," C.J. grumbled. "I have nightmares about that roof caving in on your head. The damn place is falling apart."

"The place is not falling apart." She turned, inadvertently kicking the screen and sending it clattering across the floor. At that moment, her eyes met Cliff's. He was still leaning against the counter, still close enough to the back door to be gone in two strides. But now he was grinning. Maggie looked at the screen, then back at Cliff, and covered her mouth to smother a giggle.

"What was that noise?" C.J. demanded.

"Noise?" Maggie swallowed. "I didn't hear any noise." She covered the mouth of the receiver with her hand when Cliff laughed again. "Shh," she whispered, smiling. "C.J.," she said back into the phone, knowing she needed to distract him, "the score's nearly finished."

"When?" The response was immediate and predictable. She sent Cliff a knowing nod.

"For the most part, it's polished. I'm a little hung up on the title song. If you let me get back to work, the tape'll be in your office next week."

"Why don't you deliver it yourself? We'll have lunch."

"Forget it."

He sighed. "Just thought I'd try. To show you my heart's in the right place, I sent you a present."

"A present? The Godiva?"

"You'll have to wait and see," he said evasively. "It'll be there by tomorrow morning. I expect you to be so touched you'll catch the next plane to L.A. to thank me in person."

"C.J.—"

"Get back to work. And call me," he added, clever enough to know when to retreat and when to advance. "I keep having visions of you falling off that mountain."

He hung up, leaving her, as he often did, torn between amusement and annoyance. "My agent," Maggie said as she replaced the receiver. "He likes to worry."

"I see."

Cliff remained where he was; so did she. That one silly shared moment seemed to have broken down a barrier between them. Now, in its place, was an awkwardness neither of them fully understood. He was suddenly aware of the allure of her scent, of the slender line of her throat. She was suddenly disturbed by his basic masculinity, by the memory of the firm, rough feel of his palm. Maggie cleared her throat.

"Mr. Delaney—"

"Cliff," he corrected.

She smiled, telling herself to relax. "Cliff. We seem to've gotten off on the wrong foot for some reason. Maybe if we concentrate on something that interests us both—my land—we won't keep rubbing each other the wrong way."

He found it an interesting phrase, particularly since he was imagining what it would feel like to run his hands over her skin. "All right," he agreed as he straightened from the counter. He crossed to her, wondering who he was testing, himself or her. When he stopped, she was trapped between him and the stove.

He didn't touch her, but both of them could sense what it would be like. Hard hands, soft skin. Warmth turning quickly to heat. Mouth meeting mouth with confidence, with knowledge, with passion.

"I consider your land a challenge." He said it quietly, his eyes on hers. She didn't think of mists now but of smoke—of smoke and fire. "Which is why I've decided to give this project quite a bit of my personal attention."

Her nerves were suddenly strung tight. Maggie didn't back away, because she was almost certain that was what he wanted. Instead, she met his gaze. If her eyes weren't calm, if they'd darkened with the first traces of desire, she couldn't prevent it. "I can't argue with that."

"No." He smiled a little. If he stayed, even moments longer, he knew he'd find out how her lips tasted. That might be the biggest mistake he'd ever make. Turning, he went to the back door. "Call Bog." He tossed this over his shoulder as he pushed the screen door open. "Your fingers belong on piano keys, not on putty knives."

Maggie let out a long, tense breath when the screen door slammed. Did he do that on purpose? she wondered as she pressed a hand to her speeding heart. Or was it a natural talent of his to turn women into limp rags? Shaking her head, she told herself to forget it. If there was one thing she had experience in, it was in avoiding and evading the professional lothario. She was definitely uninterested in going a few rounds with Morganville's leading contender.

With a scowl, she dropped back to her knees and picked up the putty knife. She began to hack at the tile with a vengeance. Maggie Fitzgerald could take care of herself.

Chapter 3

For the third morning in a row, Maggie was awakened by the sound of men and machinery outside her windows. It occurred to her that she'd hardly had the chance to become used to the quiet when the chaos had started.

The bulldozer had been replaced by chain saws, industrial weed eaters and trucks. While she was far from getting used to the early risings, she was resigned. By seven-fifteen she had dragged herself out of the shower and was staring at her face in the bathroom mirror.

Not so good, she decided, studying her own sleepy eyes. But then she'd been up until two working on the score. Displeased, she ran a hand over her face. She'd never considered pampering her skin a luxury or a waste of time. It was simply something she did routinely, the same way she'd swim twenty laps every morning in California.

She'd been neglecting the basics lately, Maggie decided, squinting at her reflection. Had it been over two months since she'd been in a salon? Ruefully, she tugged at the bangs that swept over her forehead. It was showing, and it was time to do something about it.

After wrapping her still-damp hair in a towel, she pulled open the mirrored medicine-cabinet door. The nearest Elizabeth Arden's was seventy miles away. There were times, Maggie told herself as she smeared on a clay mask, that you had to fend for yourself.

She was just rinsing her hands when the sound of quick, high-pitched barking reached her. C.J.'s present, Maggie thought wryly, wanted his breakfast. In her short terry-cloth robe, which was raveled at the hem, her hair wrapped in a checked towel and the clay mask hardening on her face, she started downstairs to tend to the demanding gift her agent had flown out to her. She had just reached the bottom landing when a knock on the door sent the homely bulldog puppy into a frenzy.

"Calm down," she ordered, scooping him up under one arm. "All this excitement and I haven't had my coffee yet. Give me a break." The pup lowered his head and growled when she pulled on the front door. Definitely city-oriented, she thought, trying to calm the pup. She wondered if C.J. had planned it that way. The door resisted, sticking. Swearing, Maggie set down the dog and yanked with both hands.

The door swung open, carrying her a few steps back with the momentum. The pup dashed through the closest doorway, poking his head around the frame and snarling as if he meant business. Cliff stared at Maggie as she stood, panting, in the hall. She blew out a breath, wondering what could happen next. "I thought country life was supposed to be peaceful."

Cliff grinned, tucking his thumbs in the front pockets of his jeans. "Not necessarily. Get you up?"

"I've been up for quite some time," she said loftily.

"Mmm-hmm." His gaze skimmed over her legs, nicely exposed by the brief robe, before it lingered on the puppy crouched in the doorway. Her legs were longer, he mused, than one would think, considering the overall size of her. "Friend of yours?"

Maggie looked at the bulldog, which was making fierce sounds in his throat while keeping a careful distance. "A present from my agent."

"What's his name?"

Maggie sent the cowering puppy a wry look. "Killer."

Cliff watched the pup disappear behind the wall again. "Very apt. You figure to train him as a guard dog?"

"I'm going to teach him to attack music critics." She lifted a hand to push it through her hair—an old habit—and discovered the towel. Just as abruptly, she remembered the rest of her appearance. One hand flew to her face and found the thin layer of hardened clay. "Oh, my God," Maggie murmured as Cliff's grin widened. "Oh, damn." Turning, she raced for the stairs. "Just a minute." He was treated to an intriguing glimpse of bare thighs as she dashed upstairs.

Ten minutes later, she walked back down, perfectly composed. Her hair was swept back at the side with mother-of-pearl combs; her face was lightly touched with makeup. She'd pulled on the first thing she'd come to in her still-unpacked trunk. The tight black jeans proved an interesting contrast to the bulky white sweatshirt. Cliff sat on the bottom landing, sending the cowardly puppy into ecstasy by rubbing his belly. Maggie frowned down at the crown of Cliff's head.

"You weren't going to say a word, were you?"

He continued to rub the puppy, not bothering to look up. "About what?"

Maggie narrowed her eyes and folded her arms under her breasts. "Nothing. Was there something you wanted to discuss this morning?"

He wasn't precisely sure why that frosty, regal tone appealed to him. Perhaps he just liked knowing he had the ability to make her use it. "Still want that pond?"

"Yes, I still want the pond," she snapped, then gritted her teeth to prevent herself from doing so again. "I don't make a habit of changing my mind."

"Fine. We'll be clearing out the gully this afternoon." Rising, he faced her while the puppy sat expectantly at his feet. "You didn't call Bog about the kitchen floor."

Confusion came and went in her eyes. "How do you—"

"It's easy to find things out in Morganville."

"Well, it's none of your—"

"Hard to keep your business to yourself in small towns," Cliff interrupted again. It amused him to hear her breath huff out in frustration. "Fact is, you're about the top news item in town these days. Everybody wonders what the lady from California's doing up on this mountain. The more you keep to yourself," he added, "the more they wonder."

"Is that so?" Maggie tilted her head and stepped closer. "And you?" she countered. "Do you wonder?"

Cliff knew a challenge when he heard one, and knew he'd answer it in his own time. Impulsively, he cupped her chin in his hand and ran his thumb over her jawline. She didn't flinch or draw back, but became very still. "Nice skin," he murmured, sweeping his gaze along the path his thumb took. "Very nice. You take good care of it, Maggie. I'll take care of your land."

With this, he left her precisely as she was—arms folded, head tilted back, eyes astonished.

By ten, Maggie decided it wasn't going to be the quiet, solitary sort of day she'd moved to the country for. The men outside shouted above the machinery to make themselves heard. Trucks came and went down her newly graveled lane. She could comfort herself that in a few weeks that part of the disruption would be over.

She took three calls from the Coast from friends who wondered how and what she was doing. By the third call, she was a bit testy from explaining she was scraping linoleum, papering walls, painting woodwork and enjoying it. She left the phone off the hook and went back to her putty knife and kitchen floor.

More than half of the wood was exposed now. The progress excited her enough that she decided to stick with this one job until it was completed. The floor would be beautiful, and, she added, thinking of Cliff's comments, she'd have done it herself.

Maggie had barely scraped off two more inches when there was a knock behind her. She turned her head, ready to flare if it was Cliff Delaney returned to taunt her. Instead, she saw a tall, slender woman of her own age with soft brown hair and pale blue eyes. As Maggie studied Joyce Morgan Agee, she wondered why she hadn't seen the resemblance to Louella before.

"Mrs. Agee." Maggie rose, brushing at the knees of her jeans. "Please, come in. I'm sorry." Her sneakers squeaked as she stepped on a thin layer of old glue. "The floor's a bit sticky."

"I don't mean to disturb your work." Joyce stood uncertainly in the doorway, eyeing the floor. "I would've called, but I was on my way home from Mother's."

Joyce's pumps were trim and stylish. Maggie felt the glue pull at the bottom of her old sneakers. "We can talk outside, if you don't mind." Taking the initiative, Maggie walked out into the sunshine. "Things are a little confused around here right now."

"Yes." They heard one of the workers call to a companion, punctuating his suggestion with good-natured swearing. Joyce glanced over in their direction before she turned back to Maggie. "You're not wasting any time, I see."

"No." Maggie laughed and eyed the crumbling dirt wall beside them. "I've never been very patient. For some reason, I'm more anxious to have the outside the way I want it than the inside."

"You couldn't have picked a better company," Joyce murmured, glancing over at one of the trucks with *Delaney's* on the side.

Maggie followed her gaze but kept her tone neutral. "So I'm told."

"I want you to know I'm really glad you're doing so much to the place." Joyce began to fiddle with the strap of her shoulder bag. "I can hardly remember living here. I was a child when we moved, but I hate waste." With a little smile, she looked around again and shook her head. "I don't think I could live out here. I like being in town, with neighbors close by and other children for my children to play with. Of course, Stan, my husband, likes being available all the time."

It took Maggie a moment; then she remembered. "Oh, your husband's the sheriff, isn't he?"

"That's right. Morganville's a quiet town, nothing like Los Angeles, but it keeps him busy." She smiled, but Maggie wondered why she sensed strain. "We're just not city people."

"No." Maggie smiled, too. "I guess I've discovered I'm not, either."

"I don't understand how you could give up—" Joyce seemed to catch herself. "I guess what I meant was, this must be such a change for you after living in a place like Beverly Hills."

"A change," Maggie agreed. Was she sensing undercurrents here, too, as she had with Louella's dreaminess? "It was one I wanted."

"Yes, well, you know I'm glad you bought the place, and so quickly. Stan was a little upset with my putting it on the market when he was out of town, but I couldn't see it just sitting here. Who knows, if you hadn't come along so fast, he might've talked me out of selling it."

"Then we can both be grateful I saw the sign when I did." Mentally, Maggie was trying to figure out the logistics of the situation. It seemed the house had belonged exclusively to Joyce, without her husband or her mother having any claim. Fleetingly, she wondered why Joyce hadn't rented or sold the property before.

"The real reason I came by, Miss Fitzgerald, is my mother. She told me she was here a few days ago."

"Yes, she's a lovely woman."

"Yes." Joyce looked back toward the men working, then took a deep breath. Maggie no longer had to wonder if she was sensing undercurrents. She was sure of it. "It's more than possible she'll drop in on you again. I'd like to ask you a favor, that is, if she begins to bother you, if you'd tell me instead of her."

"Why should she bother me?"

Joyce let out a sound that was somewhere between fatigue and frustration. "Mother often dwells on the past. She's never completely gotten over my father's death. She makes some people uncomfortable."

Maggie remembered the discomfort she'd felt on and off during Louella's brief visit. Still, she shook her head. "Your mother's welcome to visit me from time to time, Mrs. Agee."

"Thank you, but you will promise to tell me if—well, if you'd like her to stay away. You see, she'd often come here, even when the place was deserted. I don't want her to get in your way. She doesn't know who you are. That is—" Obviously embarrassed,

Joyce broke off. "I mean, Mother doesn't understand that someone like you would be busy."

Maggie remembered the lost eyes, the unhappy mouth. Pity stirred again. "All right, if she bothers me, I'll tell you."

The relief in Joyce's face was quick and very plain. "I appreciate it, Miss Fitzgerald."

"Maggie."

"Yes, well . . ." As if only more uncertain of her ground, Joyce managed a smile. "I understand that someone like you wouldn't want to have people dropping by and getting in the way."

Maggie laughed, thinking how many times the phone calls from California had interrupted her that morning. "I'm not a recluse," she told Joyce, though she was no longer completely sure. "And I'm not really very temperamental. Some people even consider me normal."

"Oh, I didn't mean—"

"I know you didn't. Come back when I've done something with that floor, and we'll have some coffee."

"I'd like to, really. Oh, I nearly forgot." She reached into the big canvas bag on her shoulder and pulled out a manila envelope. "Mother said you wanted to see these. Some pictures of the property."

"Yes." Pleased, Maggie took the envelope. She hadn't thought Louella would remember or bother to put them together for her. "I hoped they might give me some ideas."

"Mother said you could keep them as long as you liked." Joyce hesitated, fiddling again with the strap of her bag. "I have to get back. My youngest gets home from kindergarten at noon, and Stan sometimes comes home for lunch. I haven't done a thing to the house. I hope I see you sometime in town."

"I'm sure you will." Maggie tucked the envelope under her arm. "Give my best to your mother."

Maggie started back into the house, but as she put her hand on the doorknob, she noticed Cliff crossing to Joyce. Curiosity had her stopping to watch as Cliff took both the brunette's hands in his own. Though she couldn't hear the conversation over the din of motors, it was obvious that they knew each other well. There was a gentleness on Cliff's face Maggie hadn't seen before, and something she interpreted as concern. He bent down close, as if Joyce were speaking very softly, then touched her hair. The touch of a brother? Maggie wondered. Or a lover?

As she watched, Joyce shook her head, apparently fumbling with the door handle before she got into the car. Cliff leaned into the window for a moment. Were they arguing? Maggie wondered. Was the tension she sensed real or imaginary? Fascinated with the silent scene being played out in her driveway, Maggie watched as Cliff withdrew from the window and Joyce backed out to drive away. Before she could retreat inside, Cliff turned, and their gazes locked.

There were a hundred feet separating them, and the air was full of the sounds of men and machines. The sun was strong enough to make her almost too warm in the sweatshirt, yet she felt one quick, unexpected chill race up her spine. Perhaps it was hostility she felt. Maggie tried to tell herself it was hostility and not the first dangerous flutters of passion.

There was a temptation to cross those hundred feet and test both of them. Even the thought of it stirred her blood. He didn't move. He didn't take his eyes from her. With fingers gone suddenly numb, Maggie twisted the handle and went inside.

Two hours later, Maggie went out again. She'd never been one to retreat from a challenge, from her emotions or from trouble. Cliff Delaney seemed connected with all three. While she'd scraped linoleum, Maggie had lectured herself on letting Cliff intimidate her for no reason other than his being powerfully male and sexy.

And different, she'd admitted. Different from most of the men she'd encountered in her profession. He didn't fawn—far from it. He didn't pour on the charm. He wasn't impressed with his own physique, looks or sophistication. It must have been that difference that had made her not quite certain how to handle him.

A very direct, very frank business approach, she decided as she circled around the back of the house. Maggie paused to look at the bank fronting her house.

The vines, briars and thick sumac were gone. Piles of rich, dark topsoil were being spread over what had been a tangled jungle of neglect. The tree that had leaned toward her house was gone, stump and all. Two men, backs glistening with sweat, were setting stone in a low-spreading wall where the edge of the slope met the edge of the lawn.

Cliff Delaney ran a tight ship, Maggie concluded, and made her way through the new dirt toward the side yard. Here, too, the worst had been cleared out. An enormous bearded man in bib overalls sat atop a big yellow backhoe as easily as another might sit in an armchair. At the push of a lever, the digger went down into the gully, bit into earth and rock and came up full.

Maggie shaded her eyes and watched the procedure while the puppy circled her legs and snarled at everything in sight. Each time the digger would open its claws to drop its load, the dog would send up a ruckus of barks. Laughing, Maggie crouched down to scratch his ears and soothe him.

"Don't be a coward, Killer. I won't let it get you."

"I wouldn't get any closer," Cliff said from behind her.

She turned her head, squinting against the sun. "This is close enough." Disliking the disadvantage of looking up and into the sun, Maggie stood. "You seem to be making progress."

"We need to get the plants in and the wall of this thing solid—" he gestured toward the gully "—before the rain hits. Otherwise, you'll have a real mess on your hands."

"I see." Because he wore the frustratingly tinted glasses again, she turned from him to watch the backhoe work. "You certainly have a large staff."

Cliff's thumbs went into his pockets. "Large enough." He'd told himself he'd imagined that powerful sexual pull hours before. Now, feeling it again, he couldn't deny it.

She wasn't what he wanted, yet he wanted her. She wasn't what he would have chosen, yet he was choosing her. He could turn away logic until he'd learned what it was like to touch her.

Maggie was very aware of how close they stood. The stirring she'd felt hours before began to build again, slowly, seductively, until she felt her whole body tense with it. She understood that you could want someone you didn't know, someone you passed on the street. It all had to do with chemistry, but her chemistry had never reacted this way before. She had a wild urge to turn into his arms, to demand or offer the fulfillment, or whatever it was, that simmered between them. It was something that offered excitement and pleasure she had only glimpsed before. So she did turn, completely uncertain as to what she would say.

"I don't think I like what's happening here."

Cliff didn't pretend to misunderstand her. Neither of their minds was on the pond or the machine. "Do you have a choice?"

Maggie frowned, wishing she was more certain of her moves. He wasn't like the men she'd known before; therefore, the standard rules didn't apply. "I think so. I moved here because it was where I wanted to live, where I wanted to work. But I also moved here because I wanted to be on my own. I intend to do all those things."

Cliff studied her a moment, then gave the backhoe driver an absent wave as he shut off the machine to take his lunch break. "I took this job because I wanted to work this land. I intend to do it."

Though she didn't feel the slightest lessening of tension, Maggie nodded. "Then we understand each other."

As she started to turn away, Cliff put a hand on her shoulder, holding her still. "I think we both understand quite a bit."

The muscles in her stomach tightened and loosened like a nervous fist. With his fingers so light on the bulky sweatshirt, she shouldn't have felt anything. But hundreds of pulses sprang to life in her body. The air seemed to grow closer, hotter, the sounds of men more distant. "I don't know what you mean."

"Yes, you do."

Yes, she did. "I don't know anything about you," Maggie managed.

Cliff caught the tips of her hair in his fingers. "I can't say the same."

Maggie's temper flared, though she knew when she was being baited. "So, you believe everything you read in the tabloids and glossies." She tossed her head to free her hair from his fingers. "I'm surprised that a man who's obviously so successful and talented could be so ignorant."

Cliff acknowledged the hit with a nod. "I'm surprised a woman who's obviously so successful and talented could be so foolish."

"Foolish? What the hell's that supposed to mean?"

"It seems foolish to me to encourage the press to report every area of your life."

She clenched her teeth and tried deep breathing. Neither worked. "I don't encourage the press to do anything."

"You don't discourage them," Cliff countered.

"Discouragement *is* encouragement," she tossed back. Folding her arms under her breasts as she'd done earlier, she stared out over the open gully. "Why am I defending myself?" she muttered. "You don't know anything about it. I don't need you to know anything about it."

"I know you gave an interview about yourself and your husband weeks after his death." He heard her quick intake of breath even as he cursed himself for saying something so personal, and so uncalled-for.

"Do you have any idea how the press hammered at me during those weeks?" Her voice was low and strained, and she no longer looked at him. "Do you know all the garbage they were printing?" Her fingers tightened on her own arms. "I chose a reporter I could trust, and I gave the most honest, most straightforward interview I could manage, knowing it was my only chance to keep things from sinking lower. That interview was for Jerry. It was the only thing I had left to give him."

He'd wanted to prod, perhaps even to prick, but he hadn't

wanted to hurt. "I'm sorry." Cliff put his hand on her shoulder again, but she jerked away.

"Forget it."

This time he took both of her shoulders, turning her firmly to face him. "I don't forget blows below the belt, especially when I'm the one doing the punching."

She waited to speak until she was certain she had some control again. "I've survived hits before. My advice to you is not to criticize something you have no capacity for understanding."

"I apologized." He didn't release her shoulders when she tried to draw away. "But I'm not very good at following advice."

Maggie became still again. Somehow they had gotten closer, so that now their thighs brushed. The combination of anger and desire was becoming too strong to ignore. "Then you and I don't have any more to say to each other."

"You're wrong." His voice was very quiet, very compelling. "We haven't begun to say all there is to say."

"You work for me—"

"I work for myself," Cliff corrected.

She understood that kind of pride, admired it. But admiration wouldn't remove his hands from her shoulders. "I'm paying you to do a job."

"You're paying my company. That's business."

"It's going to be our only business."

"Wrong again," he murmured, but released her.

Maggie opened her mouth to hurl something back at him, but the dog began to bark in quick, excited yelps. She decided turning her back on him to investigate her pet was a much grander insult than the verbal one she'd planned. Without a word, she began to make her way around the slope of the gully to the pile of earth and rock and debris the backhoe had dumped.

"All right, Killer." The going was so rough that she swore under her breath as she stumbled over stones. "You'll never find anything worthwhile in that pile, anyway."

Ignoring her, the puppy continued to dig, his barking muffled as his nose went farther in, his backside wriggling with either effort or delight in the new game.

"Cut it out." She bent to pull him out of the heap and ended up sitting down hard. "Damn it, Killer." Staying as she was, she grabbed the dog with one hand, dragging him back and unearthing a small avalanche of rock.

"Will you be careful?" Cliff shouted from above her, knowing she'd been lucky not to have one of the rocks bounce off her shin.

"It's the stupid dog!" Maggie shouted back as she lost her grip on him again. "God knows what he thinks is so fascinating about this mess. Nothing but dirt and rocks," she muttered, pushing at the pile that had landed near her hip.

"Well, grab him and get back up here before you're both hurt."

"Yeah," she muttered under her breath. "You're a big help." Disgusted, she started to struggle up when her fingers slid into the worn, rounded rock her hand had rested on. Hollow, she thought curiously. Her attention torn between the gully and the dog's unrelenting barks, Maggie glanced down.

Then she began to scream, loud and long enough to send the puppy racing for cover.

Cliff's first thought as he raced down the slope to her was snakes. When he reached her, he dragged her up and into his arms in an instinctive move of protection. She'd stopped screaming, and though her breathing was shallow, Maggie grabbed his shirt before he could carry her back up the slope. "Bones," she whispered. Closing her eyes, she dropped her head on his shoulder. "Oh, my God."

Cliff looked down and saw what the machine and dog had unearthed. Mixed with the rock and debris was a pile of what might have been mistaken for long white sticks layered with dirt.

But lying on the bones, inches from where Maggie had sat, was a human skull.

Chapter 4

"I'm all right." Maggie sat at the kitchen table and gripped the glass of water Cliff had handed her. When the pain in her fingers finally registered, she relaxed them a bit. "I feel like an idiot, screaming that way."

She was still pale, he noted. Though the hands on the glass were steady now, they were still white at the knuckles. Her eyes were wide and shocked, suddenly too big for the rest of her face. He started to stroke her hair, then stuck his own hands in his pockets. "A natural enough reaction."

"I guess." She looked up and managed a shaky smile. She was cold, but prayed she wouldn't begin to shiver in front of him. "I've never found myself in that sort of . . . situation before."

Cliff lifted a brow. "Neither have I."

"No?" Somehow she'd wanted to think it had happened before. If it had, it might make it less horrible—and less personal. She looked down at the floor, not realizing until that moment that the dog lay across her feet, whimpering. "But don't you dig up a lot of—" She hesitated, not sure just how she wanted to phrase it. "Things—" Maggie decided weakly "—in your line of work?"

She was reaching, Cliff thought, and whether she knew it or not, those big brown eyes were pleading with him for some sort of easy explanation. He didn't have one to give her. "Not that kind of thing."

Their gazes held for one long, silent moment before Maggie nodded. If there was one thing she'd learned in the hard, competitive business she'd chosen, it was to handle things as they came. "So, neither of us has a tidy explanation." The little expulsion of breath was the last sign of weakness she intended to show him. "I guess the next step is the police."

"Yeah." The more determined she became to be calm, the more difficult it became for him. She was weakening something in him that he was determined to keep objective. His hands were balled into fists inside his pockets in his struggle not to touch her. Distance was the quickest defense. "You'd better call," Cliff said briskly. "I'll go out and make sure the crew keeps clear of the gully."

Again, her answer was a nod. Maggie watched as he crossed to the screen door and pushed it open. There he hesitated. He'd have cursed if he'd understood what it was he wanted to swear at. When he looked back, she saw the concern on his face she'd seen when he'd spoken to Joyce. "Maggie, are you all right?"

The question, and the tone, helped her to settle. Perhaps it had something to do with her knowing just what it was like to be pressured by another's weakness. "I will be. Thanks." She waited until the screen door banged shut behind him before she dropped her head on the table.

Good heavens, what had she walked into here? People didn't find bodies in their front yard. C.J. would've said it was totally uncivilized. Maggie choked back a hysterical giggle and straightened. The one unarguable fact she had to face was that she had found one. Now she had to deal with it. Taking deep breaths, she went to the phone and dialed the operator.

"Get me the police," she said quickly.

A few minutes later, Maggie went outside. Though she'd hoped the practical routine of reporting what she'd found would calm her, it hadn't worked. She didn't go near the gully, but she found she couldn't sit inside, waiting alone. Circling around the front of the house, she found a convenient rock and sat. The puppy stretched out in the patch of sunlight at her feet and went to sleep.

She could almost believe she'd imagined what she'd seen in that pile of dirt and rock. It was too peaceful here for anything so stark. The air was too soft, the sun too warm. Her land might be unruly, but it held a serenity that blocked out the harsher aspects of life.

Was that why she'd chosen it, Maggie wondered. Because she wanted to pretend there wasn't any real madness in the world? Here she could cocoon herself from so many of the pressures and demands that had threaded through her life for so long. Was this spot the home she'd always wanted, or was it in reality just an escape for her? She squeezed her eyes shut. If that were true, it made her weak and dishonest, two things she couldn't tolerate. Why had it taken this incident to make her question what she hadn't questioned before? As she tried to find her tranquillity again, a shadow fell over her. Opening her eyes, Maggie looked up at Cliff.

For some reason it toughened her. She wouldn't admit to him that she'd begun to doubt herself or her motives. No, not to him.

"Someone should be here soon." She linked her folded hands over one knee and looked back into the woods.

"Good." Several minutes passed while they both remained silent, looking into the trees.

Eventually, Cliff crouched down beside her. Funny, but he thought that she looked more apt to fall apart now than she had when he'd carried her into her kitchen. Reaction, he decided, had different speeds for different people. He wanted to hold her again, hard and close, as he'd done all too briefly before. The contact had made something strong and sultry move through him. Like her music—something like her music.

He wished like hell he'd turned down the job and had walked away the first time he'd seen her. Cliff looked past her to the slope that led to the gully.

"You talked to Stan?"

"Stan?" Blankly, Maggie stared at Cliff's set profile. At that moment, he was close enough to reach but seemed miles away. "Oh, the sheriff." She wished he'd touch her, just for a moment. Just a hand on her. "No, I didn't call him. I called the operator and asked for the police. She connected me with the state police in Hagerstown." She lapsed into silence, waiting for him to make some comment on her typical city response.

"Probably for the best," Cliff murmured. "I let the crew go. It'll be less confusing."

"Oh." She must've been in a daze not to notice that the trucks and men were gone. When she forced herself to look, she saw that the backhoe remained, sitting on the rise above the gully, big and yellow and silent. The sun was warm on her back. Her skin was like ice. Time to snap out of it, Maggie told herself, and straightened her shoulders. "Yes, I'm sure you're right. Should I call your office when the police say it's all right to start work again?" Her voice was businesslike. Her throat was dry with the thought of being left alone, completely alone, with what was down by the gully.

Cliff turned his head. Without speaking, he took off his sunglasses so that their eyes met. "Thought I'd hang around."

Relief washed over her. Maggie knew it must've shown in her face, but she didn't have the will to put pride first. "I'd like you to. It's stupid, but—" She glanced over in the direction of the gully.

"Not stupid."

"Maybe *weak*'s a better word," she mumbled, trying to smile.

"Human." Despite his determination not to, Cliff reached out and took her hand. The touch, one designed to comfort, to reassure her, set off a chain reaction of emotion too swift to stop.

It ran through her head that she should rise swiftly and go inside. He might stop her, or he might let her go. Maggie didn't ask herself which she wanted, nor did she move. Instead, she sat where she was, meeting his gaze and letting the sensation of torrid, liquid heat flow through her. Nothing else existed. Nothing else mattered.

She felt each of his fingers tense individually on her hand. There was a sense of power there; whether it was his or hers, she wasn't sure. Perhaps it was the melding of both. She saw his eyes darken until the irises were only shades lighter than the pupils. It was as if he were looking through her, into her chaotic thoughts. In the quiet of midafternoon, she heard each breath he drew in and expelled. The sound stirred the excitement that vibrated in the air between them.

Together they moved toward each other until mouth molded itself to mouth.

Intensity. She hadn't known anything between two people could be so concentrated, such pure sensation. She understood that if years passed, if she was blind and deaf, she would know this man just by the touch of his lips. In one instant she became intimate with the shape of his mouth, the taste and texture of his tongue. Her mouth was on his, his hand on hers, and they touched nowhere else. In that moment there was no need to.

There was an aggressiveness, even a harshness, to the kiss that Maggie hadn't expected. It held none of the sweetness, the hesitation, that first kisses often do, yet she didn't back away from it. Perhaps it was all part of the attraction that had begun the moment he'd stepped from the truck. Different, yes, he was different from the other men who'd touched her life—different still from the man she'd shared her body with. She'd known that from the first encounter. Now, with his mouth stirring her senses, she found herself grateful for it. She wanted nothing to be the same as it had been, no reminders of what she'd had once and lost. This man wouldn't pamper or worship. He was strong enough to want strength in return. She felt his tongue tangle with hers, probing deeper. Maggie reveled in the demands.

It was easy, almost too easy, to forget her delicate build, her fragile looks, when her mouth was so ardent on his. He should've known there'd be deep, restless passion in a woman who created music with such sexuality. But how could he have known that passion would call to him as though he'd been waiting for years?

It was much too easy to forget she wasn't the kind of woman he wanted in his life when her taste was filling him. Again, he should have known she'd have the power to make a man toss aside all logic, all intellect. Her lips were warm, moist, the taste as pungent as the scent of newly turned earth around them. The urge rose to take her in his arms and fulfill, there under the clear afternoon sun, all the needs that welled inside him. Cliff drew back, resisting that final painful twist of desire.

Breathless, throbbing, Maggie stared at him. Could that one searing meeting of lips have moved him as it had moved her? Were his thoughts swimming as hers were? Was his body pulsing with wild, urgent needs? She could tell nothing from his face. Though his eyes were fixed on hers, their expression was unreadable. If she asked, would he tell her that he, too, had never known a wave of passion so overwhelming or so mesmerizing? She would ask, and would know, as soon as she had the voice to question. As she sat, struggling to catch her breath, the events of the day came flashing back into her mind. Abruptly, Maggie sprang to her feet.

"God, what are we doing?" she demanded. With a hand that shook, she pushed the hair away from her face. "How can we sit here like this when that—that thing's only a few yards away?"

Cliff took her arm, turning her back to face him. "What does one have to do with the other?"

"Nothing. I don't know." With her insides churning, she looked up at him. Her emotions had always been too dominant. Though she knew it, Maggie had never been able to change it. It had been years since she'd really tried. Confusion, distress, passion, radiated from her as tangible things. "What we found, it's dreadful, unbelievably dreadful, and a few moments ago I was sitting there wondering what it would be like to make love with you."

Something flashed in his eyes, quickly controlled. Unlike Maggie, Cliff had learned long ago to channel his emotions and keep them to himself. "You obviously don't believe in evading the issue."

"Evasions take too much time and effort." After letting out a long breath, Maggie managed to match his even, casual tone. "Listen, I didn't expect that sort of—eruption," she decided. "I suppose I'm wound up over all of this, and a bit too susceptible."

"Susceptible." Her choice of words made him smile. Somehow, when she became cool and calm, he became tempted to prod. Deliberately, he lifted a hand and ran his fingertips down her cheek. Her skin was still warm with desire. "I wouldn't have described you that way. You seem to be a woman who knows what she wants and how to get it."

If he'd wanted to fire her up, he'd found the perfect key. "Stop it." In one sharp move, she pushed his hand from her face. "I've said it before—you don't know me. Every time we're together, I become more certain that I don't want you to. You're a very attractive man, Cliff. And very unlikable. I stay away from people I don't like."

It occurred to him that he'd never gone out of his way to argue with anyone before. A lot of things were changing. "In a small community like this, it's hard to stay away from anyone."

"I'll put more effort into it."

"Nearly impossible."

She narrowed her eyes and fought to keep her lips from curving. "I'm very good when I put my mind to something."

"Yeah." He put his sunglasses back on. When he grinned, the deliberate cockiness was almost too appealing to resist. "I bet you are."

"Are you trying to be smart, or are you trying to be charming?"

"I never had to try to be either one."

"Think again." Because she was having trouble controlling the grin, Maggie turned away. As luck would have it, she found herself staring out over the gully. A chill raced up her spine. Swearing, she folded her arms under her breasts. "I can't believe it," she muttered. "I can't believe I'm standing here having a ridiculous conversation when there's a—" She found she couldn't say it and detested herself. "I think the whole world must be going mad."

He wasn't going to let her get shaky on him again. When she was vulnerable, she was much more dangerous. "What's down there's been there for a long time." His voice was brisk, almost hard. "It doesn't have anything to do with you."

"It's my land," Maggie tossed back. She whirled around, eyes glowing, chin angled. "So it has everything to do with me."

"Then you better stop shaking every time you think about it."

"I'm not shaking."

Without a word, he drew her hand away from her elbow so they could both see the tremor. Furious, Maggie snatched it away again. "When I want you to touch me, I'll let you know," she said between her teeth.

"You already have."

Before she could think of an appropriate response, the dog scrambled up and began to bark furiously. Seconds later, they both heard the sound of an approaching car.

"He might make you a decent watchdog, after all," Cliff said mildly. The pup bounded around in circles like a mad thing, then hid behind the rock. "Then again . . ."

As the official car came into sight, he bent down to pat the dog on the head before he walked toward the end of the drive. Maggie hurried to keep pace. Her land, her problem, her responsibility, she told herself. *She'd* do the talking.

A trooper climbed out of the car, adjusted his hat, then broke into a grin. "Cliff, didn't expect to see you out here."

"Bob." Because the greeting didn't include a handshake, Maggie assumed the men knew each other well and saw each other often. "My company's handling the landscaping."

"The old Morgan place." The trooper looked around with interest. "Been a while since I was back here. You dig up something we should know about?"

"So it seems."

"It's the Fitzgerald place now," Maggie cut in briskly.

The trooper touched the brim of his hat and started to make a polite comment. His eyes widened when he took his first good look at her. "Fitzgerald," he repeated. "Hey, aren't you Maggie Fitzgerald?"

She smiled, though the recognition, with Cliff beside her, made her uncomfortable. "Yes, I am."

"I'll be damned. You look just like your pictures in all the magazines. I guess there isn't a song you've written I can't hum. You bought the Morgan place."

"That's right."

He pushed the hat back on his head in a gesture that made her think of cowboys. "Wait till I tell my wife. We had 'Forever' played at our wedding. You remember, Cliff. Cliff was best man."

Maggie tilted her head to look at the man beside her. "Really?"

"If you've finished being impressed," Cliff said mildly, "you might want to take a look at what's down by the gully."

Bob grinned again, all amiability. "That's why I'm here." They began to walk toward the gully together. "You know, it isn't easy to tell what's from a human and what's from an animal just by looking. Could be, ma'am, that you uncovered a deer."

Maggie glanced over at Cliff. She could still feel the way her hand had slid into the hollow opening of what she'd taken for a rock. "I wish I could think so."

"Down here," Cliff said without acknowledging the look. "The going's rough." In a smooth, calculated move, he blocked Maggie's way before she could start down. It forced her to pull up short and grab his arm for support. "Why don't you wait here?"

It would've been easy to do so. Much too easy. "It's my land," Maggie said, and, brushing by him, led the way down herself. "The dog started digging in this pile." She heard the nerves in her own voice and fought against them. "I came down to pull him away, and that's when I saw . . ." Trailing off, she pointed.

The trooper crouched down, letting out a low whistle. "Holy hell," he murmured. He turned his head, but it was Cliff he looked at, not Maggie. "It doesn't look like you dug up any deer."

"No." In a casual move, Cliff shifted so that he blocked Maggie's view. "What now?"

Bob rose. He wasn't smiling now, but Maggie thought she detected a gleam of excitement. "I'll have to call the investigation section. Those boys are going to want to take a look at this."

Maggie didn't speak when they climbed up the slope again. She waited in silence while the trooper went to his car to radio in his report. When she did speak, she deliberately avoided the reason they were all standing outside in the middle of the afternoon.

"So you two know each other," she commented as though it were any normal remark made on any normal day.

"Bob and I went to school together." Cliff watched a big black crow swoop over the trees. He was remembering the look on Maggie's face the moment before she'd begun to scream. "He ended up marrying one of my cousins a couple of years ago."

Bending over, she plucked a wildflower and began to shred it. "You have a lot of cousins."

He shrugged. The crow landed and was still. "Enough."

"A few Morgans."

That caught his attention. "A few," he said slowly. "Why?"

"I wondered if it was your connection with them that made you resent my having this land."

Cliff wondered why, when he normally respected candor, it annoyed him from her. "No."

"But you did resent it," Maggie insisted. "You resented me before you even saw me."

He had, and perhaps the resentment had grown since he'd had a taste of her. "Joyce had the right to sell this property whenever, and to whomever, she wanted."

Maggie nodded, looking down to where the puppy scrambled in the new dirt. "Is Joyce a cousin, too?"

"What are you getting at?"

Lifting her head, Maggie met his impatient look. "I'm just trying to understand small towns. After all, I'm going to be living here."

"Then the first thing you should learn is that people don't like questions. They might volunteer more information than you want to hear, but they don't like to be asked."

Maggie acknowledged this with a lift of a brow. "I'll keep that in mind." Rather pleased that she'd annoyed him, Maggie turned to the trooper as he approached.

"They're sending out a team." He glanced from her to Cliff, then over his friend's shoulder toward the gully. "Probably be here for a while, then take what they find with them."

"What then?"

Bob brought his attention back to Maggie. "Good question." He shifted his feet as he considered it. "To tell you the truth, I've never been in on anything like this before, but my guess would be they'd ship everything off to the medical examiner in Baltimore. He'd have to check the, ah, everything out before they could start an investigation."

"Investigation?" she repeated, and felt something tighten in her throat. "What kind of investigation?"

The trooper ran his thumb and forefinger down his nose. "Well, ma'am, as far as I can see, there's no reason for anything like that to be buried down in that gully unless—"

"Unless someone buried it there," Cliff finished.

Maggie stared out into the peaceful spread of greening wood across the lane. "I think we could all use some coffee," she murmured. Without waiting for an acknowledgment, she went back toward the house.

Bob took off his hat and wiped at the sweat on his forehead. "This is one for the books."

Cliff followed his friend's long look at the woman climbing the rickety front steps. "Which? Her or that?" With one hand he gestured toward the gully.

"Both." Bob took out a pack of gum and carefully unwrapped a piece. "First place, what's a woman like her, a celebrity, doing holed up here in the woods?"

"Maybe she decided she likes trees."

Bob slipped the gum into his mouth. "Must be ten, twelve acres of them here."

"Twelve."

"Looks to me like she bought more than she bargained for. Holy hell, Cliff, we haven't had anything like this down in this end of the county since crazy Mel Stickler set those barn fires. Now, in the city—"

"Taken to the fast pace, have you?"

Bob knew Cliff well enough to catch both the dig and the humor.

"I like some action," he said easily. "Speaking of which, the lady songwriter smells like heaven."

"How's Carol Ann?"

Bob grinned at the mention of his wife. "Just fine. Look, Cliff, if a man doesn't look, and appreciate, he'd better see a doctor. You're not going to tell me you haven't noticed just how nice that lady's put together."

"I've noticed." He glanced down at the rock beside him. She'd sat there when he'd kissed her. It wouldn't take any effort to remember each separate sensation that had run through him in that one moment. "I'm more interested in her land."

Bob let out a quick laugh. "If you are, you've done a lot of changing since high school. Remember when we used to come up here—those blond twins, the cheerleaders whose parents rented the place for a while? That old Chevy of yours lost its muffler right there on that turn."

"I remember."

"We had some interesting walks up there in the woods," Bob reminisced. "They were the prettiest girls in school till their daddy got transferred and they moved away."

"Who moved in after that?" Cliff wondered, half to himself. "That old couple from Harrisburg—the Faradays. They were here a long time, until the old man died and she went to live with her kids." Cliff narrowed his eyes as he tried to remember. "That was a couple months before Morgan ran off the bridge. Nobody's lived here since."

Bob shrugged; then both of them looked toward the gully. "Guess it's been ten years since anybody lived here."

"Ten years," Cliff repeated. "A long time."

They both looked over at the sound of a car. "The investigators," Bob said, adjusting his hat again. "They'll take over now."

From the corner of the porch, Maggie watched the proceedings. She'd decided that if the police crew needed her, they'd let her know. It appeared to her that they knew their business. She would just be in the way down there, Maggie reasoned as she drank another cup of black coffee.

She watched them shovel, sift and systematically bag what they'd come for. Maggie told herself that once it was off her property, she'd forget it. It would no longer concern her. She wished she could believe it. What was now being transferred into plastic bags had once been a living being. A man or a woman who'd had thoughts and feelings had lain, alone, only yards from what was now her home. No, she didn't believe she'd be able to forget that.

Before it was over, she'd have to know who that person had been, why they had died and why their grave had been on her land. She'd have to have the answers if she were to live in the home she'd chosen. She finished the last swallow of coffee as one of the police crew broke away from the group and came toward the porch. Maggie went to the steps to meet him.

"Ma'am." He nodded to her but, to her relief, didn't offer his hand. Instead, he took out a badge, flashing the cover up briefly. "I'm Lieutenant Reiker."

She thought he looked like a middle-aged accountant and wondered if he carried a gun under his jacket. "Yes, Lieutenant."

"We're just about finished up. Sorry for the inconvenience."

"That's all right." She gripped her hands together over the cup and wished she could go inside, to her music.

"I've got the trooper's report, but I wonder if you could tell me how you happened to find the remains."

Remains, Maggie thought with a shudder. It seemed a very cold word. For the second time, she related her story of the puppy's digging. She did so calmly now, without a tremor.

"You just bought the place?"

"Yes, I only moved in a few weeks ago."

"And you hired Delaney to do some landscaping."

"Yes." She looked down to where Cliff stood talking to another of the team. "The handyman I hired recommended him."

"Mmm-hmm." In a very casual way, the investigator took notes. "Delaney tells me you wanted the gully there dug out for a pond."

Maggie moistened her lips. "That's right."

"Nice place for one," he said conversationally. "I'd like to ask you to hold off on that for a while, though. We might need to come back and take another look around."

Maggie's hands twisted on the empty cup. "All right."

"What we'd like to do is block off that area." He hitched at his belt, then settled one foot on the step above the other. "Some chicken wire," he said easily, "to keep your dog and any other stray animal from digging around in there."

And people, Maggie thought, deciding it didn't take a genius to read between the lines. Before the day was over, this would be the biggest news flash in the county. She was learning fast. "Do whatever you need to do."

"We appreciate the cooperation, Miss Fitzgerald." He twirled the pen in his fingers, hesitating.

"Is there something else?"

"I know it's a bad time," he said with a sheepish smile, "but I can't pass it up. Would you mind signing my pad? I was a big fan of your mother's, and I guess I know most all of your songs, too."

Maggie laughed. It was far better to laugh. The day had been a series of one ludicrous event after another. "Of course." She took the offered pad and pen. "Would you like me to say anything special?"

"Maybe you could just write—to my good friend Harvey."

Before she could oblige, she glanced up and caught Cliff's eyes on her. She saw his lips twist into something between a sneer and a smile. With a silent oath, she signed the pad and handed it back.

"I don't know much about this kind of thing," she began briskly, "but I'd appreciate it if you kept me informed on whatever's being done."

"We'll have the medical examiner's report in a few days." Pocketing his pad, the investigator became solidly professional again. "We'll all know more then. Thanks for your time, Miss Fitzgerald. We'll be out of your way as soon as we can."

Though she felt Cliff's gaze still on her, Maggie didn't look over. Instead, she turned and walked back into the house. Moments later, music could be heard through the open windows.

Cliff remained where he was, though he'd answered all the questions that he could answer. His thoughts were focused on the sounds coming from the music room. It wasn't one of her songs, he concluded, but something from the classics, something that required speed, concentration and passion. Therapy, he wondered, frowning up at the window. With a shrug, he started toward his car. It wasn't his concern if the lady was upset. Hadn't she told him she'd moved back here to be on her own?

Turning his head, he saw the investigators preparing to leave. Within moments, he reflected, she'd be alone. The music pouring out of the windows was tense, almost desperate. Swearing, Cliff stuffed his keys back in his pocket and strode toward the steps.

She didn't answer his knock. The music played on. Without giving it a second thought, he pushed open the front door. The house vibrated with the storm coming from the piano. Following it into the music room, he watched her from the doorway.

Her eyes were dark, her head was bent, though he didn't think she even saw the keys. Talent? There was no denying it, any more than there could be any denying her tension or her vulnerability. Later, he might ask himself why all three made him uncomfortable.

Perhaps he did want to comfort her, he told himself. He'd do the same for anyone, under the circumstances. She didn't have to mean anything to him for him to want to offer a diversion. Strays and wounded birds had always been weaknesses of his. Dissatisfied with his own logic, Cliff waited until she'd finished.

Maggie looked up, startled to see him in the doorway. Damn her nerves, she thought, carefully folding her hands in her lap. "I thought you'd gone."

"No. They have."

She tossed the hair out of her eyes and hoped she looked composed. "Was there something else?"

"Yeah." He walked over to run a finger over the piano keys. No dust, he noted, in a house nearly choked with it. Her work was obviously of first importance.

When he didn't elaborate, Maggie frowned. Cliff preferred the impatience he saw in her eyes now. "What?"

"I had a steak in mind."

"I beg your pardon?"

The cool response made his lips curve. Yes, he definitely preferred her this way. "I haven't eaten."

"Sorry." Maggie began to straighten her sheet music. "I don't happen to have one handy."

"There's a place about ten miles out of town." He took her arm to draw her to her feet. "I have a feeling they'd treat a steak better than you would, anyway."

She pulled away, stood her ground and studied him. "We're going out to dinner?"

"That's right."

"Why?"

He took her arm again, so that he wouldn't ask himself the same question. "Because I'm hungry," Cliff said simply.

Maggie started to resist, though he didn't appear to notice. Then it struck her how much she wanted to get out, to get away, just for a little while. Sooner or later, she'd have to be alone in the house, but right then—No, right then, she didn't want to be alone anywhere.

He knew, understood, and whatever his approach, Cliff was offering her exactly what she needed.

Though their thoughts weren't particularly calm, neither of them spoke as they walked through the door together.

Chapter 5

Maggie set aside the next day to complete the title song for the movie score. She made a conscious effort to forget everything that had happened the day before. Everything. She wouldn't think of what had been buried and unearthed so close to her house, nor would she think of police or investigators or medical examiners.

In exactly the same way, she refused to think of Cliff, of the one wildly exciting kiss or of the oddly civilized dinner they'd shared. It was difficult to believe that she'd experienced both with the same man.

Today, she was Maggie Fitzgerald, writer of songs, creator of music. If she thought of only that, *was* only that, perhaps she could convince herself that everything that had happened yesterday had happened to someone else.

She knew there were men outside spreading seed, planting. There were shrubs going in, mulch being laid, more brush being cleared. If the landscape timbers she'd seen brought in that morning meant what she thought, construction was about to begin on her retaining wall.

None of that concerned her. The score demanded to be completed, and she'd complete it. The one form of discipline she understood perfectly was that a job had to be done no matter what went on around you. She'd seen her father direct a movie when his equipment had broken down and his actors had thrown tantrums.

She'd known her mother to perform while running a fever. Much of her life might have been lived in a plush, make-believe world, but she'd learned responsibility.

The score came first today, and the title song would be written. Perhaps she'd even add some clever little aside to C.J. at the end of the tape before she mailed it off.

It certainly wouldn't do to mention what was going on in her side yard, Maggie thought as she meticulously copied notes onto staff paper. C.J. wouldn't be able to find enough antacids in L.A. to handle it for him. Poor man, she mused, he'd been worried about the roof caving in on her. In a totally unexpected way, it certainly had. If he knew there'd been policemen swarming over her land with plastic bags, he'd catch the next plane and drag her back to L.A.

She wondered if Cliff would've dragged her from the house the night before if she hadn't gone voluntarily. Fortunately, it hadn't been an issue, because Maggie thought him perfectly capable of it. Yet he'd been the ideal dinner companion. While she hadn't expected consideration from him, he'd been considerate. She hadn't expected subtle kindness, but it had been there. Finding both had made it difficult to remember she considered him an unlikable man.

They hadn't spoken of what had been found on her property that day, nor had there been any speculation on the whys and hows. They hadn't discussed his work or hers, but had simply talked.

Looking back, Maggie couldn't say precisely what they'd talked about, only that the mood had been easy. So easy, she had almost forgotten the passion they'd pulled from each other in the quiet afternoon sunlight. Almost forgotten. The memory had been there, quietly nagging at her throughout the evening. It had made her blood move a little faster. It had made her wonder if he'd felt it, too.

Maggie swore and erased the last five notes she'd copied down. C.J. wouldn't appreciate the fact that she was mixing her bass and tenor. She was doing exactly what she'd promised herself she wouldn't do, and as she'd known it would, the upheaval of yesterday was affecting her work. Calmly, she took deep breaths until her mind was clear again. The wisest course was to switch the recorder back on to play and start from the beginning. Then the knock on the front door disrupted her thoughts. Quiet country life. She asked herself where she'd ever heard that expression as she went to answer.

The gun on the man's hip made her stomach twist. The little badge pinned to the khaki shirt told her he was the sheriff. When she took her gaze up to his face, she was surprised by his looks. Blond, tanned, with blue eyes fanned by lines that spoke of humor or sun. For a moment, she had the insane notion that C.J. had sent him out from central casting.

"Miss Fitzgerald?"

She moistened her lips as she tried to be rational. C.J. worried too much for practical jokes. Besides, the gun looked very, very real. "Yes."

"I'm Sheriff Agee. Hope you don't mind me dropping by."

"No." She tried a polite smile, but found it strained. Guns and badges and official vehicles. Too many police in too short a time, Maggie told herself.

"If it wouldn't put you out too much, I'd like to come in and talk to you for a few minutes."

It did put her out. She wanted to say it did, then close the door on him and everything he wanted to talk about. *Coward*, she told herself, and stepped back to let him in. "I suppose you're here about what we found yesterday." Maggie put her shoulder to the door to shut it. "I don't know what I can tell you."

"I'm sure it was a nasty experience, Miss Fitzgerald, and one you'd just as soon forget." His voice held just the right trace of sympathy mixed with professionalism. She decided he knew his business. "I wouldn't feel I was doing my duty as sheriff or as a neighbor if I didn't give you whatever help I can."

Maggie looked at him again. This time her smile came a bit more easily. "I appreciate that. I can offer you coffee, if you don't mind the mess in the kitchen."

He smiled and looked so solid, so pleasant, Maggie almost forgot the gun at his hip. "I never turn down coffee."

"The kitchen's down here," she began, then laughed. "I don't have to tell you, do I? You'd know this house as well as I do."

He fell into step beside her. "Tell you the truth, I've been around the outside, hacking at the weeds now and again or hunting, but I've only been inside a handful of times. The Morgans moved out when Joyce was still a kid."

"Yes, she told me."

"Nobody's lived here for more'n ten years. Louella just let it go after the old man died." He glanced up at the cracked ceiling paint. "She held it in trust till Joyce inherited it at twenty-five. You probably heard I held Joyce off from selling."

"Well . . ." Uncertain how to respond, Maggie busied herself at the stove.

"Guess I thought we'd fix it up eventually, rent it out again." To her, he sounded like a man who knew about dreams but never found the time for them. "But a big old place like this needs a lot of time and money to put right. Joyce probably did the right thing, selling out."

"I'm glad she did." After switching on the coffee-maker, Maggie indicated a chair.

"With Bog handling repairs and Delaney working on the grounds, you picked the right men." When Maggie just looked at him, the sheriff grinned again. "Nothing travels fast in small towns but news."

"No, I suppose not."

"Look, what happened yesterday . . ." He paused, clearing his throat. "I know it must be rough on you. I gotta tell you, Joyce was worked up about it. A lot of people who'd find something like that a stone's throw from their house would just pull up stakes and take off."

Maggie reached in the cabinets for cups. "I'm not going anywhere."

"Glad to hear it." He was silent a moment, watching her pour the coffee. Her hands looked steady enough. "I understand Cliff was here yesterday, too."

"That's right. He was overseeing some of the work."

"And your dog dug up—"

"Yes." Maggie set both cups on the table before she sat down. "He's just a puppy. Right now he's asleep upstairs. Too much excitement."

The sheriff waved away her offer of cream, sipping the coffee black. "I didn't come to press you for details. The state police filled me in. I just wanted to let you know I was as close as the phone if you needed anything."

"I appreciate that. I'm not really familiar with the procedure, but I suppose I should've called you yesterday."

"I like to take care of my own territory," he said slowly, "but with something like this—" He shrugged. "Hell, I'd've had to call in the state, anyway." She watched his wedding ring gleam dully in the sunlight. Joyce had had a matching one, Maggie recalled. Plain and gold and solid. "Looks like you're redoing this floor."

Maggie looked down blankly. "Oh, yes, I took up the old linoleum. I've got to get to the sanding."

"You call George Cooper," the sheriff told her. "He's in the book. He'll get you an electric sander that'll take care of this in no time. Just tell him Stan Agee gave you his name."

"All right." She knew the conversation should've eased her mind, but her nerves were jumping again. "Thank you."

"Anything else you need, you just give us a call. Joyce'll want to have you over for dinner. She bakes the best ham in the county."

"That'd be nice."

"She can't get over someone like you moving here to Morganville." He sipped at his coffee while Maggie's grew cold. While he leaned back in the chair, relaxed, she sat very straight with tension. "I don't keep up with music much, but Joyce knows all of your songs. She reads all those magazines, too, and now somebody who's in them's living in her old house." He glanced idly at the back door. "You ought to speak to Bog about putting some dead bolts on."

She looked over at the screen, remembering the hinges needed oiling. "Dead bolts?"

With a laugh, he finished off his coffee. "That's what happens when you're sheriff. You're always thinking of security. We've got a nice, quiet community, Miss Fitzgerald. Wouldn't want you to think otherwise. But I'd feel better knowing you had some good solid locks on the doors, since you're back here alone." Rising, he tugged absently at his holster. "Thanks for the coffee. You just remember to call if you need anything."

"Yes, I'll remember."

"I'll go on out this way and let you get back to work. You call George Cooper, now."

"All right." Maggie walked to the back door with him. "Thank you, Sheriff."

For a moment she just stood there by the door, her head resting against the jamb. She hated knowing she could be so easily worked up. The sheriff had come to reassure her, to show her that the community she'd chosen to live in had a concerned, capable law enforcer. Now her nerves were raw from talking to so many police. So many police, Maggie mused, just as it had been when Jerry died. All the police, all the questions. She thought she'd been over it, but now everything was coming back again, much too clearly.

"Your husband drove off the road, Mrs. Browning. We haven't located his body yet, but we're doing everything we can. I'm sorry."

Yes, there'd been sympathy at first, Maggie remembered. She'd had sympathy from the police, from her friends, Jerry's friends. Then questions: "Had your husband been drinking when he left the house?" "Was he upset, angry?" "Were you fighting?"

God, hadn't it been enough that he'd been dead? Why had they picked and pulled at all the reasons? How many reasons could there be for a twenty-eight-year-old man to turn his car toward a cliff and drive over it?

Yes, he'd been drinking. He'd done a lot of drinking since his career had started to skid and hers had kept climbing. Yes, they'd been fighting, because neither of them had understood what had happened to the dreams they'd once had. She'd answered their questions; she'd suffered the press until she had thought she'd go mad.

Maggie squeezed her eyes tight. That was over, she told herself. She couldn't bring Jerry back and solve his problems now. He'd found his own solution. Turning from the door, she went back to the music room.

In her work she found the serenity and the discipline she needed. It had always been that way for her. She could escape into the music so that her emotions found their outlet. She could train her mind on timing and structure. Her drive had always been to release the emotions, hers by the creation of a song and the listener's by hearing it. If she was successful in that, she needed no other ambition.

Talent wasn't enough in itself, she knew. It hadn't been enough for Jerry. Talent had to be harnessed by discipline; discipline, guided by creativity. Maggie used all three now.

As time passed, she became absorbed in the music and in the goal she'd set. The title song had to be passionate, full of movement and sexuality, as the title itself suggested. When it was played, she wanted it to stir the senses, touch off needs, build longings.

No one had been signed to perform it yet, so she was free to use whatever style she chose. She wanted something bluesy, and in her mind she could hear the moan of a sax. Sexy, sultry. She wanted the quiet wail of brass and the smoky throb of bass. Late the night before, when she'd been restless, she'd written down a few phrases. Now she experimented with them, twining words to music.

Almost at once she knew she'd found the key. The key was unexplained passion, barely controlled. It was desire that promised to rip aside anything civilized. It was the fury and heat that a man and woman could bring to each other until both were senseless from it. She had the key now, Maggie thought as her pulse began to pound with the music, because she'd experienced it herself. Yesterday, on the rise, in the sun, with Cliff.

Madness. That was the word that streamed through her mind.

Desire was madness. She closed her eyes as words and melody flowed through her. Hadn't she felt that madness, the sweetness and the ache of it, when his mouth had moved on hers? Hadn't she wanted to feel him against her, flesh to flesh? He'd made her think of dark nights, steamy, moonless nights when the air was so thick you'd feel it pulse on your skin. Then she hadn't thought at all, because desire was madness.

She let the words come, passionate, wanton promises that simmered over the heat of the music. Seductive, suggestive, they poured out of her own needs. Lovers' words, desperate words, were whispered out in her low, husky voice until the room was charged with them. No one who heard would be unmoved. That was her ambition.

When she was finished, Maggie was breathless and moved and exhilarated. She reached up to rewind the recorder for playback when, for the second time, she saw Cliff standing in the doorway.

Her hand froze, and her pulse, already fast, went racing. Had she called him with the song? she wondered frantically. Was the magic that strong? When he said nothing, she switched off the recorder and spoke with studied calm. "Is it an accepted habit in the country for people to walk into homes uninvited?"

"You don't seem to hear the door when you're working."

She acknowledged this with an inclination of her head. "That might mean I don't like to be disturbed when I'm working."

"It might." Disturbed. The word almost made him laugh. Perhaps he had disturbed her work, but that was nothing compared to what the song had done to him—to what watching her sing had done to him. It had taken every ounce of his control not to yank her from the piano stool and take her on the littered, dusty floor. He came closer, knowing before it reached him that her scent would be there to add to her allure.

"I lost quite a bit of time yesterday." Maggie swallowed whatever was trying to block her voice. Her body was still throbbing, still much too vulnerable from the passion she'd released. "I have a deadline on this score."

He glanced down at her hands. He wanted to feel them stroke over him with the same skill she'd used on the piano keys. Slowly, he took his gaze up her arms, over the curve of her shoulder to her face. For both of them, it was as if he'd touched her.

Her breath wasn't steady; her eyes weren't calm. That was as he wanted it now. No matter how often or how firmly he told himself to back off from her, Cliff knew he was reaching a point when it would be impossible. She wasn't for him—he could convince himself of that. But they had something that had to be freed and had to be tasted.

"From what I heard," he murmured, "you seem to be finished."

"That's for me to decide."

"Play it back." It was a challenge. He saw from her eyes that she knew it. A challenge could backfire on either of them. "The last song—I want to hear it again."

Dangerous. Maggie understood the danger. As she hesitated, his lips curved. It was enough. Without a word, she punched the rewind button. The song was a fantasy, she told herself as the tape hurried backward. It was a fantasy, just as the film was a fantasy. The song was for the characters in a story and had nothing, absolutely nothing, to do with her. Or with him. She flicked the recorder to play.

She'd listen objectively, Maggie decided as the music began to spill into the room. She'd listen as a musician, as a technician. That was what her job demanded. But she found, as her own voice began to tempt her, that she was listening as a woman. Rising, she walked to the window and faced out. When a hunger was this strong, she thought, distance could mean everything.

> *Wait for night when the air's*
> *hot and there's madness*
> *I'll make your blood swim*
> *Wait for night when passion rises like*
> *a flood in the heat dance*
> *Desire pours over the rim*

He listened, as he had before, and felt his system respond to the music and the promises that low voice made. He wanted all that the song hinted at. All that, and more.

When Cliff crossed the room, he saw her tense. He thought he could feel the air snap, hissing with the heat the song had fanned. Before he reached her, Maggie turned. The sun at her back shot a nimbus around her. In contrast, her eyes were dark. Like night, he thought. Like her night music. The words she'd written filled the room around them. It seemed those words were enough.

He didn't speak, but circled the back of her neck with his hand. She didn't speak, but resisted, forcing her body to stiffen. There was anger in her eyes now, as much for herself as for him. She'd taken herself to this point by allowing her own needs and fantasies to clear the path. It wasn't madness she wanted, Maggie told herself as she drew back. It was stability. It wasn't the wild she sought, but serenity. He wouldn't offer those things.

His fingers only tightened as she pulled back. That surprised them both. He'd forgotten the rules of a civilized seduction, just as he'd forgotten he'd only come there to see how she was. The music, the words, made the vulnerability that had concerned him a thing of the past. Now he felt strength as his fingers pressed into her skin. He saw challenge in her stance, and a dare, mixed with the fury in her eyes. Cliff wanted nothing less from her.

He stepped closer. When she lifted a hand in protest, he took her wrist. The pulse throbbed under his hand as intensely as the music throbbed on the air. Their eyes met, clashed, passion against passion. In one move, he pulled her against him and took her mouth.

She saw the vivid colors and lights she'd once imagined. She tasted the flavor of urgent desire. As her arms pulled him yet closer to her, Maggie heard her own moan of shuddering pleasure. The world was suddenly honed down to an instant, and the instant went on and on.

Had she been waiting for this? This mindless, melting pleasure? Were these sensations, these emotions, what she'd poured out into music for so long? She could find no answers, only more needs.

He'd stopped thinking. In some small portion of his brain, Cliff knew he'd lost the capacity to reason. She made him feel, outrageously, so that there was no room for intellect. His hands sought her, skimming under her shirt to find the soft, heated skin he knew he'd dreamed about. She strained against him, offering more. Against his mouth, he felt her lips form his name. Something wild burst inside him.

He wasn't gentle, though as a lover he'd never been rough before. He was too desperate to touch to realize that he might bruise something more fragile than he. The kiss grew savage. He knew he'd never be able to draw enough from her to satisfy him. More, and still more, he wanted, though her mouth was as crazed and demanding as his.

He was driving her mad. No one had ever shown her a need so great. Hunger fueled hunger until she ached with it. She knew it could consume her, perhaps both of them. With a fire so hot, they could burn each other out and be left with nothing. The thought made her moan again, and cling. She wanted more. Yet she feared to take more and find herself empty.

"No." His lips at her throat were turning her knees to water. "No, this is crazy," she managed.

He lifted his head. His eyes were nearly black now, and his breathing was unsteady. For the first time, Maggie felt a twinge of fear. What did she know of this man? "You called it madness," he murmured. "You were right."

Yes, she'd been right, and it had been him she'd thought of when she'd written the words. Yet she told herself it was sanity she needed. "It's not what either of us should want."

"No." His control was threatening to snap completely. Deliberately, he ran a hand down her hair. "But it's already too far along to stop. I want you, Maggie, whether I should or not."

If he hadn't used her name—Until then she hadn't realized that he could say her name and make her weak. As needs welled up again, she dropped her head on his chest. It was that artless, unplanned gesture that cleared his frenzied thoughts and tugged at something other than desire.

This was the kind of woman who could get inside a man. Once she did, he'd never be free of her. Knowing that, he fought back the overwhelming need to hold her close again. He wanted her, and he intended to have her. That didn't mean he'd get involved. They both knew that what had ignited between them would have to be consummated sooner or later. It was basic; it was simple. And they'd both walk away undamaged.

Whereas the arousal he'd felt hadn't worried him, the tenderness he was feeling now did. They'd better get things back on the right road. He took her by the shoulders and drew her back.

"We want each other." It sounded simple when he said it. Cliff was determined to believe it could be.

"Yes." She nodded, almost composed again. "I'm sure you've learned, as I have, that you can't have everything you want."

"True enough. But there's no reason for either of us not to have what we want this time."

"I can think of a few. The first is that I barely know you."

He frowned as he studied her face. "Does that matter to you?"

Maggie jerked away so quickly his hands fell to his sides. "So, you do believe everything you read." Her voice was brittle now, and her eyes were cold. "Los Angeles, land of sinning and sinners. I'm sorry to disappoint you, Cliff, but I haven't filled my life with nameless, faceless lovers. This fills my life." She slapped her hand down on the piano so that papers slid off onto the floor. "And since you read so much, since you know so much about me, you'll know that up to two years ago I was married. I had a husband, and as ridiculous as it sounds, was faithful for six years."

"My question didn't have anything to do with that." His voice was so mild in contrast to hers that she stiffened. Maggie had learned to trust him the least when he used that tone. "It was more personal, as in you and me."

"Then let's just say I have a rule of thumb not to hop into bed with men I don't know. You included."

He crossed the room, then laid his hand over hers on the piano. "Just how well do you have to know me?"

"Better, I think, than I ever will." She had to fight the urge to snatch her hand away. She'd made a fool of herself enough for one day. "I have another rule about steering clear of people who don't like who and what I am."

He looked down at the hand beneath his. It was pale, slender and strong. "Maybe I don't know who and what you are." His gaze lifted to lock on hers. "Maybe I intend to find out for myself."

"You'll have to have my cooperation for that, won't you?"

He lifted a brow, as if amused. "We'll see."

Her voice became only more icy. "I'd like you to leave. I've a lot of work to do."

"Tell me what you were thinking about when you wrote that song."

Something fluttered over her face so quickly he couldn't be certain if it was panic or passion. Either would have suited him.

"I said I want you to leave."

"I will—after you tell me what you were thinking of."

She kept her chin angled and her eyes level. "I was thinking of you."

He smiled. Taking her hand, he brought her palm to his lips. The unexpected gesture had thunderbolts echoing in her head. "Good," he murmured. "Think some more. I'll be back."

She closed her fingers over her palm as he walked away. He'd given her no choice but to do as he'd asked.

It was late, late into the night, when she woke. Groggy, Maggie thought it had been the dream that had disturbed her. She cursed Cliff and rolled onto her back. She didn't want to dream of him. She certainly didn't want to lie awake in the middle of the night, thinking of him.

Staring up at the ceiling, she listened to the quiet. At times like this, it struck her how alone she was. There were no servants sleeping downstairs, as there had been all her life. Her closest neighbor was perhaps a quarter of a mile away through the woods. No all-night clubs or drugstores, she mused. So far, she'd yet to even deal with getting an outside antenna for television. She was on her own, as she'd chosen.

Then why, Maggie wondered, did her bed suddenly seem so empty and the night so long? Rolling to her side, she struggled to shake off the mood and her thoughts of Cliff.

Overhead, a board creaked, but she paid no attention. Old houses made noises at night. Maggie had learned that quickly. Restless, she shifted in bed and lay watching the light of the waning moon.

She didn't want Cliff there, with her. Even allowing herself to think that she did was coming too close to dangerous ground. It was true her body had reacted to him, strongly. A woman couldn't always control the needs of her body, but she could control the direction of her thoughts. Firmly, she set her mind on the list of chores for the next day.

When the sound came again, she frowned, glancing automatically at the ceiling. The creaks and groans rarely disturbed her, but then, she'd always slept soundly in this house. Until Cliff Delaney, she thought, and determinedly shut her eyes. The sound of a door shutting quietly had them flying open again.

Before panic could register or reason overtake it, her heart was lodged in her throat, pounding. She was alone, and someone was in the house. All the nightmares that had ever plagued a woman alone in the dark loomed in her mind. Her fingers curled into the sheets as she lay stiffly, straining to hear.

Was that a footstep on the stairs, or was it all in her imagination? As terror flowed into her, she thought of the gully outside. She bit down on her lip to keep herself from making a sound. Very slowly, Maggie turned her head and made out the puppy sleeping at the foot of the bed. He didn't hear anything. She closed her eyes again and tried to even her breathing.

If the dog heard nothing that disturbed him, she reasoned, there was nothing to worry about. Just boards settling. Even as she tried to convince herself, Maggie heard a movement downstairs. A soft squeak, a gentle scrape. The kitchen door? she asked herself as the panic buzzed in her head. Fighting to move slowly and quietly, she reached for the phone beside the bed. As she held it to her ear, she heard the buzz that reminded her she'd left the kitchen extension off the hook earlier so as not to be disturbed. Her phone was as good as dead. Hysteria bubbled and was swallowed.

Think, she ordered herself. *Stay calm and think.* If she was alone, with no way to reach help, she had to rely on herself. How many times in the past few weeks had she stated that she could do just that?

She pressed a hand against her mouth so that the sound of her own breathing wouldn't disturb her concentrated listening. There was nothing now, no creaks, no soft steps on wood.

Careful to make no sound, she climbed out of bed and found the fireplace poker. Muscles tense, Maggie propped herself in the chair, facing the door. Gripping the poker in both hands, she prayed for morning.

Chapter 6

After a few days, Maggie had all but forgotten about the noises in her house. As early as the morning after the incident, she'd felt like a fool. She'd been awakened by the puppy licking her bare feet while she sat, stiff and sore from the night in the chair. The fireplace poker had lain across her lap like a medieval sword. The bright sunlight and birdsong had convinced her she'd imagined everything, then had magnified every small noise the way a child magnifies shadows in the dark. Perhaps she wasn't quite as acclimated to living alone as she'd thought. At least she could be grateful she'd left the downstairs extension off the hook. If she hadn't, everyone in town would know she was a nervous idiot.

If she had nerves, Maggie told herself, it was certainly understandable under the circumstances. People digging up skeletons beside her house, the local sheriff suggesting she lock her doors, and Cliff Delaney, Maggie added, keeping her up at night. The only good thing to come out of the entire week was the completed score. She imagined that C.J. would be pleased enough with the finished product not to nag her about coming back to L.A., at least for a little while.

Maggie decided the next constructive thing to do was to take the tape and sheet music she'd packaged to the post office and mail it off. Perhaps later she'd celebrate her first songs written in her new home.

She enjoyed the trip to town and took it leisurely. The narrow little roads were flanked by trees that would offer a blanket of shade in a few short weeks. Now the sun streamed through the tiny leaves to pour white onto the road. Here and there the woods were interrupted by fields, brown earth turned up. She could see farmers working with their tractors and wondered what was being planted. Corn, hay, wheat? She knew virtually nothing of that aspect of the home she'd chosen. Maggie thought it would be interesting to watch things grow until the summer or autumn harvest.

She saw cows with small calves nursing frantically. There was a woman carrying a steel bucket to what must have been a chicken coop. A dog raced along a fenced yard, barking furiously at Maggie's car.

Her panic of a few nights before seemed so ridiculous she refused to think of it.

She passed a few houses, some of them hardly more than cabins, others so obviously new and modern they offended the eyes. She found herself resenting the pristine homes on lots where trees had been cleared. Why hadn't they worked with what was there, instead of spoiling it? Then she laughed at herself. She was sounding too much like Cliff Delaney. People had a right to live where and how they chose, didn't they? But she couldn't deny that she preferred the old weathered brick or wood homes surrounded by trees.

As she drove into Morganville, she noted the homes were closer together. That was town life, she decided. There were sidewalks here, and a few cars parked along the curb. People kept their lawns trimmed. Maggie decided that from the look of it, there was quite a bit of pride and competition among the flower gardens. It reminded her to check her own petunias.

The post office was on the corner, a small redbrick building with a two-car parking lot. Beside it, separated by no more than a two-foot strip of grass, was the Morganville bank. Two men stood beside the outside mailbox, smoking and talking. They watched as Maggie pulled into the lot, as she stepped out of the car and as she walked toward the post office. Deciding to try her luck, she turned her head and flashed them a smile.

"Good morning."

"Morning," they said in unison. One of them pushed back his fishing cap. "Nice car."

"Thank you."

She walked inside, pleased that she had had what could pass for a conversation.

There was one woman behind the counter already engaged in what appeared to be casual gossip with a younger woman who toted a baby on her hip. "No telling how long they've been there," the postmistress stated, counting out stamps. "Nobody's lived out there since the Faradays, and that's been ten years last month. Old lady Faraday used to come in for a dollar's worth of stamps once a week, like clockwork. 'Course, they were cheaper then." She pushed the stamps across the counter. "That's five dollars' worth, Amy."

"Well, I think it's spooky." The young mother jiggled the baby on her hip while he busied himself gurgling at Maggie. Gathering up the stamps, she stuffed them into a bag on her other shoulder. "If I found a bunch of old bones in my yard, I'd have a For Sale sign up the next day." Hearing the words, Maggie felt some of her pleasure in the day fade. "Billy said some drifter probably fell in that gully and nobody ever knew about it."

"Could be. Guess the state police'll figure it out before long." The postmistress closed the conversation by turning to Maggie. "Help you?"

"Yes." Maggie stepped up to the counter. The young woman gave her one long, curious look before she took her baby outside. "I'd like to send this registered mail."

"Well, let's see what it weighs." The postmistress took the package and put it on the scale. "You want a return receipt?"

"Yes, please."

"Okay." She took the pencil from behind her ear to run the tip along a chart taped to the scale. "Cost you a bit more, but you'll know it got there. Let's see, it's going to zone—" She broke off as she caught the return address on the corner of the package. Her gaze lifted, focusing sharply on Maggie, before she began to fill out the form. "You're the songwriter from California. Bought the Morgan place."

"That's right." Because she wasn't sure what to say after the conversation she'd overheard, Maggie left it at that.

"Nice music." The postmistress wrote in meticulously rounded letters. "Lot of that stuff they play I can't even understand. I got some of your mama's records. She was the best. Nobody else comes close."

Maggie's heart warmed, as it always did when someone spoke of her mother. "Yes, I think so, too."

"You sign this here." As she obeyed, Maggie felt the postmistress's eyes on her. It occurred to her that this woman saw every piece of correspondence that came to or from her. Though it was an odd feeling, she found it wasn't unpleasant. "Big old house, the Morgan place." The woman figured the total on a little white pad. "You settling in all right out there?"

"Bit by bit. There's a lot to be done."

"That's the way it is when you move into a place, 'specially one's been empty so long. Must be a lot different for you."

Maggie lifted her head. "Yes. I like it."

Perhaps it was the direct eyes or perhaps it was the simple phrasing, but the postmistress seemed to nod to herself. Maggie felt as though she'd found her first full acceptance. "Bog'll do well by you. So will young Delaney."

Maggie smiled to herself as she reached for her wallet. Small towns, she thought. No secrets.

"You had a shock the other day."

Because she'd been expecting some kind of comment, Maggie took it easily. "I wouldn't care to have another like it."

"Nope, guess nobody would. You just relax and enjoy that old house," the postmistress advised. "It was a showcase in its day. Louella always kept it fine. Let the police worry about the rest of it."

"That's what I'm trying to do." Maggie pocketed her change. "Thank you."

"We'll get this off for you right away. You have a nice day."

Maggie was definitely feeling pleased with herself when she walked back outside. She took a deep breath of soft spring air, smiled again at the two men still talking beside the mailbox, then turned toward her car. The smile faded when she saw Cliff leaning against the hood.

"Out early," he said easily.

He'd told her it was difficult to avoid anyone in a town that size. Maggie decided it was his accuracy that annoyed her. "Shouldn't you be working somewhere?"

He grinned and offered her the bottle of soda he held. "Actually, I just came off a job site and was on my way to another." When she made no move to take the soda, he lifted the bottle to his lips again and drank deeply. "You don't see too many of these in Morganville." He tapped a finger against the side of her Aston Martin.

She started to move around him to the driver's door. "If you'll excuse me," she said coolly, "I'm busy."

He stopped her effortlessly with a hand on her arm. Ignoring her glare, as well as the interested speculation of the two men a few yards away, Cliff studied her face. "You've shadows under your eyes. Haven't you been sleeping?"

"I've been sleeping just fine."

"No." He stopped her again, but this time he lifted a hand to her face, as well. Though she didn't seem to know it, every time her fragile side showed, he lost ground. "I thought you didn't believe in evasions."

"Look, I'm busy."

"You've let that business in the gully get to you."

"Well, what if I have?" Maggie exploded. "I'm human. It's a normal reaction."

"I didn't say it wasn't." The hand on her face tilted her chin back a bit farther. "You fire up easily these days. Is it just that business that has you tense, or is there something else?"

Maggie stopped trying to pull away and stood very still. Maybe he hadn't noticed the men watching them, or the postmistress in the window, but she had. "It's none of your business whether I'm tense or not. Now, if you'll stop making a scene, I have to go home and work."

"Do scenes bother you?" Amused now, he drew her closer. "I wouldn't have thought so, from the number of times you've had your picture snapped."

"Cliff, cut it out." She put both hands on his chest. "For heaven's sake, we're standing on Main Street."

"Yeah. And we've just become the ten-o'clock bulletin."

A laugh escaped before she even knew it was going to happen. "You get a real kick out of that, don't you?"

"Well . . ." He took advantage of her slight relaxing and wrapped his arms around her. "Maybe. I've been meaning to talk to you."

A woman walked by with a letter in her hand. Maggie noticed that she took her time putting it into the box. "I think we could find a better place." At his snort of laughter, she narrowed her eyes. "I didn't mean that. Now, will you let go?"

"In a minute. Remember when we went out to dinner the other night?"

"Yes, I remember. Cliff—" She turned her head and saw that the two men were still there, still watching. Now the woman had joined them. "This really isn't funny."

"Thing is," he continued easily, "we have this custom around here. I take you out to dinner, then you reciprocate."

Out of patience, she wriggled against him and found that only made her blood pressure rise. "I haven't the time to go out to dinner right now. I'll get back to you in a few weeks."

"I'll take potluck."

"Potluck?" she repeated. "At *my* house?"

"Good idea."

"Wait a minute. I didn't say—"

"Unless you can't cook."

"Of course I can cook," she tossed back.

"Fine. Seven o'clock?"

She aimed her most deadly, most regal stare. "I'm hanging wallpaper tonight."

"You have to eat sometime." Before she could comment, he kissed her, briefly but firmly enough to make a point. "See you at seven," he said, then strolled over to his truck. "And, Maggie," he added through the open window, "nothing fancy. I'm not fussy."

"You—" she began, but the roar of the truck's engine drowned her out. She was left standing alone, fuming, in the center of the parking lot. Knowing there were at least a dozen pair of eyes on her, Maggie kept her head high as she climbed into her own car.

She cursed Cliff repeatedly, and expertly, on the three-mile drive back to her house.

Maggie expected the men from Cliff's crew to be there when she returned. The discreet black car at the end of her driveway, however, was unexpected. She discovered as she pulled alongside it that she wasn't in the mood for visitors, not for neighbors calling to pay their respects or for curiosity-seekers. She wanted to be alone with the sander she'd rented from George Cooper.

As she stepped from the car, she spotted the rangy man with the salt-and-pepper hair crossing her front yard from the direction of the gully. And she recognized him.

"Miss Fitzgerald."

"Good morning. Lieutenant Reiker, isn't it?"

"Yes, ma'am."

What was the accepted etiquette, Maggie wondered, when you came home and found a homicide detective on your doorstep? Maggie decided on the practical, marginally friendly approach. "Is there something I can do for you?"

"I'm going to have to ask for your cooperation, Miss Fitzgerald." The lieutenant kept his weight on one foot, as if his hips were troubling him. "I'm sure you'd like to get on with all your landscaping plans, but we want you to hold off on the pond a while longer."

"I see." She was afraid she did. "Can you tell me why?"

"We've received the medical examiner's preliminary report. We'll be investigating."

It might've been easier not to ask, not to know. Maggie wasn't certain she could live with herself if she took the coward's way out that she was obviously being offered. "Lieutenant, I'm not sure how much you're at liberty to tell me, but I do think I have a right to know certain things. This is my property."

"You won't be involved to any real extent, Miss Fitzgerald. This business goes back a long way."

"As long as my land's part of it, I'm involved." She caught herself worrying the strap of her bag, much as Joyce had done on her visit. She forced her hands to be still. "It'd be easier for me, Lieutenant, if I knew what was going on."

Reiker rubbed his hand over his face. The investigation was barely under way, and he already had a bad taste in his mouth. Maybe things that'd been dead and buried for ten years should just stay buried. Some things, he decided grimly. Yes, some things.

"The medical examiner determined that the remains belonged to a Caucasian male in his early fifties."

Maggie swallowed. That made it too real. Much too real. "How long—" she began, but had to swallow again. "How long had he been there?"

"The examiner puts it at about ten years."

"As long as the house has been empty," she murmured. She brought herself back, telling herself that it wasn't personal. Logically, practically, it had nothing to do with her. "I don't suppose they could determine how he died?"

"Shot," Reiker said flatly, and watched the horror fill her eyes. "Appears to've been a thirty-gauge shotgun, probably at close range."

"Good God." Murder. Yet hadn't she known it, sensed it almost from the first instant? Maggie stared out into the woods and watched two squirrels race up the trunk of a tree. How could it have happened here? "After so many years—" she began, but had to swallow yet again. "After so many years, wouldn't it be virtually impossible to identify the—him?"

"He was identified this morning." Reiker watched as she turned to him, pale, her eyes almost opaque. It gave him a bad feeling. He told himself it was because, like every other man in the country, he'd had a fantasy love affair with her mother twenty years before.

He told himself it was because she was young enough to be his daughter. At times like this, he wished he'd chosen any other line of work.

"We found a ring, too, an old ring with a lot of fancy carving and three small diamond chips. An hour ago, Joyce Agee identified it as her father's. William Morgan was murdered and buried in that gully."

But that was wrong. Maggie dragged a hand through her hair and tried to think. No matter how bluntly, how practically, Reiker put it, it was wrong. "That can't be. I was told that William Morgan had an accident—something about a car accident."

"Ten years ago, his car went through the guardrail of the bridge crossing into West Virginia. His car was dragged out of the Potomac, but not his body. His body was never found . . . until a few days ago."

Through the rail, into the water, Maggie thought numbly. Like Jerry. They hadn't found Jerry's body, either, not for nearly a week. She'd lived through every kind of hell during that week. As she stood, staring straight ahead, she felt as though she were two people in two separate times. "What will you do now?"

"There'll be an official investigation. It has nothing to do with you, Miss Fitzgerald, other than we need for you to keep that section of your property clear. There'll be a team here this afternoon to start going over it again, just in case we missed something."

"All right. If you don't need anything else—"

"No, ma'am."

"I'll be inside."

As she walked across the lawn toward the house, she told herself that something that had happened ten years before had nothing to do with her. Ten years before, she'd been dealing with her own tragedy, the loss of her parents. Unable to resist, she looked back over her shoulder at the gully as she climbed the steps to the porch.

Joyce Agee's father, Maggie thought with a shudder. Joyce had sold her the house without knowing what would be discovered.

She thought of the pretty, tense young woman who had been grateful for a simple kindness to her mother. Compelled, Maggie went to the pad scrawled with names and numbers beside the phone. Without hesitating, she called the number for Joyce Agee. The voice that answered was soft, hardly more than a whisper. Maggie felt a stab of sympathy.

"Mrs. Agee—Joyce, this is Maggie Fitzgerald."

"Oh . . . Yes, hello."

"I don't want to intrude." Now what? Maggie asked herself. She had no part of this, no link other than a plot of land that had lain neglected for a decade. "I just wanted you to know that I'm terribly sorry, and if there's anything I can do . . . I'd like to help."

"Thank you, there's nothing." Her voice hitched, then faltered. "It's been such a shock. We always thought—"

"Yes, I know. Please, don't think you have to talk to me or be polite. I only called because somehow—" She broke off, passing a hand over her hair. "I don't know. I feel as though I've set it all off."

"It's better to know the truth." Joyce's voice became suddenly calm. "It's always better to know. I worry about Mother."

"Is she all right?"

"I'm not—I'm not sure." Maggie sensed fatigue now, rather than tears. She understood that form of grief, as well. "She's here now. The doctor's with her."

"I won't keep you, then. Joyce, I understand we hardly know each other, but I would like to help. Please let me know if I can."

"I will. Thank you for calling."

Maggie replaced the receiver. That accomplished nothing, she reflected. It accomplished nothing, because she didn't know Joyce Agee. When you grieved, you needed someone you knew, the way she'd needed Jerry when her parents had been killed. Though she knew Joyce had a husband, Maggie thought of Cliff and the way he'd taken the woman's hands, the look of concern on his face, when he'd spoken to her. He'd be there for her, Maggie mused, and wished she knew what they meant to each other.

To give her excess energy an outlet, she switched on the rented sander.

The sun was low, the sky rosy with it, when Cliff drove toward the old Morgan property. His mind was full of questions. William Morgan murdered. He'd been shot, buried on his own property; then someone had covered the trail by sending his car into the river.

Cliff was close enough to the Morgans and to the people of Morganville to know that every other person in town might've wished William Morgan dead. He'd been a hard man, a cold man, with a genius for making money and enemies. But could someone who Cliff knew, someone he'd talk to on the street any day of the week, have actually murdered him?

In truth, he didn't give a damn about the old man, but he worried about Louella and Joyce—especially Joyce. He didn't like to see her the way she'd been that afternoon, so calm, so detached, with nerves snagged at the edge. She meant more to him than any other woman he'd known, yet there seemed to be no way to help her now. That was for Stan, Cliff thought, down-shifting as he came to a corner.

God knew if the police would ever come up with anything viable. He didn't have much faith in that after ten years. That meant Joyce would have to live with knowing that her father had been murdered and that his murderer still walked free. Would she, Cliff mused, look at her neighbors and wonder?

Swearing, Cliff turned onto the lane that led to the Morgan place. There was someone else he worried about, he thought grimly, though he didn't have the excuse of a long, close friendship with this woman.

Damned if he wanted to worry about Maggie Fitzgerald. She was a woman from another place, who liked glittery parties and opening nights. Where he'd choose solitude, she'd choose crowds. She'd want champagne; he, cold beer. She'd prefer trips to Europe;

he, a quiet ride down the river. She was the last person he needed to worry about.

She'd been married to a performer who'd flamed like a comet and who'd burned out just as quickly. Her escorts had been among the princes of the celebrity world. Tuxedos, silk scarves and diamond cuff links, he thought derisively. What the hell was she doing in the middle of a mess like this? And what the hell, he asked himself, was she doing in his life?

He pulled up behind her car and stared broodingly at her house. Maybe with all that was going on she'd decide to go back West. He'd prefer it that way. Damned if he didn't want to believe he would. She had no business crashing into his thoughts the way she had lately. That music. He let out a long stream of curses as he remembered it. That night music. Cliff knew he wanted her the way he'd wanted no woman before. It was something he couldn't overcome. Something he could barely control.

So why was he here? Why had he pushed his way into a meeting she hadn't wanted? Because, he admitted, when he thought of the way it had been between them, he didn't want to overcome it. Tonight he didn't want control.

As he walked toward the front door, he reminded himself that he was dealing with a woman who was different from any he'd known. Approach with caution, he told himself, then knocked at the front door.

From the other side, Maggie gripped the knob with both hands and tugged. It took two tries before she opened the door, and by that time Killer was barking nonstop.

"You should have Bog take care of that," Cliff suggested. He bent down to ruffle the dog's fur. Killer flopped on his back, offering his belly.

"Yeah." She was glad to see him. Maggie told herself she would've been glad to see anyone, but when she looked at him, she knew it was a lie. All through the afternoon she'd waited. "I keep meaning to."

He saw tension in the way she stood, in the way one hand still gripped the doorknob. Deliberately, he gave her a cocky smile. "So, what's for dinner?"

She let out a quick laugh as some of the nerves escaped. "Hamburgers."

"Hamburgers?"

"You did invite yourself," she reminded him. "And you did say not to fuss."

"So I did." He gave Killer a last scratch behind the ears, then rose.

"Well, since it's my first dinner party, I thought I'd stick with my speciality. It was either that or canned soup and cold sandwiches."

"If that's been your staple since you moved in, it's no wonder you're thin."

Frowning, Maggie glanced down at herself. "Do you realize you make a habit of criticizing?"

"I didn't say I didn't like thin women."

"That's not the point. You can come back and complain while I cook the hamburgers."

As they walked down the hall, Cliff noticed a few bare spots where she'd removed strips of wallpaper. Apparently she was serious about taking on the overwhelming job of redoing the house. When they passed the music room, he glanced in at her piano and wondered why. She was in the position of being able to hire a fleet of decorators and craftsmen. The job could be done in weeks, rather than the months, even years, it promised to take this way. The freshly sanded floor in the kitchen caught his eye.

"Nice job." Automatically, he crouched down to run his fingers over the floor's surface. The dog took this as an invitation to lick his face.

Maggie lifted a brow. "Well, thank you."

Catching the tone, he looked up at her. He couldn't deny that he'd been giving her a hard time from the outset. He had his reasons. The primary one as Cliff saw it now was her effect on him. "The question is," he said, rising again, "why you're doing it."

"The floor needed it." She turned to the counter to begin making patties.

"I meant why *you're* doing it."

"It's my house."

He wandered over to stand beside her. Again, he found himself watching her hands. "Did you sand your own floors in California?"

"No." Annoyed, she set the patties under the broiler. "How many can you eat?"

"One'll do. Why are you sanding floors and hanging wallpaper?"

"Because it's my house." Maggie grabbed a head of lettuce from the refrigerator and began to shred it for salad.

"It was your house in California, too."

"Not the way this is." She dropped the lettuce and faced him. Impatience, annoyance, frustration—the emotions were plainly on the surface for him to see. "Look, I don't expect you to understand. I don't *care* if you understand. This house is special. Even after everything that's happened, it's special."

No, he didn't understand, but he discovered he wanted to. "The police have contacted you, then."

"Yes." She began to shred lettuce with a vengeance. "That investigator, Lieutenant Reiker, was here this morning." Her fingers dug into the cold, wet leaves. "Damn it, Cliff, I feel gruesome. I called Joyce and felt like an idiot, an intruder. There was nothing I could say."

"Did you?" he murmured. Strange that Joyce hadn't said anything about it, he thought. Then again, Joyce had said very little to him. "There isn't anything for you to say." He put his hands on her shoulders and felt the tension ripple. "This is something Joyce and her mother and the police have to deal with. It's nothing to do with you."

"I tell myself that," she said quietly. "Intellectually, I know it's true, but—" She turned, because she needed someone. Because, she admitted, she needed him. "It happened right outside. I'm involved, connected, whether I want to be or not. A man was murdered a few yards from my house. He was killed in a spot where I'd planned to put a nice quiet pond, and now—"

"And now," Cliff said, interrupting, "it's ten years later."

"Why should that matter?" she demanded. "My parents were killed ten years ago—Time doesn't make any difference."

"That," he countered, less gently than he'd intended, "had everything to do with you."

With a sigh, she allowed herself the weakness of resting her head against him. "I know how Joyce is feeling now. Everywhere I look, something draws me into this."

The more Maggie talked of Joyce, the less Cliff thought of the quiet brunette, and the more he thought of Maggie. His fingers tangled in her hair. It wasn't desire he felt now, but an almost fierce, protective urge he'd never expected. Perhaps there was something he could do, he decided, drawing her away.

"You didn't know William Morgan."

"No, but—"

"I did. He was a cold, ruthless man who didn't believe in words like *compassion* or *generosity*." Deliberately, he set Maggie aside and tended to the meat under the broiler himself. "Half the town would've cheered ten years ago if it hadn't been for Louella. She loved the old man. Joyce loved him, too, but both of them feared him every bit as much. The police won't have an easy time proving who killed him, and the town won't care. I detested him myself, for a lot of reasons."

She didn't like knowing that he could speak of a man's murder so calmly, so coldly. But then, as she'd told him herself before, they really didn't understand each other. To keep her hands busy, Maggie went back to the salad. "Joyce?" she asked casually.

He glanced at her sharply, then leaned on the counter again. "Yeah, for one. Morgan believed in discipline. Old-fashioned discipline. Joyce was like my kid sister. When I caught Morgan going at her with a belt when she was sixteen, I threatened to kill him myself."

He said it so casually Maggie's blood froze. He saw the doubts and the questions in her eyes when she looked at him.

"And so," Cliff added, "as the stories go, did half the population of Morganville. No one grieved when they fished William Morgan's car out of the river."

"No one has the right to take a life," Maggie said in a shaky voice. "Not their own or anyone else's."

He remembered that they had fished her husband's car out of the water, too. He remembered that the final verdict had been suicide. "You'd be better off not making comparisons," he said roughly.

"They seem to make themselves."

"What happened to Jerry Browning was a tragic waste of a life and of a talent. Do you plan on taking the blame for that, too?"

"I never took the blame," Maggie said wearily.

"Did you love him?"

Her eyes were eloquent, but her voice was steady. "Not enough."

"Enough to be faithful to him for six years," Cliff countered.

She smiled as her own words came back to her. "Yes, enough for that. Still, there's more to love than loyalty, isn't there?"

His hand was gentle again when he touched her face. "You said you hadn't taken the blame."

"Responsibility and blame are different things."

"No." He shook his head. "There's no responsibility or blame this time, either. Don't you think it's the height of egotism to feel responsible for someone else's actions?"

She started to snap at him, but the words hit home. "Maybe. Maybe it is." It wasn't easy, but she shook off the mood and smiled. "I think the hamburgers are done. Let's eat."

Chapter 7

Maggie found the kitchen cozy with the smell of hot food and the patter of raindrops that had just begun to strike the windows. When she thought of it, she decided she'd never really experienced coziness before. Her parents had lived on a grand scale: huge, elegant rooms and huge, elegant parties; boisterous, eccentric friends. With her own home in Beverly Hills, Maggie had followed the same pattern. Extravagance might've been what she needed during that phase of her life, or it might've been a habit. She wasn't sure when it had begun to wear on her, any more than she was certain if she'd ever been as relaxed as she was at that moment, eating in her half-finished kitchen with a man she wasn't quite sure of.

He was strong, she mused. Perhaps she'd never allowed a strong man into her life. Her father had been strong, Maggie remembered. He'd been the type of man who could do and get precisely what he wanted simply because he wanted it. The strength hadn't been a physical one, but one of personality and will. But then, her mother had matched him with her own combination of grit and exuberance. Maggie had never seen a more perfect relationship than theirs.

Theirs had been an all-consuming, enduring love, with qualities of practicality, compassion and fire. They'd never competed, never envied each other's success. Support, she thought. Perhaps that had been the real key to the quality and lasting power of their relationship. Unquestioning mutual support. She hadn't found that in her own marriage, and she'd come to think her parents had been unique.

Something had happened to the balance in her relationship with Jerry. As he'd grown weaker, she'd grown stronger. Eventually, they'd come to a point where all the support had been on her side and all the need on his. Yet she'd stayed, because it had been impossible to forget that they'd been friends. Friends don't break promises.

She wondered, as she studied Cliff, what sort of friend he would be. And she wondered, though she tried not to, what he would be like as a lover.

"What're you thinking of?"

The question came so abruptly that Maggie almost overturned her glass. Quickly, she sorted out her thoughts and chose the least personal. She could hardly tell him what had been the last thing on her mind. "I was thinking," she began, picking up her wine again, "how cozy it is eating here in the kitchen. I'll probably demote the dining room to the last thing on my list."

"That's what you were thinking?" By the way he held her gaze, she knew he sensed there'd been other things.

"More or less." A woman who'd been interviewed and questioned all her life knew how to evade and dodge. Lifting the bottle, she filled Cliff's glass again. "The Bordeaux's another present from my agent. Or another bribe," she added.

"Bribe?"

"He wants me to give up this mad scheme of camping out in the wilderness and come back to civilization."

"He thinks he can persuade you with puppies and French wine?"

With a bubbling laugh, Maggie sipped. "If I weren't so attached to this place, either one might've worked."

"Is that what you are?" Cliff asked thoughtfully. "Attached?"

At the question, her eyes stopped laughing, and her soft, wide mouth sobered. "In your business you should know that some things root quickly."

"Some do," he agreed. "And some that do can't acclimate to the new territory."

She tapped the side of her glass with a fingertip, wishing she understood why his doubts dug at her so deeply. "You don't have much faith in me, do you?"

"Maybe not." He shrugged as if to lighten a subject he wasn't so certain of any longer. "In any case, I'm finding it interesting to watch you make the adjustments."

She decided to go with his mood. "How'm I doing?"

"Better than I'd thought." He lifted his glass in a half toast. "But it's early yet."

She laughed, because arguing seemed like a waste of time. "Were you born cynical, Cliff, or did you take lessons?"

"Were you born an optimist?"

Both brows lifted to disappear under the fringe of sable bangs. *"Touché,"* Maggie said. No longer interested in the meal, she studied him, finding that while his face was very much to her liking, she still couldn't judge him by his eyes. Too much control, she thought. A person would only get inside his head if he or she was invited. "You know," she began slowly, "after I'd stopped being annoyed, I decided I was glad you were coming by this evening." Now she grinned. "I don't know when I might've opened the wine otherwise."

This time he grinned. "I annoy you?"

"I think you're well aware of that," Maggie returned dryly. "And that for your own personal reasons it pleases you to do so."

Cliff tasted the wine again. It was warm and rich, reminding him of her mouth. "Actually, I do."

He said it so easily that Maggie laughed again. "Is it just me, or is annoying people a hobby of yours?"

"Just you." Over the rim of his glass, he studied her. She'd pinned her hair up in a loose Gibson style that accentuated her delicate, old-fashioned features. She wore some dark contouring shadow that made her eyes seem even larger, but her mouth was naked. This was a woman, Cliff thought, who knew how to accentuate her own looks to the best advantage, subtly, so that a man would be caught before he analyzed what was Maggie and what was illusion. "I like your reactions," Cliff continued after a moment. "You don't like to lose your temper."

"So you like to provoke me until I do."

"Yeah." He smiled again. "That about sizes it up."

"Why?" she demanded in a voice filled with exasperated amusement.

"I'm not immune to you," Cliff said, so quietly her fingers tightened on the stem of her glass. "I wouldn't like to think you were immune to me."

She sat for a moment, stirred and baffled. Before her emotions could rise any closer to the surface, she stood and began to clear the table. "No, I'm not. Would you like more wine or some coffee?"

His hands closed over hers on the dishes. Slowly, he rose, his gaze fixed on her face. Maggie felt as though the kitchen had shrunk in size. Like Alice in the rabbit hole, she thought confusedly, unsure whether to sample that tempting little bottle or not. The patter of rain outside seemed to grow to a roar.

"I want to make love with you."

She wasn't a child, Maggie told herself. She was an adult, and men had wanted her before. She'd resisted temptations before. But had any ever been quite so alluring? "We've already been through this."

His hands tightened on hers when she tried to turn away. "But we never resolved it."

No, she couldn't turn away, or run away, from a man like this, Maggie realized. She'd have to stand her ground. "I was sure we had. Perhaps coffee would be best, since you have to drive this evening and I have to work."

Cliff took the dishes and set them back on the table. With her hands empty, Maggie found herself at a loss. She folded her arms under her breasts, a habit Cliff had discovered she used whenever she was upset or disturbed. At the moment, he didn't care which she was, as long as she wasn't unmoved.

"We haven't resolved it," he repeated, and plucked a pin from her hair. "We haven't begun to resolve it."

Though her eyes remained steady, she backed up when he stepped closer. It made him feel as though he were stalking her, an odd and thrilling sensation. "I really thought I'd made myself clear," Maggie managed, in what sounded to her like a firm, dismissive tone.

"It's clear when I touch you." Cliff backed her up against the counter, then pulled another pin from her hair. "It's clear when you look at me like you're looking at me now."

Maggie's heart began to pound at the base of her throat. She was weakening; she felt it in the heaviness of her limbs, the lightness in her head. Desire was temptation, and temptation a seduction in itself. "I didn't say I didn't want you—"

"No, you didn't," Cliff interrupted. When he drew out the next pin, her hair fell heavily to her shoulders and lay there, dark and tousled. "I don't think lying comes easily to you."

How could she have been so relaxed a few moments before and so tense now? Every muscle in her body was taut in the effort to combat what seemed to be inevitable. "No, I don't lie." Her voice was lower, huskier. "I said I didn't know you. I said you didn't understand me."

Something flashed into him. Perhaps it was rage; perhaps it was need. "I don't give a damn how little we know each other or how little we understand each other. I know I want you." He gathered her hair in one hand. "I only have to touch you to know you want me."

Her eyes grew darker. Why did it always seem her desire was mixed with anger and, though she detested it, a certain weakness she couldn't control? "Can you really believe it's that simple?"

He had to. For the sake of his own survival, Cliff knew, he had to keep whatever was between them purely physical. They'd make love through the night until they were exhausted. In the morning, the need and the bond would be gone. He had to believe it. Otherwise . . . He didn't want to dwell on otherwise. "Why should it be complicated?" he countered.

The anger and the longing flowed through her. "Why indeed?" Maggie murmured.

The room had lost its cozy ambience. Now she felt she'd suffocate if she didn't escape it. Her eyes were stormy, his almost brutally calm, but she kept her gaze level on his while her thoughts raged. Why should she feel the need to rationalize, to romanticize? she asked herself. She wasn't an innocent young girl with misty dreams, but an adult, a widow, a professional woman who'd learned to live with reality. In reality, people took what they wanted, then dealt with the consequences. Now so would she.

"The bedroom's upstairs," she told him, and, brushing by him, walked out of the kitchen.

Disturbed, Cliff frowned after her. This was what he wanted, he thought. The lack of complications. Yet her abrupt acceptance had been so unexpected, so cool. No, he realized as he started after her, that wasn't what he wanted.

Maggie was at the base of the steps before he caught up with her. When she looked over her shoulder, he saw the fury in her eyes. The moment he took her arm, he felt the tension. This, he discovered, was what he wanted. He didn't want her cool, emotionless agreement or a careless acquiescence. He wanted to build that fury and tension until the passion that spawned them broke through. Before the night was over, he'd draw it all from her and purge himself, as well.

In silence, they climbed the stairs to the second floor.

The rain fell, strong and steady, against the windows and the newly seeded earth below. The sound made Maggie think of the subtle rhythmic percussion she'd imagined in the arrangement of the song she'd just completed. There was no moon to guide the way, so she moved from memory. Darkness was deep and without shadows. She didn't look when she entered the bedroom, but she knew Cliff was still beside her.

What now? she thought with sudden panic. What was she doing, bringing him here, to the single spot she considered purely private? He might learn more than she wanted before he left again, yet she might learn nothing more than she already knew. They wanted each other; it was unexplainable. It was undeniable.

As her nerves stretched tighter, Maggie was grateful for the dark. She didn't want him to see the doubts that would be clear on her face. As the need grew stronger, she knew she wouldn't have been able to conceal that, either. Darkness was better, she told herself, because it was anonymous. When he touched her, her body went rigid with a dozen conflicting emotions.

Feeling it, Cliff ran his hands over the slope of her shoulders, down to her lower back. He found he didn't want her to be too relaxed, to be too yielding. Not yet. He wanted to know she struggled against something deeper, something unnamed, even as he did.

"You don't want to give in to this," Cliff said quietly. "Or to me."

"No." Yet she felt the tremor, not fear but pleasure, course through her body when he slipped his hands under her thin wool sweater. "No, I don't."

"What choice is there?"

She could see his face through the gloom of darkness, close, very close, to hers. "Damn you," she whispered. "There's none at all."

He slid his hands up her naked back, through the neck opening of her sweater, until his fingers found her hair. "No, not for either of us."

His body was firm against hers. His voice, soft and low, was faintly edged with anger. She caught the scent of soap, sharp, unrepentantly male, that lingered on his skin. His face was mysterious, indistinct in the darkness. He might've been anyone. As Maggie felt the next fierce pull of desire, she almost wished he was.

"Make love with me," she demanded. A decision made quickly, freely, would leave no room for regrets. "Take me now. It's all either of us wants."

Was it? The question had barely formed in his mind when his mouth was on hers. Then there were no questions, just flame and flash and power. Understanding, if there had been any before, dimmed. Reason vanished. Sensation, and only sensation, ruled. While perhaps both of them had expected it, they were caught in a maelstrom in which neither of them had any control. Racked by it, they fell together onto the bed and let the fire rage.

He could find no gentleness to give her, but it seemed she neither demanded nor expected any. He wanted her naked but not vulnerable, soft but not yielding. If he had spoken the needs aloud, she could have been no more than what he'd asked for. As she arched against him, her lips clung in a wild, urgent kiss that was only a prelude to passion. He pulled at her clothes, forgetting finesse, then caught his breath when, in an equal frenzy, she began to strip him.

Clothes were tossed aside as if they were meaningless. Her scent rose up from her skin, from her hair, clouding whatever logic he might have tried to regain. The mattress swayed and dipped as they rolled over it, mindless now of the rain, of the dark, of time and place.

Then they were naked, heated flesh to heated flesh. The desperation grew in each to have all there could be of the other. Whispered demands, labored breathing, moans and sighs of pleasure, drowned out the sound of falling rain. Her body was small and supple and surprisingly strong. All three aspects combined to drive him mad.

This was what it meant to be consumed. Maggie knew it as his hands skimmed over her, inciting thrill after thrill. She hungered, no, starved, for each new demand. Greedy for what pleasure he would give and what pleasure she would take, she allowed him whatever he wanted. She felt no shame, no hesitation, in tasting, in touching, in asking for more or in taking it.

If his body had been designed to her wish, it could have been no more perfect. She reveled in the leanness, the cords of muscle, the long, narrow bones that ran along his hips. Wherever, whenever, she touched, she could almost feel the blood throb under his skin.

She wanted to know he had no more control than she. She wanted to know they were both victims of their own combined power. The fuse that had been lit between them with a look was burning quickly. Desire was madness, and if the words she'd written were true, she'd cast aside her reason for it.

With a savageness they both craved, they came together, fighting to prolong an outrageous passion, greedy to capture that final flash of pleasure. She thought of whirlpools and high winds and the bellow of thunder. She felt the spin, the speed and heard the roar. Then both her mind and body shuddered from the last violent surge.

Love? Maggie thought some dim time later, when her thoughts began to clear again. If this was making love, she'd been innocent all her life. Could something with so gentle a name have such a violent effect on the body? Hers was pulsing and throbbing as if she'd raced up one side of a mountain and fallen off the other. She'd written songs about love, songs about passion, yet she'd never fully understood her own words until now.

Until now, she thought, when the man who lay beside her had dared her to live her own fantasies. With him she'd found the answer to the dark, driving needs that gave the grit, or the wistfulness, to most of her music. She understood, but understanding opened the door to dozens of questions.

Maggie ran a hand up her own body, astonished at the lingering sense of power and of wonder. How long had she been waiting for this night to come? Perhaps it was possible for passion to lie dormant, unexplored, until it was triggered by a certain person at a certain time.

Maggie thought of the film her music would score. It had been that way for the female character. She'd been content with life, almost smug, until one day a man had entered it, a man she'd shared little common ground with, a man who'd ignited a spark that had changed everything. It hadn't mattered that the woman was intelligent, successful, independent. The man, merely by existing, had altered the scope and pattern of her life.

If the same thing was happening to her, there was still time to stop it before she, too, became so consumed by needs, so ruled by desire, that nothing would ever be the same again.

In the film, the relationship had spawned violence. Instinct told her that there was something between her and Cliff that could do the same. There was little moderation in either of them. It was extremes, she knew, that played havoc with human nature.

Maybe fate had brought her to this serene little plot of land with its undertones of violence. The same fate might have brought her to this taciturn, physical man who seemed connected with both the tranquillity and the danger. The question now was whether she was strong enough to deal with the consequences of each.

What, Maggie asked herself while she stared into the darkness, would happen next?

Because nothing was as he'd expected it, Cliff was silent. He'd wanted passion, but he'd never imagined the scope of it. He'd wanted what her song had whispered of, but the reality had been much more dramatic than any words or any melody. He'd been certain that once the tension between them had been released, once the lure had been accepted, the needs would lessen.

It was true his body was sated with a pleasure more intense than anything he'd known, but his mind—Cliff closed his eyes, wishing his mind would rest as easy. But it was too full of her. So full that he knew even a touch would set his body raging again. That kind of need was a shade too close to dependence for comfort. They had nothing to offer each other, he reminded himself, nothing but outrageous mutual desire.

And suddenly he remembered a line from her song. "Desire is madness."

If he could have stopped himself, he wouldn't have touched her again. He was already reaching for her.

"You're cold," he murmured, automatically drawing her against him to warm her.

"A bit." There was an awkwardness she didn't know how to alleviate and a need she didn't know how to explain.

"Here." He tugged the tangled spread over her, then pulled her close again. "Better?"

"Yes." Her body relaxed against his, even as her thoughts continued to race.

They lapsed into silence again, neither knowing quite how to deal with what had flared between them. Cliff listened to the rain beat against the window glass, adding to the sense of isolation. Even on a clear night, he knew, you would see no light from a neighboring house. "Are you having trouble staying out here alone?"

"Trouble?" Maggie hedged. She wanted to stay exactly as she was, wrapped close around him, warm and safe and untroubled. She didn't want to think now of staying in the big house alone, of sleeping alone.

"This place is more isolated than most around here." How soft she was, he thought. It brought him an odd sort of contentment to feel her hair lie against his shoulder. "A lot of people, even if they were raised here, would have trouble being this far back and alone, especially after everything that's happened."

No, she didn't want to talk about it. Maggie closed her eyes, reminding herself that she'd come here determined to take care of herself, to deal with whatever came. She drew a deep breath, but when she started to shift away, Cliff held her still.

"You are having trouble."

"No. No, not really." Her biggest problem at the moment was to keep her mind and body from wanting more of him. Opening her eyes again, she stared at the rain-drenched window. "I'll admit I've had a couple of restless nights since—well, since we started to dig the pond. It isn't easy knowing what happened in that gully ten years ago, and I have a very active imagination."

"Part of the job?" He turned toward her a bit more, so that her leg slid casually between his. Her skin was smooth as polished glass.

"I suppose." She laughed, but he thought he detected nerves in it. "One night I was certain I heard someone in the house."

He stopped stroking her hair, drawing her back far enough to see her eyes. "In the house?"

"Just my imagination," she said with a shrug. "Boards creaking in the attic, stealthy footsteps on the stairs, doors opening and closing. I worked myself up into quite a state."

He didn't like the sound of it, even in her dismissive tone of voice. "Don't you have a phone in this room?" Cliff demanded.

"Well, yes, but—"

"Why didn't you call the police?"

Maggie sighed and wished she'd never mentioned anything about it. He sounded like a cranky older brother scolding his scatterbrained sister. "Because I'd left the kitchen extension off the hook. I'd been trying to work that afternoon, and—" The word scatterbrained flowed back into her head. Embarrassed, she trailed off. "Anyway, it's better that I didn't call. I felt like an idiot in the morning in any case."

Imagination or not, Cliff reflected, she was still a woman alone, isolated, and everyone in a ten-mile radius knew it. "Are you locking your doors?"

"Cliff—"

"Maggie." He rolled until she was on her back and he was looking down at her. "Are you locking your doors?"

"I wasn't," she said, annoyed. "But after the sheriff came by, I—"

"Stan was here?"

A breath hissed out between her teeth. "Damn it, do you know how often you cut me off in the middle of a sentence?"

"Yes. When did Stan come by?"

"The day after the state police were here. He wanted to reassure me." She wasn't cold now, not with the way his body was pressed against hers. Desire began to stir again, not too quiet, not too slow. "He seems to know his job."

"He's been a good sheriff."

"But?" Maggie prompted, sensing more.

"Just a personal thing," Cliff murmured, shifting away again. Maggie felt the chill return immediately.

"Joyce," she said flatly, and started to rise. Cliff's arm came out to pin her down.

"You have a habit of saying little and implying a lot." His voice was cool now, his hold firm. "It's quite a talent."

"It seems we have little to say to each other."

"I don't have to explain myself to you."

She lay stiff and still. "I'm not asking you to."

"The hell you aren't." Angry, he sat up, drawing her with him so that the cover dropped away. Her skin was pale, her hair like a flood of night over her shoulders. Despite a strong will and a keen sense of privacy, he felt compelled to clarify. "Joyce's been like my sister. When she married Stan, I gave her away. I'm godfather to her oldest girl. It might be difficult for you to understand that kind of friendship."

It wasn't. It had been like that between herself and Jerry. The friendship had gradually deteriorated during marriage, because the marriage had been a mistake. "No, I understand it," Maggie said quietly. "I don't understand why you seem so concerned about her."

"That's my business."

"It certainly is."

He swore again. "Look, Joyce has been going through a difficult time. She never wanted to stay in Morganville. When she was a kid, she'd had ideas about going to the city and studying to be an actress."

"She wanted to act?"

"Pipe dreams, maybe." Cliff moved his shoulders. "Maybe not. She let them go when she married Stan, but she's never been happy staying in Morganville. One of the reasons she sold the house was so they'd have enough money to move. Stan won't budge."

"They could compromise."

"Stan doesn't understand how important it is to her to get away from here. She was eighteen when she married. Then she had three children over the next five years. She spent the first part of her life following her father's rules, the second caring for her children and her mother. A woman like you wouldn't understand that."

"I'm sick of that!" Maggie exploded, jerking away from him. "I'm sick to death of you putting me in some category. Pampered celebrity with no conception of how real people feel or live." Anger rocketed through her, so quick and powerful she never thought to repress it. "What kind of man are you, going to bed with a woman you haven't an ounce of respect for?"

Stunned by the sudden, passionate outburst, he watched her spring from the bed. "Wait a minute."

"No, I've made enough mistakes for one evening." She began to search for her clothes among those scattered on the floor. "You had your dinner and your sex," she said in a brittle tone. "Now get out."

Fury rose so that he had to fight it back. She was right, Cliff told himself. He'd come to take her to bed; that was all. Intimacy didn't always equal closeness. He wasn't interested in being close to her or in becoming involved with anything more than her body. Even as he thought it, the emptiness of it washed over him. The contentment he'd felt so briefly vanished. He could hear her unsteady breathing as she pulled on her sweater. Reaching for his clothes, he tried to concentrate on the sound of the rain instead.

"We're not finished, you and I," he murmured.

"Aren't we?" Enraged, aching, Maggie turned. She could feel the tears well in her eyes, but felt secure in the darkness. The sweater skimmed her thighs, leaving the length of her legs naked. She knew what he thought of her, and this time would give him the satisfaction of believing he was right. "We went to bed, and it was good for both of us," she said easily. "Not all one-night stands are as successful. You get a high rating as a lover, Cliff, if that helps your ego."

This time there was no controlling the temper that roared into him. Grabbing both her arms, he pulled her toward him. "Damn you, Maggie."

"Why?" she tossed back. "Because I said it first? Go home and curl up with your double standard, Cliff. I don't need it."

Everything she said hit home, and hit hard. If he stayed, he wasn't certain what he might do. Throttle her? It was tempting. Drag her back to bed and purge himself of the angry desire that pounded in him? More temptation. As he held her, he wasn't sure if it was he who was shaking or her, but he knew if he stayed, something volatile, perhaps irrevocable, would burst.

Dropping his hands, he walked from the room. "Lock your doors," he called out, and cursed her as he strode down the stairs.

Maggie wrapped her arms around herself and let the tears overflow. It was much too late for locks, she thought.

Chapter 8

For the next few days, Maggie worked like a Trojan. Her kitchen floor was sealed, making it her first fully and successfully completed project. She added three fresh strips of wallpaper to her bedroom, found a rug for the music room and cleaned the trim in the downstairs hall.

In the evenings, she worked at her piano until she was too tired to see the keys or hear her own music. She kept her phone off the hook. All in all, she decided, the life of a recluse had its advantages. She was productive, and no one interfered with the flow of her days. It became almost possible to believe that was what she wanted and no more.

Perhaps she was pushing herself. She might admit that, but she wouldn't admit she did so to prevent herself from thinking about her night with Cliff. That had been a mistake. It wasn't wise to dwell on mistakes.

She saw no one, spoke to no one, and told herself she was content to go on that way indefinitely.

But of course complete solitude lasts only so long. Maggie was painting the window trim in the music room when she heard the sound of an approaching car. She debated whether she might just ignore the caller until he or she went away again. As a beginning recluse, it was certainly her right. Then she recognized the old Lincoln.

Setting the paint bucket on the drop cloth at her feet, Maggie went to the front door to meet Louella Morgan.

She looked even more frail this time, Maggie mused. Her skin seemed almost translucent against the tidy white hair. It was an odd, somewhat eerie combination of youth and age. As Maggie watched, Louella looked over toward the gully. For a moment she seemed like a statue, unmoving, unblinking, unbreathing. When Maggie saw her take a step toward the fenced-off section, she walked outside.

"Good morning, Mrs. Morgan."

Louella glanced up, her eyes focusing slowly. The hand she lifted to pat at her hair shook lightly. "I wanted to come."

"Of course." Maggie smiled and hoped she was doing the right thing. "Please come in. I was about to fix some coffee."

Louella walked up the sagging steps Maggie had yet to contact Bog about. "You've made some changes."

Unsure which route to take, she decided on light, cheerful chatter. "Yes, inside and out. The landscapers work faster than I do." Killer stood in the doorway, snarling and backing up. Maggie hushed him as they went inside.

"This wallpaper was here when we moved in," Louella murmured, looking around the hall. "I always meant to change it."

"Did you?" Maggie led her gently toward the living room as she spoke. "Perhaps you could give me some suggestions. I haven't quite made up my mind yet."

"Something warm," Louella said softly. "Something warm, with subtle color, so people would feel welcome. That's what I wanted."

"Yes, I'm sure that's just what it needs." She wanted to put her arm around the woman and tell her she understood. Perhaps it was kinder not to.

"A house like this should smell of lemon oil and flowers."

"It will," Maggie told her, wishing she could change the scent of dust and paint.

"I always felt it should be filled with children." She gazed around the room with the kind of misty concentration that made Maggie think she was seeing it as it had been more than twenty years before. "Children give a house its personality, you know, more than its decorating. They leave their mark on it."

"You have grandchildren, don't you?" Maggie steered her toward the sofa.

"Yes, Joyce's children. The baby's in school now. Time goes so quickly for the young. You've looked at the pictures?" Louella asked suddenly.

"The pictures?" Maggie's brow creased, then cleared. "Oh, yes, I've really only had a chance to glance at them. I've been a bit tied up." Remembering, she walked to the mantel and retrieved the envelope. "Your roses looked beautiful. I'm not sure I'd have that kind of talent."

Louella took the envelope and stared down at it. "Roses need love and discipline. Like children."

Maggie decided against another offer of coffee. Instead, she sat down beside Louella. "Perhaps if we looked at them together it would help."

"Old pictures." Louella opened the flap and drew them out. "There's so much to see in old pictures if you know where to look. Early spring," she murmured, looking down at the first snapshot. "You see, the hyacinths are blooming, and the daffodils."

Maggie studied the square, pristine black and white, but it was the man and small girl who caught her attention rather than the flowers. He was tall, broad in the chest, with a sharp-boned, lantern-jawed face. The suit he wore was severe and proper. Beside him, the little girl wore a frilly dress, ribboned at the waist with black strap shoes and a flowered bonnet.

It must've been Easter, Maggie concluded. The little girl smiled determinedly at the camera. Joyce would've been around four then, Maggie calculated, and perhaps a bit uncomfortable in the organdy and flounces. William Morgan didn't look cruel, she thought as she studied his set, unreadable face. He simply looked untouchable. She fought back a shudder and spoke lightly.

"I want to plant some bulbs myself. Things should be a little more settled by fall."

Louella said nothing as she turned over the next picture. This time Maggie was looking at a young Louella. The style of hair and dress told her the picture was more than twenty years old. The lopsided angle of the shot made her suspect that Joyce had taken it as a child.

"The roses," Louella murmured, running a finger over the picture where they grew in profusion. "Gone now, with no one to care for them."

"Do you have a garden now?"

"Joyce does." Louella set the picture aside and took up another. "I tend it now and then, but it isn't the same as having your own."

"No, it's not, but Joyce must be grateful for your help."

"She's never been easy in town," Louella said, half to herself. "Never easy. A pity she took after me rather than her father."

"She's lovely," Maggie told her, searching for something to say. "I hope to see more of her. Her husband suggested that we have dinner."

"Stan's a good man. Solid. He's always loved her." The sad, elusive smile touched her lips. "He's been kind to me."

When she turned over the next picture, Maggie felt her stiffen. She saw the smile freeze rather than fade. Looking down, she saw William Morgan and a young, perhaps teenaged Stan Agee. This more recent photo was in color, and the trees in the background were vibrant with fall. The two men were dressed in flannel shirts and caps, and each wore a drab-colored vest with what looked to Maggie like small weights around the hem. Each carried a shotgun.

Shells, not weights, Maggie realized as she looked at the vests again. They must've been hunting. And they stood, she noted, near the slope of the gully. Disturbed, she looked at the trees again, at the tapestry she wanted to see for herself.

"Joyce would've taken this," Louella murmured. "She hunted with her father. He taught her how to handle guns before she was twelve. It didn't matter that she hated them—she learned to please him. William looks pleased," Louella continued, though Maggie couldn't see it. "He liked to hunt this land. Now we know he died here. Here," she repeated, placing a palm over the picture. "Not three miles away, in the river. He never left his land. Somehow I think I always knew."

"Mrs. Morgan." Maggie set the pictures aside and laid a hand on her arm. "I know this must be difficult for you; it must be like going through it all over again. I wish there was something I could do."

Turning her head, Louella fixed Maggie with a long, unsmiling stare. "Put in your pond," she said flatly. "Plant your flowers. That's as it should be. The rest is over."

When she started to rise, Maggie found herself more disturbed by the emotionless reply than she would've been with a bout of tears. "Your pictures," she began helplessly.

"Keep them." Louella walked to the doorway before she turned. "I've no need for them anymore."

Should she have been depressed? Maggie wondered as she listened to the car drive away. Was her reaction normal empathy for another's tragedy, or was she allowing herself to become personally involved again? Over the last few days, she'd nearly convinced herself that the Morgan business had nothing to do with her. Now, after one brief contact, it was beginning again.

Yet it was more than a sense of involvement, Maggie admitted as she rubbed her arms to bring back warmth. There'd been something eerie in the way Louella had looked at the pictures. As if, Maggie reflected, she'd been putting the people in them to rest, though only one was dead.

Imagination again, she scolded herself. An overactive one. Yet hadn't there been something odd in the way Louella had studied that last snapshot? It had been as if she'd been searching for details, looking for something. With a frown, Maggie walked over and sifted through the pictures herself, stopping when she came to the color print.

There was William Morgan again, his hair a bit thinner, his eyes a bit sterner than they'd been in the Easter photo. Sheriff Agee stood beside him, hardly more than a boy, his build not quite filled out, his hair a little shaggy. He'd looked even more like a beachcomber in his youth, Maggie decided, though he held the gun as if he were very familiar with firearms. Looking at him, Maggie could easily see why Joyce had fallen for him hard enough to give up dreams of fame and fortune. He was young, handsome, with a trace of cocky sexuality around his mouth.

She could understand, too, why Joyce had feared and obeyed and struggled to please the man beside him. William Morgan looked straight at the camera, legs spread, the gun held in both hands. Cliff had described him as a hard, cold man. Maggie had no trouble believing him, but it didn't explain why Louella had been so disturbed by this one picture. Or why, Maggie added, she herself became uneasy when she looked at it.

Annoyed by her own susceptibility, she started to study the picture more closely when the rumble outside warned of another approaching vehicle.

When it rains it pours, she thought bad-temperedly. Tossing the picture carelessly on top of the others, she walked to the window. When Cliff's pickup came into view, the flare of excitement left her shaken. *Oh, no*, Maggie warned herself. *Not again. A woman who makes the same mistake twice deserves what she gets.* Determined, she picked up her brush and began to paint in long, hard strokes. Let him knock all he wanted, she thought with an angry toss of her head. She had work to do.

Minutes passed, but he didn't come to her door. Maggie continued to paint, telling herself it didn't matter to her what he was doing outside. When she tried to lean closer to the window to look through, paint smeared from the sill to her jeans. Swearing, she wiped at it and made it worse.

She didn't give a damn about Cliff Delaney, Maggie told herself. But she did care about having people wander around on her land. It was her right to go out and see what he was up to and order him away, she told herself as she set down her brush. If he were only checking on how her grass was growing, she fumed as she headed for the door, he should still have the courtesy to announce himself.

By not announcing himself, he was denying her the satisfaction of ignoring him.

She yanked open the door but didn't, as she'd expected, see him bending over the little green sprouts that had begun to shoot up through the topsoil. Neither was he looking out over the plugs of phlox or the juniper shrubs on her front bank. Perhaps, Maggie thought with a frown, he'd gone around to check on the last project to be completed, the crown vetch on her eroding rear bank.

Annoyed that she hadn't thought of that in the first place, she started to turn back into the house when a movement near the gully caught her eye. For an instant, basic, primitive fear that slept in her awoke. She thought of ghouls and phantoms and legends of shades that never rest. In the next instant she recognized Cliff. As infuriated as she was embarrassed by her own reaction, she went to confront him.

As she drew closer, Maggie saw the willow, slender, small and tenderly green. Cliff was setting the ball of roots into a hole he'd dug out of the rocky soil with a pick and shovel. He stood perhaps six feet from the slope of the gully, his shirt tossed carelessly on the ground. She could see the muscles in his back ripple as he began to shovel dirt back into the hole. The twinge of her stomach told her that her reaction to him was no less powerful now than it had been before they'd made love.

Maggie straightened her shoulders and angled her chin. "What're you doing?"

Because he continued to shovel without breaking rhythm, she decided he'd known she was coming. "Planting a tree," Cliff said easily.

Her eyes narrowed dangerously. "I can see that. As far as I remember, I didn't order a willow from you."

"No." He knelt down to mound and smooth the dirt at the base of the tree. She watched his hands, knowing now what they could do on her body. It seemed he had the same talent with soil. "No charge."

Impatient with his nonanswers and with her own growing arousal, she folded her arms. "Why are you planting a tree I didn't buy?"

Satisfied that the willow was secure, he rose. Leaning casually on the shovel, he studied her. No, he hadn't gotten her out of his system, Cliff decided. Seeing her again didn't relieve the knots of tension he'd been living with for days. Somehow he'd known it wouldn't, but he'd had to try. "Some people might call it a peace offering," he told her at length, then watched her mouth open and close again.

Maggie looked at the tree. It was so young, so fragile, but one day she would see it in full sweep, spreading over her pond, and— She stopped, realizing that it was the first time she'd thought of going through with the pond since the discovery. He must have known that, just as he'd known the willow might be enough to make her see the beauty and serenity again. Most of her anger had drained before she remembered to hold on to any of it.

"A peace offering," she repeated, running a finger down one delicate leaf. "Is that what you call it?"

Her voice had been cool, but he saw that her eyes had already started to warm. He wondered how many strong men she'd slain with that one look. "Maybe." He sliced the shovel into the ground where it stood, tilting slightly to the left. "Got anything cold in there to drink?"

It was an apology, Maggie decided, perhaps the only kind a man like him could give. It only took her five seconds to decide to accept it. "Maybe," she said in an equal tone, then turned to walk back toward the house. A smile curved her lips when he fell into step beside her. "Your men did an excellent job," she continued while they circled around toward the rear of the house. "I'm anxious to see how the stuff over the retaining wall's going to look."

"Crown vetch," Cliff supplied before he stopped to check the job, as she'd suspected he would. "You should see something come through in four or five more days. It'll spread fast enough to cover this bank before summer's over." He kept his hands in his back pockets as he studied the work his men had done and thought of the woman beside him. "You've been busy?"

Maggie lifted a brow. "I suppose so. The house needs a lot of attention."

"Seen the paper?"

"No," she said, puzzled. "Why?"

Cliff shrugged, then walked ahead to the screen door to open it. "There was a big story on finding William Morgan buried on his old land. Land," he continued when Maggie moved by him into the kitchen, "recently purchased by a celebrated songwriter."

She turned sharply. "They had my name?"

"Yeah, it was mentioned—several times."

"Damn," she whispered, and, forgetting he'd asked for a drink, she dropped into a chair. "I'd wanted to avoid that." Half hopefully, she glanced up. "The local paper?"

Helping himself, Cliff went to the refrigerator and searched out a soda. "Morganville doesn't have a paper. There were stories in the *Frederick Post* and the *Herald Mail*." As he twisted off the top, he nodded toward the phone sitting off the hook. "If you hadn't done that, you'd have already answered a flood of calls from reporters." And from himself, Cliff thought silently. In the past twenty-four hours, he'd called her a dozen times. He'd vacillated between being frantic and furious every time he'd gotten a busy signal. What kind of woman left her phone off the hook for hours at a time? One who was independent of the outside world, he mused, or one who was hiding from it. Lifting the bottle, he drank. "That your escape route these days?"

In defense, Maggie rose and slammed the receiver back in place. "I don't need to escape from anything. You said yourself that this whole business doesn't have anything to do with me."

"So I did." He examined the liquid left in the bottle. "Maybe you were escaping from something else." He shifted his gaze until it locked on hers. "Were you hiding from me, Maggie?"

"Certainly not." She swept over to the sink and began to scrub the paint splatters from her hands. "I told you, I've been busy."

"Too busy to answer the phone?"

"The phone's a distraction. If you want to start an argument, Cliff, you can just take your peace offering and—" The phone shrilled behind her so that she ended her suggestion with an oath. Before she could answer it herself, Cliff had picked up the phone.

"Yes?" He watched the fury spring into her eyes as he leaned on the counter. He'd missed that, he discovered, just as he'd missed the subtle sexiness of the scent she wore. "No, I'm sorry, Miss Fitzgerald isn't available for comment." He replaced the receiver while Maggie wiped her damp hands on her jeans.

"I can screen my own calls, thank you. When I want a liaison, I'll let you know."

He drank from the bottle again. "Just saving you some aggravation."

"I don't want you or anyone to save me aggravation," she fumed. "It's my aggravation, and I'll do whatever I want with it." He grinned, but before she could think of any retaliation, the phone rang again. "Don't you dare," she warned. Shoving him aside, she answered herself.

"Hello."

"Damn it, Maggie, you've been leaving the phone off the hook again."

She let out a huff of breath. A reporter might've been easier to deal with. "Hello, C.J. How are you?"

"I'll tell you how I am!"

Maggie drew the phone back from her ear and scowled at Cliff. "There's no need for you to hang around."

He took another long sip from the bottle before he settled back comfortably. "I don't mind."

"Maggie!" C.J.'s voice vibrated in her ear. "Who the hell are you talking to?"

"Nobody," she mumbled, deliberately turning her back on Cliff. "You were going to tell me how you were."

"For the past twenty-four hours I've been frantic trying to get through to you. Maggie, it's irresponsible to leave your phone off the hook when people're trying to reach you."

There was a bag of cookies on the counter. Maggie dug into it, then bit into one with a vengeance. "Obviously I left it off the hook so I couldn't be reached."

"If I hadn't gotten you this time, I was going to send a telegram, and I'm not even sure they deliver telegrams in that place. What the hell have you been doing?"

"I've been working," she said between her teeth. "I can't work when the phone's ringing off the wall and people are forever coming by. I moved out here to be alone. I'm still waiting for that to happen."

"That's a nice attitude," he tossed back. In Los Angeles, C.J. searched through his desk drawer for a roll of antacids. "You've got people all over the country worried about you."

"Damn it, people all over the country don't have to worry about me. I'm fine!"

"You sound fine."

With an effort, Maggie controlled her precarious temper. When she lost it with C.J., she invariably lost the bout, as well. "I'm sorry I snapped at you, C.J., but I'm tired of being criticized for doing what I want to do."

"I'm not criticizing you," he grumbled over the peppermint-flavored pill. "It's just natural concern. For God's sake, Maggie, who wouldn't be concerned after that business in the paper?"

She tensed and, without thinking, turned back to face Cliff. He was watching her intently, the neck of the bottle held loosely in his fingers. "What business in the paper?"

"About that man's—ah, what was left of that man being dug up on your property. Good God, Maggie, I nearly had a heart attack when I read it. Then, not being able to reach you—"

"I'm sorry." She dragged a hand through her hair. "I'm really sorry, C.J. I didn't think it would hit the papers, at least not out there."

"So what I didn't know wouldn't hurt me?"

She smiled at the offended tone of voice. "Yes, something like that. I'd've called you with the details if I'd realized the news would get that far."

"Get this far?" he retorted, unappeased. "Maggie, you know that anything with your name in it's going to hit the press on both sides of the Atlantic."

She began to rub one finger slowly up and down her right temple. "And you know that was one of the reasons I wanted to get out."

"Where you live isn't going to change that."

She sighed. "Apparently not."

"Besides, that doesn't have anything to do with what's happened now," C.J. argued. He pressed a hand to his nervous stomach and wondered if a glass of Perrier would calm him. Maybe scotch would be a better idea.

"I haven't seen the paper," Maggie began in an even tone, "but I'm sure the whole thing was blown out of proportion."

"Blown out of proportion?" Again, she had to move the receiver back from her ear. A few steps away, Cliff heard C.J.'s voice clearly. "Did you or did you not stumble over a pile of—of bones?"

She grimaced at the image. "Not exactly." She had to concentrate harder on keeping her voice calm. "Actually, it was the dog that found them. The police came right out and took over. I really haven't been involved." She saw Cliff lift a brow at her final statement but made no comment.

"Maggie, it said that man had been murdered and buried right there, only yards from your house."

"Ten years ago." She pressed her fingers more firmly against her temple.

"Maggie, come home."

She closed her eyes, because his voice held the kind of plea that was hard to resist. "C.J., I am home."

"Damn it, how am I supposed to sleep at night thinking of you alone out in the middle of nowhere? For God's sake, you're one of the most successful, wealthiest, most celebrated women in the world, and you're living in Dogpatch."

"If I'm successful, wealthy and celebrated, I can live wherever I want." She struggled against temper again. However he phrased it, whatever his tone, the concern was real. It was better to concentrate on that. "Besides, C.J., I have the vicious guard dog you sent me." She looked down to where Killer was sleeping peacefully at Cliff's feet. When she lifted her gaze, she found herself smiling into Cliff's face. "I couldn't be safer."

"If you hired a bodyguard—"

Now she laughed. "You're being an old woman again. The last thing I need's a bodyguard. I'm fine," she went on quickly before he could comment. "I've finished the score, I've a dozen ideas for new songs running around in my head, and I'm even considering another musical. Why don't you tell me how brilliant the score was?"

"You know it's brilliant," he mumbled. "It's probably the best thing you've done."

"More," she insisted. "Tell me more. My ego's starving."

He sighed, recognizing defeat. "When I played it for the producers, they were ecstatic. It was suggested that you come out and supervise the recording."

"Forget it." She began to pace to the sink and back again.

"Damn it, we'd come to you, but there's no studio in Hicksville."

"Morganville," she corrected mildly. "You don't need me for the recording."

"They want you to do the title song."

"What?" Surprised, she stopped her restless pacing.

"Now listen to me before you say no." C.J. straightened in his chair and put on his best negotiator's voice. "I realize you've always refused to perform or record, and I've never pressed you. But this is something I really think you should consider. Maggie, that song's dynamite, absolute dynamite, and nobody's going to be able to put into it what you did. After I played the tape, everyone in the room needed a cold shower."

Though she laughed, Maggie couldn't quite put the idea aside. "I can think of a half-dozen artists who could deliver that number, C.J. You don't need me."

"I can think of a dozen who could deliver it," he countered. "But not like you. The song needs you, Maggie. At least you could think about it."

She told herself she'd already refused him enough for one day. "Okay, I'll think about it."

"You let me know in a week."

"C.J.—"

"Okay, okay, two weeks."

"All right. And I'm sorry about the phone."

"You could at least get one of those hateful answering machines."

"Maybe. Take care of yourself, C.J."

"I always do. Just take your own advice."

"I always do. Bye." She hung up, heaving a long sigh. "I feel like I've just been taken to task by the school principal."

Cliff watched her pick up a folded dish towel, crumple it, then set it down again. "You know how to handle him."

"I've had plenty of practice."

"What's C.J. stand for?"

"Constant Jitters," she murmured, then shook her head. "No, to tell you the truth, I haven't any idea."

"Does he always give you a hard time?"

"I suppose." She picked up the dish towel again. "It seems the news hit the papers on the Coast. Then, when he couldn't reach me . . ." She trailed off, frowning out the window.

"You're tense."

She dropped the cloth over the edge of the sink. "No."

"Yes," Cliff corrected. "I can see it." Reaching out, he ran his hand down the side of her neck to the curve of her shoulder. "I can feel it."

The brush of his fingers made her skin hum. Slowly, she turned her head. "I don't want you to do that."

Deliberately, he took his other hand on a like journey, so that he could knead at the tension in both of her shoulders. Was it her nerves he sought to soothe or his own? "To touch you?" he said quietly. "It's difficult not to."

Knowing she was already weakening, Maggie lifted her hands to his wrists. "Put some effort into it," she advised as she tried to push him aside.

"I have for the past few days." His fingers pressed into her skin and released, pressed and released, in a rhythm that caused her bones to liquefy. "I decided it was a misdirection of energy when I could put the same effort into making love to you."

Her mind was starting to haze, her breath beginning to tremble. "We've nothing to give each other."

"We both know better than that." He lowered his head so that his lips could brush along the temple he'd seen her stroke while on the phone.

A sigh escaped before she stopped it. This wasn't what she wanted—it was everything she wanted. "Sex is—"

"A necessary and enjoyable part of life," Cliff finished before he moved his lips down to tease hers.

So this was seduction, Maggie thought as her mind began to float. This was arousal without will. She knew she wasn't resisting, but yielding, melting, submitting, just as she knew that when surrender was complete, her bridges would be in flames behind her.

"We'll only be two people sharing a bed," she murmured. "There's nothing else."

Whether it was a question or a statement, Cliff tried to believe it was true. If there was more, it wouldn't end, and he'd find himself tangled around a woman he barely understood for the rest of his life. If there were only needs, he could relinquish his control and race with them. If there was only desire, he could take whatever he wanted with no consequences. When she was softening and heating in his arms, what did he care for consequences?

"Let me feel you," he murmured against her lips. "I want your skin under my hands, smooth and hot, your heart pounding."

Anything, she thought dizzily. She'd give him anything, as long as he stayed close like this, as long as his mouth continued that dark, desperate, delirious seduction of her senses. He tugged her T-shirt over her head, then ran his hands down her sides, up again, so that the friction had her nearly mad for more. His shirt scraped against her taut nipples until his hands came between them to possess.

He could feel her heart beat now, and she could hear it pounding in her own head. Her thighs pressed against his with only two layers of thin, soft denim between. She could remember every slope and plane of his body, how it had felt warm and urgent and naked on hers.

He smelled of work and the outdoors, traces of sweat and turned earth. As the scent raced through her senses, she took her lips over his face and throat to draw in the taste.

Uncivilized, like the land that held them both. Alluring and not quite tamed, like the thick woods that surrounded them. If she thought at all, this was how she thought of the need that burned between them. There was danger in both, and pleasure and wonder. Throwing aside all reason, Maggie gave herself to it.

"Now," she demanded huskily. "I want you now."

With no sense of time or place, no hesitation, they lowered onto the floor. The struggle with clothes only added to the aura of desperation and unrelenting desire that sprang back whenever they touched. Warmth against warmth, they found each other.

When the phone shrilled on the wall beside them, neither heard. Whether it was by choice or the will of fate, there was nothing for either of them but each other.

A tremble, a moan, a rough caress, the scent and fury of passion; that was their world. Urgently and more urgently, they sought the taste and touch of each other, as if the hunger would never abate, as if neither would allow it to. The floor was hard and smooth beneath them. They rolled over it as if it were layered with feathers. Sunlight streamed in, falling over them. They explored all the secrets of the night.

Man for woman, woman for man—time had no place and place no meaning. Hot and open, his mouth found hers, and finding it, he burned with the need to possess her completely. His fingers dug into her hips as he shifted her on top of him so that her skin slid tantalizingly over his. He felt her throb, just as he felt the flood of passion beat against the weakened dam of his control. At the moment of joining, her body arched back in stunned pleasure. The pace was frenetic, leaving them both helpless and raging. On and on they drove each other, mercilessly, ruthlessly.

Through half-closed eyes, Cliff saw her shudder with the speed of the crest. Then he was swept up with her in the power of the ultimate heat dance.

Chapter 9

Had hours passed, or was his sense of time still distorted? Cliff tried to gauge the hour by the slant of the sun through the window, but couldn't be sure. He felt more than rested; he felt vitalized. Turning his head, he watched Maggie as she slept beside him. Though his own actions were vague in his mind, like a half dream that blurs on awakening, he could remember carrying her upstairs where they'd tumbled into bed. Wrapped around each other, they'd fallen into an exhausted sleep. Yes, that part was vague, he mused, but the rest—

On the kitchen floor. He ran a hand over his face, uncertain if he was pleased or astonished. Cliff discovered he was both.

He'd made love to her on the kitchen floor like a frantic teenager in the first spin of desire. By the time a man of experience had reached his thirties, he should be able to show a bit more control, use a bit more finesse. Yet he'd had neither both times he'd made love with her. Cliff wasn't certain that would change if he'd loved her a hundred times. She had some power over him that went deep and triggered frenzy rather than style. And yet . . . Because she was asleep and unaware, he brushed the hair from her cheek so that he could see more of her face. Looking at her was becoming a habit he wasn't sure could be easily broken. Yet when they lay quiet like this, he was overwhelmed by a sense of protective tenderness. As far as he could remember, no other woman had elicited either response from him before. The knowledge wasn't comfortable.

Perhaps it was because when she slept as she did now, she looked frail, defenseless, small. He'd never been able to resist fragility. When she was in his arms, she was all fire and flare, with a power so potent she seemed indestructible. Challenges were something else he'd never been able to resist.

Just who was Maggie Fitzgerald? Cliff wondered while he traced the shape of her mouth with a fingertip. He wouldn't have said she was beautiful, yet her face had the power to both stun and haunt a man. He hadn't expected her to be kind or compassionate, yet he'd seen the qualities in her. He hadn't expected her to be self-sufficient, yet she was proving to be just that under an uneasy set of circumstances.

He frowned and unconsciously drew her closer. Maggie murmured but slept on. Though he'd told her that she had no connection with what had happened there ten years before, Cliff didn't like knowing she was alone in the big, remote house. Knowing Morganville was a quiet, settled town didn't change that. Even the quiet, the settled, had undercurrents. That had been made plain in the past two weeks.

Whoever had killed William Morgan had gone unpunished for a decade. Whoever had murdered him had probably walked the streets of town, chatted outside the bank, cheered at Little League games. It wasn't a pleasant thought. Nor was it pleasant to conclude that whoever had killed once might do anything necessary to go on living a quiet, settled life in a town where everyone knew your name and your history. It might be a cliché about the murderer returning to the scene of the crime, but—

She woke up alone, her mind still disoriented. Was it morning? she wondered groggily. When she shifted, lifting both hands to push back her hair, she felt the sweet heaviness in her limbs that came from lovemaking. Abruptly awake, she looked over to see the bed beside her empty.

Perhaps she'd been dreaming. But when she felt the sheets beside her, they were still warm, and when she turned her face into the pillow, his scent lingered on the case.

They'd made love on the kitchen floor, she remembered with a reaction that directly paralleled Cliff's. But she also remembered quite clearly the sensation of being carried up the stairs, gently, as if she'd been something precious. It was a warm memory, different from the erotic scene that had preceded it. A memory like that was something she could hold on to during some long, restless night in the future.

But he'd left, saying nothing.

Grow up, Maggie, she ordered herself. *Be sensible.* From the beginning she'd known this wasn't romance but desire. The only thing she'd gain from dwelling on the first was pain. Romance was for the impractical, the vulnerable, the naive. Hadn't she spent a great deal of her time training herself to be none of those things?

He didn't love her; she didn't love him. There was a twinge in her stomach at the second denial that had her biting her lip. No, she insisted, she didn't love him. She couldn't afford to.

He was a hard man, though she'd seen some softer aspects of him. He was intolerant, impatient and more often rude than not. A woman didn't need to fix her heart on a man like that. In any case, he'd made it clear that he wanted her body, and her body only. Twice she'd made the decision to give it to him, so she had no right to regrets, even though he'd left without a word.

Maggie flung her arms over her eyes and refused to acknowledge the growing fear that she'd already given him more than her body, without either of them being aware of it.

Then she heard it, the soft creak directly overhead. Slowly, she lowered her arms, then lay still. When it came the second time, the panic fluttered in her throat. She was awake, it was midafternoon, and the sounds came from the attic, not her imagination.

Though she was shaking, she climbed quietly out of bed. This time she wouldn't cower in her room while someone invaded her home. This time, she thought, moistening her lips as she slipped into her T-shirt, she'd find out who it was and what they wanted. Cold and clearheaded, she took the poker from the fireplace and slipped into the hallway.

The attic stairs were to her right. When she saw that the door at the top was open, fear sliced through her again. It hadn't been opened since she'd moved in. Shaking, determined, she took a firmer grip on the poker and started up the stairs.

At the doorway, she paused, hearing the faint whisper of movement inside. She pressed her lips together, swallowed, then stepped inside.

"Damn it, Maggie, you could hurt someone with that thing."

She jumped back, banging smartly into the door-jamb. "What are you doing up here?" she demanded as Cliff scowled back at her.

"Just checking. When's the last time you were up here?"

She expelled a breath, releasing pent-up tension. "Never. It's far down on my lists of priorities, so I haven't been up since I moved in."

He nodded, taking another glance around. "Someone has."

For the first time, she looked into the room. As she'd suspected, it contained little more than dust and cobwebs. It was high enough that Cliff could stand upright with an inch or so to spare, though at the sides it sloped down with the pitch of the roof. There was an old rocker that might prove interesting after refinishing, a sofa that was hopeless, two lamps without shades and a large upright traveling chest.

"It doesn't look as though anyone's been up here for years."

"More like a week," Cliff corrected. "Take a look at this."

He walked toward the chest, and making a face at the layer of dust on the floor, Maggie padded after him in her bare feet. "So?" she demanded. "Joyce mentioned that there were some things up here she didn't have any use for. I told her not to bother with them, that I'd take care of hauling them out when I was ready."

"I'd say someone already took something out." Cliff crouched in front of the dust-covered chest, then pointed.

Annoyed, stifling the urge to sneeze, Maggie bent toward the dust-covered chest. Then she saw it. Just near the lock, and very faint, was the imprint of a hand. "But—"

Cliff grabbed her wrist before she could touch the imprint herself. "I wouldn't."

"Someone was here," she murmured. "I didn't imagine it." Struggling for calm, she looked back at Cliff. "But what could anyone have wanted up here, in this thing?"

"Good question." He straightened, but kept her hand in his.

She wanted to play it light. "How about a good answer?"

"I think we might see what the sheriff thinks."

"You think it has something to do with—the other thing."

Her voice was steady enough, but with his fingers on her wrist, he knew her pulse wasn't. "I think it's odd that everything's happening at once. Coincidences are curious things. You wouldn't be smart to let this one go."

"No." This wasn't ten years ago, she thought. This was now. "I'll call the sheriff."

"I'll do it."

She stopped in the doorway, bristling. "It's my house," she began.

"It certainly is," Cliff agreed mildly, then stunned her by running both hands up her naked thighs to her hips. "I don't mind looking at you half dressed, but it's bound to distract Stan."

"Very funny."

"No, very beautiful." While she stared, wide-eyed, he lowered his head and kissed her with the first true gentleness he'd shown. She didn't move or speak when he lifted his head again. Her eyes were still open. "I'll call the sheriff," Cliff said roughly. "You get some pants on."

Without waiting for her reply, he was heading down the steps, leaving her staring after him. Dazed, Maggie lifted a finger to trace over her own lips. That, she decided, had been as unexpected and as difficult to explain as anything else that had happened between them.

Utterly confused, Maggie left the poker tilted against the door and went back to her room. She couldn't have known he could kiss like that—tenderly, exquisitely. If she couldn't have known that, she couldn't have known that her heart could stop beating and her lungs could choke up. The totally different kiss had brought on a totally different reaction. This reaction, she knew, had left her without any form of defense.

A passionate, aggressive demand she could meet with passion and aggression of her own. There they were equal, and if she had no control, neither did he. Urgency would be met with urgency, fire with fire, but tenderness . . . What would she do if he kissed her like that again? And how long would she have to wait until he did? A woman could fall in love with a man who kissed like that.

Maggie caught herself. Some women, she corrected, hastily dragging on her jeans. Not her. She wasn't going to fall in love with Cliff Delaney. He wasn't for her. He wanted no more than—

Then she remembered that he hadn't left without a word. He hadn't left at all.

"Maggie!"

The voice from the bottom of the stairs had her jolting. "Yes." She answered him while she stared at her own astonished face in the mirror.

"Stan's on his way."

"All right, I'm coming down." In a minute, she added silently, in just a minute. Moving like someone who wasn't sure her legs could be trusted, she sat on the bed.

If she was falling in love with him, she'd better admit it now, while there was still time to do something about it. Was there still time? It washed over her that her time had been up days before, perhaps longer. Perhaps it had been up the moment he'd stepped out of his truck onto her land.

Now what? she asked herself. She'd let herself fall for a man she hardly knew, barely understood and wasn't altogether sure she liked a great deal of the time. He certainly didn't understand her and didn't appear to want to.

Yet he'd planted a willow in her yard. Perhaps he understood more than either of them realized. Of course, there couldn't be anything between them, really, she reminded herself hastily. They were poles apart in attitude. Still, for the moment, she had no choice but to follow her heart and hope that her mind would keep her somewhat level. As she rose, Maggie remembered fatalistically that it never had before.

It was quiet downstairs, but as soon as she came to the landing, she smelled coffee. She stood there a moment, wondering if she should be annoyed or pleased that Cliff was making himself at home. Unable to decide, she walked back to the kitchen.

"Want a cup?" Cliff asked as she entered. He was already leaning against the counter in his habitual position, drinking one of his own.

Maggie lifted a brow. "As a matter of fact, I would. Have any trouble finding what you needed?"

He ignored the sarcasm and reached in a cupboard for another cup. "Nope. You haven't eaten lunch."

"I generally don't." She came up behind him to pour the cup herself.

"I do," he said simply. With a naturalness Maggie thought bordered on arrogance, he opened the refrigerator and began to search through it.

"Just help yourself," she muttered before she scalded her tongue on the coffee.

"You'd better learn to stock up," Cliff told her when he found her supplies discouragingly slim. "It isn't unusual to get snowed in on a back road like this for a week at a time in the winter."

"I'll keep that in mind."

"You eat this stuff?" he asked, pushing aside a carton of yogurt.

"I happen to like it." She strode over, intending to slam the refrigerator door whether his hand was inside or not. Cliff outmaneuvered her by plucking out a single chicken leg, then stepping aside. "I'd just like to mention you're eating my dinner."

"Want a bite?" Apparently all amiability, he held out the drumstick. Maggie concentrated on keeping her lips from curving. "No."

"Funny." Cliff took a bite and chewed thoughtfully. "Just coming into this kitchen seems to work up my appetite."

She shot him a look, well aware that she was now standing on the spot where they'd made wild love only a short time before. If he was trying to get a rise out of her, he was succeeding. If he was trying to distract her from what they'd discovered in the attic, he was succeeding, as well. Either way, Maggie found she couldn't resist him.

Deliberately, she took a step closer, running her hands slowly up his chest. It was time, she decided, to give him back a bit of his own. "Maybe I'm hungry, after all," she murmured, and, rising on her toes, brushed her lips teasingly over his.

Because he hadn't expected the move from her, Cliff did nothing. From the start he'd stalked and seduced. She was the lady, the crown princess with the wanton passion men often fantasize about on long, dark nights. Now, looking into those deep, velvet eyes, he thought her more of a witch. And who, he wondered as his blood began to swim, had been stalked and seduced?

She took his breath away—just the scent of her. She made his reason cloud—just the touch of her. When she looked at him like this, her eyes knowing, her lips parted and close, she was the only woman he wanted, the only woman he knew. At times like this, he wanted her with a fire that promised never to be banked. Quite suddenly and quite clearly, she terrified him.

"Maggie." He put a hand up to ward her off, to draw her closer; he'd never know, for the dog began to bark, and the rumble of a car laboring up the lane sounded from outside. Cliff dropped the hand to his side again. "That'll be Stan."

"Yes." She studied him with an open curiosity he wasn't ready to deal with.

"You'd better get the door."

"All right." She kept her gaze direct on his for another moment, rather pleased with the uncertainty she saw there. "You coming?"

"Yeah. In a minute." He waited until she had gone, then let out a long, uneasy breath. That had been too close for comfort. Too close to what, he wasn't certain, but he was certain he didn't like it. With his appetite strangely vanished, Cliff abandoned the drumstick and picked up his coffee. When he noticed his hands weren't quite steady, he downed the contents in one swallow.

Well, she certainly had enough to think about, Maggie mused as she walked down the hall. The sheriff was at her door again, Cliff was standing in her kitchen looking as though he'd been struck with a blunt instrument, and her own head was so light from a sense of—was it power?—that she didn't know what might happen next. Her move to the country certainly hadn't been quiet. She'd never been more stimulated in her life.

"Miss Fitzgerald."

"Sheriff." Maggie scooped Killer up in one arm to quiet his barking.

"Quite a beast you've got there," he commented. Then, holding out a hand, he allowed the puppy to sniff it cautiously. "Cliff gave me a call," he continued. "Said it looked like somebody's broken into the house."

"That seems to be the only explanation." Maggie stepped back to struggle with both the puppy and the door. "Although it doesn't make any sense to me. Apparently someone was in the attic last week."

"Last week?" Stan took care of the door himself, then rested his hand lightly, it seemed negligently, on the butt of his gun. "Why didn't you call before?"

Feeling foolish, Maggie set the dog down, giving him an impatient nudge on the rear that sent him scampering into the music room. "I woke up sometime in the middle of the night and heard noises. I admit it panicked me at the time, but in the morning . . ." She trailed off and shrugged. "In the morning, I thought it'd been my imagination, so I more or less forgot the whole thing."

Stan listened, and his nod was both understanding and prompting. "And now?"

"I happened to mention it to Cliff this . . . ah . . . this morning," she finished. "He was curious enough to go up into the attic."

"I see." Maggie had the feeling he saw everything, very well.

"Stan." Cliff strode down the hall from the kitchen, looking perfectly at ease. "Thanks for coming by."

I should've said that, Maggie thought, but before she could open her mouth again, the men were talking around her.

"Just part of the job," Stan stated. "You're doing quite a job yourself on the grounds outside."

"They're coming along."

Stan gave him a crooked, appealing smile. "You've always liked a challenge."

They knew each other well enough that Cliff understood he referred to the woman, as well as her land. "Things would be dull without them," he said mildly.

"Heard you found something in the attic."

"Enough to make me think someone's been poking around."

"I'd better have a look."

"I'll show you," Maggie said flatly, then, sending Cliff a telling look, led the way upstairs.

When they came to the attic door, Stan glanced down at the poker still leaning against it. "Somebody could trip over that," he said mildly.

"I must have left it there before." Ignoring Cliff's grin, she picked it up and held it behind her back.

"Doesn't look like anyone's been up here in a long time," Stan commented as he brushed a cobweb away from his face.

"I haven't been up at all until today." Maggie shivered as a large black spider crawled sedately up the wall to her left. She hadn't admitted to anyone yet that the prospect of insects and mice was primarily what had kept her out. "There's been so much else to do in the house." Deliberately, she stepped farther away from the wall.

"Not much up here." Stan rubbed a hand over his chin. "Joyce and I cleared out everything we were interested in when she first inherited. Louella already had everything she wanted. If you haven't been up," he continued, peering slowly around, "how do you know anything's missing?"

"I don't. It's this." For the second time, Maggie crossed the dusty floor to the trunk. This time it was she who crouched down and pointed.

Stan bent down over her, close enough that she could smell the simple department-store aftershave he wore. She recognized it and, on a wave of nostalgia, remembered her mother's driver had worn it, too. For no other reason, her sense of trust in him was confirmed.

"That's curious," Stan murmured, careful not to smear the faint outline. "Did you open this?"

"Neither of us touched it," Cliff said from behind.

With another nod, Stan pushed the button on the latch. His other hand came up automatically, stopping just short of gripping the trunk in the same spot the handprint was. "Looks like somebody did." Cautiously, he put his hand on the closure and tugged. "Locked." Sitting back on his haunches, he frowned at the trunk. "Damn if I can remember what's in this thing or if there's a key. Joyce might know—more'n likely Louella, though. Still . . ." With a shake of his head, he straightened. "It doesn't make much sense for somebody to break in and take something out of this old trunk, especially now that the house is occupied for the first time in ten years." He looked back at Maggie. "Are you sure nothing's missing from downstairs?"

"No—that is, I don't think so. Almost everything I shipped out's still in crates."

"Wouldn't hurt to take a good look."

"All right." She started back toward the second floor, realizing she hoped something would be missing. That would make sense; that would be tangible. The faint handprint on the trunk and no explanation gave her a queasy feeling in the stomach. A cut-and-dried burglary would only make her angry.

With the two men following, she went into her bedroom, checking her jewelry first. Everything was exactly as it should've been. In the next bedroom were crates that at a glance she could see were untouched and unopened.

"That's all up here. There's more crates downstairs and some paintings I haven't had reframed yet."

"Let's take a look."

Going with the sheriff's suggestion, Maggie headed for the stairs again.

"I don't like it," Cliff said to Stan in an undertone. "And you don't think she's going to find anything missing downstairs."

"Only thing that makes sense is a burglary, Cliff."

"A lot of things haven't made sense since we started digging in that gully."

Stan let out a quiet breath, watching Maggie's back as she descended the steps. "I know, and a lot of times there just aren't any answers."

"Are you going to tell Joyce about this?"

"I might have to." Stan stopped at the base of the stairs, running a hand over the back of his neck as though there were tension or weariness there. "She's a strong woman, Cliff. I guess I didn't know just how strong until this business started. I know when we first got married, a lot of people thought I did it for her inheritance."

"Not anyone who knew you."

Stan shrugged. "Anyway, that died down after a while, died completely after I became sheriff. I guess there were times I wondered whether Joyce ever thought it."

"She'd have told me if she had," Cliff said bluntly.

With a half laugh, Stan turned to him. "Yes, she would've at that."

Maggie came back into the hall from the music room. "There's nothing missing in there, either. I've a few things in the living room, but—"

"Might as well be thorough," Stan told her, then strode across the hall and over the threshold. "Doing some painting?" he asked when he noticed the can and brush by the window.

"I'd planned to have all the trim done in here today," she said absently as she examined a few more packing boxes, "but then Mrs. Morgan stopped by, and—"

"Louella," Stan interrupted.

Because he was frowning, Maggie began to smooth it over. "Yes, though she didn't stay very long. We just looked over the pictures she'd lent me." Distracted, she picked up the stack. "Actually, I'd wanted to show these to you, Cliff. I wondered if you could tell me how to deal with getting some climbing roses like these started."

With the men flanking her, Maggie flipped through the snapshots.

"Louella certainly had a feel for making flowers look like they'd grown up on their own," she murmured. "I don't know if I have the talent for it."

"She always loved this place," Stan said. "She—" Then he stopped when she flipped to the color shot of himself and Morgan. "I'd forgotten about that one," he said after a moment. "Joyce took that the first day of deer season."

"Louella mentioned that she hunted."

"She did," Cliff put in, "because he wanted her to. Morgan had an—affection for guns."

And died by one, Maggie thought with a shudder. She turned the pictures facedown. "There's nothing missing anywhere that I can see, Sheriff."

He stared down at the pile of photos. "Well, then, I'll do a check of the doors and windows, see if anything's been forced."

"You can look," Maggie said with a sigh, "but I don't know if the doors were locked, and half the windows at least were open."

He gave her the look parents give children when they do something foolish and expected. "I'll just poke around, anyway. Never can tell."

When he'd gone out, Maggie flopped down on the sofa and lapsed into silence. As if he had nothing better to do, Cliff wandered to the clock on the mantel and began to wind it. Killer came out from under the sofa and began to dance around his legs. The tension in the room was palpable. Maggie had almost given up wondering if it would ever be resolved.

Why would anyone break into an old trunk that had been neglected for years? Why had Cliff been in on the discovery, just as he'd been in on the discovery in the gully? What had caused her to fall in love with him, and would this need between them fade, as flash fires had a habit of doing? If she could understand any of it, perhaps the rest would fall into place and she'd know what move to make.

"There doesn't seem to be any forced entry," Stan said as he came back into the room. "I'll go into town, file a formal report and get to work on this, but—" He shook his head at Maggie. "I can't promise anything. I'd suggest you keep your doors locked and give some more thought to those dead bolts."

"I'll be staying here for the next few days," Cliff announced, throwing Stan and Maggie into surprised silence. He continued as if he hadn't noticed the reaction his statement caused. "Maggie won't be alone, though it would seem that whatever was wanted in the house was taken."

"Yeah." Stan scratched his nose, almost concealing a grin. "I'd better get back. I'll just let myself out."

Maggie didn't rouse herself to say goodbye but stared at Cliff until the front door shut. "Just what do you mean, you'll be staying here?"

"We'll have to do some grocery shopping first. I can't live off what you keep in that kitchen."

"Nobody asked you to live off it," she said, springing to her feet. "And nobody asked you to stay here. I don't understand why I have to keep reminding you whose house and land this is."

"Neither do I."

"You told *him*," she continued. "You just as good as announced to the town in general that you and I—"

"Are exactly what we are," Cliff finished easily. "You'd better get some shoes on, if we're going to town."

"I'm not going to town, and you're not staying here."

He moved so quickly she was caught completely off guard. His hands closed over both her arms. "I'm not letting you stay here alone until we know exactly what's going on."

"I've told you before I can take care of myself."

"Maybe you can, but we're not putting it to the test right now. I'm staying."

She gave him a long stare. The truth was she didn't want to be alone. The truth was, she wanted him, perhaps too much for her own good. Yet he was the one insisting, she thought as her temper began to cool. Since he was insisting, perhaps he cared more than he was willing to admit. Maybe it was time she took a gamble on that.

"If I let you stay . . ." she began.

"I am staying."

"If I let you stay," she repeated coolly, "you have to cook dinner tonight."

He lifted a brow, and the grip on her arms relaxed slightly. "After sampling your cooking, you won't get any argument."

Refusing to be insulted, she nodded. "Fine. I'll get my shoes."

"Later." Before she knew what he was up to, they were tumbling back onto the sofa. "We've got all day."

Chapter 10

Maggie considered it ironic that she'd just begun to become accustomed to living alone and she was no longer living alone. Cliff made the transition unobtrusively. No fuss, no bother. A brisk, rather subtle sense of organization seemed to be a part of his makeup. She'd always respected organized people—from a safe distance.

He left early each morning, long before she considered it decent for a person to be out of his bed. He was quiet and efficient and never woke her. Occasionally, when she groped her way downstairs later in the morning, she'd find a scrawled note next to the coffeepot.

"Phone was off the hook again," it might say. Or "Milk's low. I'll pick some up."

Not exactly love letters, Maggie thought wryly. A man like Cliff wouldn't put his feelings down on paper the way she was compelled to. It was just one more area of opposition between them.

In any case, Maggie wasn't certain Cliff had any feelings about her other than impatience and an occasional bout of intolerance. Though there were times she suspected she touched some of his softer edges, he didn't act much like a lover. He brought her no flowers, but she remembered he'd planted a willow tree. He gave her no smooth, clever phrases, but she remembered the look she'd sometimes catch in his eyes. He wasn't a poet, he wasn't a romantic, but that look, that one long, intense look, said more than most women ever heard.

Perhaps, despite both of them, she was beginning to understand him. The more she understood, the more difficult it became to control a steadily growing love. He wasn't a man whose emotions could be pushed or channeled. She was a woman who, once her feelings were touched, ran with them in whatever direction they went.

Though she'd lived in the house outside of Morganville for only a month, Maggie understood a few basics of small-town life. Whatever she did became common knowledge almost before she'd done it. Whatever it was she did would draw a variety of opinions that would lead to a general consensus. There were a few key people whose opinion could sway that consensus. Cliff, she knew, was one of them, if he chose to bother. Stan Agee and the postmistress were others. It didn't take her long to discover that Bog was another whose opinion was sought and carefully weighed.

The politics in Morganville might've been on a smaller scale than those in Southern California's music industry, but Maggie saw that they ran in the same vein. In L.A., however, she'd been second-generation royalty, while here she was an outsider. An outsider, she knew, whose notoriety could be either scorned or accepted. To date, she'd been fortunate, because most of the key people had decided to accept. Thinking of small, close-knit towns, she realized she'd taken a chance on that acceptance by living with Cliff.

Not living with, Maggie corrected as she spread adhesive on her newly stripped bathroom floor. He wasn't living with her; he was staying with her. There was a world of difference between the two. He hadn't moved in, bag and baggage, nor had there been any discussion about the length of his stay. It was, she decided, a bit like having a guest whom you didn't feel obligated to entertain or impress.

Unnecessarily, and through his own choice, he'd opted to be her bodyguard. And at night, when the sun went down and the woods were quiet, her body was his. He accepted her passion, her hungers and desires. Perhaps, just perhaps, one day he might accept her emotions, which raged just as hot, and just as high. First he had to come to understand her as she was beginning to understand him. Without that, and the respect that went with it, emotions and desires would wither and die.

Maggie set the next square of tile into position, then sat back to judge the outcome. The stone-patterned ceramic was rustic and would leave her free to use an infinite range of color combinations. She wanted nothing in her home to be too restricted or regimented, just as she wanted to do most of the changes and improvements herself.

Looking at the six pieces of tile she'd installed, Maggie nodded. She was becoming quite handy these days. Though her pansies had never recovered, they were her only major failure.

Pleased and ready for more, Maggie debated whether to mix up another batch of adhesive or to start the next wall of paper in her bedroom. There was only a wall and a half left to cover, she remembered; then it would be time to make a decision on curtains. Priscillas, cafés, Cape Cods . . . Nothing monumental, most people would say, she mused, but then she'd always left such things up to decorators before. Now, if something didn't work, she had no one to blame but herself.

With a laugh, she reached into the box of tiles again, swearing halfheartedly as she scraped her finger against a sharp edge. The price of being your own handyman, Maggie decided, going to the sink to run water over the cut. Maybe it was time to turn in the tiles for wallpaper and paste.

When the dog began to bark, she knew that either project would have to wait. Resigned, she turned off the tap just as the sound of a car reached her. Going to the tiny latticed window, she watched Lieutenant Reiker pull around the last curve.

Why was he back? she wondered, frowning. There couldn't possibly be any more information she could give him. When he didn't approach the house immediately, Maggie stayed where she was. He walked along the path of flagstone Cliff's crew had set just that week. When he reached the end, he didn't turn toward the

porch, but looked out over the gully. Slowly, he drew out a cigarette, then lit it with a short wooden match. For several moments
he just stood there, smoking and watching the dirt and rocks as
if they had the answers he wanted. Then, before she could react,
he turned and looked directly up at the window where she stood.
Feeling like an idiot, she started down to meet him.

"Lieutenant." Maggie went cautiously down the porch steps and
onto the sturdy new flagstone.

"Miss Fitzgerald." He flipped the cigarette stub into the tangle
of brush near the gully. "Your place is coming along. Hard to believe what it looked like a few weeks ago."

"Thank you." He looked so harmless, so pleasant. She wondered
if he carried a gun in a shoulder holster under his jacket.

"Noticed you planted a willow over there." But he looked at her,
not at the gully. "It shouldn't be much longer before you can have
your pond put in."

Like Reiker, Maggie didn't look toward the gully. "Does that
mean the investigation's almost over?"

Reiker scratched along the side of his jaw. "I don't know if I'd
say that. We're working on it."

She bit back a sigh. "Are you going to search the gully again?"

"I don't think it's going to come to that. We've been through
it twice now. Thing is—" He stopped, shifting his weight to ease
his hip. "I don't like loose ends. The more we look into this thing,
the more we find. It's hard to tie up ends that've been dangling for
ten years."

Was this a social call or an official one? she wondered, trying
not to be annoyed. Maggie could remember how embarrassed
he'd been when he'd asked for her autograph. At the moment, she
didn't need a fan. "Lieutenant, is there something I can do?"

"I wondered if you'd had anyone coming around, someone you
know, maybe someone you don't know."

"Coming around?"

"The murder happened here, Miss Fitzgerald, and the more we

dig, the more people we find who had reason to kill Morgan. A lot of them still live in town."

She folded her arms under her breasts. "If you're trying to make me uneasy, Lieutenant, you're doing a good job."

"I don't want to do that, but I don't want to keep you in the dark, either." He hesitated, then decided to go with his instincts. "We discovered that Morgan withdrew twenty-five thousand cash from his bank account on the day he disappeared. His car was found, now his body's been found, but the money's never showed up."

"Twenty-five thousand," Maggie murmured. A tidy sum, even tidier ten years ago. "You're telling me you think the money was the motive for murder?"

"Money's always a motive for murder, and it's a loose end. We're checking a lot of people out, but it takes time. So far, nobody around here's ever flashed that kind of money." He started to reach for another cigarette, then apparently changed his mind. "I've got a couple of theories . . ."

She might've smiled if her head wasn't beginning to ache. "And you'd like to tell me?"

"Whoever killed Morgan was smart enough to cover his tracks. He might've been smart enough to know that coming up with twenty-five thousand dollars wouldn't go unnoticed in a town like this. Maybe, just maybe, he panicked and got rid of the money. Or maybe he hid it so he could wait a good long time, until any rumors about Morgan had died down—then it'd just be waiting for him."

"Ten years is a very long time, Lieutenant."

"Some people're more patient than others." He shrugged. "It's just a theory."

But it made her think. The attic, and the trunk and the handprint. "The other night—" she began, then stopped.

"Something happen the other night?" he prompted.

It was foolish not to tell him, to feel as though, if she did, she would be forging another link in the chain that bound her to everything that had happened. He was, after all, in charge of the investigation. "Well, it seems someone broke in and took something out of a trunk in the attic. I didn't realize it until days later—then I reported it to Sheriff Agee."

"That was the thing to do." His gaze lifted to the dormer window. "He come up with anything?"

"Not really. He did find a key. That is, his wife found one somewhere. He came back and opened the trunk, but it was empty."

"Would you mind if I had a look myself?"

She wanted it over, yet it seemed every step she took brought her in deeper. "No, I don't mind." Resigned, Maggie turned to lead him into the house. "It seems odd that anyone would hide money in the attic, then wait until someone was living here to claim it."

"You bought the place almost as soon as the sign was posted," Reiker reminded her.

"But it was nearly a month before I'd moved in."

"I heard Mrs. Agee kept quiet about the sale. Her husband didn't like the idea."

"You hear a lot of things, Lieutenant."

He gave her the slow, half-embarrassed smile he'd given her when he'd asked for her autograph. "I'm supposed to."

Maggie lapsed into silence until they reached the second floor. "The attic's up here. For what it's worth, I haven't found anything missing in the house."

"How'd they get in?" he asked as he began to climb the steeper, more narrow staircase.

"I don't know," she mumbled. "I wasn't locking my doors."

"But you are now?" He looked back over his shoulder.

"Yes, I'm locking them."

"Good." He went directly to the trunk, and, crouching down, studied the lock. The handprint had faded back to dust. "You say Mrs. Agee had the key?"

"Yes, or one of them. It seems this trunk belonged to the last people who rented the house, an old couple. The woman left it here after her husband died. Apparently there were at least two keys, but Joyce could only find one of them."

"Hmm." Reiker opened the now-unlocked trunk and peered inside, much as he'd peered into the gully. And it, Maggie thought, was just as empty now.

"Lieutenant, you don't really think there's a connection between this and—what you're investigating?"

"I don't like coincidences," he muttered, echoing Cliff's earlier statement. "You say the sheriff's looking into it?"

"Yes."

"I'll talk to him before I head back. Twenty-five thousand doesn't take up much room," he said. "It's a big trunk."

"I don't understand why anyone would let it sit in one for ten years."

"People're funny." He straightened, grunting a little with the effort. "Of course, it's just a theory. Another is that Morgan's mistress took the money and ran."

"His mistress?" Maggie repeated blankly.

"Alice Delaney," Reiker said easily. "She'd been having an affair with Morgan for five or six years. Funny how people'll talk once you get them started."

"Delaney?" Maggie said it quietly, hoping she'd heard incorrectly.

"That's right. As a matter of fact, it's her son who's been doing your landscaping. Coincidences," he repeated. "This business is full of them."

Somehow she managed to remain composed as they walked back downstairs. She spoke politely when he told her again how much he admired her music. Maybe she even smiled when she closed the door on him. When she was alone, Maggie felt her blood turn to ice, then drain.

Cliff's mother had been Morgan's mistress for years; then she'd disappeared, right after his death? Cliff would've known. Everyone would've known, she thought, and covered her face with both hands. What had she fallen into, and how would she ever get out again?

Maybe he was going crazy, but Cliff was beginning to think of the long, winding drive up the hill as going home. He'd never have believed he could consider the old Morgan place as home. Not with the way he'd always felt about William Morgan. Nor would he have believed the woman who lived there could make him think that way. It seemed a great deal was happening that he could neither stop nor harness. Yet staying with Maggie had been his own choice, just as leaving again would be—when he was ready. From time to time he found he needed to remind himself that he could and would leave again.

Yet when she laughed, the house was so warm. When she was angry, it was so full of energy. When she sang—when she worked in the music room in the evening, Cliff thought. When the woods were quiet, before the moon had risen, she'd play. She'd sing snatches of words, sentences, phrases, as she composed. Long before she'd finished, he'd find himself in a frenzy of need. He wondered how she worked hour after hour, day after day, with such passion and feeling driving her.

It was the discipline, Cliff decided. He'd never expected her to be so disciplined about her music. The talent he'd admired all along, but in the few days he'd lived with her, he'd learned that she drove herself hard in the hours she worked.

A contrast, Cliff decided. It was an implausible contrast to the woman who jumped sporadically from one project to another in that big, dusty house. She left walls half papered, ceilings half painted. There were crates and boxes everywhere, most of which hadn't been touched. Rolls of supplies were tucked into every corner. He'd say her work on the house was precise, even creative, to the point where she'd leave off for something new.

She wasn't like anyone he'd ever known, and he realized that somewhere along the way he'd begun to understand her. It had been easier when he could dismiss her as a spoiled Hollywood princess who'd bought a dilapidated country house on a whim or for a publicity stunt. He knew now that she'd bought the house for no other reason than she'd loved it.

Perhaps she was a bit spoiled. She tended to give orders a little too casually. When she didn't get her own way, she tended to bristle or to freeze up. Cliff grinned. The same could be said of himself, he admitted.

To give Maggie her due, she hadn't run from the trouble or unpleasantness that had begun so shortly after she'd moved in. If he'd seen another woman stick as Maggie was sticking, he'd have said she'd indeed taken root. Cliff still had his doubts. Perhaps he fostered them purposely, because if he believed Maggie Fitzgerald would stay in Morganville, he might have to admit he wanted her to. He might have to admit that coming home every night to a woman who made him laugh and fume and throb wasn't something he'd give up without a fight.

He drove the last few yards, then stopped at the edge of the drive. The phlox was blooming on the bank. The new grass was like a green shadow over the soil. Maggie's petunias were a splash of color.

They'd both put part of themselves into the land already, he realized. Perhaps that in itself was a bond that would be difficult to break. Even as he stepped out of the truck, he wanted her, just the scent, just the softness of her. There was nothing he could do to change it.

There was no music. Cliff frowned as he slowly climbed the front steps. Maggie was always at her piano at this time of day. There were times he'd come back earlier and work on the yard himself. He'd know it was five o'clock, because that's when the music would begin, and it would continue for no less than an hour, often longer. Cliff looked at his watch: 5:35 p.m. Uneasy, he turned the knob on the front door.

Of course it was unlocked, he thought, annoyed. He'd left her a note that morning, telling her none of his crew would be there that day and to keep the doors locked. Senseless woman, he thought as he shoved the door open. Why couldn't she get it through her head that she was completely isolated here? Too many things had happened, and simply by living in this house, she was in the center of them.

Quiet. Too damn quiet, Cliff realized as annoyance began to

fade into anxiety. The dog wasn't barking. The house had that echoing, empty feeling almost everyone can sense but can't explain. Though instinct told him no one was there, he began to go from room to room, calling her. Her name bounced back off the walls in his own voice and taunted him.

Where the hell was she, Cliff demanded as he took the stairs two at a time to check the second floor. He didn't like to admit that he could feel panic at nothing more than coming home to an empty house, but panic was exactly what he felt. Every day that week he'd been sure he'd had a crew, or part of one, working outside until he'd been there. He hadn't wanted her left alone, but because he couldn't explain it, Cliff had broken the ritual that day. And now he couldn't find her.

"Maggie!" Desperately, he searched the second floor, not even certain what he expected, or wanted, to find. He'd never experienced this kind of raw, basic fear. He only knew the house was empty and his woman was gone. A pair of her shoes sat carelessly in the center of the bedroom rug. A blouse was tossed negligently over a chair. The earrings he'd watched her take off the night before still lay on the dresser, beside a silver-backed brush engraved with her mother's initials. The room held her scent; it always did.

When he saw the new tiles in the bathroom, he tried to calm himself. In her helter-skelter way, she'd started a new project. But where in the hell—

Then, in the bowl of the sink, he saw something that stopped his heart. Against the pristine white porcelain were three drops of blood. He stared while panic swirled through him, making his head swim and his skin ice.

From somewhere outside, the dog began to bark frantically. Cliff was racing down the steps, not even aware that he called her name again and again.

He saw her as soon as he burst through the back door. She was coming slowly through the woods to the east, the dog dancing around her legs, leaping and nipping. She had her hands in her pockets, her head down. His mind took in every detail while the combination of fear and relief made his legs weak.

He ran toward her, seeing her head lift as he called her again. Then he had her in his arms, holding tight, closing his eyes and just feeling her, warm and whole and safe. He was too overcome with emotions that had no precedent to notice that she stood stiff and unyielding against him.

He buried his face in the soft luxury of her hair. "Maggie, where've you been?"

This was the man she'd thought she was beginning to understand. This was the man she was beginning to love. Maggie stared straight ahead over his shoulder to the house beyond. "I went for a walk."

"Alone?" he demanded irrationally, drawing her back. "You went out alone?"

Everything turned cold; her skin, her manner, her eyes. "It's my land, Cliff. Why shouldn't I go out alone?"

He caught himself before he could rage that she should've left him a note. What was happening to him? "There was blood in the sink upstairs."

"I cut my finger on a tile."

He found he wanted to rage at her for that. She had no business hurting herself. "You're usually playing this time of day," he managed.

"I'm not locked into a routine any more than I'm locked into the house. If you want a placid little female who's waiting to fall at your feet every night when you come home, you'd better look somewhere else." Leaving him staring, she broke away and went into the house.

Calmer but more confused, Cliff went into the kitchen to see her pouring a drink. Scotch, he noted, another first. With his mind a bit clearer, he could see that the normal color was absent from her cheeks and that her shoulders were stiff with tension. This time he didn't go to her or touch her.

"What's happened?"

Maggie swirled the scotch once before she swallowed.

She found it too warm, too strong, but she sipped again. "I don't know what you mean." The kitchen was too small. Maggie took the glass and went out. The air was warm and soft. Outside there were no walls or ceilings to make her feel closed in. Circling around, she sat down on the spread of new grass. She'd sit here in the summer, Maggie thought, and read—Byron, if that was her mood. She'd let the sun fall over her, the silence cloak her, and read until she slept. Maggie continued to look out over the woods when Cliff's shadow slanted over her.

"Maggie, what's wrong with you?"

"I'm having a mood," she said flatly. "You'd expect spoiled celebrities to have moods, wouldn't you?"

Keeping his temper in check, Cliff sat down beside her, then took her chin in his hand. He waited until their eyes had met and held. "What?"

She'd known she'd have to tell him. It was the not knowing what there would be afterward that left her insides cold and knotted. "Lieutenant Reiker was here today," she began, but carefully removed Cliff's hand from her face.

Cliff swore, cursing himself for leaving her alone. "What'd he want?"

Maggie shrugged and sipped at the scotch again. "He's a man who doesn't like loose ends. Apparently he's been finding quite a number. It seems William Morgan withdrew twenty-five thousand dollars from his bank account on the day he was murdered."

"Twenty-five thousand?"

He sounded surprised, Maggie noted. Genuinely surprised. She recognized his expression, that thoughtful, narrow-eyed look that meant he was considering all the details and angles. How could she be certain of anything any longer? "The money was never recovered. One of Reiker's theories is that the murderer hid it away, patiently waiting until people forgot about Morgan."

Cliff's eyes sharpened. Automatically, he turned his head and looked back to the house. "Here?"

"Possibly."

"Ten years is a damn long time to sit on twenty-five thousand," Cliff muttered. Still, he didn't care for loose ends, either. "Did you tell him about the trunk in the attic?"

"Yes, he had a look at it himself."

He touched her shoulder, just his fingertips, so lightly that the touch offered whatever support she might want to take. "It's upset you." Maggie said nothing, nor did she look at him. Tension began to work at his own muscles. "There's more."

"There's always more," Maggie said quietly. Now she looked at him; she had to. "He mentioned that Morgan's mistress had disappeared right after his death." She felt Cliff's fingers tighten convulsively on her shoulder just as she felt the waves of anger.

"She wasn't his mistress," Cliff said tightly. "My mother might've been foolish enough to fall in love with a man like Morgan, she might've been unwise enough to sleep with him, but she wasn't his mistress."

"Why didn't you tell me before?" Maggie demanded. "Why did you wait until I found out this way?"

"It doesn't have anything to do with you or with anything that's happened here." As restless anger swarmed in him, he rose.

"Coincidences," Maggie said quietly, but Cliff turned and stared down at her. "Weren't you the one who said not to trust coincidences?"

He was trapped, by an old anger and by a pair of depthless brown eyes. Again he found himself compelled to explain what he'd never explained before. "My mother was lonely and very vulnerable after my father died. Morgan knew how to exploit that. I was living outside of D.C. at the time. If I'd been here, I might've stopped it." Resentment welled up and was controlled. "He knew how to play on weaknesses, and he played on my mother's. When I found out they were lovers, I wanted to kill him."

He said it as he had once before, coldly, calmly. Maggie swallowed on a dry throat. "She was already too involved for anything to be done, deluded into believing she loved him, or maybe she did love him. Other intelligent women had. She'd been friends with Louella for years, but that didn't matter. When they found his car in the river, she snapped."

It was painful to look back on it, but Maggie's solemn brown eyes insisted he go on. "She didn't disappear—she came to me. She was frantic, and for the first time since she'd become involved with Morgan, she was seeing clearly again. Shame affects different people in different ways. My mother broke all ties with Morganville and everyone in it. She knew her relationship with Morgan wasn't a secret, and now that it was over, she simply couldn't face the gossip. She's still in D.C. She has a new life, and I don't want any of this to touch her."

Was he always so unflaggingly protective of the women in his life? Maggie wondered. Joyce, his mother . . . Where, she wondered, did she fit in? "Cliff, I understand how you feel. My mother was one of the most precious people in my life, too. But there might not be anything you can do about it. They're reconstructing what happened ten years ago, and your mother has a part in it."

But that wasn't all she was thinking, Cliff realized. Deliberately, he sat down beside her, struggling to keep the tension from his fingers when he took her shoulders. "You're wondering how much a part I might've had in it."

"Don't." She tried to stand, but he held her still.

"It's possible that I could've shot Morgan to end a destructive relationship with my mother."

"You hated him."

"Yes."

Her eyes never left his. They looked deep, searching. Logic might implicate him; his own temperament might make him suspect. Maggie stared into the smoky gray of his eyes and believed what she saw. "No," she murmured, drawing him against her. "No, I understand you too well."

Her faith—the warm flood of it—almost destroyed him. "Do you?"

"Maybe too well," she murmured. "I was so frightened before." Closing her eyes, she drew in the familiar scent of him. He was real, he was solid, and for as long as she could hold on, he was hers. "Not now, not now that you're here."

He could feel the pull, that slow, gentle pull. If he wasn't careful, he'd soon forget there was anything or anyone but her in his life. "Maggie." His fingers were already tangling in her hair. "You shouldn't trust without questions."

"It isn't trust with questions," she countered. She wanted it to be only the two of them, with the rest of the world locked out, forgotten. Framing his face with her hands, she drew his mouth down to hers.

She'd expected fire, aggression, but his lips were soft and sweet. Confused, moved, Maggie drew back to stare at him. The eyes that had fascinated her from the beginning held hers as seconds edged closer to a minute. She was lost in the mists and the smoke. Without a word, he brought her close again.

With his eyes on hers, he lightly traced the shape of her face with a fingertip. This, he discovered, was the only face he ever needed to see again. Lightly, he outlined the shape of her lips. These, he knew, were the only lips he'd ever need to taste. With a gentleness he'd shown to no other lover, he laid her back. This was the only body he ever wanted to possess.

Tenderness left her stunned, weak. His mouth lingered on hers, but with such poignancy, the kiss alone made her bones liquefy. The grass was cool beneath her, the sun warm. Swimming in emotion, Maggie closed her eyes while his lips traveled over her face.

Had she ever been touched like this before? As if she were spun glass, his hands stroked over her. As if she were the rarest of delicacies, his lips tasted. And she was helplessly caught in the silken web that was more love than passion.

"Cliff—"

She might've told him, if his lips hadn't captured hers with a sweetness that left her speechless.

He'd never felt a stronger need to savor. It was as if each moment could be stretched to an hour as long as they lay together in the fragrant spring grass. The color in her cheeks was delicate; the sunlight combed through her hair. The look in her eyes was one no man could resist. It told him as clearly as words that she was his. He had only to claim. Knowing it, he moved only more slowly and touched only more reverently.

He undressed her while his kisses continued to hold her in the honey-steeped prison of pleasure. When she was naked, he watched how the sun streamed over her skin. Her large, expressive eyes were half closed. He could feel the pliancy in her body when, with a sigh, she lifted her hands to help him undress.

The raw, primitive need she so often incited in him didn't rise up. Instead, she drew out the softer emotions he normally held back. He wanted only to please her.

Gently, he lowered his mouth to her breast. He could hear her heartbeat increase in pace as he lingered there with his tongue tracing, his teeth nibbling. The tip grew taut, so that when he drew it into his mouth, he heard her breath shudder out, then catch again. Her hand moved through his hair as she lay back, saturated with sensation.

Her body was like a treasure to be discovered and admired before possession. Slowly, almost leisurely, he took those moist kisses and gentle hands over it, stopping, lingering, when he felt her shuddering response. He knew she was steeped in that dim, heavy world where passions hover around the edges and desires lick temptingly, like tiny tongues of fire. He wanted to keep her there for hours or days or years.

Her thighs were slender and long and pearl-white. He loitered there, nudging them both closer, still closer to the edge. But not yet.

She'd forgotten where she was. Though her eyes were half opened, she saw nothing but mists and dreams. She could feel, oh, yes, she could feel each stroke of his hand, each warm brush of lips.

She could hear gentle murmurs, quiet sighs that might've been his or hers. There was no reason to ever feel or hear anything else. She was slowly, inevitably, being drawn through the sweetness and into the heat. She began to crave it.

He felt the change in her body, heard the change in the breaths that whispered through her lips. He swept his mouth farther up her thigh, but still he didn't hurry. She would have all he had to give before they were finished.

She arched, catapulted with the sudden intensity of pleasure. She crested, quickly, shatteringly, with an abandonment of self and will. He wanted, demanded, just that. Before she could settle, he drove her up again until the madness once more began to creep into both of them. Cliff held it off, almost delirious with the knowledge that he could give her what a woman might only dream of. Her body was alive with sensations only he could bring to her. Her mind was swirling with thoughts of only him.

Knowing it, reveling in it, he slipped into her, taking her with a tenderness that lasted and lasted and lasted.

Chapter 11

Saturday morning, Maggie decided she could lie there, half dozing, until it was Saturday afternoon. She could feel the weight of Cliff's arm across her waist, his warm breath fluttering over her cheek. Without opening her eyes, she snuggled closer, wallowing in lazy contentment.

If she'd been certain he could be so gentle, she'd have fallen in love with him willingly. But how satisfying it was to have discovered it after her heart had already been lost. He had such emotion in him. Perhaps he was cautious with it, but she could love him much more comfortably knowing it was there and that now and again, unexpectedly, it would reach out to her.

No, it wasn't flowery phrases she wanted, but his stability. She didn't need smooth charm. When a woman found a man who was capable of such passion and such tenderness, she'd be a fool to want to change him in any way. Maggie Fitzgerald, she thought with a little satisfied smile, was no fool.

"What're you smiling at?"

Opening her eyes, Maggie looked directly into Cliff's. Because his were alert and direct, she knew he'd been awake for some time. She tried to blink away the mists and smiled again. "It feels good," she murmured, snuggling even closer. "You feel good."

He ran a hand down her back, over her hip and thigh. Yes, it felt very good. "Soft," Cliff said quietly. "So soft and smooth."

He wondered how he'd gone so many years without being able to touch her like this, when she was lazy and warm and naked. He felt no tension in her, none of the subtle little signs he'd grown so adept at spotting. The need was very strong in him to keep that tension away for as long as he could. She'd walked unwittingly into a whirlpool, and somehow he was connected with it. If it was only for a day, he'd keep the problems at bay.

He rolled, pressed her down into the mattress so that she laughingly murmured a complaint. "Are you going to cook breakfast?" he demanded.

Maggie pillowed her head on her hands, giving him arrogant look for arrogant look. "You don't like my cooking."

"I've decided to be tolerant this morning."

"Have you?" She arched a brow. "How lucky for me."

"Floppy bacon and sloppy eggs," he told her before he nuzzled at her neck.

She shifted, enjoying the rough feel of the night's growth of beard against her skin. "What?"

"I don't like my bacon too crisp—" he nipped at the pulse in her throat "—or my eggs too set."

With a sigh, she closed her eyes again. She wanted to bottle this moment, so that she could take it out again whenever she needed to feel content. "I like my bacon so crisp it crumbles, and I don't like eggs at all."

"They're good for you." Cliff took his lips up her throat to nibble at her ear. "Might put some meat on you." As he spoke, he took his hand down her side again.

"Complaining?"

"Uh-uh." He ran his hand back up again so that his fingers brushed the side of her breast. "Though you do tend toward the lean side. We could build you up with three square meals a day and some exercise."

"No one needs three meals a day," she began, a bit huffily. "And as for exercise—"

"Do you like to dance?"

"Yes, but I—"

"Not much muscle," he noted, pinching her arm. "How's your endurance?"

She gave him a saucy look. "You should know."

With a laugh, he pressed his lips to hers. "You've a very quick, very wicked mind."

"Thanks."

"Now, about dancing. Ever been in a contre line?"

"A what?"

"I thought so." He shook his head, then shifted so that he could look down at her with pity. "Country dancing, Maggie."

Her brows drew together. "Square dancing?"

"No." It was time to educate the lady, Cliff decided, and drew her up to a sitting position. Her hair flowed wildly over her shoulders, the way he liked it best. "Square dancing's more formal, more regimented, than country dancing, but there'd be traditional music and a caller."

Maggie ran a finger up his chest. "Swing your partner and do-si-do?"

He felt the little thrill inch along his skin behind the trail of her finger. Did she know it? he wondered. From the smile that hovered on her lips, he thought she knew it very well. "Among other things."

Maggie linked her hands around his neck and let her head fall back so that she could look at him from beneath lowered lashes. "I'm sure it's all very fascinating, but I don't know why we're doing all this talking when you could be kissing me."

For an answer he gave her a long, searing kiss that left her breathless and pleased. "Because," he said, and nipped at her ear, "I want to go dancing with you."

Sighing, content, Maggie enjoyed the sensation of feeling her own blood begin to sizzle. "Where and when?"

"Tonight, in the park outside of town."

"Tonight?" She opened one eye. "Dancing in the park?"

"It's a tradition." He laid her back again but kept himself propped up so that his hand was free to skim her body. "A sort of

Founder's Day celebration combined with rites of spring. Most of the town'll show. There'll be dancing till midnight, then a potluck supper. Then . . ." He cupped her breast, enjoying the way her eyes clouded when he brushed a fingertip over the point. "There's dancing till dawn for anybody who can handle it."

"Until dawn?" Intrigued and already hopelessly aroused, Maggie arched under him.

"You've danced until dawn before, I imagine."

He'd said the wrong thing or used the wrong tone, because her body stiffened. No, he didn't want to bring up their differences now. At the moment, he could hardly recognize them. He lay down beside her and cradled her in his arms. "We could watch the sun come up," he murmured. "And the stars go out."

She lay against him, but her mind was clear now. The doubts had returned. "You never mentioned this to me before."

"I didn't think you'd be much interested in country dances and potluck suppers. I guess I realized I was wrong."

It was another kind of apology. Maggie accepted this one as easily as she had the first. Smiling again, she tilted her head back from him. "Are you asking me for a date?"

He liked it when her eyes held that half teasing, half challenging light. "Looks like it."

"I'd love to."

"Okay." Her hair fell onto his shoulder. Absently, he twisted the end around his finger. "Now, about breakfast."

She grinned, lowering her mouth to his. "We'll have it for lunch."

She didn't know what she expected, but Maggie looked forward to an evening out, away from the house, an evening to spend with other people. After her brief stab at being a hermit, she'd discovered that she could indeed take total command of her own needs. Being able to live with herself for long periods of time simply showed her that she didn't always have to in order to prove her independence. Perhaps she hadn't been attempting to learn anything with the dramatic change in her lifestyle, but she'd learned something, anyway.

She could take charge of the tiny details of day-to-day living that she'd always left to others, but she didn't have to cut herself off from everyone to do it.

No, she didn't know what to expect, perhaps a quaint little festival with tinny music and warm lemonade in paper cups. She didn't expect to be particularly impressed. She certainly didn't expect to be enchanted.

The line of cars that sloped down the winding drive to the park surprised her. She'd thought most of the people in town would simply walk. When she mentioned it to Cliff, he shrugged and negotiated his pickup into a spot behind a yellow van.

"They come from all over the county, and from as far away as D.C. and Pennsylvania."

"Really?" Pursing her lips, she climbed out of the truck into the warm, clear night. There'd be a full moon, though the sun was just beginning to set. She wondered if the town had planned it that way or if it had been the luck of the draw. Either way, it was one more thing to be enjoyed. Putting her hand in Cliff's, she began to walk with him to the crest of the hill.

As she watched, the sun dropped lower behind the mountains in the west. She'd seen the sun sink gloriously into the sea and been awed by the colors and brilliance of sunsets in the snow-covered Alps. She'd seen the desert vibrate with color at dusk and cities glow with twilight. Somehow, watching the gold and mauve and pink layer over what were hardly more than foothills of a great range, she was more deeply affected. Perhaps it was foolish, perhaps it was fanciful, but she felt more a part of this place, more involved with the coming of this night, than she'd been of any other. On impulse, she threw her arms around Cliff's neck and held on.

Laughing, he put his hands on her hips. "What's this for?"

"It feels good," she said, echoing her morning words.

Then with a bang that shattered the silence, the music burst out. As a musician, she recognized each individual instrument—violin, banjo, guitar, piano. As a music lover, she felt her excitement leap.

"It's fabulous!" she exclaimed, drawing quickly away. "Absolutely fabulous. Hurry, I have to see." Maggie grabbed his hand and raced the rest of the way up the hill.

Her first impression was of a maze of people, two hundred, perhaps two hundred fifty, crowded together in a covered pavilion. Then she saw they were in lines, six, no, eight, she realized after a quick count. There would be a line of men facing a line of women, and so on, until they simply ran out of room. And they were moving to the music in a system that looked both confusing and fluid.

Some of the women wore skirts that flared out as they dipped, swayed or spun. Others wore jeans. Men's attire was no more consistent and no more formal than the women's. Some of the dancers wore sneakers, while a great many more wore what seemed to be old-fashioned black leather shoes that tied and had thick, sturdy heels. Still others wore what looked like Chinese slippers with a single strap across the instep. It didn't seem to matter what was worn; everyone moved. Petticoats flashed, heels stomped, laughter rang out.

A woman stood at the edge of a small wooden stage in front of the band and belted out instructions in a singsong voice. Maggie might not have understood most of the words, but she understood rhythm. Already she was itching to try it herself.

"But how do they know what to do?" she shouted over the music. "How do they understand her?"

"It's a sequence of moves repeated over and over," Cliff told her. "Once you've got the sequence down, you don't even need a caller; she just adds to it."

A sequence, Maggie mused and tried to find it. At first, she only saw bodies moving in what seemed a helter-skelter pattern, but gradually she began to see the repetition. Counting off the beats, she concentrated on one couple while trying to anticipate their next move. It pleased her to be able to find the sequence, just as the music pleased her ear and the swirling colors pleased her eye. She could smell a mixture of colognes, men's and women's, and the bursting fragrance of the spring flowers that skirted the pavilion.

As the sun dropped lower, the lights, strung overhead, spilled over the dancers. The floor vibrated under her feet so that she felt she was already dancing herself. With Cliff's arm around her, she watched with the undiluted fascination of discovering something new and exciting. She recognized the postmistress. The rather severe-looking middle-aged woman spun by like a dervish and flirted like a young girl.

Flirtation was part of it, Maggie realized as she began to watch faces instead of feet and bodies. Eye contact was essential, as were the saucy smiles she noted and the quick head tosses. It was, as perhaps dances had always been, a kind of mating ritual.

He hadn't thought she'd be fascinated or excited, but he recognized both in the look in her eyes. It gave Cliff overwhelming pleasure to know he'd brought that to her. Her face was flushed, her body already moving to the beat, and her eyes were everywhere at once. She didn't make him think of Maggie Fitzgerald, star baby and glamorous celebrity, but of Maggie, a woman he could hold on to and dance with until the sun came up again.

When the music ended, Maggie burst into raucous applause with everyone else. Laughing, her face tilted back, she grabbed his hand. "I have to try the next one, even if I make a fool of myself."

"Just listen to the calls and follow the music," he said simply as the lines began to form again. "They always run through the dance once before the music starts."

She listened as the next dance sequence was explained by the caller. Though she didn't understand half of the terms, Maggie tried to link them in her mind with the moves that followed. As Cliff guided her slowly through the paces, she enjoyed the sense of camaraderie and the lack of inhibitions around her.

Though she could sense that she was being watched with speculation and interest, Maggie refused to be perturbed by it. They had a right to look, she decided. It was, after all, the first time she'd participated in a town function, and she was being partnered by a man everyone seemed to know.

"This one's called, 'Whiskey before Breakfast,'" the caller sang out. "If you've tried it, you know it ain't as good for you as dancing." She stomped her foot on the platform, one, two, three, and the music began.

The dance was fast and exuberant. Maggie was caught up in the moves before she'd fully registered them. Right, then left; join left hands with your corner and turn around twice. Pass through. Balance and swing.

The first time Cliff whirled her around, she felt the rush of air on her face and laughed.

"Watch my eyes," he warned. "Or you'll be too dizzy to stand up."

"I like it!" she tossed back, then "Whoops!" as she botched the next step and hurried to keep up with the rest of the line.

She didn't mind the sense of confusion or the crowd. Shoulders bumped, feet tangled, her waist was gripped, and she was whirled around by people she'd never met. Teenagers danced with grandmothers. Ladies in frilly dresses swirled with men in jeans with bandannas in their back pockets. Obviously anyone was welcome to line up and dance, and Maggie had already noticed that women picked men for partners just as often as men picked women. It was a free-for-all, and the rules were loose.

As the steps became more repetitive and more instinctive, she began to enjoy it even more. Her steps became more animated, her concentration less focused on the moves and more on the music. She could see why it drove people to dance. Feet couldn't be still with that rhythm jangling out. She knew, as Cliff grabbed her and swung her in fast circles, that she could've danced for hours.

"That's it," he said, laughing as she clung to him.

"Already?" She was breathless but not nearly finished. "It was wonderful, but too short. When do we do another?"

"Anytime you like."

"Now," she told him, sliding in as new lines formed.

She was fitting in as if she'd been to country dances in rural parks all her life. Perhaps he shouldn't have been surprised; she'd proved him wrong time and time again in his preconception of her. Yet in other ways, Cliff mused, he'd been right. She had an elegance that was too ingrained to be missed, whether she was scraping linoleum or lying in his arms. There was a polish that came from affluence and classy schools that set her apart from the other women around her. For days he'd been telling himself that it was that difference that attracted him as much as it put his back up. He couldn't explain the reason for either. He couldn't explain now, as he watched her begin the next dance as if she'd been moving to the call all her life, why she made him uneasy.

Circumstances, he told himself, and turned her back and around in a butterfly swing. The circumstances almost from the moment they'd met had been uneasy. That was bound to affect the way he felt when he looked at her—when he thought of her. And he thought of her, Cliff admitted, more often than he should; he looked at her less often than he wanted to.

Living with her for the past few days had given him the odd sensation of having something he hadn't known he'd wanted. There was something just a little too appealing about waking each morning with her warm beside him, about coming home to Maggie and her music. It would be wiser, much wiser, if he remembered those differences between them. No real common ground, he told himself again. But when she whirled into his arms, laughing, it was as though he'd been waiting for her.

The first few dances were a blur of color and sound and music. Maggie let herself go, realizing it had been weeks since she'd felt this free of tension and trouble. She'd danced in trendy clubs with celebrities, twirled in ballrooms with royalty, but she knew she'd never had as much simple fun as she was having now, following the caller and the fiddle.

As she turned to her next partner, she found her hand gripped by Stan Agee. Without his badge and gun, he might've been an attractive athlete in his prime. For a reason Maggie couldn't analyze, she tensed immediately on contact.

"Glad to see you're out, Miss Fitzgerald."

"Thank you." Determined not to give in to the mood, she smiled, lifting a hand to his shoulder as he began the spin. She caught his scent, the familiar department-store cologne, but it didn't soothe her.

"You catch on fast."

"It's wonderful. I can't believe I've missed it all my life." Out of the corner of her eye, she saw Cliff spinning with Joyce. The tension wouldn't dissolve.

"Save out a dance for me," he ordered before they whirled back to their original partners for the next step.

The moment he touched her, Cliff felt the rigidity of her muscles. "What's wrong?"

"Nothing." It was nothing, Maggie told herself, because she couldn't explain it. But now, as she swirled and turned from one pair of arms to another, it came to her that each time she danced with someone, she might be dancing with a murderer. How was she to know? It could be anyone—the real estate agent who'd sold her the house, the butcher who'd recommended the pork chops only the day before, the postmistress, the bank teller. How was she to know?

Maggie's mind began to whirl. For an instant, her eyes locked on Lieutenant Reiker's as he stood on the sidelines, watching. Why here? she asked herself as she was snatched up and spun again. Why would he come here? Perhaps he was watching her—but why? Protecting her—from what?

Then she was in Cliff's arms again, grateful that her feet could follow the mindless repetition of the dance while her thoughts raced in dozens of directions. Hadn't Cliff said people came from all over to this all-night festival? Maybe Reiker was a country-dance enthusiast. More likely, she thought grimly, he'd wanted to see all the townspeople together, observe, dissect. She shuddered. It was his job, she reminded herself. He was only doing his job. But how she wished he'd go away.

There was Louella, seeming to float through the dance. Rather than verve, she had a restrained dignity in her movements that was both lovely and uncomfortable to watch. Lovely, Maggie realized, because Louella had the grace of a natural dancer. Uncomfortable—though she wasn't able to put her finger on it, Maggie sensed there was something beneath the restraint that struggled for release.

Fanciful, she berated herself. She was being foolish and fanciful, imagining things that weren't there. But the feeling of discomfort was persistent. She was being watched, she knew. By Reiker? Stan Agee, Joyce, Louella? By everyone, Maggie thought. They all knew one another; they'd all known William Morgan. She was the outsider who'd uncovered what had been dead and buried for a decade. Logic indicated that at least one of them would resent her for that—perhaps all of them.

Suddenly, the music was too loud, the steps were too fast and the air was too full of scent.

Then she was caught up in Bog's short, wiry arms and spun at a breathless pace. "You're a good spinner, Miss Maggie," he told her, grinning and showing several gaps instead of teeth. "One helluva spinner."

Looking down into his homely, wrinkled face, she broke into a grin of her own. She was being ridiculous. No one resented her. Why should they? She wasn't involved in a tragedy that was ten years old. It was time she stopped looking beneath the surface and accepted things as she saw them. "I love to spin!" she shouted to Bog, leaning back into it. "I could spin for hours."

He gave a cackling laugh and released her for the next sequence. The music built, but it no longer seemed too loud. The tempo increased, but she could've danced faster and faster. When it was over, she had her hands linked around Cliff's neck and was laughing.

There was no tension in her now, but there had been. He thought he understood the reason. Deliberately, he steered her away from the Agees and Louella. "I could use a beer."

"Sounds perfect. I'd like to watch another one, anyway. It's the best show in town."

"You want a beer?"

Maggie glanced up, brow lifted. "Aren't I allowed?"

He shrugged and passed a man in overalls a dollar. "You just don't look like the beer type."

"You type too easily," Maggie countered, watching as beer was tapped from a wooden keg into paper cups.

"Maybe," he murmured as she sipped at the froth. "You're having a good time?"

"Yes." She laughed over the rim. The beer was lukewarm, but it was wet. Her foot was already tapping. They'd added a mandolin, she noticed. The sound was sweet and old-fashioned. "Didn't you think I would?"

"I thought you'd enjoy the music." He leaned against the wall so that he could see her with the dancers at her back. "I thought you needed to get out. But I didn't expect you to take to all this as if you'd been born doing it."

She lowered her half-empty cup and gave him a solemn smile. "When are you going to stop putting me in that shiny glass cage, Cliff? I'm not a delicate hothouse flower or a spoiled Hollywood bitch. I'm Maggie Fitzgerald, and I write music."

The look held for a long time while the music pulsed around them. "I think I know who you are." Lifting a hand, he ran the back of it down her cheek. "I think I know Maggie Fitzgerald. It might've been safer for both of us with you in that glass cage."

She felt the heat rise. It only took a touch. "We'll have to see, won't we?" With one brow still lifted in question, she touched her cup to his. "To new understanding?"

"All right." He cradled her chin in his hand before he kissed her. "We'll give it a shot."

"Miss Fitzgerald?"

Maggie turned to see a short man in his early twenties running a felt hat around and around in his hands. Until that moment, she'd been so intent on Cliff that she hadn't noticed the music had stopped. "You're the piano player." Her eyes lit, and the smile that could stun so unexpectedly curved on her lips. "You're wonderful."

He'd been nervous before; now he was overwhelmed. "I just— Thank you," he managed, staring at her with his soul in his eyes.

She doesn't even know it, Cliff realized. She wasn't aware that she could make a man want to grovel. Sipping his beer, he watched the piano player try to find his voice again.

"I couldn't believe it when I heard you were here."

"I live here," she told him simply.

The way she said it, so matter-of-factly, had Cliff looking at her again. She'd said it before, countless times in countless ways, but he realized now he hadn't listened. Yes, she lived here. She'd chosen to live here just as he had. It hardly mattered where she'd lived or how she'd lived before. She was here now because she'd chosen to be. And she was staying. For the first time, he fully believed it.

"Miss Fitzgerald . . ." The piano player crushed the brim of his hat in his fingers, torn between pleasure and anxiety. "I just wanted you to know it's great having you here. We don't want to push you into anything, but if you'd like to play anything, anything at all—"

"Are you asking?" she interrupted.

The boy stumbled over uncertain ground. "We just wanted you to know that if you'd like—"

"I don't know any of the songs," she told him, taking a last sip of beer. "Do you trust me to improvise?"

His mouth dropped open. "Are you kidding?"

She laughed and handed her cup to Cliff. "Hang on to this."

He shook his head, leaning back against the wall as she walked to the stage with the piano player. She had a habit of giving orders, he mused. Then he thought of the look of stunned admiration in the boy's eyes. Maybe it was worth it.

She played for an hour. It was, she discovered, as much fun making the music as it was dancing to it. She enjoyed the challenge of the unfamiliar music and the freewheeling style. Before she'd gone through the second number, Maggie had decided to write one of her own.

From the vantage point of the stage, she could see the dancers. She saw Louella again, partnered by Stan. Automatically, she searched the crowd for Joyce and found her facing Cliff. As if she'd known he'd be there, her gaze was drawn to the left. Reiker leaned against a post, smoking, watching the dancers.

Who? Maggie wondered. Who is he watching? As the lines merged and shifted, she couldn't be sure, only that the direction of his gaze rested on where Stan danced with Louella and Cliff with Joyce.

If he saw one of them as a murderer, it didn't show in his eyes. They were calm and steady and made Maggie's stomach queasy. Deliberately, she turned her head and concentrated on the music.

"I didn't expect to lose my partner to a piano," Cliff said when the music paused again.

Maggie sent him an arch look. "You didn't appear to lack for any."

"A lone man's easy prey around here." Grabbing her hand, he drew her to her feet. "Hungry?"

"Is it midnight already?" Maggie pressed a hand to her stomach. "I'm starving."

They piled their plates high, though the light was so dim it was impossible to tell what they were eating until it was tasted. They sat on the grass under a tree and chatted easily to the people who passed by. It was easy, Maggie thought. They were just people drawn to one place by music. Again she felt a sense of camaraderie and connection. Leaning back, Maggie scanned the crowd.

"I don't see Louella."

"Stan would've taken her home," Cliff said between bites. "She never stays past midnight. He'll come back."

"Mmm." Maggie sampled what turned out to be Waldorf salad.

"Miss Fitzgerald."

Maggie set down her fork as Reiker crouched down beside her. "Lieutenant."

"I enjoyed your playing." He gave her the quiet smile that had her cursing her reaction to him. "I've listened to your music for years, but I never expected to be able to hear you play."

"I'm glad you liked it." She knew she should leave it at that, but felt compelled to go on. "I haven't noticed you dancing."

"Me?" The smile turned sheepish. "No, I don't dance. My wife, now, she likes to come."

Maggie felt herself relax. So the explanation had been a simple one, an innocent one. "Most people who appreciate music like to dance."

"I'd like to. My feet don't." His gaze shifted to Cliff. "I want to thank you for your cooperation. It might help us tie up a few loose ends."

"Whatever I can do," Cliff said briskly. "We'd all like this business tied up."

Reiker nodded, then, with some effort, rose. "I hope you'll play some more before the night's over, Miss Fitzgerald. It's a real pleasure listening to you."

When he was gone, Maggie let out a long breath. "It isn't fair that he makes me uncomfortable. He's only doing his job." She began to pick at her food again when Cliff remained silent. "What did he mean by cooperation?"

"I contacted my mother. She's coming up Monday to give a statement."

"I see. That must be difficult for her."

"No." Cliff shrugged it off. "It was ten years ago. It's behind her. It's behind all of us," he added quietly, "but one."

Maggie closed her eyes on a shudder. She wouldn't think of it now, not tonight. "Dance with me again," she insisted when the musicians began to tune. "There are hours yet before dawn."

She never tired, even after the moon began to set. The music and the movement gave her the release she needed for nervous energy. Some dancers faded; others became only more exuberant as the night grew later. The music never stopped.

As the sky began to lighten, there were no more than a hundred dancers left on their feet. There was something mystical, something powerful, in watching the sun rise from behind the mountains while the music poured onto the air. As the light grew rosy with the new day, the last waltz was called.

Cliff folded Maggie in his arms and circled the floor. He could feel the life vibrate from her—exciting, strong. Once she'd stopped, he thought as he gathered her closer, she'd sleep for hours.

She moved with him, snug against him. Her heartbeat was steady, her hair soft. He watched the colors spread over the mountains to the east. Then she tilted back her head and smiled at him.

And when he realized he was in love with her, Cliff was stunned and speechless.

Chapter 12

Maggie might've noticed Cliff's abrupt withdrawal if she hadn't been so full of the night and the music. "I can't believe it's over. I've hours more dancing in me."

"You'll be asleep before you're home," Cliff told her, but made certain he wasn't touching her. He must be crazy, falling in love with a woman like her. She couldn't decide whether to hang wallpaper or lay tile. She gave orders. She wore silk under her jeans. He must be crazy.

But she could dance with him through the night. There was a ridge of strength and courage under the delicate features. She made music that was part heaven and part sin. Hadn't he known, and hadn't he fought so hard, because he'd known almost from the first that she was a woman he'd never get out of his mind?

Now she was climbing into the cab of his pickup and resting her head against his shoulder as if it belonged there. It did belong there. Though the acceptance didn't come easily to him, Cliff put his arm around her, drawing her closer. She belonged there.

"I don't know when I've had such a good time." The energy was draining out of her swiftly. Through sheer will, Maggie kept her eyes open.

"The music's still running around in your head."

She tilted her head so that she could see his profile. "I think you are beginning to understand me."

"Some."

"Some's enough." She yawned hugely. "It was fun playing to-night. You know, I've always avoided performing, mainly because I knew it would only open the door for more comparisons. But tonight . . ."

Cliff frowned, not certain if he liked the drift. "You're thinking of performing?"

"No, not on a regular basis. If I'd had a drive to do it, I'd have done it long before this." She shifted into a more comfortable po-sition. "But I've decided to take C.J.'s advice and do the title song for *Heat Dance*. It's a compromise, a recording rather than a per-formance. And I do feel rather personally toward that song."

"You decided this tonight?"

"I've been leaning toward it for quite a while. It seems foolish to live by rules so strict you can't do something you really want to do. I really want to do that song." As her head began to droop, she noticed they were turning into her lane. "It'll mean flying back to L.A. for a few days for the taping, which'll thrill C.J." She gave a sleepy laugh. "He'll pull out every trick in the book to keep me from coming back."

Cliff felt the panic in his chest. He pulled the truck up at the end of the drive and set the brake. "I want you to marry me."

"What?" Half-asleep, Maggie shook her head, certain she'd misunderstood.

"I want you to marry me," Cliff repeated, but this time he took her shoulders so that she wasn't slumped down in the seat any lon-ger. "I don't care if you record a dozen songs. You're going to marry me before you go back to California."

To say she was stunned would've been an immeasurable un-derstatement. Maggie stared at him as if one of them had lost his mind. "I must be a little foggy at the moment," she said slowly. "Are you saying you want to marry me?"

"You know damn well what I'm saying." It was too much to know the fear of losing her just when he'd realized he couldn't live without her. He couldn't be calm; he couldn't be rational; he couldn't let her go without a pledge that she'd come back. "You're not going to California until you marry me."

Trying to clear her mind, Maggie drew back. "Are you talking about my doing a recording, or are we talking marriage? One has to do with my business, the other with my life."

Frustrated that she was calm when he couldn't be, Cliff dragged her back. "From now on, your life is my business."

"No." That sounded too familiar. "No, I don't want someone looking out for me, if that's what you mean. I won't take that kind of responsibility again, or that kind of guilt."

"I don't know what the hell you're talking about," Cliff exploded. "I'm telling you you're going to marry me."

"That's just it—you can't *tell* me!" She jerked away from him, and the sleepiness in her eyes had turned to fire. "Jerry told me we were getting married, and I went along because it seemed like the thing to do. He was my best friend. He'd helped me get over the death of my parents, encouraged me to write again. He wanted to take care of me." Maggie dragged a hand through her hair. "And I let him, until things started going downhill and he couldn't even take care of himself. I couldn't help him then. The pattern had been set, and I couldn't help him. Not again, Cliff. I won't be put in that glass cage again."

"This has nothing to do with your first marriage and nothing to do with cages," Cliff tossed back. "You can damn well take care of yourself, but you're going to marry me."

Her eyes narrowed into slits as she held down her own uncertain temper. "Why?"

"Because I'm telling you."

"Wrong answer." With a toss of her head, she was out of the truck and had slammed the door. "You can go cool off or go sleep it off or whatever you want," she told him coldly. "I'm going to bed." Turning on her heel, she strode up the shaky front steps to the door. As she turned the handle, she heard the sound of his truck descending the hill. *Let him go*, Maggie told herself before she could turn around and call him back. *You can't let yourself be pushed around that way.* When a man thinks he can order a woman to marry him, he deserves exactly what she'd given him, Maggie decided. A good swift kick in the ego. Imagine bringing up marriage out of the blue that way, she thought as she shoved open the front door. Marriage, not love. He dangled marriage at her as though it were a carrot at the end of a stick. She wasn't biting. If he wanted her, really wanted her, he'd have to do a hell of a lot better.

I love you. She leaned her head against the door and told herself she wouldn't cry. That's all it would've taken; that's all he'd needed to say. Understanding. No, she decided as she straightened again, they were still a long way from understanding each other.

Why wasn't the dog barking, she wondered grumpily as she pushed the door shut again. Terrific watchdog he'd turned out to be. Annoyed, she turned toward the steps, planning on a hot bath and a long sleep, when a scent stopped her. Candle wax, Maggie thought, puzzled. Roses? Odd, she thought. Her imagination was good, but not good enough to conjure up scents. She crossed toward the living room and stopped in the doorway.

Louella sat very straight and very prim in a high-backed chair. Her hands were neatly folded in the lap of the same misty-gray dress she'd worn for dancing. Her skin was so pale that the shadows under her eyes looked like bruises. The eyes themselves seemed to stare straight through Maggie. On the table beside her there were candles burning, the tapers hardly more than stubs now, with the wax pooled heavily on the base of the holders. A vase of fresh roses sat nearby, so that the breeze through the open window carried the scent through the room.

After the first shock, Maggie tried to bring her thoughts to order. It had been obvious from the first that Louella wasn't completely well. She'd have to be handled gently, Maggie thought, and so she approached her as one might a wounded bird.

"Mrs. Morgan," she said quietly, then cautiously touched a hand to her shoulder.

"I've always liked candlelight." Louella spoke in her calm, soft voice. "So much prettier than a lamp. I'd often burn candles in the evening."

"They're lovely." Maggie kept her tone gentle as she knelt beside her. "But it's morning now."

"Yes." Louella looked blankly at the sun-filled window. "I often sit up through the night. I like the sounds. The woods make such music at night."

Perhaps if she'd thought it through, Maggie wouldn't have questioned. She would simply have led Louella out to her car and driven her home. But she didn't think it through. "Do you often come here at night, Mrs. Morgan?"

"Sometimes I'll drive," she said dreamily. "Sometimes, if the night's as clear and warm as this, I'll walk. I used to walk a great deal as a girl. Joyce used to love to toddle on the paths in the woods when she was just a baby."

Maggie moistened her lips. "Do you come back here often, Mrs. Morgan, at night?"

"I know I should stay away. Joyce has told me so all along. But—" Louella sighed, and the small, sad smile touched her mouth. "She has Stan. Such a good man—they take care of each other. That's what marriage is, you know, loving and taking care of each other."

"Yes." Helplessly, Maggie watched as Louella's hands grew agitated in her lap.

"William wasn't a loving man. He just wasn't made that way. I wanted Joyce to have a loving man, like Stan." She lapsed into silence, closing her eyes and breathing shallowly so that Maggie thought she slept. Deciding it was best to call the Agees, she started to rise, when Louella's hand closed over hers.

"I followed him here that night," she whispered. Now her eyes were intense, fully focused. Maggie's mouth went dry.

"Followed him?"

"I didn't want anything to happen. Joyce loved him so."

Maggie struggled to keep her voice low and even, her eyes steady. "You followed your husband here?"

"William was here," Louella told her. "He was here, and he had the money. I knew he was going to do something dreadful, something he'd have gotten away with because of who he was. There had to be an end to it." Her fingers tightened convulsively on Maggie's, then relaxed just as abruptly as her head fell back. "Of course, the money couldn't be buried with him. I thought, no, if they find him, they shouldn't find the money. So I hid it."

"Here," Maggie managed. "In the attic."

"In the old trunk. I forgot all about it," Louella said as fatigue washed through her voice. "Forgot until a few weeks ago, when they dug in the gully. I came and took the money out and burned it, as I should've burned it ten years ago."

Maggie looked down at the hand that lay limply on hers. It was frail, the blue veins showing sharply against the thin ivory skin. Could that hand have pulled a trigger, sending a bullet into a man? Maggie shifted her gaze to Louella's face and saw it was now serene in sleep.

What do I do? Maggie asked herself as she laid Louella's hand carefully back in her lap. Call the police? Maggie looked at the peacefully sleeping, fragile figure in the chair. No, she couldn't; she didn't have the steel for it. She'd call Joyce.

She went to the phone and asked the operator for Joyce's number. There was no answer at the Agee house. Maggie sighed and glanced over her shoulder into the living room at Louella, who was still sleeping. She hated to do it, but she had to call Lieutenant Reiker. When she couldn't get hold of him, either, she left a message with his office.

Coming back into the living room, Maggie gasped as a figure moved toward her. "Oh, you frightened me."

"Sorry." Stan looked with concern from Maggie to his mother-in-law. "I came in the back. The dog's sleeping pretty heavily in the kitchen. Looks like Louella might've given him part of a sleeping pill to keep him quiet."

"Oh." Maggie made an instinctive move toward the kitchen.

"He's all right," Stan assured her. "He'll just be a little groggy when he wakes up."

"Sheriff—Stan," she decided, hoping the lack of formality would make it easier for him. "I was just about to call you. I think Louella's been here most of the night."

"I'm sorry." He rubbed his own sleep-starved eyes. "She's been getting steadily worse since this business started. Joyce and I don't want to put her in a home."

"No." Concerned, she touched his arm. "But she told me she wanders at night, and—" Maggie broke off and circled the room. Could she tell him what Louella had said? He was her son-in-law, but he was still the sheriff. The badge and the gun he wore reminded her.

"I heard what she told you, Maggie."

She turned, her eyes filled with compassion and concern. "What should we do? She's so fragile. I can't bear to be a part of having her punished for something that happened so long ago. And yet, if she killed . . ." With her conscience tearing her in different directions, she turned again.

"I don't know." Stan looked at Louella while he rubbed the back of his neck. "What she told you doesn't have to be true."

"But it makes sense," Maggie insisted. "She knew about the money. If she'd hid it in the trunk, then forgotten about it, blocked it out because it reminded her—" Maggie shook her head and forced herself to continue. "Stan, it's the only explanation for the break-in here." She covered her face with her hands as her sense of right and wrong battled. "She needs help," Maggie said abruptly. "She doesn't need police or lawyers. She needs a doctor."

Relief ran over Stan's face. "She'll get one. The best one Joyce and I can find."

Shaky, uncertain, Maggie rested a hand on the table. "She's devoted to you," she murmured. "She always speaks so highly of you, of how you love Joyce. I think she'd do anything she could to keep both of you happy."

As she spoke, Maggie's gaze was drawn down to where her palm rested—on the color snapshot of Morgan and Stan, near the gully.

It would all be laid to rest now, she thought as she stared down at the photo. Louella had suffered enough, been punished enough for—

Distracted, she narrowed her eyes and looked closer. Why it came to her now, Maggie would never know, but she remembered Reiker's words. "We found a ring, too, an old ring with a lot of fancy carving and three small diamond chips . . . Joyce Agee identified it as her father's."

But in the picture William Morgan wasn't wearing the ring. Stan Agee was.

She looked up, her eyes dry and clear with the knowledge.

He didn't have to look at the picture under her hand. He'd already seen. "You should've let it go, Maggie."

She didn't stop to think, to reason; she only reacted. In a dead run, she headed for the front door. The move was so unexpected, she was into the hall with her hand on the knob before he'd taken the first step. As the door stuck, she cursed it, cursed her own inefficiency for not having it seen to weeks before. As she started to tug a second time, Stan's hand closed over her arm.

"Don't." His voice was low and strained. "I don't want to hurt you. I have to think this through."

With her back to the door, Maggie stared at him. She was alone in the house with a murderer. Alone, she thought desperately, except for a fragile old woman who loved him enough to have shielded him for ten years. Maggie watched him rest his hand on the butt of his gun.

"We'd better sit down."

Cliff drank his second cup of coffee and wished it was bourbon. If he'd tried to make a fool of himself over a woman, he could've done no better. Drinking in the strong, bitter taste, he scowled down at the laminated counter in the café. The scent of frying eggs and sausage did nothing for his appetite.

How could he have botched it so badly? What woman in

her right mind, he asked himself, would respond favorably to a shouted, angry proposal? Maggie had given him the heave-ho, and now that he'd cooled off a bit, he couldn't blame her.

Still, he wasn't one of the fancy crowd she'd run with in L.A., he reminded himself. He wasn't going to change his manners for her any more than he expected her to change for him. She'd chosen to change her life before he'd been a part of it.

Chosen, Cliff thought again, cursing himself. She'd chosen her home, and he'd never seen anyone put down roots so quickly. He shouldn't have panicked at the mention of the recording in L.A. She'd be back. The land was as important to her as it was to him. Perhaps that had been their first bond, though they both insisted they'd had no common ground.

She'd be back, Cliff told himself again. He'd been an idiot to think bullying her into marriage would assure that. Maggie wouldn't be bullied, and she was here to stay. Those were two of the reasons he loved her.

He should have told her that, he thought, pushing the unwanted coffee aside. He could have found the words to tell her he'd been in love with her for weeks and that at dawn, with the morning light spilling over her face, he'd realized it. It had taken his breath away, stolen his senses, made him weak. He could've found the words to tell her.

Straightening from the counter, he checked his watch. She'd had an hour's sleep. Cliff decided a woman didn't need any more than that for a proper proposal of marriage. He tossed the money on the counter and began to whistle.

He continued to whistle as he took the road through town, until Joyce dashed into the street and frantically hailed him.

"Oh, Cliff!"

Though he'd stopped the car in the middle of the street, he was halfway out of it as he spoke. "What is it, one of the kids?"

"No, no." Struggling for calm, Joyce gripped his arms. She, too, hadn't changed from the dance, but the hair she'd worn up was now escaping its pins and falling in clumps. "It's my mother," she managed after a moment. "She hasn't been in bed all night—and Stan, I can't find Stan anywhere."

"We'll find Louella." Cliff brushed the hair from her face as he'd done since she'd been a child. "She might have been restless and gone for a walk. With the excitement last night—"

"Cliff." Joyce gripped his arms tighter. "I think she went out to the old place. I'm dead sure of it—it wouldn't be the first time."

He thought of Maggie with a little ripple of unease. "Maggie's home," he said soothingly. "She'll look out for her."

"She's been getting worse." Joyce's breath began to shudder. "Oh, Cliff, I thought I was doing the right thing, the only thing."

"What're you talking about?"

"I lied to the police. I lied before I'd thought it through, but I know I'd do the same thing again." She pressed her fingers to her eyes briefly, then dropped them. When she looked at Cliff now, she looked at him with a surface calm that was deadly. "I know who killed my father. I've known for weeks. Mother—it seems Mother's known for ten years."

"Get in," he ordered. He was thinking of Maggie now, of Maggie alone in the house, surrounded by woods. "Tell me while we drive."

Maggie's back was stiff and straight as she sat on a low bench. Moving only her eyes, she watched Stan pace the room. She wanted to believe he wouldn't hurt her. But he'd killed once, ten years before. Now he'd have to deal with her or pay for it.

"I never wanted Joyce to sell this house." He paced to the window, then back to the center of the room. "I never wanted it. The money meant nothing to me. Her money—her father's money—never has. How could I've guessed she'd get it into her head to put it on the market when I was out of town?"

He ran a hand over his shirt and left faint streaks. He's sweating, Maggie noted. It didn't help her nerves.

"She lied to the police about the ring."

Maggie moistened her lips. "She loves you."

"She didn't know—I'd never told her all these years. Then,

when I finally had to, she stood by me. A man can't ask for more than that." He paced again, so that the soles of his shoes hitting hardwood and rug were the only sounds. "I didn't murder him," Stan said flatly. When he looked at Maggie, his eyes were glazed with fatigue. "It was an accident."

She gripped that, clung to that. "Then if you go to the police and explain—"

"Explain?" Stan cut her off. "Explain that I killed a man, buried him and drove his car into the river?" He rubbed the heels of his hands over his face. "I was only twenty," he began. "Joyce and I'd been in love for two years. Morgan had already made it clear that there couldn't be anything between us, so we saw each other in secret. When Joyce found out she was pregnant, there couldn't be any more secrets."

He leaned against the window and stared into the room. "We should've known there was something wrong when he took it so well, but we were both so relieved, both so thrilled at the idea of being married and starting a family, that we never caught on. He told us to keep it quiet for a few weeks while he arranged for the wedding."

Maggie remembered the stern face from the photograph. "But he didn't mean it."

"No, both of us were too wrapped up in each other to remember what kind of man he was." Stan kept moving in the same line, to the window, back to the center of the room, to the window again. "He said he was having trouble with groundhogs up at his old place. I was young and eager to do anything to keep on the right side of him. I told him I'd bring my shotgun one evening after work and take care of them."

He saw Maggie shudder and glance at the pistol on his hip. "It was dusk when he drove up. I didn't expect him. When he got out of the car, I remember thinking he looked like an undertaker, all in black with shiny shoes. He was carrying a little metal box that he set down on the stump of a tree near the gully. He didn't waste any time," Stan continued. "He told me outright that he'd never let a small-town nobody like me marry his daughter. He said he was going to send her away. Sweden or somewhere. She'd have the baby and give it away. He didn't expect me to keep quiet for nothing. He told me he had twenty-five thousand in the box. I was to take it and disappear."

So the twenty-five thousand had been payoff money, blackmail. Yes, she could believe that the man in the photo had thought money would ensure anything.

"I got frantic. I couldn't believe he was threatening to take away everything I'd ever wanted. He could've done it, too." Stan wiped at the sweat that beaded on his upper lip. "He would've done it without a second thought. I shouted at him. I told him he wasn't going to take Joyce and our baby away from me. I told him we'd go away, we didn't need his filthy money. He opened the cash box and showed me all those bills, as if it would tempt me. I knocked it out of his hands."

His breath was coming quickly now, heavily, as if he were reliving that moment—the anger, the despair. Maggie felt her pity well up to tangle with her fear.

"He never lost his temper. Never once. He just bent down and scooped the money back in the box. He thought I wanted more. He never understood, wasn't capable of understanding. When it got to the point where he saw I wasn't going to take the money and go away, he picked up my gun just as calmly as he'd picked up the box. I knew, as sure as I'd ever know anything, that he'd kill me where I stood and he'd get away with it. Somehow he'd get away with it. All I could think was that I'd never see Joyce again, never hold our baby. I grabbed for the gun—it went off over my shoulder. We started struggling."

He was panting now, his eyes glazed. Maggie could visualize the struggle between man and boy as clearly as if it were happening in front of her eyes. She shut them. Then she saw the scene in the film she'd scored in which overpowering need had erupted into irrevocable violence. But this was real and needed no music to spark the drama.

"He was strong—that old man was strong. I knew I'd be dead if I didn't get the gun away. Somehow—" Stan dragged both his hands up his face and into his hair. "Somehow I had it in my hands and was falling back. I'll never forget—it was like a dream, a nightmare. I was falling back, and the gun went off."

She could picture it, all too clearly. Both sympathetic and afraid, Maggie dared to speak. "But it was an accident, self-defense."

He shook his head as his hands dropped back to his side, back, she noted with a tremor, near the gun on his hip. "I was twenty, scraping pennies. I'd just killed the most important man in town, and there was twenty-five thousand dollars in a box next to his body. Who'd have believed me? Maybe I panicked, maybe I did the only sensible thing, but I buried him and his money in the gully, then sent his car into the river."

"Louella . . ." Maggie began.

"I didn't know she'd followed me. I guess she knew Morgan better than anyone and understood he'd never let me marry Joyce. I didn't know she'd watched everything from the woods. Maybe if I had, things would've been different. It seemed she never really came out of the shock of losing her husband—now I understand better. She'd seen it all—then, for some reason of her own, she'd dug out the cash box and hidden it in the house. I guess she was protecting me all these years."

"And Joyce?"

"She never knew." Stan shook his head and tugged at the collar of his shirt as if it were too tight. "I never told her. You have to understand. I love Joyce. I've loved her since she was a girl. There's nothing I wouldn't do for her if I could. If I'd told her everything, everything he'd threatened to do and what had happened, she might have thought—she might not have believed it was an accident. I couldn't have lived with that. For years I've done everything I could to make up for what happened in that gully. I dedicated myself to the law, to the town. I've been the best father, the best husband, I know how to be."

He picked up the color snapshot and crushed it in his hand.

"That damn picture. Damn ring. I was so wired up I didn't notice I'd lost it until days afterward. My grandfather's ring." He rubbed a hand over his temple. "Ten years later it's dug up with Morgan. Do you know how I felt when I learned that Joyce had identified it as her father's? She knew," he said passionately. "She knew it was mine, but she stood behind me. She never questioned me, and when I told her everything, she never doubted me. All these years—I've lived with it all these years."

"You don't have to live with it anymore." Maggie spoke calmly, though her heart was in her throat. He was strung so tight she couldn't gauge when he might snap or what he might do. "People respect you, know you. Louella saw everything. She'd testify."

"Louella's on the edge of a complete breakdown. Who knows if she'd be capable of making a coherent sentence if all this comes out? I have to think of Joyce, of my family, of my reputation." A muscle began to jerk in his cheek as he stared at Maggie. "There's so much at stake," he whispered. "So much to protect."

She watched his hand hover over the butt of his gun.

Cliff started up the steep lane at full speed, spitting gravel. Joyce's breathless story told him one vital thing. Maggie was caught in the middle of violence and passion that had simmered underground for ten years. If it erupted today, she'd be alone—alone because he'd been a fool. As he rounded the top curve, a man stepped into the path of the car, forcing him to brake. Swearing, Cliff stormed out of the car.

"Mr. Delaney," Reiker said mildly. "Mrs. Agee."

"Where's Maggie?" Cliff demanded, and would've moved past him if Reiker hadn't stopped him with a surprisingly strong grip.

"She's inside. At the moment, she's fine. Let's keep it that way."

"I'm going up."

"Not yet." He gave Cliff a long, steely look before he turned to Joyce. "Your mother's inside, Mrs. Agee. She's fine, sleeping. Your husband's in there, too."

"Stan." Joyce looked toward the house, taking an instinctive step forward.

"I've been keeping a close eye on things. Your husband told Miss Fitzgerald everything."

Cliff's blood iced. "Damn it, why haven't you gotten her out?"

"We're going to get her out. We're going to get them all out. Quietly."

"How do you know he won't hurt her?"

"I don't—if he's pushed. I want your help, Mrs. Agee. If your husband loves you as much as he says, you're the key." He looked toward the house. "He'd have heard the car. Better let him know you're here."

Inside the house, Stan had Maggie by the arm, holding her close as he stood at the window. She could feel his muscles jumping, hear his breath whistling. As terror washed over her, she closed her eyes and thought of Cliff. If he'd come back, everything would be all right. If he came back, the nightmare would end.

"Someone's out there." Stan jerked his head toward the open window, and his free hand opened and closed on the butt of his gun. "I can't let you talk to anyone. You have to understand. I can't risk it."

"I won't." His fingers dug into her arm so that the pain kept her head clear. "Stan, I want to help you. I swear I only want to help. If you hurt me, it'll never be over."

"Ten years," he muttered, straining to see any movement outside. "Ten years and he's still trying to ruin my life. I can't let him."

"Your life will be ruined if you do anything to me." *Be logical*, Maggie told herself as waves of panic threatened to overtake her. *Be calm.* "It wouldn't be an accident this time, Stan. This time you'd be a murderer. You'd never make Joyce understand."

His fingers tightened until she had to dig her teeth into her lower lip to keep from crying out. "Joyce stood behind me."

"She loves you. She believes in you. But if you hurt me, everything would change."

She felt him tremble. The grip on her arm loosened fractionally. As Maggie watched, Joyce walked up over the rise toward the house. At first, she thought she was hallucinating; then she heard Stan's breath catch. He saw her, too.

"Stan." Joyce's hand moved on her throat, as if she could make her voice stronger. "Stan, please come out."

"I don't want you involved in this." Stan's fingers were like iron on Maggie's arm again.

"I am involved. I've always been involved. I know everything you did you did for me."

"Damn it." He pressed his face against the window glass, pounding one fist steadily against the frame. "He can't ruin everything we've built."

"No, he can't." Joyce came closer to the house, measuring each step. In all the years she'd known her husband, she'd never heard despair in his voice. "Stan, he can't touch us now. We're together. We'll always be together."

"They'll take me away from you. The law." He squeezed his eyes tighter. "I've done my best by the law."

"Everyone knows that. Stan, I'll be with you. I love you. You're everything to me, my whole life. Please, please, don't do anything I'd be ashamed of."

Maggie felt him tense as he straightened from the window. The muscle was still working in his cheek. There was a line of sweat over his lip he no longer bothered to wipe away. He stared out the window, at Joyce, then over at the gully.

"Ten years," he whispered. "But it's still not over."

His fingers worked sporadically on Maggie's arm. Numb with fear, she watched as he drew the gun out of its holster. His eyes met hers, cold, clear blue, without expression. Perhaps she would've begged for her life, but she knew, as any prey knows, that mercy comes at the hunter's whim.

His expression never changed as he set the gun down on the sill and released her arm. Maggie felt her blood begin to pump again, fast and hot. "I'm going outside," Stan said flatly, "to my wife."

Weak with relief, Maggie sank down on the piano stool. Without even the energy to weep, she buried her face in her hands.

"Oh, Maggie." Then Cliff's arms were around her, and she could feel the hard, fast beat of his heart. "That was the longest ten minutes of my life," he murmured as he began to run wild kisses over her face. "The longest."

She didn't want explanations. He was here; that was enough. "I kept telling myself you'd come. It kept me sane."

"I shouldn't have left you alone." He buried his face in her hair and drew in the scent.

She held him tighter. "I told you I could take care of myself."

He laughed, because she was in his arms and nothing had changed. "Yes, you did. It's over now." He framed her face in his hands so that he could study it. Pale, he noticed. The eyes were shadowed but steady. His Maggie was a woman who could take care of herself. "Reiker was outside, long enough to get the drift of what was going on. He's taking all three of them."

She thought of Louella's pale face, Stan's anguished eyes, Joyce's trembling voice. "They've been punished enough."

"Maybe." He ran his hands up her arms, just to assure himself she was whole and safe. "If he'd hurt you—"

"He wouldn't have." She shook her head and clung again. "He couldn't have. I want the pond, Cliff," she said fiercely. "I want you to put in the pond quickly, and I want to see the willow draping over it."

"You'll have it." He drew her back again. "And me? Will you have me, Maggie?"

She took a deep breath, letting his fingers rest on her face again. Again, she thought. She would try again and see if he understood. "Why should I?"

His brows drew together, but he managed to swallow the oath that came to mind. Instead, he kissed her, hard and long. "Because I love you."

She let out a trembling breath. She was indeed home. "That was the right answer."

This Magic Moment

Chapter 1

He'd chosen it for the atmosphere. Ryan was certain of it the moment she saw the house on the cliff. It was stone gray and solitary. It turned its back on the Pacific. It wasn't a symmetrical structure, but rambling, with sections of varying heights rising up here and there, giving it a wild sort of grace. High at the top of a winding cliff road, with the backdrop of an angry sky, the house was both magnificent and eerie.

Like something out of an old movie, Ryan decided as she shifted into first to take the climb. She had heard Pierce Atkins was eccentric. The house seemed to testify to that.

All it needs, she mused, is a thunderclap, a little fog and the howl of a wolf; just some minor special effects. Amused at the thought, she drew the car to a stop and looked the house over again. You wouldn't see many like it only a hundred and fifty miles north of L.A. You wouldn't, she corrected silently, see many like it anywhere.

The moment she slid from the car, the wind pulled at her, whipping her hair around her face and tugging at her skirt. She was tempted to go to the seawall and take a look at the ocean but hurried up the steps instead. She hadn't come to admire the view.

The knocker was old and heavy. It gave a very impressive thud when she pounded it against the door. Ryan told herself she wasn't the least bit nervous but switched her briefcase from hand to hand as she waited. Her father would be furious if she walked away without Pierce Atkins's signature on the contracts she carried. No, not furious, she amended. Silent. No one could use silence more effectively than Bennett Swan.

I'm not going to walk away empty-handed, she assured herself. I know how to handle temperamental entertainers. I've spent years watching how it's done and—

Her thoughts were cut off as the door opened. Ryan stared. Staring back at her was the largest man she had ever seen. He was at least six foot five, with shoulders that all but filled the doorway. And his face. Ryan decided he was, indisputably, the ugliest human being she had ever seen. His broad face was pale. His nose had obviously been broken and had reknit at an odd angle. His eyes were small, a washed-out brown that matched his thick mat of hair. Atmosphere, Ryan thought again. Atkins must have chosen him for atmosphere.

"Good afternoon," she managed. "Ryan Swan. Mr. Atkins is expecting me."

"Miss Swan." The slow, barrel-deep voice suited him perfectly. When the man stepped back, Ryan found herself fighting a reluctance to enter. Storm clouds, a hulking butler and a brooding house on a cliff. Oh, yes, she decided. Atkins knows how to set the stage.

She walked in. As the door closed behind her, Ryan took a quick glimpse around.

"Wait here," the laconic butler instructed and walked, lightly for a big man, down the hall.

"Of course, thank you very much," she muttered to his back.

The walls were white and draped with tapestries. The one nearest her was a faded medieval scene depicting the young Arthur drawing the sword from the stone, with Merlin the Enchanter highlighted in the background. Ryan nodded. It was an exquisite piece of work and suited to a man like Atkins. Turning, she found herself staring at her own reflection in an ornate cheval glass.

It annoyed her to see that her hair was mussed. She represented Swan Productions. Ryan pushed at the stray misty blond wisps.

The green of her eyes had darkened with a mixture of anxiety and excitement. Her cheeks were flushed with it. Taking a deep breath, she ordered herself to calm down. She straightened her jacket.

Hearing footsteps, she quickly turned away from the mirror. She didn't want to be caught studying herself or attempting last-minute repairs. It was the butler again, alone. Ryan repressed a surge of annoyance.

"He'll see you downstairs."

"Oh." Ryan opened her mouth to say something else, but he was already retreating. She had to scramble to keep up.

The hall wound to the right. Ryan's heels clicked quickly as she trotted to match the butler's pace. Then he stopped so abruptly, she nearly collided with his back.

"Down there." He had opened a door and was already walking away.

"But . . ." Ryan scowled after him, then made her way down the dimly lighted steps. Really, this was ridiculous, she thought. A business meeting should be conducted in an office, or at least in a suitable restaurant. Show business, she mused scornfully.

The sound of her own footfalls echoed back at her. There was no sound at all from the room below. Oh, yes, she concluded, Atkins knows how to set the stage. She was beginning to dislike him intensely. Her heart was hammering uncomfortably as she rounded the last curve in the winding staircase.

The lower floor was huge, a sprawling room with crates and trunks and paraphernalia stacked all around. The walls were paneled and the floor was tiled, but no one had bothered with any further decoration. Ryan looked around, frowning, as she walked down the last of the steps.

He watched her. He had the talent for absolute stillness, absolute concentration. It was essential to his craft. He also had the ability to sum up a person quickly. That, too, was part of his profession. She was younger than he had expected, a fragile-looking woman, small in stature, slight in build, with clouds of pale hair and a delicately molded face. A strong chin.

She was annoyed, he noted, and not a little apprehensive. A smile tugged at his mouth. Even after she began to wander around the room, he made no move to go to her. Very businesslike, he thought, with her trim, tailored suit, sensible shoes, expensive briefcase and very feminine hands. Interesting.

"Miss Swan."

Ryan jolted, then swore at herself. Turning in the direction of the voice, she saw only shadows.

"You're very prompt."

He moved then, and Ryan saw that he stood on a small stage. He wore black and blended with the shadows. With an effort, she kept the annoyance from her voice. "Mr. Atkins." Ryan went toward him then, fixing on a trained smile. "You have quite a house."

"Thank you."

He didn't come down to her but stood on the stage. Ryan was forced to look up at him. It surprised her that he was more dramatic in person than on tape. Normally, she had found the reverse to be true. She had seen his performances. Indeed, since her father had taken ill and reluctantly turned Atkins over to her, Ryan had spent two entire evenings watching every available tape on Pierce Atkins.

Dramatic, she decided, noting a raw-boned face with a thick, waving mane of black hair. There was a small scar along his jawline, and his mouth was long and thin. His brows were arched with a slight upsweep at the tips. But it was the eyes under them which held her. She had never seen eyes so dark, so deep. Were they gray? Were they black? Yet it wasn't their color that disconcerted her, it was the absolute concentration in them. She felt her throat go dry and swallowed in defense. She could almost believe he was reading her mind.

He had been called the greatest magician of the decade, some said the greatest of the last half of the century. His illusions and escapes were daring, flashy and unexplainable. It was a common thing to hear of him referred to as a wizard. Staring into his eyes, Ryan began to understand why.

She shook herself free of the trance and started again. She didn't believe in magic. "Mr. Atkins, my father apologizes for not being able to come himself. I hope—"

"He's feeling better."

Confused, she stopped. "Yes. Yes, he is." She found herself staring again.

Pierce smiled as he stepped down to her. "He phoned an hour ago, Miss Swan. Long-distance dialing, no telepathy." Ryan glared before she could stop herself, but his smile only widened. "Did you have a nice drive?"

"Yes, thank you."

"But a long one," he said. "Sit." Pierce gestured to a table, then took a chair behind it. Ryan sat opposite him.

"Mr. Atkins," she began, feeling more at ease now that business was about to begin. "I know my father has discussed Swan Productions' offer with you and your representative at length, but perhaps you'd like to go over the details again." She set her briefcase on the table. "I could clarify any questions you might have."

"Have you worked for Swan Productions long, Miss Swan?"

The question interrupted the flow of her presentation, but Ryan shifted her thoughts. Entertainers often had to be humored. "Five years, Mr. Atkins. I assure you, I'm qualified to answer your questions and negotiate terms if necessary."

Her voice was very smooth, but she was nervous. Pierce saw it in the careful way she folded her hands on the table. "I'm sure you're qualified, Miss Swan," he agreed. "Your father isn't an easy man to please."

Surprise and a trace of apprehension flickered into her eyes. "No," she said calmly, "which is why you can be sure of receiving the best promotion, the best production staff, the best contract available. Three one-hour television specials over three years, guaranteed prime time, with a budget that ensures quality." She paused only for a moment. "An advantageous arrangement for you and for Swan Productions."

"Perhaps."

He was looking at her too closely. Ryan forced herself not to fidget. Gray, she saw. His eyes were gray—as dark as was possible without being black.

"Of course," she continued, "your career has been aimed primarily at live audiences in clubs and theaters. Vegas, Tahoe, the London Palladium and so forth."

"An illusion means nothing on film, Miss Swan. Film can be altered."

"Yes, I realize that. To have any impact, a trick has to be performed live."

"Illusion," Pierce corrected. "I don't do tricks."

Ryan stopped. His eyes were steady on hers. "Illusion," she amended with a nod. "The specials would be broadcast live, with a studio audience as well. The publicity—"

"You don't believe in magic, do you, Miss Swan?" There was the slightest of smiles on his mouth, the barest trace of amusement in his voice.

"Mr. Atkins, you're a very talented man," she said carefully. "I admire your work."

"A diplomat," he concluded, leaning back. "And a cynic. I like that."

Ryan didn't feel complimented. He was laughing at her without making the smallest attempt to conceal it. Your job, she reminded herself as her teeth clenched. Do your job. "Mr. Atkins, if we could discuss the terms of the contract—"

"I don't do business with anyone until I know who they are."

Ryan let out a quick breath. "My father—"

"I'm not talking to your father," Pierce interrupted smoothly.

"I didn't think to type up a bio," she snapped, then bit her tongue. Damn! She couldn't afford to lose her temper. But Pierce grinned, pleased.

"I don't think that will be necessary." He had her hand in his before she realized what he was doing.

"Nevermore."

The voice from behind had Ryan jolting in her chair.

"That's just Merlin," Pierce said mildly as she twisted her head.

There was a large black myna bird in a cage to her right. Ryan took a deep breath and tried to steady her nerves. The bird was staring at her.

"Very clever," she managed, eyeing the bird with some reservation. "Did you teach him to talk?"

"*Mmm.*"

"Buy you a drink, sweetie?"

Wide-eyed, Ryan gave a muffled laugh as she turned back to Pierce. He merely gave the bird a careless glance. "I haven't taught him manners."

She struggled not to be amused. "Mr. Atkins, if we could—"

"Your father wanted a son." Ryan forgot what she had been about to say and stared at him. "That made it difficult for you." Pierce was looking into her eyes again, her hand held loosely in his. "You're not married, you live alone. You're a realist who considers herself very practical. You find it difficult to control your temper, but you work at it. You're a very cautious woman, Miss Swan, slow to trust, careful in relationships. You're impatient because you have something to prove—to yourself and to your father."

His eyes lost their intense directness when he smiled at her. "A parlor game, Miss Swan, or telepathy?" When Pierce released her hand, Ryan pulled it from the table into her lap. She hadn't cared for his accuracy.

"A little amateur psychology," he said comfortably, enjoying her stunned expression. "A basic knowledge of Bennett Swan and an understanding of body language." He shrugged his shoulders. "No trick, Miss Swan, just educated guesswork. How close was I?"

Ryan gripped her hands together in her lap. Her right palm was still warm from his. "I didn't come here to play games, Mr. Atkins."

"No." He smiled again, charmingly. "You came to close a deal, but I do things in my own time, in my own way. My profession encourages eccentricity, Miss Swan. Humor me."

"I'm doing my best," Ryan returned, then took a deep breath and sat back. "I think it's safe to say that we're both very serious about our professions."

"Agreed."

"Then you understand that it's my job to sign you with Swan, Mr. Atkins." Perhaps a bit of flattery would work, she decided. "We want you because you're the best in your field."

"I'm aware of that," he answered without batting an eye.

"Aware that we want you or that you're the best?" she found herself demanding.

He flashed her a very appealing grin. "Of both."

Ryan took a deep breath and reminded herself that entertainers were often impossible. "Mr. Atkins," she began. With a flutter of wings, Merlin swooped out of his cage and landed on her shoulder. Ryan gasped and froze. "Oh, God," she murmured. This was too much, she thought numbly. Entirely too much.

Pierce frowned at the bird as it settled its wings. "Odd, he's never done that with anyone before."

"Aren't I lucky," Ryan muttered, sitting perfectly still. Did birds bite? she wondered. She decided she didn't care to wait to find out. "Do you think you could—ah, persuade him to perch somewhere else?"

A slight gesture of Pierce's hand had Merlin leaving Ryan's shoulder to land on his own.

"Mr. Atkins, please, I realize a man in your profession would have a taste for—atmosphere." Ryan took a breath to steady herself, but it didn't work. "It's very difficult to discuss business in—in a dungeon," she said with a sweep of her arm. "With a crazed raven swooping down on me and . . ."

Pierce's shout of laughter cut her off. On his shoulder the bird settled his wings and stared, steely-eyed, at Ryan. "Ryan Swan, I'm going to like you. I work in this dungeon," he explained good-naturedly. "It's private and quiet. Illusions take more than skill; they take a great deal of planning and preparation."

"I understand that, Mr. Atkins, but—"

"We'll discuss business more conventionally over dinner," he interrupted.

Ryan rose as he did. She hadn't planned to stay more than an hour or two. It was a good thirty-minute drive down the cliff road to her hotel.

"You'll stay the night," Pierce added, as if he had indeed read her thoughts.

"I appreciate your hospitality, Mr. Atkins," she began, following as he walked back to the stairs, the bird remaining placidly on his shoulder. "But I have a reservation at a hotel in town. Tomorrow—"

"Do you have your bags?" Pierce stopped to take her arm before he mounted the steps.

"Yes, in the car, but—"

"Link will cancel your reservation, Miss Swan. We're in for a storm." He turned his head to glance at her. "I wouldn't like to think of you driving these roads tonight."

As if to accentuate his words, a blast of thunder greeted them as they came to the top of the stairs. Ryan murmured something. She wasn't certain she wanted to think of spending the night in this house.

"Nothing up my sleeve," Merlin announced.

She shot him a dubious look.

Chapter 2

Dinner did much to put Ryan's mind at rest. The dining room was huge, with a roaring fire at one end and a collection of antique pewter at the other. The long refectory table was set with Sèvres china and Georgian silver.

"Link's an excellent cook," Pierce told her as the big man set a Cornish hen in front of her. Ryan caught a glimpse of his huge hands before Link left the room. Cautiously, she picked up her fork.

"He's certainly quiet."

Pierce smiled and poured a pale gold wine into her glass. "Link only talks when he has something to say. Tell me, Miss Swan, do you enjoy living in Los Angeles?"

Ryan looked over at him. His eyes were friendly now, not intense and intrusive, as they had been before. She allowed herself to relax. "Yes, I suppose I do. It's convenient for my work."

"Crowded?" Pierce cut into the poultry.

"Yes, of course, but I'm used to it."

"You've always lived in L.A.?"

"Except when I was in school."

Pierce noted the slight change in tone, the faintest hint of resentment no one else might have caught. He went on eating. "Where did you go to school?"

"Switzerland."

"A beautiful country." He reached for his wine. *And she didn't care to be shipped off,* he thought. "Then you began to work for Swan Productions?"

Frowning, Ryan stared into the fire. "When my father realized I was determined, he agreed."

"And you're a very determined woman," Pierce commented.

"Yes," she admitted. "For the first year, I shuffled papers, went for coffee, and was kept away from the talent." The frown vanished. A gleam of humor lit her eyes. "One day some papers came across my desk, quite by mistake. My father was trying to sign Mildred Chase for a miniseries. She wasn't cooperating. I did a little research and went to see her." Laughing with the memory, she sent Pierce a grin. "*That* was quite an experience. She lives in this fabulous place in the hills—guards, a dozen dogs. She's very 'old Hollywood.' I think she let me in out of curiosity."

"What did you think of her?" he asked, mainly to keep her talking, to keep her smiling.

"I thought she was wonderful. A genuine *grande dame*. If my knees hadn't been shaking, I'm sure I would have curtsied." A light of triumph covered her face. "And when I left two hours later, her signature was on the contract."

"How did your father react?"

"He was furious." Ryan picked up her wine. The fire sent a play of shadow and light over her skin. She was to think of the conversation later and wonder at her own expansiveness. "He raged at me for the better part of an hour." She drank, then set down the glass. "The next day, I had a promotion and a new office. Bennett Swan appreciates people who get things done."

"And do you," Pierce murmured, "get things done, Miss Swan?"

"Usually," she returned evenly. "I'm good at handling details."

"And people?"

Ryan hesitated. His eyes were direct again. "Most people."

He smiled, but his look remained direct. "How's your dinner?"

"My . . ." Ryan shook her head to break the gaze, then glanced down at her plate. She was surprised to see she had eaten a healthy portion of the hen. "It's very good. Your . . ." She looked back at him again, not certain what to call Link. *Servant? Slave?*

"Friend," Pierce put in mildly and sipped his wine.

Ryan struggled against the uncomfortable feeling that he saw inside her brain. "Your friend is a marvelous cook."

"Appearances are often deceiving," Pierce pointed out, amused. "We're both in professions that show an audience something that isn't real. Swan Productions deals in illusions. So do I." He reached toward her, and Ryan sat back quickly. In his hand was a long-stemmed red rose.

"Oh!" Surprised and pleased, Ryan took it from him. Its scent was strong and sweet. "I suppose that's the sort of thing you have to expect when you have dinner with a magician," she commented and smiled at him over the tip of the bud.

"Beautiful women and flowers belong together." The wariness that came into her eyes intrigued him. A very cautious woman, he thought again. He liked caution, respected it. He also enjoyed watching people react. "You're a beautiful woman, Ryan Swan."

"Thank you."

Her answer was close to prim and had his mouth twitching. "More wine?"

"No. No, thank you, I'm fine." But her pulse was throbbing lightly. Setting the flower beside her plate, she went back to her meal. "I've rarely been this far up the coast," she said conversationally. "Have you lived here long, Mr. Atkins?"

"A few years." He swirled the wine in his glass, but she noted he drank very little. "I don't like crowds," he told her.

"Except at a performance," she said with a smile.

"Naturally."

It occurred to Ryan, when Pierce rose and suggested they sit in the parlor, that they hadn't discussed the contract. She was going to have to steer him back to the subject.

"Mr. Atkins . . ." she began as they entered. "Oh! What a beautiful room!"

It was like stepping back to the eighteenth century. But there were no cobwebs, no signs of age. The furniture shone, and the flowers were fresh. A small upright piano stood in a corner with sheet music open. There were small, blown-glass figurines on the mantel. A menagerie, she noted on close study—unicorns, winged horses, centaurs, a three-headed hound. No conventional animals in Pierce Atkins's collection. Yet the fire in the grate was sedate, and the lamp standing on a piecrust table was certainly a Tiffany. It was a room Ryan would have expected to find in a cozy English country house.

"I'm glad you like it," Pierce said, standing beside her. "You seemed surprised."

"Yes. The outside looks like a prop from a 1945 horror movie, but . . ." Ryan stopped herself, horrified. "Oh, I'm sorry, I didn't mean . . ." But he was grinning, obviously delighted with her observation.

"It was used for just that more than once. That's why I bought it."

Ryan relaxed again as she wandered around the room. "It did occur to me that you might have chosen it for the atmosphere."

Pierce lifted a brow. "I have an—affection for things others take at face value." He stepped to a table where cups were already laid out. "I can't offer you coffee, I'm afraid. I don't use caffeine. The tea is herbal and very good." He was already pouring as Ryan stepped up to the piano.

"Tea's fine," she said absently. It wasn't printed sheet music on the piano, she noted, but staff paper. Automatically, she began to pick out the handwritten notes. The melody was hauntingly romantic. "This is beautiful." Ryan turned back to him. "Just beautiful. I didn't know you wrote music."

"I don't." Pierce set down the teapot. "Link does." He watched Ryan's eyes widen in astonishment. "Face value, Miss Swan?"

She lowered her eyes to her hands. "You make me quite ashamed."

"I've no intention of doing that." Crossing to her, Pierce took her hand again. "Most of us are drawn to beauty."

"But you're not?"

"I find surface beauty appealing, Miss Swan." Quickly, thoroughly, he scanned her face. "Then I look for more."

Something in the contact made her feel odd. Her voice wasn't as strong as it should have been. "And if you don't find it?"

"Then I discard it," he said simply. "Come, your tea will get cold."

"Mr. Atkins." Ryan allowed him to lead her to a chair. "I don't want to offend you. I can't afford to offend you, but . . ." She let out a frustrated breath as she sat. "I think you're a very strange man."

He smiled. She found it compelling, the way his eyes smiled a split second before his mouth. "You'd offend me, Miss Swan, if you didn't think so. I have no wish to be ordinary."

He was beginning to fascinate her. Ryan had always been careful to keep her professional objectivity when dealing with talent. It was important not to be awed. If you were awed, you'd find yourself adding clauses to contracts and making rash promises.

"Mr. Atkins, about our proposition."

"I've given it a great deal of thought." A crash of thunder shook the windows. Ryan glanced over as he lifted his cup. "The roads will be treacherous tonight." His eyes came back to Ryan's. Her hands had balled into fists at the blast. "Do storms upset you, Miss Swan?"

"No, not really." Carefully, she relaxed her fingers. "But I'm grateful for your hospitality. I don't like to drive in them." Lifting her cup, she tried to ignore the slashes of lightning. "If you have any questions about the terms, I'd be glad to go over them with you."

"I think it's clear enough." He sipped his tea. "My agent is anxious for me to accept the contract."

"Oh?" Ryan had to struggle to keep the triumph from her voice. It would be a mistake to push too soon.

"I never commit myself to anything until I'm certain it suits me. I'll tell you what I've decided tomorrow."

She nodded, accepting. He wasn't playing games, and she sensed that no agent, or anyone, would influence him beyond a certain point. He was his own man, first and last.

"Do you play chess, Miss Swan?"

"What?" Distracted, she looked up again. "I beg your pardon?"

"Do you play chess?" he repeated.

"Why, yes, I do."

"I thought so. You know when to move and when to wait. Would you like to play?"

"Yes," she agreed without hesitation. "I would."

Rising, he offered his hand and led her to a table by the windows. Outside, the rain hurled itself against the glass. But when she saw the chessboard already set up, she forgot the storm.

"They're exquisite!" Ryan lifted the white king. It was oversized and carved in marble. "Arthur," she said, then picked up the queen. "And Guinevere." She studied the other pieces. "Lancelot the knight, Merlin the bishop, and, of course, Camelot." She turned the castle over in her palm. "I've never seen anything like these."

"Take the white," he invited, seating himself behind the black. "Do you play to win, Miss Swan?"

She took the chair opposite him. "Yes, doesn't everyone?"

He gave her a long, unfathomable look. "No. Some play for the game."

After ten minutes Ryan no longer heard the rain on the windows. Pierce was a shrewd player and a silent one. She found herself watching his hands as they slid pieces over the board. They were long, narrow hands with nimble fingers. He wore a gold ring on his pinky with a scrolled symbol she didn't recognize. Ryan had heard it said those fingers could pick any lock, untie any knot. Watching them, she thought they were more suited for tuning a violin. When she glanced up, she found him watching her with his amused, knowing smile. She channeled her concentration on her strategy.

Ryan attacked, he defended. He advanced, she countered. Pierce was pleased to have a well-matched partner. She was a cautious player, given to occasional bursts of impulse. He felt her game-playing reflected who she was. She wouldn't be easily duped or easily beaten. He admired both the quick wits and the strength he sensed in her. It made her beauty all the more appealing.

Her hands were soft. As he captured her bishop, he wondered

idly if her mouth would be, too, and how soon he would find out. He had already decided he would; now it was a matter of timing. Pierce understood the invaluable importance of timing.

"Checkmate," he said quietly and heard Ryan's gasp of surprise.

She studied the board a moment, then smiled over at him. "Damn, I didn't see that coming. Are you sure you don't have a few extra pieces tucked up your sleeve?"

"Nothing up my sleeve," Merlin cackled from across the room. Ryan shot him a glance and wondered when he had joined them.

"I don't use magic when skill will do," Pierce told her, ignoring his pet. "You play well, Miss Swan."

"You play better, Mr. Atkins."

"This time," he agreed. "You interest me."

"Oh?" She met his look levelly. "How?"

"In several ways." Sitting back, he ran a finger down the black queen. "You play to win, but you lose well. Is that always true?"

"No." She laughed but rose from the table. He was making her nervous again. "Do you lose well, Mr. Atkins?"

"I don't often lose."

When she looked back, he was standing at another table handling a pack of cards. Ryan hadn't heard him move. It made her uneasy.

"Do you know Tarot cards?"

"No. That is," she corrected, "I know they're for telling fortunes or something, aren't they?"

"Or something." He gave a small laugh and shuffled the cards gently. "Mumbo jumbo, Miss Swan. A device to keep someone's attention focused and to add mystery to quick thinking and observation. Most people prefer to be fooled. Explanations leave them disappointed. Even most realists."

"You don't believe in those cards." Ryan walked over to join him. "You know you can't tell the future with pasteboard and pretty colors."

"A tool, a diversion." Pierce lifted his shoulders. "A game, if you like. Games relax me." Pierce fanned the oversized cards in a quick, effective gesture, then spread them on the table.

"You do that very well," Ryan murmured. Her nerves were tight again, but she wasn't sure why.

"A basic skill," he said easily. "I could teach you quickly enough. You have competent hands." He lifted one, but it was her face he examined, not her palm. "Shall I pick a card?"

Ryan removed her hand. Her pulse was beginning to race. "It's your game."

With a fingertip, Pierce drew out a card and flipped it faceup. It was the Magician. "Confidence, creativity," Pierce murmured.

"You?" Ryan said flippantly to conceal the growing tension.

"So it might seem." Pierce laid a finger on another card and drew it out: The High Priestess. "Serenity," he said quietly. "Strength. You?"

Ryan shrugged. "Simple enough for you to draw whatever card you like after you've stacked the deck."

Pierce grinned, unoffended. "The cynic should choose the next to see where these two people will end. Pick a card, Miss Swan," he invited. "Any card."

Annoyed, Ryan plucked one and tossed it faceup on the table. After a strangled gasp, she stared at it in absolute silence. The Lovers. Her heart hammered lightly at her throat.

"Fascinating," Pierce murmured. He wasn't smiling now, but he studied the card as if he'd never seen it before.

Ryan took a step back. "I don't like your game, Mr. Atkins."

"Hmmm?" He glanced up distractedly, then focused on her. "No? Well then . . ." He carelessly flipped the cards together and stacked them. "I'll show you to your room."

Pierce had been as surprised by the card as Ryan had been. But he knew reality was often stranger than any illusion he could devise. He had work to do, a great deal of final planning for his engagement in Las Vegas in two weeks time. Yet as he sat in his room, he was thinking of Ryan, not of the mechanics of his craft.

There was something about her when she laughed, something brilliant and vital. It appealed to him the same way her low-key, practical voice had appealed to him when she spoke of contracts and clauses.

He already knew the contract backward and forward. He wasn't a man to brush aside the business end of his profession. Pierce signed his name to nothing unless he understood every nuance. If the public saw him as mysterious, flashy and odd, that was all to the good. The image was part illusion, part reality. That was the way he preferred it. He had spent the second half of his life arranging things as he preferred them.

Ryan Swan. Pierce stripped off his shirt and tossed it aside. He wasn't certain about her just yet. He had fully intended to sign the contracts until he had seen her coming down the stairs. Instinct had made him hesitate. Pierce relied heavily on his instincts. Now he had some thinking to do.

The cards didn't influence him. He could make cards stand up and dance if that's what he wanted. But coincidence influenced him. It was odd that Ryan had turned over the card symbolizing lovers when he had been thinking what she would feel like in his arms.

With a laugh, he sat down and began to doodle on a pad of paper. The plans he was forming for a new escape would have to be torn up or revised, but it relaxed him to turn it over in his mind, just as he turned Ryan over in his mind.

It might be wise to sign her papers in the morning and send her on her way. He didn't care to have a woman intrude on his thoughts. But Pierce didn't always do what was wise. If he did, he would still be playing the club field, pulling rabbits out of his hat and colored scarves out of his pocket at union scale. Now he turned a woman into a panther and walked through a brick wall.

Poof! he thought. Instant magic. And no one remembered the years of frustration and struggle and failure. That, too, was exactly as he wanted it. There were few who knew where he had come from or who he had been before he was twenty-five.

Pierce tossed aside the pencil. Ryan Swan was making him uneasy. He would go downstairs and work until his mind was clear. It was then he heard her scream.

Ryan undressed carelessly. Temper always made her careless. Parlor tricks, she thought furiously and pulled down the zipper of her skirt. Show people. She should be used to their orchestrations by now.

She remembered a meeting with a well-known comedian the month before. He had tried out a twenty-minute routine on her before he had settled down to discuss plans for a guest appearance on a Swan Production presentation. All the business with the Tarot cards had been just a show, designed to impress her, she decided and kicked off her shoes. Just another ego trip for an insecure performer.

Ryan frowned as she unbuttoned her blouse. She couldn't agree with her own conclusions. Pierce Atkins didn't strike her as an insecure man—on stage or off. And she would have sworn he had been as surprised as she when she had turned over that card. Ryan shrugged out of her blouse and tossed it over a chair. Well, he was an actor, she reminded herself. What else was a magician but a clever actor with clever hands?

She remembered the look of his hands on the black marble chess pieces, their leanness, their grace. She shook off the memory. Tomorrow she would get his name on that contract and drive away. He had made her uneasy; even before the little production with the cards, he had made her uneasy. Those eyes, Ryan thought and shivered. There's something about his eyes.

It was simply that he had a very strong personality, she decided. He was magnetic and yes; very attractive. He'd cultivated that, just as he had no doubt cultivated the mysterious air and enigmatic smile.

Lightning flashed, and Ryan jolted. She hadn't been completely honest with Pierce: storms played havoc with her nerves. Intellectually, she could brush it aside, but lightning and thunder always had her stomach tightening. She hated the weakness, a primarily feminine weakness. Pierce had been right; Bennett Swan had wanted a son. Ryan had gone through her life working hard to make up for being born female.

Go to bed, she ordered herself. Go to bed, pull the covers over your head and shut your eyes. Purposefully, she walked over to draw the drapes. She stared at the window. Something stared back. She screamed.

Ryan was across the room like a shot. Her damp palms skidded off the knob. When Pierce opened the door, she fell into his arms and held on.

"Ryan, what the hell's going on?" He would have drawn her away, but the arms around his neck were locked tight. She was very small without her heels. He could feel the shape of her body as she pressed desperately against him. Through concern and curiosity, Pierce experienced a swift and powerful wave of desire. Annoyed, he pulled her firmly away and held her arms.

"What is it?" he demanded.

"The window," she managed, and would have been back in his arms again if he hadn't held her off. "At the window by the bed."

Setting her aside, he walked to it. Ryan put both hands to her mouth and backed into the door, slamming it.

She heard Pierce's low oath as he drew up the glass and reached outside. He pulled in a very large, very wet black cat. On a moan, Ryan slumped against the door.

"Oh, God, what next?" she wondered aloud.

"Circe." Pierce set the cat on the floor. She shook herself once, then leaped onto the bed. "I didn't realize she was outside in this." He turned to look at Ryan. If he had laughed at her, she would never have forgiven him. But there was apology in his eyes, not amusement. "I'm sorry. She must have given you quite a scare. Can I get you a brandy?"

"No." Ryan let out a long breath. "Brandy doesn't do anything for acute embarrassment."

"Being frightened is nothing to be embarrassed about."

Her legs were still shaking, so she stayed propped against the door. "You might warn me if you have any more pets." Making the effort, she managed a smile. "That way, if I wake up with a wolf in bed with me, I can shrug it off and go back to sleep."

He didn't answer. As she watched, his eyes drifted slowly down her body. Ryan became aware she wore only a thin silk teddy. She straightened bolt upright against the door. But when his eyes came back to hers, she couldn't move, couldn't speak. Her breath had started to tremble before he took the first step toward her.

Tell him to go! her mind shouted, but her lips wouldn't form the words. She couldn't look away from his eyes. When he stopped in front of her, her head tilted back so that the look continued to hold. She could feel her pulse hammer at her wrists, at her throat, at her breast. Her whole body vibrated with it.

I want him. The knowledge stunned her. *I've never wanted a man the way I want him.* Her breath was audible now. His was calm and even. Slowly, Pierce took his finger to her shoulder and pushed aside the strap. It fell loosely on her arm. Ryan didn't move. He watched her intensely as he brushed aside the second strap. The bodice of the teddy fluttered to the points of her breasts and clung tenuously. A careless movement of his hand would have it falling to her feet. She stood transfixed.

Pierce lifted both hands, pushing the hair back from her face. He let his fingers dive deep into it. He leaned closer, then hesitated. Ryan's lips trembled apart. He watched her eyes shut before his mouth touched hers.

His lips were firm and gentle. At first they barely touched hers, just tasted. Then he lingered for a moment, keeping the kiss soft. A promise or a threat; Ryan wasn't certain. Her legs were about to buckle. In defense, she curled her hands around his arms. There were muscles, hard, firm muscles that she wouldn't think of until much later. Now she thought only of his mouth. He was barely kissing her at all, yet the shock of the impact winded her.

Degree by aching degree he deepened the kiss. Ryan's fingers tightened desperately on his arms. His mouth brushed over hers, then came back with more pressure. His tongue feathered lightly over hers. He only touched her hair, though her body tempted him. He drew out every ounce of pleasure with his mouth alone.

He knew what it was to be hungry—for food, for love, for a woman—but he hadn't experienced this raw, painful need in years. He wanted the taste of her, only the taste of her. It was at once sweet and pungent. As he drew it inside him, he knew there would come a time when he would take more. But for now her lips were enough.

When he knew he had reached the border between backing away and taking her Pierce lifted his head. He waited for Ryan to open her eyes.

Her green eyes were darkened, cloudy. He saw that she was as stunned as she was aroused. He knew he could take her there, where they stood. He had only to kiss her again, had only to brush aside the brief swatch of silk she wore. But he did neither. Ryan's fingers loosened, then her hands dropped away from his arms. Saying nothing, Pierce moved around her and opened the door. The cat leaped off the bed to slip through the crack before Pierce shut it behind him.

Chapter 3

By morning the only sign of the storm was the steady drip of water from the balcony outside Ryan's bedroom window. She dressed carefully. It was important that she be perfectly poised and collected when she went downstairs. It would have been easier if she could have convinced herself that she had been dreaming—that Pierce had never come to her room, that he had never given her that strange, draining kiss. But it had been no dream.

Ryan was too much a realist to pretend otherwise or to make excuses. A great deal of what had happened had been her fault, she admitted as she folded yesterday's suit. She had acted like a fool, screaming because a cat had wanted in out of the rain. She had thrown herself into Pierce's arms wearing little more than shattered nerves. And lastly and most disturbing she had made no protest. Ryan was forced to concede that Pierce had given her ample time to object. But she had done nothing, made no struggle, voiced no indignant protest.

Maybe he had hypnotized her, she thought grimly as she brushed her hair into order. The way he had looked at her, the way her mind had gone blank . . . With a sound of frustration, Ryan tossed the brush into her suitcase. You couldn't be hypnotized with a look.

If she was to deal with it, she first had to admit it. She had wanted him to kiss her. And when he had, her senses had ruled her. Ryan clicked the locks on the suitcase, then set it next to the door. She would have gone to bed with him. It was a cold, hard fact, and there was no getting around it. Had he stayed, she would have made love with him—a man she had known for a matter of hours.

Ryan drew a deep breath and gave herself a moment before opening the door. It was a difficult truth to face for a woman who prided herself on acting with common sense and practicality. She had come to get Pierce Atkins's name on a contract, not to sleep with him.

You haven't done either yet, she reminded herself with a grimace. And it was morning. Time to concentrate on the first and forget the second. Ryan opened the door and started downstairs.

The house was quiet. After peeking into the parlor and finding it empty, she continued down the hall. Though her mind was set on finding Pierce and completing the business she had come for, an open door to her right tempted her to stop. The first glance drew a sound of pleasure from her.

There were walls—literally walls—of books. Ryan had never seen so many in a private collection, not even her father's. Somehow she knew these books were more than an investment, they were read. Pierce would know each one of them. She walked into the room for a closer look. There was a scent of leather and of candles.

The Unmasking of Robert-Houdin, by Houdini; *The Edge of the Unknown*, by Arthur Conan Doyle; *Les Illusionnistes et Leurs Secrets*. These and dozens of other books on magic and magicians Ryan expected. But there was also T. H. White, Shakespeare, Chaucer, the poems of Byron and Shelley. Scattered among them were works by Fitzgerald, Mailer and Bradbury. Not all were leather bound or aged and valuable. Ryan thought of her father, who would know what each of his books cost, down to the last dollar and who had read no more than a dozen in his collection.

He has very eclectic taste, she mused as she wandered the room. On the mantelpiece were carved, painted figures she recognized as inhabitants of Tolkien's Middle Earth. There was a very modern metal sculpture on the desk.

Who is this man? Ryan wondered. Who is he really? Lyrical, fanciful, with hints of a firm realist beneath. It annoyed her to realize just how badly she wanted to discover the full man.

"Miss Swan?"

Ryan swung around to see Link filling the doorway. "Oh, good morning." She wasn't certain if his expression was disapproving or if it was simply her impression of his unfortunate face. "I'm sorry," she added. "Shouldn't I have come in here?"

Link lifted his massive shoulders in a shrug. "He would have locked it if he wanted you to stay out."

"Yes, of course," Ryan murmured, not certain if she should feel insulted or amused.

"Pierce said you can wait for him downstairs after you've had breakfast."

"Has he gone out?"

"Running," Link said shortly, "He runs five miles every day."

"Five miles?" But Link was already turning away. Ryan dashed across the room to keep up.

"I'll make your breakfast," he told her.

"Just coffee—tea," she corrected, remembering. She didn't know what to call him but realized that she would soon be too breathless from trying to keep pace with him to call him anything. "Link." Ryan touched his arm, and he stopped. "I saw your work on the piano last night." He was looking at her steadily, without any change of expression. "I hope you don't mind." He shrugged again. Ryan concluded he used the gesture often in place of words. "It's a beautiful melody," she continued. "Really lovely."

To her astonishment, he blushed. Ryan hadn't thought it possible for a man of his size to be embarrassed. "It's not finished," he mumbled, with his wide, ugly face growing pinker.

Ryan smiled at him, touched. "What is finished is beautiful. You have a wonderful gift."

He shuffled his feet, then mumbled something about getting her tea and lumbered off. Ryan smiled at his retreating back before she walked to the dining room.

Link brought her toast, with a grumble about her having to eat something. Ryan finished it off dutifully, thinking of Pierce's remark about face value. If nothing else came of her odd visit, she had learned something. Ryan didn't believe she would ever again make snap decisions about someone based on appearance.

Though she deliberately loitered over the meal, there was still no sign of Pierce when Ryan had finished. Reluctance to brave the lower floor again had her sipping at cold tea and waiting. At length, with a sigh, she rose, picked up her briefcase and headed down the stairs.

Someone had switched on the lights, and Ryan was grateful. The room wasn't brilliantly illuminated; it was too large for the light to reach all the corners. But the feeling of apprehension Ryan had experienced the day before didn't materialize. This time she knew what to expect.

Spotting Merlin standing in his cage, she walked over to him. The door of the cage was open, so she stood cautiously to the side as she studied him. She didn't want to encourage him to perch on her shoulder again, particularly since Pierce wasn't there to lure him away.

"Good morning," she said, curious as to whether he'd talk to her when she was alone.

Merlin eyed her a moment. "Buy you a drink, sweetie?"

Ryan laughed and decided Merlin's trainer had an odd sense of humor. "I don't fall for that line," she told him and bent down until they were eye to eye. "What else can you say?" she wondered out loud. "I bet he's taught you quite a bit. He'd have the patience for it." She grinned, amused that the bird seemed to be listening attentively to her conversation. "Are you a smart bird, Merlin?" she demanded.

"Alas, poor Yorick!" he said obligingly.

"Good grief, the bird quotes *Hamlet*." Shaking her head, Ryan turned toward the stage. There were two large trunks, a wicker hamper and a long, waist-high table. Curious, Ryan set down her briefcase and mounted the stairs. On the table was a deck of playing cards, a pair of empty cylinders, wine bottles and glasses and a pair of handcuffs.

Ryan picked up the playing cards and wondered fleetingly how he marked them. She could see nothing, even when she held them up to the light. Setting them aside, she examined the handcuffs. They appeared to be regulation police issue. Cold, steel, unsympathetic. She searched the table for a key and found none.

Ryan had done her research on Pierce thoroughly. She knew there wasn't supposed to be a lock made that could hold him. He had been shackled hand and foot and stuffed into a triple-locked steamer trunk. In less than three minutes he had been out, unmanacled. Impressive, she admitted, still studying the cuffs. Where was the trick?

"Miss Swan."

Ryan dropped the handcuffs with a clatter as she spun around. Pierce stood directly behind her. But he couldn't have come down the stairs, she thought. She would have heard, or certainly seen. Obviously, there was another entrance to his workroom. And how long, she wondered, had he been standing and watching? He was doing no more than that now while the cat busied herself by winding around his ankles.

"Mr. Atkins," she managed in a calm enough voice.

"I hope you slept well." He crossed to the table to join her. "The storm didn't keep you awake?"

"No."

For a man who had just run five miles, he looked remarkably fresh. Ryan remembered the muscles in his arms. There was strength in him, and obviously stamina. His eyes were very steady, almost measuring, on hers. There was no hint of the restrained passion she had felt from him the night before.

Abruptly, Pierce smiled at her, then gestured with his hand. "What do you see here?"

Ryan glanced at the table again. "Some of your tools."

"Ah, Miss Swan, your feet are always on the ground."

"I like to think so," she returned, annoyed. "What should I see?"

He seemed pleased with her response and poured a small amount of wine into a glass. "The imagination, Miss Swan, is an incredible gift. Do you agree?"

"Yes, of course." She watched his hands carefully. "To a point."

"To a point." He laughed a little and showed her the empty cylinders. "Can there be restrictions on the imagination?" He slipped one cylinder inside the other. "Don't you find the possibilities of the power of the mind over the laws of nature interesting?" Pierce placed the cylinders over the wine bottle, watching her.

Ryan was frowning at his hands now. "As a theory," she replied.

"But only a theory." Pierce slipped one cylinder out and set it over the wineglass. Lifting the first cylinder, he showed her that the bottle remained under it. "Not in practice."

"No." Ryan kept her eyes on his hands. He could hardly pull anything off right under her nose.

"Where's the glass, Miss Swan?"

"It's there." She pointed to the second cylinder.

"Is it?" Pierce lifted the tube. The bottle stood under it. With a sound of frustration, Ryan looked at the other tube. Pierce lifted it, revealing the partially filled glass. "They seem to have found the theory more viable," he stated and dropped the cylinders back in place.

"That's very clever," she said, irritated that she had stood inches away and not seen the trick.

"Would you care for some wine, Miss Swan?"

"No, I . . ."

Even as she spoke, Pierce lifted the cylinder. There, where she had just seen the bottle, stood the glass. Charmed despite herself, Ryan laughed. "You're very good, Mr. Atkins."

"Thank you."

He said it so soberly, Ryan looked back at him. His eyes were calm and thoughtful. Intrigued, she tilted her head. "I don't suppose you'd tell me how you did it."

"No."

"I didn't think so." She lifted the handcuffs. The briefcase at the foot of the stage was, for the moment, forgotten. "Are these part of your act, too? They look real."

"They're quite real," he told her. He was smiling again, pleased that she had laughed. He knew it was a sound he would be able to hear clearly whenever he thought of her.

"There's no key," Ryan pointed out.

"I don't need one."

She passed the cuffs from hand to hand as she studied him. "You're very sure of yourself."

"Yes." The hint of amusement in the word made her wonder what twist his thoughts had taken. He held out his hands, wrists close. "Go ahead," he invited. "Put them on."

Ryan hesitated only a moment. She wanted to see him do it— right there in front of her eyes. "If you can't get them off," she said as she snapped the cuffs into place, "we'll just sit down and talk about those contracts." She glanced up at him, eyes dancing. "When you've signed them, we can send for a locksmith."

"I don't think we'll need one." Pierce held up the cuffs, dangling and open.

"Oh, but how . . ." She trailed off and shook her head. "No, that was too quick," she insisted, taking them back from him. Pierce appreciated the way her expression changed from astonishment to doubt. It was precisely what he had expected from her. "You had them made." She was turning them over, searching closely. "There must be a button or something."

"Why don't you try it?" he suggested and had the cuffs snapped on her wrists before she could decline. Pierce waited to see if she'd be angry. She laughed.

"I talked myself right into that one." Ryan gave him a good-humored grimace, then concentrated on the cuffs. She jiggled her wrists. "They certainly feel real enough." Though she tried several different angles, the steel held firmly shut. "If there's a button," she muttered, "you'd have to dislocate your wrist to get to it." She tugged another moment, then tried to slip her hands through the opening. "All right, you win," she announced, giving up. "They're real." Ryan grinned up at him. "Can you get me out of these?"

"Maybe," he murmured, taking her wrists in his hands.

"That's a comforting answer," she returned dryly, but they both felt her pulse leap as his thumb brushed over it. He continued to stare down at her until she felt the same draining weakness she had experienced the night before. "I think," she began, her voice husky as she struggled to clear it. "I think you'd better . . ." The sentence trailed off as his fingers traced the vein in her wrist. "Don't," she said, not even certain what she was trying to refuse.

Silently, Pierce lifted her hands, slipping them over his head so that she was pressed against him.

She wouldn't allow it to happen twice. This time she would protest. "No." Ryan tugged once, uselessly, but his mouth was already on hers.

This time his mouth wasn't so patient or his hands so still. Pierce held her hips as his tongue urged her lips apart. Ryan fought against the helplessness—a helplessness that had more to do with her own needs than the restraints on her wrists. She was responding totally. Under the pressure of his, her lips were hungry. His were cool and firm while hers heated and softened. She heard him murmur something as he dragged her closer. An incantation, she thought dizzily. He was bewitching her; there was no other explanation.

But it was a moan of pleasure, not of protest, that slipped from her when his hands trailed up to the sides of her breasts. He drew slow, aching circles before his thumbs slipped between their bodies to stroke over her nipples. Ryan pressed closer, nipping at his bottom lip as she craved more. His hands were in her hair, pulling her head back so that his lips had complete command of hers.

Perhaps he was magic. His mouth was. No one else had ever made her ache and burn with only a kiss.

Ryan wanted to touch him, to make him hunger as desperately as she. She fretted against the restraints on her wrists, only to find her hands were free. Her fingers could caress his neck, run through his hair.

Then, as quickly as she had been captured, she was released. Pierce had his hands on her shoulders, holding her away.

Confused, still aching, Ryan stared up at him. "Why?"

Pierce didn't answer for a moment. Absently, he caressed her shoulders. "I wanted to kiss Miss Swan. Last night I kissed Ryan."

"You're being ridiculous." She started to jerk away, but his hands were suddenly firm.

"No. Miss Swan wears conservative suits and worries about contracts. Ryan wears silk and lace underneath and is frightened of storms. The combination fascinates me."

His words troubled her enough to make her voice cool and sharp. "I'm not here to fascinate you, Mr. Atkins."

"A side benefit, Miss Swan." He grinned, then kissed her fingers. Ryan jerked her hand away.

"It's time we settled our business one way or the other."

"You're right, Miss Swan." She didn't like the hint of amusement or the way he emphasized her name. Ryan found she no longer cared whether or not he signed the papers she carried. She simply wanted to shake loose of him.

"Well, then," she began and stooped to pick up her briefcase.

Pierce laid his hand over hers on the handle. His fingers closed gently. "I'm willing to sign your contracts with a few adjustments."

Ryan schooled herself to relax. Adjustments normally meant money. She'd negotiate with him and be done with it. "I'll be glad to discuss any changes you might want."

"That's fine. I'll want to work with you directly. I want you to handle Swan's end of the production."

"Me?" Ryan's fingers tightened on the handle again. "I don't get involved with the production end. My father—"

"I'm not going to work with your father, Miss Swan, or any other producer." His hand was still gently closed over hers, with the contracts between them. "I'm going to work with you."

"Mr. Atkins, I appreciate—"

"I'll need you in Vegas in two weeks."

"In Vegas? Why?"

"I want you to watch my performances—closely. There's nothing more valuable to an illusionist than a cynic. You'll keep me sharp." He smiled. "You're very critical. I like that."

Ryan heaved a sigh. She would have thought criticism would annoy, not attract. "Mr. Atkins, I'm a businesswoman, not a producer."

"You told me you were good at details," he reminded her amiably. "If I'm going to break my own rule and perform on television, I want someone like you handling the details. More to the point," he continued, "I want *you* handling the details."

"You're not being practical, Mr. Atkins. I'm sure your agent would agree. There are any number of people at Swan Productions who are better qualified to produce your special. I don't have any experience in that end of the business."

"Miss Swan, do you want me to sign your contracts?"

"Yes, of course, but—"

"Then make the changes," he said simply. "And be at Caesars Palace in two weeks. I have a week's run." Stooping, he lifted the cat into his arms. "I'll look forward to working with you."

Chapter 4

When she stalked into her office at Swan Productions four hours later, Ryan was still fuming. He had nerve, she decided. She would give him top of the list for nerve. He thought he had her boxed into a corner. Did he really imagine he was the only name talent she could sign for Swan Productions? What outrageous conceit! Ryan slammed her briefcase down on her desk and flopped into the chair behind it. Pierce Atkins was in for a surprise.

Leaning back in her chair, Ryan folded her hands and waited until she was calm enough to think. Pierce didn't know Bennett Swan. Swan liked to run things his own way. Advice could be considered, discussed, but he would never be swayed on a major decision. As a matter of fact, she mused, he would more than likely go in the opposite direction he was pushed. He wouldn't appreciate being told who to put in charge of a production. Particularly, Ryan thought ruefully, when that person was his daughter.

There was going to be an explosion when she told her father of Pierce's conditions. Her only regret was that the magician wouldn't be there to feel the blast. Swan would find another hot property to sign, and Pierce could go back to making wine bottles disappear.

Ryan brooded into space. The last thing she wanted to do was worry about rehearsal calls and shooting schedules—and all the thousands of other niggling details involved in producing an hour show—not to mention the outright paranoia of it being a live telecast. What did she know about dealing with technical break-downs and union rules and set designing? Producing was a complicated job. She had never had any desire to try her hand at that end of the business. She was perfectly content with the paperwork and preproduction details.

She leaned forward again, elbows on the desk, and cupped her chin in her hands. How foolish it is, she mused, to lie to yourself. And how fulfilling it would be to follow through on a project from beginning to end. She had ideas—so many ideas that were constantly being restricted by legal niceties.

Whenever she had tried to convince her father to give her a chance on the creative side, she had met the same unyielding wall. She didn't have the experience; she was too young. He conveniently forgot that she had been around the business all of her life and that she would be twenty-seven the following month.

One of the most talented directors in the business had done a film for Swan that had netted five Oscars. And he'd been twenty-six, Ryan remembered indignantly. How could Swan know if her ideas were gold or trash if he wouldn't listen to them? All she needed was one opportunity.

No, she had to admit that nothing would suit her better than to follow a project from signing to wrap party. But not this one. This time she would cheerfully admit failure and toss the contracts and Pierce Atkins right back in her father's lap. There was enough Swan in her to get her back up when given an ultimatum.

Change the contracts. With a snort of derision, Ryan flipped open her briefcase. He overplayed his hand, she thought, and now he'll . . . She stopped, staring down at the neatly stacked papers inside the case. On top of them was another long-stemmed rose.

"Now how did he . . ." Ryan's own laughter cut her off. Leaning back, she twirled the flower under her nose. He was clever, she mused, drawing in the scent. Very clever. But who the devil was he? What made him tick? Sitting there in her tailored, organized office, Ryan decided she very much wanted to know. Perhaps it would be worth an explosion and a bit of conniving to find out.

There were depths to a man who spoke quietly and could command with his eyes alone. Layers, she thought. How many layers would she have to peel off to get to the core of him? It would be risky, she decided, but . . . Shaking her head, Ryan reminded herself that she wasn't going to be given the opportunity to find out, in any case. Swan would either sign him on his own terms or forget him. She drew out the contracts, then snapped the briefcase shut. Pierce Atkins was her father's problem now. Still, she kept the rose in her hand.

The buzzer on her phone reminded her she didn't have time for daydreaming. "Yes, Barbara."

"The boss wants to see you."

Ryan grimaced at the intercom. Swan would have known she was back the moment she passed the guard at the gate. "Right away," she agreed. Leaving the rose on her desk, Ryan took the contracts with her.

Bennett Swan smoked an expensive Cuban cigar. He liked expensive things. More, he liked knowing his money could buy them. If there were two suits of equal cut and value, Swan would choose the one with the biggest price tag. It was a matter of pride.

The awards in his office were also a matter of pride. Swan Productions was Bennett Swan. Oscars and Emmys proved he was a success. The paintings and sculptures his art broker had advised him to purchase showed the world that he knew the value of success.

He loved his daughter, would have been shocked if anyone had said otherwise. There was no doubt in his mind that he was an excellent father. He had always given Ryan everything his money could buy: the best clothes, an Irish nanny when her mother had died, an expensive education, then a comfortable job when she had insisted on working.

He had been forced to admit that the girl had more on the ball than he had expected. Ryan had a sharp brain and a way of cutting through the nonsense and getting to the heart of a matter. It proved to him that the money spent on the Swiss school had been well spent. Not that he would begrudge his daughter the finest education. Swan expected results.

He watched the smoke curl from the tip of his cigar. Ryan had paid off for him. He was very fond of his daughter.

She knocked, then entered when he called out. He watched her cross the wide space of thick carpet to his desk. A pretty girl, he thought. Looks like her mother.

"You wanted to see me?" She waited for the signal to sit. Swan wasn't a big man but had always made up for his lack of size with expansiveness. The wide sweep of his arm told her to sit. His face was still handsome in the rugged, outdoorsy manner women found appealing. He had put on a bit of flesh in the last five years and had lost a bit of hair. Essentially, however, he looked the same as Ryan's earliest memory of him. Looking at him, she felt the familiar surge of love and frustration. Ryan knew too well the limitations of her father's affection for her.

"You're feeling better?" she asked, noting that his bout with the flu hadn't left any mark of sickness on him. His face was healthily ruddy, his eyes clear. With another sweeping gesture, he brushed the question aside. Swan was impatient with illness, particularly his own. He didn't have time for it.

"What did you think of Atkins?" he demanded the moment Ryan was settled. It was one of the small concessions Swan made to her, the asking of her opinion on another. As always, Ryan thought carefully before answering.

"He's a unique man," she began in a tone that would have made Pierce smile. "He has extraordinary talent and a very strong personality. I'm not sure that one isn't the cause for the other."

"Eccentric?"

"No, not in the sense that he does things to promote an eccentric image." Ryan frowned as she thought of his house, his life-style. *Face value.* "I think he's a very deep man and one who lives precisely as he chooses. His profession is more than a career. He's dedicated to it the way an artist is to painting."

Swan nodded and blew out a cloud of expensive smoke. "He's hot box office."

Ryan smiled and shifted the contracts. "Yes, because he's probably the best at what he does; plus he's dynamic on stage and a bit mysterious off it. He seems to have locked up the beginnings of his life and tossed away the key. The public loves a puzzle. He gives them one."

"And the contracts?"

Here it comes, Ryan thought, bracing herself. "He's willing to sign, but with certain conditions. That is, he—"

"He told me about his conditions," Swan interrupted.

Ryan's carefully thought out dissertation was thrown to the winds. "He told you?"

"Phoned a couple of hours ago." Swan plucked the cigar from his mouth. The diamond on his finger shot light as he eyed his daughter. "He says you're cynical and dedicated to details. That's what he claims he wants."

"I simply don't believe his tricks were anything but clever staging," Ryan countered, annoyed that Pierce had spoken to Swan before she had. She felt, uncomfortably, as if she were playing chess again. He'd already outmatched her once. "He has a habit of incorporating his magic into the everyday. It's effective, but distracting at a business meeting."

"Insulting him seems to have turned the trick," Swan commented.

"I didn't insult him!" At that Ryan rose with the contracts in her hand. "I spent twenty-four hours in that house with talking birds and black cats, and I didn't insult him. I did everything I could to get his name on these except letting him saw me in half." She dropped the papers on her father's desk. "There are limits to what I'll do to humor the talent, no matter how hot they are at the box office."

Swan steepled his fingers and watched her. "He also said he didn't mind your temper. He doesn't like to be bored."

Ryan bit off the next words that sprang to mind. Carefully, she sat back down. "All right, you told me what he said to you. What did you say to him?"

Swan took his time answering. It was the first time anyone connected with the business had referred to Ryan's temper. Swan knew she had one and knew, too, that she kept it scrupulously controlled on the job. He decided to let it pass. "I told him we'd be glad to oblige him."

"You . . ." Ryan choked on the word and tried again. "You agreed? Why?"

"We want him. He wants you."

No explosion, she thought, not a little confused. What spell had Pierce used to manage this one? Whatever it was, she told herself grimly, she wasn't under it. She rose again. "Do I have any say in this?"

"Not as long as you work for me." Swan gave the contracts an idle glance. "You've been itching to do something along these lines for a couple of years," he reminded her. "I'm giving you your chance. And," he looked up then and met her eyes, "I'll be watching you closely. If you mess it up, I'll pull you."

"I'm not going to mess it up," she retorted, barely controlling a new wave of fury. "It'll be the best damn special Swan's ever produced."

"Just see that it is," he warned. "And that you don't go over budget. Take care of the changes and send the new contracts to his agent. I want him signed before the end of the week."

"He will be." Ryan scooped up the papers before she headed for the door.

"Atkins said you two would work well together," Swan added as she yanked the door open. "He said it was in the cards."

Ryan shot an infuriated glance over her shoulder before she marched out, slamming the door behind her.

Swan grinned a little. She certainly did favor her mother, he thought, then pushed a button to summon his secretary. He had another appointment.

If there was one thing Ryan detested, it was being manipulated. By the time her temper had cooled and she was back in her office, it dawned on her how smoothly both Pierce and her father had maneuvered her. She didn't mind it as much from Swan—he had had years to learn that to suggest she might not be able to handle something was the certain way to see that she did. Pierce was a different matter. He didn't know her at all, or shouldn't have. Yet he had handled her, subtly, expertly, in the same the-hand-is-quicker-than-the-eye fashion he had handled the empty cylinders. He had what he wanted. Ryan drafted out the new contracts and brooded.

She had gotten past that one little point, and she had what she wanted as well. She decided to look at the entire matter from a new angle. Swan Productions would have Pierce sewed up for three prime-time specials, and she would have her chance to produce. *Ryan Swan, Executive Producer.* She smiled. Yes, she liked the sound of it. She said it again to herself and felt the first stirring of excitement. Pulling out her date book, Ryan began to calculate how quickly she could tie up loose ends and devote herself to the production.

Ryan had plowed through an hour's paperwork when the phone interrupted her. "Ryan Swan," she answered briskly, balancing the receiver on her shoulder as she continued to scribble.

"Miss Swan, I've interrupted you."

No one else called her *Miss Swan* in just that way. Ryan broke off the sentence she had been composing and forgot it. "That's all right, Mr. Atkins. What can I do for you?"

He laughed, annoying her instantly.

"What's so funny?"

"You've a lovely business voice, Miss Swan," he said with the trace of humor still lingering. "I thought, with your penchant for detail, you'd like to have the dates I'll need you in Vegas."

"The contracts aren't signed yet, Mr. Atkins," Ryan began primly.

"I open on the fifteenth," he told her as if she hadn't spoken. "But rehearsals begin on the twelfth. I'd like you there for them as well." Ryan frowned, marking down the dates. She could almost

236 • Nora Roberts

see him sitting in his library, holding the cat in his lap. "I close on the twenty-first." She noted idly that the twenty-first was her birthday.

"All right. We could begin outlining the production of the special the following week."

"Good." Pierce paused a moment. "I wonder if I could ask you for something, Miss Swan."

"You could ask," Ryan said cautiously.

Pierce grinned and scratched Circe's ears. "I have an engagement in L.A. on the eleventh. Would you come with me?"

"The eleventh?" Ryan shifted the phone and turned back the pages of her desk calendar. "What time?"

"Two o'clock."

"Yes, all right." She marked it down. "Where should I meet you?"

"I'll pick you up—one-thirty."

"One-thirty. Mr. Atkins . . ." She hesitated, then picked up the rose on her desk. "Thank you for the flower."

"You're welcome, Ryan."

Pierce hung up, then sat for a moment, lost in thought. He imagined Ryan was holding the rose even now. Did she know that her skin was as soft as its petals? Her face, just at the jawline—he could still clearly feel its texture on his fingertips. He ran them down the cat's back. "What did you think of her, Link?"

The big man continued to push books back into place and didn't turn. "She has a nice laugh."

"Yes, I thought so, too." Pierce could remember the tone of it perfectly; it had been unexpected, a stark contrast to her serious expression of a moment before. Both her laugh and her passion had surprised him. He remembered the way her mouth had heated under his. He hadn't been able to work at all that night, thinking of her upstairs in bed with only that swatch of silk covering her.

He didn't like having his concentration disturbed, yet he was pulling her back. Instinct, he reminded himself. He was still following his instinct.

"She said she liked my music," Link murmured, still shuffling books.

Pierce glanced up, bringing his thoughts back. He knew how sensitive Link was about his music. "She did like it, very much. She thought the melody you'd left on the piano was beautiful."

Link nodded, knowing Pierce would tell him nothing but the truth. "You like her, don't you?"

"Yes," Pierce answered absently as he stroked the cat. "Yes, I believe I do."

"I guess you must want to do this TV thing."

"It's a challenge," Pierce replied.

Link turned then. "Pierce?"

"*Hmmm?*"

He hesitated to ask, afraid he already knew the answer. "Are you going to do the new escape in Las Vegas?"

"No." Pierce frowned, and Link felt a flood of relief. Pierce remembered that he'd been trying to work on that particular escape the night Ryan had stayed in his house in the room just down the hall from his own. "No, I haven't worked it all out yet." Link's relief was short-lived. "I'll use it for the special instead."

"I don't like it." It came out quickly, causing Pierce to look up again. "Too many things can go wrong."

"Nothing's going to go wrong, Link. It just needs some more work before I use it in the act."

"The timing's too close," Link insisted, taking an uncharacteristic step by arguing. "You could make some changes or just postpone it. I don't like it, Pierce," he said again, knowing it was useless.

"You worry too much," Pierce assured him. "It's going to be fine. I just have a few more things to work out."

But he wasn't thinking of the mechanics of his escape. He was thinking of Ryan.

Chapter 5

Ryan caught herself watching the clock. *One-fifteen.* The days before the eleventh had gone quickly. She had been up to her ears in paperwork, often working ten hours a day trying to clear her desk before the trip to Las Vegas. She wanted a clear road and no lingering contractual problems hanging over her head once she began work on the special. She would make up for lack of experience by giving the project all of her time and attention.

She still had something to prove—to herself, to her father, and now, to Pierce. There was more to Ryan Swan than contracts and clauses.

Yes, the days had gone quickly, she mused, but this last hour . . . *one-seventeen.* With a sound of annoyance, Ryan pulled out a file folder and opened it. She was watching the clock as if she were waiting for a date rather than a business appointment. That was ridiculous. Still, when the knock came, her head shot up and she forgot the neatly typed pages in the folder. Pushing away a surge of anticipation, Ryan answered calmly.

"Yes, come in."

"Hi, Ryan."

She struggled with disappointment as Ned Ross strolled into the room. He gave her a polished smile.

"Hello, Ned."

Ned Ross—thirty-two, blond and personable with casual California chic. He let his hair curl freely and wore expensive designer slacks with quiet silk shirts. No tie, Ryan noted. It went against his image, just as the subtle whiff of breezy cologne suited it. Ned knew the effects of his charm, which he used purposefully.

Ryan chided herself half-heartedly for being critical and returned his smile, though hers was a great deal cooler.

Ned was her father's second assistant. For several months, up to a few weeks ago, he had also been Ryan's constant escort. He had wined and dined her, given her a few thrilling lessons in surfing, showed her the beauty of the beach at sunset and made her believe she was the most attractive, desirable woman he had ever met. It had been a painful disillusionment when she had discovered he was more interested in cultivating Bennett Swan's daughter than Ryan herself.

"The boss wanted me to check in with you, see how things were shaping up before you take off for Vegas." He sat on the corner of her desk, then leaned over to give her a light kiss. He still had plans for his boss's daughter. "And I wanted to say goodbye."

"All my work's cleared up," Ryan told him, casually shifting the file folder between them. It was still difficult to believe that the attractive, tanned face and amiable smile masked an ambitious liar. "I intended to bring my father up to date myself."

"He's tied up," Ned told her easily and picked up the folder to flip through it. "Just took off for New York. Something on a location shoot he wants to see to personally. He won't be back until the end of the week."

"Oh." Ryan looked down at her hands. He might have taken a moment to call her, she thought, then sighed. When had he ever? And when would she ever stop expecting him to? "Well, you can tell him everything's taken care of." She took the folder back from him and set it down again. "I've a report written out."

"Always efficient." Ned smiled at her again but made no move to leave. He knew too well he had made a misstep with Ryan and had some lost ground to cover. "So, how do you feel about moving up to producer?"

"I'm looking forward to it."

"This Atkins," Ned continued, overlooking the coolness, "he's kind of a strange guy, isn't he?"

"I don't know him well enough to say," Ryan said evasively. She found she didn't want to discuss Pierce with Ned. The day she had spent with him was hers, personally. "I have an appointment in a few minutes, Ned," she continued, rising. "So if you'd—"

"Ryan." Ned took her hands in his as he had habitually done when they had dated. The gesture had always made her smile. "I've really missed you these past weeks."

"We've seen each other several times, Ned." Ryan allowed her hands to lie limply in his.

"Ryan, you know what I mean." He massaged her wrists gently but felt no increase in her pulse. His voice softened persuasively. "You're still angry with me for making that stupid suggestion."

"About using my influence with my father to have you head the O'Mara production?" Ryan lifted a brow. "No, Ned," she said evenly, "I'm not angry with you. I heard Bishop was given the job," she added, unable to resist the small jibe. "I hope you're not too disappointed."

"That's not important," he replied, masking his annoyance with a shrug. "Let me take you to dinner tonight." Ned drew her a fraction closer, and Ryan didn't resist. Just how far, she wondered, would he go? "That little French place you like so much. We could go for a drive up the coast and talk."

"Doesn't it occur to you that I might have a date?"

The question stopped him from lowering his mouth to hers. It hadn't occurred to him that she would be seeing anyone else. He was certain that she was still crazy about him. He had spent a lot of time and effort leading her to that end. He concluded she wanted to be persuaded.

"Break it," he murmured and kissed her softly, never noticing that her eyes stayed open and cold.

"No."

Ned hadn't expected a flat, unemotional refusal. He knew from experience that Ryan's emotions were easily tapped. He'd been prepared to disappoint a very friendly assistant director to be with Ryan again. Off guard, he raised his head to stare at her. "Come on, Ryan, don't be—"

"Excuse me." Ryan whipped her hands from Ned's and looked to the doorway. "Miss Swan," Pierce said with a nod.

"Mr. Atkins." She was flushed and furious to have been caught in a compromising situation in her own office. Why hadn't she told Ned to shut the door when he had come in? "Ned, this is Pierce Atkins. Ned Ross is my father's assistant."

"Mr. Ross." Pierce moved into the room but didn't extend his hand.

"A pleasure to meet you, Mr. Atkins." Ned flashed a smile. "I'm a big fan."

"Are you?" Pierce gave him a polite smile that made Ned feel as though he had been thrust into a very cold, very dark room.

His eyes faltered, then he turned back to Ryan. "Have a good time in Vegas, Ryan." He was already heading to the door. "Nice to have met you, Mr. Atkins."

Ryan watched Ned's hurried retreat with a frown. He had certainly lost his characteristic laid-back style. "What did you do to him?" she demanded when the door shut.

Pierce lifted a brow as he crossed to her. "What do you think I did?"

"I don't know," Ryan muttered. "But whatever you did to him don't ever do it to me."

"Your hands are cold, Ryan." He took them in his. "Why didn't you just tell him to go?"

He unnerved her when he called her Ryan. He unnerved her when he called her Miss Swan in the lightly mocking tone he used. Ryan looked down at their joined hands. "I did—that is, I was . . ." She caught herself, amazed that she was stammering out an explanation. "We'd better go if you're going to make your engagement, Mr. Atkins."

"Miss Swan." Pierce's eyes were full of humor as he lifted her hands to his lips. They were no longer cold. "I've missed that serious face and professional tone." Leaving her with nothing to say, Pierce took her arm and led her from the room.

Once they had settled in his car and joined the streaming traffic, Ryan tried for casual conversation. If they were going to be working closely together, she had to establish the correct relationship and quickly. *Queen's pawn to bishop two*, she thought, remembering the chess game. "What sort of engagement do you have this afternoon?"

Pierce stopped at a red light and glanced at her. His eyes met hers with brief but potent intensity. "A gig's a gig," he said enigmatically. "You're not fond of your father's assistant."

Ryan stiffened. He attacked, she defended. "He's good at his job."

"Why did you lie to him?" Pierce asked mildly when the light turned. "You could have told him you didn't want to have dinner with him instead of pretending you had a date."

"What makes you think I was pretending?" Ryan countered impulsively, hurt pride in her voice.

Pierce downshifted into second to take a corner and maneuvered his way around the point. "I simply wondered why you felt you had to."

Ryan didn't care for his calmness. "That's my affair, Mr. Atkins."

"Do you think we could drop the 'Mr. Atkins' for the afternoon?" Pierce pulled off into a lot and guided the car into a parking space. Then, turning his head, he smiled at her. He was, Ryan decided, entirely too charming when he smiled in just that way.

"Maybe," she agreed when her lips curved in response. "For the afternoon. Is Pierce your real name?"

"As far as I know." With this, he slid from the car. When Ryan climbed out her side, she noted they were in the parking lot of Los Angeles General Hospital.

"What are we doing here?"

"I have a show to do." Pierce took a black bag, not unlike one a doctor might use, from the trunk. "Tools of the trade," he told

Ryan as she gave it a curious study. "No hypos or scalpels," he promised and held out a hand to her. His eyes were on hers, patient as she hesitated. Ryan accepted his hand, and together they walked through the side door.

Wherever Ryan had expected to spend the afternoon, it hadn't been in the pediatric ward of L.A. General. Whatever she had expected of Pierce Atkins, it hadn't been a communion with children. After the first five minutes, Ryan saw that he gave them much more than a show and a bagful of tricks. He gave himself.

Why, he's a beautiful man, she realized with something of a jolt. He plays in Vegas for thirty-five dollars a head, crams Covent Garden, but he comes here just to give a bunch of kids a good time. There were no reporters to note his humanitarianism and write it up in tomorrow's columns. He was giving his time and his talent for nothing more than bringing happiness. Or perhaps more accurately, she thought, relieving unhappiness.

That was the moment, though she didn't realize it, when Ryan fell in love.

She watched as he slipped a ball in and out of his fingers with continual motion. Ryan was as fascinated as the children. With a quick movement of his hand, the ball vanished, only to be plucked from the ear of a boy who squealed in delight.

His illusions were unsophisticated, flashy little bits of business an amateur could have performed. The ward was noisy with gasps and giggles and applause. It obviously meant more to Pierce than the thundering approval he heard on stage after a complicated feat of magic. His roots were there, among children. He had never forgotten it. He remembered too well the antiseptic and floral smell of a sick room and the confinement of a hospital bed. Boredom, he thought, could be the most debilitating disease there.

"You'll notice I brought along a beautiful assistant," Pierce pointed out. It took Ryan a moment to realize he meant her. Her eyes widened in astonishment, but he only smiled. "No magician travels without one. Ryan." He held out a hand, palm up. Amid giggles and applause, she had no choice but to join him.

"What are you doing?" she demanded in a quick whisper.

"Making you a star," he said easily before turning back to the audience of children in beds and wheelchairs. "Ryan will tell you she keeps her lovely smile by drinking three glasses of milk every day. Isn't that so, Ryan?"

"Ah—yes." She glanced around at the expectant faces. "Yes, that's right." *What is he doing?* She'd never had so many large, curious eyes on her at one time.

"I'm sure everyone here knows how important it is to drink milk."

This was answered by some unenthusiastic agreements and a few muffled moans. Pierce looked surprised as he reached in his black bag and pulled out a glass already half-filled with white liquid. No one questioned why it hadn't spilled. "You do all drink milk, don't you?" He got laughter this time, along with more moans. Shaking his head, Pierce pulled out a newspaper and began to fashion it into a funnel. "This is a very tricky business. I don't know if I can make it work unless everyone promises to drink his milk tonight."

Immediately a chorus of promises sprang out. Ryan saw that he was as much Pied Piper as magician, as much psychologist as entertainer. Perhaps it was all the same. She noticed that Pierce was watching her with a lifted brow.

"Oh, I promise," she said agreeably and smiled. She was as entranced as the children.

"Let's see what happens," he suggested. "Do you suppose you could pour the milk from that glass into here?" he asked Ryan, handing her the glass. "Slowly," he warned, winking at the audience. "We wouldn't want to spill it. It's magic milk, you know. The only kind magicians drink." Pierce took her hand and guided it, holding the top of the funnel just above her eye level.

His palm was warm and firm. There hung about him some scent she couldn't place. It was of the outdoors, of the forest. Not pine, she decided, but something darker, deeper, closer to the earth. Her response to it was unexpected and unwanted. She tried to concentrate on holding the glass directly above the opening of the funnel. A few drops of milk dripped out of the bottom.

"Where do you buy magic milk?" one of the children wanted to know.

"Oh, you can't buy it," Pierce said gravely. "I have to get up very early and put a spell on a cow. There, now, that's good." Smoothly, Pierce dropped the empty glass back into his bag. "Now, if all's gone well . . ." He stopped, then frowned into the funnel. "This was my milk, Ryan," he said with a hint of censure. "You could have had yours later."

As she opened her mouth to speak, he whipped the funnel open. Automatically, she gasped and stepped back to keep from being splashed. But the funnel was empty.

The children shrieked in delight as she gasped at him. "She's still beautiful," he told the audience as he kissed Ryan's hand. "Even if she is greedy."

"I poured that milk myself," she stated later as they walked down the hospital corridor to the elevator. "It was dripping through the paper. I *saw* it."

Pierce nudged her into the elevator. "The way things seem and the way things are. Fascinating, isn't it, Ryan?"

She felt the elevator begin its descent and stood in silence for a moment. "You're not entirely what you seem, either, are you?"

"No. Who is?"

"You did more for those kids in an hour than a dozen doctors could have done." He looked down at her as she continued. "And I don't think it's the first time you've done this sort of thing."

"No."

"Why?"

"Hospitals are a hell of a place to be when you're a child," he said simply. It was all the answer he would give her.

"They didn't think so today."

Pierce took her hand in his again when they reached the first level. "There's no tougher audience than children. They're very literal-minded."

Ryan had to laugh. "I suppose you're right. What adult would have thought to ask you where you buy your magic milk?" She shot Pierce a look. "I thought you handled that one rather smoothly."

"I've had a bit of practice," he told her. "Kids keep you on your toes. Adults are more easily distracted by some clever patter and flash." He smiled down at her. "Even you. Though you watch me with very intriguing green eyes."

Ryan looked across the parking lot as they stepped outside. When he looked at her, it wasn't easy to focus on anything but him when he spoke. "Pierce, why did you ask me to come with you today?"

"I wanted your company."

Ryan turned back to him. "I don't think I understand."

"Do you have to?" he asked. In the sunlight her hair was the color of early wheat. Pierce ran his fingers through it, then framed her face with his hands as he had done that first night. "Always?"

Ryan's heart pounded in her throat. "Yes, I think . . ."

But his mouth was already on hers, and she could think no longer. It was just as it had been the first time. The gentle kiss drew everything from her. She felt a warm, fluttering ache pass through her as his fingers brushed her temple and then traveled to just under her heart. People walked by them, but she never knew. They were shadows, ghosts. The only things of substance were Pierce's mouth and hands.

Was it the wind she felt, or his fingers gliding over her skin? Did he murmur something, or had she?

Pierce drew her away. Ryan's eyes were clouded. They began to clear and focus as if she were coming out of a dream. He wasn't ready for the dream to end. Bringing her back, he took her lips again and tasted the dark, mysterious flavor of her.

He had to fight with the need to crush her against him, to savage her warm, willing mouth. She was a woman made for a gentle touch. Desire tore at him, and he suppressed it. There were times when he was locked in a dark, airless box that he had to push back the need to rush, the urge to claw his way out. Now he almost felt the same hint of panic. *What was she doing to him?* The question ran through his mind even as he brought her closer. Pierce knew only that he wanted her with a desperation he hadn't thought himself capable of.

Was there silk next to her skin again? Thin, fragile silk lightly scented with the fragrance she wore? He wanted to make love to her by candlelight or in a field with the sun pouring over her. Dear God, how he wanted her.

"Ryan, I want to be with you." The words were whispered inside her mouth and made her tremble. "I need to be with you. Come with me now." With his hands he tilted her head to another angle and kissed her again. "Now, Ryan. Let me love you."

"Pierce." She was sinking and struggling to find solid ground. She leaned against him even as she shook her head. "I don't know you."

Pierce controlled a sudden wild desire to drag her to his car, to take her back to his home. To his bed. "No." He said it as much to himself as to Ryan. Drawing her away, he held her by the shoulders and studied her. "No, you don't. And Miss Swan would need to." He didn't like the erratic beating of his heart. Calm and control were intimate parts of his work, and therefore, of him. "When you know me," he told her quietly, "we'll be lovers."

"No." Ryan's objection sprang from his matter-of-fact tone, not from the statement. "No, Pierce, we won't be lovers unless it's what I want. I make deals on contracts, not in my personal life."

Pierce smiled, more relaxed with her annoyance than he would have been with malleability. Anything that came too easily he suspected. "Miss Swan," he murmured as he took her arm. "We've already seen the cards."

Chapter 6

Ryan arrived in Las Vegas alone. She had insisted on it. Once her nerves had settled and she had been able to think practically, she had decided it would be unwise to have too much personal contact with Pierce. When a man was able to make you forget the world around you with a kiss, you kept your distance. That was Ryan Swan's new rule.

Through most of her life she had been totally dominated by her father. She had been able to do nothing without his approval. He might not have given her his time, but he had always given her his opinion. And his opinion had been law.

It was only upon reaching her early twenties that Ryan had begun to explore her own talents, her own independence. The taste of freedom had been very sweet. She wasn't about to allow herself to be dominated again, certainly not by physical needs. She knew from experience that men weren't particularly trustworthy. Why should Pierce Atkins be any different?

After paying off the cab, Ryan took a moment to look around. It was her first trip to Vegas. Even at ten in the morning it was an eye-opener. The Strip stretched long in both directions, and lining it were names like The Dunes, The Sahara, The MGM. The hotels vied for attention with gushing fountains, elaborate neon and fabulous flowers.

Billboards announced famous names in huge letters. Stars, stars,

stars! The most beautiful women in the world, the most talented performers, the most colorful, the most exotic—they were all here. Everything was packed together; an adult amusement park circled by desert and ringed by mountains. The morning sun baked the streets; at night the neon would light them.

Ryan turned and looked at Caesars Palace. It was huge and white and opulent. Above her head in enormous letters was Pierce's name and the dates of his engagements. What sort of feeling did it give a man like him, she wondered, to see his name advertised so boldly?

She lifted her bags and took the moving walkway that would transport her past the glittering fountain and Italian statues. In the morning quiet she could hear the water spurt up and splash down. She imagined that at night the streets would be noisy, filled with cars and people.

The moment she entered the hotel lobby, Ryan heard the whirl and chink of the slot machines. She had to curb a desire to walk into the casino for a look instead of going to the front desk.

"Ryan Swan." She set down her suitcases at the foot of the long counter. "I have a reservation."

"Yes, Miss Swan." The desk clerk beamed at her without checking his files. "The bellboy will take your bags." He signaled, then handed a key to the answering bellboy. "Enjoy your stay, Miss Swan. Please let us know if there's anything we can do for you."

"Thank you." Ryan accepted the clerk's deference without a thought. When people knew she was Bennett Swan's daughter, they treated her like a visiting dignitary. It was nothing new and only mildly annoying.

The elevator took her all the way to the top floor with the bellboy keeping a respectful silence. He led the way down the corridor, unlocked the door, then stepped back to let her enter.

Ryan's first surprise was that it wasn't a room but a suite. Her second was that it was already occupied. Pierce sat on the sofa working with papers he had spread out on the table in front of him.

"Ryan." He rose, then, going to the bellboy, handed him a bill. "Thank you."

"Thank *you*, Mr. Atkins."

Ryan waited until the door shut behind him. "What are you doing here?" she demanded.

"I have a rehearsal scheduled this afternoon," he reminded her. "How was your flight?"

"It was fine," she told him, annoyed with his answer and with the suspicions that were creeping into her mind.

"Can I get you a drink?"

"No, thank you." She glanced around the well-appointed room, took a brief glimpse out the window, then gestured broadly. "What the hell is this?"

Pierce lifted a brow at her tone but answered mildly. "Our suite."

"Oh, no," she said with a definite shake of her head. "*Your* suite." Picking up her bags, she headed for the door.

"Ryan." It was the calm quality of his voice that stopped her— and that snapped her temper.

"What a very small, very dirty trick!" Ryan dropped her bags with a thud and turned on him. "Did you really think you could change my reservation and—and—"

"And what?" he prompted.

She gestured around the room again. "Set me up here with you without me making a murmur? Did you really think I'd pop cozily into your bed because you arranged it so nicely? How *dare* you! How dare you lie to me about needing me to watch you perform when all you wanted was for me to keep your bed warm!"

Her voice had changed from low accusation to high fury before Pierce grabbed her wrist. The strength in his fingers had her gasping in surprise and alarm. "I don't lie," Pierce said softly, but his eyes were darker than she had ever seen them. "And I don't need tricks to find a woman for my bed."

She didn't try to free herself. Instinct warned her against it, but she couldn't control her temper. "Then what do you call this?" she tossed back.

"A convenient arrangement." He felt her pulse racing under his fingers. Anger made his voice dangerously cool.

"For whom?" she demanded.

"We'll need to talk over a number of things in the next few days." He spoke with quiet deliberation, but his grip never slackened. "I don't intend to run down to your room every time I have something to say to you. I'm here to work," he reminded her. "And so are you."

"You should have consulted me."

"I didn't," he countered icily. "And I don't sleep with a woman unless she wants me to, Miss Swan."

"I don't appreciate you taking it upon yourself to change arrangements without discussing it with me first." Ryan stood firm on this, though her knees were threatening to tremble. His fury was all the more frightening in its restraint.

"I warned you before, I do things in my own way. If you're nervous, lock your door."

The jibe made her voice sharp. "A lot of good that would do with you. A lock would hardly keep you out."

His fingers tightened on her wrist quickly, painfully, before he tossed it aside. "Perhaps not." Pierce opened the door. "But a simple *no* would."

He was gone before Ryan could say any more. She leaned back against the door as the shudders ran through her. Until that moment she hadn't realized how badly she had been frightened. She was accustomed to dealing with histrionic bursts of temper or sulky silences from her father. But this . . .

There had been ice-cold violence in Pierce's eyes. Ryan would rather have faced the raging, shouting fury of any man than the look that could freeze her.

Without knowing she did so, Ryan rubbed her wrist. It throbbed lightly in each separate spot that Pierce's fingers had gripped. She had been right when she had said she didn't know him. There was more to him than she had ever guessed. Having uncovered one layer, she wasn't entirely certain she could deal with what she had discovered. For another moment she leaned against the door, waiting for the shaking to stop.

She looked around the room. Perhaps she had been wrong to

have reacted so strongly to a harmless business arrangement, she finally decided. Sharing a suite was essentially the same thing as having adjoining rooms. If that had been the case, she would have thought nothing of it.

But he had been wrong, too, she reminded herself. They might have come to an easy agreement about the suite if he had only discussed it with her first. She had promised herself when she had left Switzerland that she would no longer be directed.

And Pierce's phrasing had worried her. *He didn't sleep with a woman unless she wanted him to.* Ryan was too aware that they both knew she wanted him.

A simple *no* would keep him out. Yes, she mused as she picked up her bags. That she could depend on. He would never force himself on any woman—very simply, he would have no need to. She wondered how long it would be before she forgot to say no.

Ryan shook her head. The project was as important to Pierce as it was to her. It wasn't smart to start off by bickering over sleeping arrangements or worrying about remote possibilities. She knew her own mind. She went to unpack.

When Ryan went down to the theatre, the rehearsal was already underway. Pierce held center stage. There was a woman with him. Even though she was dressed plainly in jeans and a bulky sweatshirt, Ryan recognized the statuesque redhead who was Pierce's assistant. On the tapes, Ryan recalled, she had worn brief, sparkling costumes or floaty dresses. *No magician travels without a beautiful assistant.*

Hold on, Ryan, she warned herself. No business of yours. Quietly, she walked down and took a seat in the center of the audience. Pierce never glanced in her direction. Hardly aware of what she did, Ryan began to think of camera angles and sets.

Five cameras, she thought, and nothing too showy in the background. Nothing glittery to pull attention away from him. Something dark, she decided. Something to enhance the image of wizard or warlock rather than showman.

It came as a complete surprise to her when Pierce's assistant drifted slowly backward until she was lying horizontally in thin air. Ryan stopped planning and watched. He used no patter now but only gestures—wide, sweeping gestures that brought black capes and candlelight to mind. The woman began revolving, slowly at first and then with greater speed.

Ryan had seen the illusion on tape, but seeing it in the flesh was a totally different experience. There were no props to distract from the two at stage center, no costumes, music or flashing lights to enhance the mood. Ryan discovered she was holding her breath and forced herself to let it out. The woman's cap of red curls fluttered as she spun. Her eyes were closed, her face utterly peaceful while her hands were folded neatly at her waist. Ryan watched closely, looking for wires, for gimmicks. Frustrated, she leaned forward.

She couldn't prevent a small gasp of appreciation as the woman began to roll over and over as she continued to spin. The calm expression on her face remained unchanged, as if she slept rather than whirled and circled three feet above the stage floor. With a gesture, Pierce stopped the motion, bringing her vertical again, slowly, until her feet touched the stage. When he passed his hand in front of her face, she opened her eyes and grinned.

"How was it?"

Ryan almost jolted at the commonplace words that bounced cheerfully off the theater walls.

"Good," Pierce said simply. "It'll be better with the music. I want red lights, something hot. Start soft and then build with the speed." He gave these orders to the lighting director before turning back to his assistant. "We'll work on the transportation."

For an hour Ryan watched, fascinated, frustrated and undeniably entertained. What seemed to her flawless, Pierce repeated again and again. With each illusion, he had his own ideas of the technical effects he wanted. Ryan could see that his creativity didn't stop at magic. He knew how to use lighting and sound to enhance, accent, underline.

A perfectionist, Ryan noted. He worked quietly, without the dynamics he exuded in a performance. Nor was there the careless ease about him she had seen when he had entertained the children. He was working. It was a plain and simple fact. A wizard, perhaps, she mused with a smile, but one who pays his dues with long hours and repetition. The longer she watched, the more respect she felt.

Ryan had wondered what it would be like to work with him. Now she saw. He was relentless, tireless and as fanatical about details as she was herself. They were going to argue, she predicted and began to look forward to it. It was going to be one hell of a show.

"Ryan, would you come up, please?"

She was startled when he called her. Ryan would have sworn he hadn't known she was in the theater. Fatalistically, she rose. It was beginning to appear that there was nothing he didn't know. As Ryan came forward, Pierce said something to his assistant. She gave a quick, lusty laugh and kissed him on the cheek.

"At least I get to stay all in one piece on this run," she told him, then turned to grin at Ryan as she mounted the stage.

"Ryan Swan," Pierce said, "Bess Frye."

On closer study Ryan saw the woman wasn't a beauty. Her features were too large for classic beauty. Her hair was brilliantly red and cropped into curls around a large-boned face. Her eyes were almost round and shades darker than Ryan's green. Her make-up was as exotic as her clothes were casual, and she was nearly as tall as Pierce.

"Hi!" There was a burst of friendliness in the one word. Bess extended her hand to give Ryan's an enthusiastic shake. It was hard to believe that the woman, as solid as a redwood, had been spinning three feet above the stage. "Pierce has told me all about you."

"Oh?" Ryan glanced over at him.

"Oh, yeah." She rested an elbow on his shoulder as she spoke to Ryan. "Pierce thinks you're real smart. He likes the brainy type, but he didn't say you were so pretty. How come you didn't tell me she was so pretty, sweetie?" It didn't take Ryan long to discover that Bess habitually spoke in long, explosive bursts.

"And have you accuse me of seeing a woman only as a stage prop?" He dipped his hands into his pockets.

Bess gave another burst of lusty laughter. "He's smart, too," she confided to Ryan, giving Pierce a squeeze. "You're going to be the producer on this special?"

"Yes." A little dazed by the overflowing friendliness, Ryan smiled. "Yes, I am."

"Good. About time we had a woman running things. I'm surrounded by men in this job, sweetie. Only one woman in the road crew. We'll have a drink sometime soon and get acquainted."

Buy you a drink, sweetie? Ryan remembered. Her smile became a grin. "I'd like that."

"Well, I'm going to see what Link's up to before the boss decides to put me back to work. See you later." Bess strode off stage—six feet of towering enthusiasm. Ryan watched her all the way.

"She's wonderful," Ryan murmured.

"I've always thought so."

"She seems so cool and reserved on stage." Ryan smiled up at Pierce. "Has she been with you long?"

"Yes."

The warmth Bess had brought was rapidly fading. Clearing her throat, Ryan began again. "The rehearsal went very well. We'll have to discuss which illusions you plan to incorporate into the special and whatever new ones you intend to develop."

"All right."

"There'll have to be some adjustments, naturally, for television," she continued, trying to overlook his monosyllabic responses. "But basically I imagine you want a condensed version of your club act."

"That's right."

In the short time Ryan had known Pierce, she had come to learn he possessed a natural friendliness and humor. Now he was looking at her with his eyes guarded, obviously impatient for her to leave. The apology she had planned couldn't be made to this man.

"I'm sure you're busy," she said stiffly and turned away. It hurt, she discovered, to be shut out. He had no right to hurt her. Ryan left the stage without looking back.

Pierce watched her until the doors at the back of the theatre swung shut behind her. With his eyes still on the door, he crushed the ball he held in his hand until it was flat. He had very strong fingers, strong enough to have snapped the bones of her wrist instead of merely bruising it.

He hadn't liked seeing those bruises. He didn't like remembering how she had accused him of trying to take her by deceit. He had never had to take any woman by deceit. Ryan Swan would be no different.

He could have had her that first night with the storm raging outside and her body pressed close to his.

And why didn't I? he demanded of himself and tossed the mangled ball aside. Why hadn't he taken her to bed and done all the things he had so desperately wanted to do? Because she had looked up at him with her eyes full of panic and acceptance. She had been vulnerable. He had realized, with something like fear, that he had been vulnerable, too. And still she haunted his mind.

When she had walked into the suite that morning, Pierce had forgotten the careful notes he had been making on a new illusion. He had seen her, walking in wearing one of those damn tailored suits, and he had forgotten everything. Her hair had been windblown from the drive, like the first time he had seen her. And all he had wanted to do was hold her—to feel the small, soft body yield against his.

Perhaps his anger had started to grow even then, to fire up with her words and accusing eyes.

He shouldn't have hurt her. Pierce stared down at his empty hands and swore. He had no right to mark her skin—the ugliest thing a man could do to a woman. She was weaker than he, and he had used that—used his temper and his strength, two things he had promised himself long, long ago he would never use on a woman. In his mind no provocation could justify it. He could blame no one but himself for the lapse.

He couldn't dwell on it or on Ryan any longer and continue to work. He needed his concentration. The only thing to do was to put their relationship back where Ryan had wanted it from the beginning. They would work together successfully, and that would be all. He had learned to control his body through his mind. He could control his needs, his emotions, the same way.

With a final oath Pierce walked back to talk with his road crew about props.

Chapter 7

Las Vegas was difficult to resist. Inside the casinos it was neither day nor night. Without clocks and with the continual clinking of slots, there was a perpetual timelessness, an intriguing disorientation. Ryan saw people in evening dress continuing a night's gambling into late morning. She watched thousands of dollars change hands at the blackjack and baccarat tables. More than once she held her breath while the roulette wheel spun with a small fortune resting on the caprices of the silver ball.

She learned that the fever came in many forms—cool, dispassionate, desperate, intense. There was the woman feeding the nickel slot machine and the dedicated player tossing the dice. Smoke hung in the air over the sounds of winning and of losing. The faces would change, but the mood remained. Just one more roll of the dice, one more pull of the lever.

The years in the prim Swiss school had cooled the gambling blood Ryan had inherited from her father. Now, for the first time, Ryan felt the excitement of the urge to test Lady Luck. She refused it, telling herself she was content to watch. There was little else for her to do.

She saw Pierce onstage at rehearsals and hardly at all otherwise. It was amazing to her that two people could share a suite and so rarely come into contact with each other. No matter how early she rose, he was already gone. Once or twice after she was long in bed,

Ryan heard the quick click of the lock on the front door. When they spoke, it was only to discuss ideas on how to alter his club act for television. Their conversations were calm and technical.

He's trying to avoid me, she thought the night of his opening performance, and doing a damn good job of it. If he had wanted to prove that sharing a suite meant nothing personal, he had succeeded beautifully. That, of course, was what she wanted, but she missed the easy camaraderie. She missed seeing him smile at her.

Ryan decided to watch the show from the wings. There she would have a perfect view and be in a position to note Pierce's timing and style while getting a backstage perspective. Rehearsals had given her an insight into his work habits, and now she would watch him perform from as close to his point of view as she could manage. She wanted to see more than the audience or a camera would see.

Careful to stay out of the way of the stagehands and grips, Ryan settled herself into a corner and watched. From the first wave of applause as he was introduced, Pierce had his audience in the palm of his hand. My God, he's beautiful! she thought as she studied his style and flare. Dynamic, dramatic, his personality alone would have held the audience. The charisma he possessed was no illusion but as integral a part of him as the color of his hair. He dressed in black, as was his habit, needing no brilliant colors to keep eyes glued to him.

He spoke as he performed. Patter, he would have called it, but it was much more. He tuned the mood with words and cadence. He could string them along, then dazzle them completely—a shot of flame from his naked palm, a glittering silver pendulum that swung, unsupported, in thin air. He was no longer pragmatic, as he had been in rehearsals, but dark and mysterious.

Ryan watched as he was padlocked into a duffel bag, slipped into a chest and chained inside. Standing on it, Bess pulled up a curtain and counted to twenty. When the curtain dropped, Pierce himself stood on the chest in a complete costume change. And, of course, when he unlocked the chest and bag, Bess was inside. He called it transportation. Ryan called it incredible.

His escapes made her uneasy. Watching volunteers from the audience nail him into a sturdy packing crate she herself had examined had her palms dampening. She could imagine him in the dark, airless box and feel her own breath clogging in her lungs. But his freedom was accomplished in less than two minutes.

For the finale, he locked Bess in a cage, curtaining it and levitating it to the ceiling. When he brought it down moments later, there was a sleek young panther in her place. Watching him, seeing the intensity of his eyes, the mysterious hollows and shadows on his face, Ryan almost believed he had transcended the laws of nature. For that moment before the curtain came down, the panther was Bess and he was more enchanter than showman.

Ryan wanted to ask him, convince him to explain just this one illusion in terms she could understand. When he came offstage and their eyes held, she swallowed the words.

His face was damp from the lights and his own concentration. She wanted to touch him, finding, to her own astonishment, that watching him perform had aroused her. The drive was more basic and more powerful than anything she had ever experienced. She could imagine him taking her with his strong, clever hands. Then his mouth, his impossibly sensual mouth, would be on hers, taking her to that strange, weightless world he knew. If she went to him now—offered, demanded—would she find him as hungry as herself? Would he say nothing, only lead her away to show her his magic?

Pierce stopped in front of her, and Ryan stepped back, shaken by her own thoughts. Her blood was heated, churning under her skin, demanding that she make the move toward him. Aware, aroused but unwilling, she kept her distance.

"You were marvelous," she said but heard the stiffness in the compliment.

"Thank you." Pierce said nothing more as he moved past her.

Ryan felt pain in her palms and discovered she was digging her nails into her flesh. This has got to stop, she told herself and turned to go after him.

"Hey, Ryan!" She stopped as Bess poked her head out of her dressing room. "What did you think of the show?"

"It was wonderful." She glanced down the corridor; Pierce was already out of reach. Perhaps it was for the best. "I don't suppose you'd let me in on the secret of the finale?" she asked.

Bess laughed. "Not if I value my life, sweetie. Come on in; talk to me while I change."

Ryan obliged, closing the door behind her. The air tingled with the scents of greasepaint and powder. "It must be quite an experience, being turned into a panther."

"Oh, Lord, Pierce has turned me into everything imaginable that walks, crawls or flies; he's sawed me to pieces and balanced me on swords. In one gag he had me sleeping on a bed of nails ten feet above the stage." As she spoke, she stripped out of her costume with no more modesty than a five-year-old.

"You must trust him," Ryan commented as she looked around for an empty chair. Bess had a habit of strewing her things over all available space.

"Just toss something out of your way," she suggested as she plucked a peacock blue robe from the arm of a chair. "Trust Pierce?" she continued as she belted the robe. "He's the best." Sitting at the vanity, she began to cream off her stage make-up. "You saw how he is at rehearsals."

"Yes." Ryan folded a crumpled blouse and set it aside. "Exacting."

"That's not the half of it. He works out his illusions on paper, then goes over them again and again in that dungeon of his before he even thinks about showing anything to me or Link." She looked at Ryan with one eye heavily mascaraed and the other naked. "Most people don't know how hard he works because he makes it look so easy. That's the way he wants it."

"His escapes," Ryan began as she straightened Bess's clothes. "Are they dangerous?"

"I don't like some of them." Bess tissued off the last of the cream. Her exotic face was unexpectedly young and fresh. "Getting out of manacles and a straightjacket is one thing." She shrugged as she rose. "But I've never liked it when he does his version of Houdini's Water Torture or his own A Thousand Locks."

"Why does he do it, Bess?" Ryan set a pair of jeans aside but continued to roam the room restlessly. "His illusions would be enough."

"Not for Pierce." Bess dropped the robe, then snapped on a bra. "The escapes and the danger are important to him. They always have been."

"Why?"

"Because he wants to test himself all the time. He's never satisfied with what he did yesterday."

"Test himself," Ryan murmured. She had sensed this herself but was a long way from understanding it. "Bess, how long have you been with him?"

"Since the beginning," Bess told her as she tugged on jeans. "Right from the beginning."

"Who is he?" Ryan demanded before she could stop herself. "Who is he really?"

With a shirt hanging from her fingertips, Bess gave Ryan a sudden, penetrating glance. "Why do you want to know?"

"He . . ." Ryan stopped, not knowing what to say. "I don't know."

"Do you care about him?"

Ryan didn't answer at once. She wanted to say no and shrug it off. She had no reason to care. "Yes, I do," she heard herself say. "I care about him."

"Let's go have a drink," Bess suggested and pulled on her shirt. "We'll talk."

"Champagne cocktails," Bess ordered when they slipped into a booth in the lounge. "I'm buying." She pulled out a cigarette and lit it. "Don't tell Pierce," she added with a wink. "He frowns on the use of tobacco. He's a fanatic about body care."

"Link told me he runs five miles every day."

"An old habit. Pierce rarely breaks old habits." Bess drew in smoke with a sigh. "He's always been really determined, you know? You could see it, even when he was a kid."

"You knew Pierce when he was a boy?"

"We grew up together—Pierce, Link and me." Bess glanced up at the waitress when their cocktails were served. "Run a tab," she directed and looked back at Ryan. "Pierce doesn't talk about back then, not even to Link or me. He's shut it off—or tried to."

"I thought he was trying to promote an image," Ryan murmured.

"He doesn't need to."

"No." Ryan met her eyes again. "I suppose he doesn't. Did he have a difficult childhood?"

"Oh, boy." Bess took a long drink. "And then some. He was a real puny kid."

"Pierce?" Ryan thought of the hard, muscled body and stared.

"Yeah." Bess gave a muffled version of her full-throated laugh. "Hard to believe, but true. He was small for his age, skinny as a rail. The bigger kids tormented him. They needed someone to pick on, I guess. Nobody likes growing up in an orphanage."

"Orphanage?" Ryan pounced on the last word. Studying Bess's open, friendly face, she felt a flood of sympathy. "All of you?"

"Oh, hell." Bess shrugged. Ryan's eyes were full of eloquent distress. "It wasn't so bad, really. Food, a roof over your head, plenty of company. It's not like you read about in that book, that *Oliver Twist*."

"Did you lose your parents, Bess?" Ryan asked with interest rather than the sympathy she saw was unwanted.

"When I was eight. There wasn't anybody else to take me. It was the same with Link." She continued with no trace of self-pity or regret. "People want to adopt babies, mostly. Older kids aren't placed so easily."

Lifting her drink, Ryan sipped thoughtfully. It would have been twenty years ago, before the current surge of interest in adoptable children. "What about Pierce?"

"Things were different with him. He had parents. They wouldn't sign, so he was unadoptable."

Ryan's brows creased with confusion. "But if he had parents, what was he doing in an orphanage?"

"Courts took him away from them. His father . . ." Bess let out a long stream of smoke. She was taking a chance, talking like this. Pierce wasn't going to like it if he found out. She could only hope it paid off. "His father used to beat his mother."

"Oh, my God!" Ryan's horrified eyes clung to Bess's. "And— and Pierce?"

"Now and again," Bess answered calmly. "But mostly his mother. First he'd hit the booze, then he'd hit his wife."

A surge of raw pain spread in the pit of her stomach. Ryan lifted her drink again. Of course she knew such things happened, but her world had always been so shielded. Her own parents might have ignored her a great deal of her life, but neither had ever lifted a hand to her. True, her father's shouting had been frightening at times, but it had never gone beyond a raised voice and impatient words. She had never dealt with physical violence of any sort firsthand. Though she tried to conceive the kind of ugliness Bess was calmly relating, it was too distant.

"Tell me," she asked finally. "I want to understand him."

It was what Bess wanted to hear. She gave Ryan a silent vote of approval and continued. "Pierce was five. This time his father beat his mother badly enough to put her in the hospital. Usually, he locked Pierce in a closet before he started on one of his rages, but this time he knocked him around a little first."

Ryan controlled the need to protest what she was hearing but kept silent. Bess watched her steadily as she spoke. "That's when the social workers took over. After the usual paperwork and court hearings, his parents were judged unfit, and he was placed in the orphanage."

"Bess, his mother." Ryan shook her head, trying to think it through. "Why didn't she leave his father and take Pierce with her? What kind of woman would—"

"I'm not a psychiatrist," Bess interrupted. "As far as Pierce ever knew, she stayed with his father."

"And gave up her child," Ryan murmured. "He must have felt so completely rejected, so frightened and alone."

What sort of damage does that do to a small mind? she wondered. What sort of compensations does a child like that make? Did he escape from chains and trunks and safes because he had once been a small boy locked in a dark closet? Did he continually seek to do the impossible because he had once been so helpless?

"He was a loner," Bess continued as she ordered another round. "Maybe that's one of the reasons the other kids tormented him. At least until Link came." Bess grinned, enjoying this part of her memories. "Nobody ever touched Pierce when Link was in sight. He's always been twice as big as anyone else. And that face!"

She laughed again, but there was nothing callous in the sound. "When Link first came, none of the other kids would go near him. Except Pierce. They were both outcasts. So was I. Link's been attached to Pierce ever since. I really don't know what might have happened to him without Pierce. Or to me."

"You really love him, don't you?" Ryan asked, drawn close in spirit to the large, exuberant redhead.

"He's my best friend," Bess answered simply. "They let me into their little club when I was ten." She smiled over the rim of her glass. "I saw Link coming and climbed up a tree. He scared me to death. We called him the Missing Link."

"Children can be cruel."

"You betcha. Anyway, just as he was passing underneath, the branch broke and I fell out. He caught me." She leaned forward, cupping her chin on her hands. "I'll never forget that. One minute I'm falling a mile a minute, and the next he's holding me. I looked up at that face and got ready to scream blue blazes. Then he laughed. I fell in love on the spot."

Ryan swallowed champagne quickly. There was no mistaking the dreamy look in Bess's eyes. "You—you and Link?"

"Well, me, anyway," Bess said ruefully. "I've been nuts about the big lug for twenty years. He still thinks I'm Little Bess. All six feet of me." She grinned and winked. "But I'm working on him."

"I thought you and Pierce . . ." Ryan began, then trailed off.

"Me and Pierce?" Bess let loose with one of her lusty laughs, causing heads to turn. "Are you kidding? You know enough about show business to cast better than that, sweetie. Do I look like Pierce's type?"

"Well, I . . ." Embarrassed by Bess's outspoken humor, Ryan shrugged. "I wouldn't have any idea what his type would be."

Bess laughed into her fresh drink. "You look smarter than that," she commented. "Anyway, he was always a quiet kid, always— what's the word?" Her forehead furrowed in thought. "Intense, you know? He had a temper." Grinning again, she rolled her eyes. "He gave a black eye for every one he got in the early days. But as he got older, he'd hold back. It was pretty clear he'd made up his mind not to follow in his old man's footsteps. When Pierce makes up his mind, that's it."

Ryan remembered the cold fury, the iced-over violence, and began to understand.

"When he was about nine, I guess, he had this accident." Bess drank, then scowled. "At least that's what he called it. He went head first down a flight of stairs. Everybody knew he'd been pushed, but he'd never say who. I think he didn't want Link to do something he could have gotten in trouble for. The fall hurt his back. They didn't think he'd walk again."

"Oh, no!"

"Yeah." Bess took another long drink. "But Pierce said he was going to walk. He was going to run five miles every day of his life."

"Five miles," Ryan murmured.

"He was determined. He worked at therapy like his life depended on it. Maybe it did," she added thoughtfully. "Maybe it did. He spent six months in the hospital."

"I see." She was seeing Pierce in the pediatric ward, giving himself to children, talking to them, making them laugh. Bringing them magic.

"While he was in, one of the nurses gave him a magic set. That was it." Bess toasted with her glass. "A five-dollar magic set. It was like he'd been waiting for it, or it was waiting for him. By the time he got out, he could do things a lot of guys in the club field have trouble with." Love and pride mingled in her voice. "He was a natural."

Ryan could see him, a dark, intense boy in a white hospital bed, perfecting, practicing, discovering.

"Listen." Bess laughed again and leaned forward. Ryan's eyes were speaking volumes. "Once when I visited him in the hospital, he set the sheet on fire." She paused as Ryan's expression became one of horror. "I swear, I *saw* it burning. Then he patted it with his hand." She demonstrated with her palm on the table. "Smoothed it out, and there was nothing. No burn, no hole, not even a singe. The little creep scared me to death."

Ryan found herself laughing despite the ordeal he must have experienced. He'd beaten it. He'd won. "To Pierce," she said and lifted her glass.

"Damn right." Bess touched rims before she tossed off the champagne. "He took off when he was sixteen. I missed him like crazy. I never thought I'd see him or Link again. I guess it was the loneliest two years of my life. Then, one day I was working in this diner in Denver, and he walks in. I don't know how he found me, he never said, but he walks in and tells me to quit. I was going to go work for him."

"Just like that?" Ryan demanded.

"Just like that."

"What did you say?"

"I didn't say anything. It was Pierce." With a smile, Bess signaled the waitress again. "I quit. We went on the road. Drink up, sweetie, you're one behind."

Ryan studied her a moment, then obliged by finishing off her drink. It wasn't every man who could command that sort of unquestioning loyalty from a strong woman. "I usually stop at two," Ryan told her, indicating the cocktail.

"Not tonight," Bess announced. "I always drink champagne when I get sentimental. You wouldn't believe some of the places we played those first years," she went on. "Kids' parties, stag parties, the works. Nobody handles a rowdy crowd like Pierce. When he looks at a guy, then whips a fireball out of his pocket, the guy quiets down."

"I imagine so," Ryan agreed and laughed at the image. "I'm not even sure he'd need the fireball."

"You got it," Bess said, pleased. "Anyway, he always knew he was going to make it, and he took Link and me along. He didn't have to. That's just the kind of man he is. He doesn't let many people in close, but the ones he does, it's forever." She stirred the champagne quietly a moment. "I know Link and me could never keep up with him up here, you know?" Bess tapped her temple. "But it doesn't matter to Pierce. We're his friends."

"I think," Ryan said slowly, "he chooses his friends very well."

Bess sent her a brilliant smile. "You're a nice lady, Ryan. A real lady, too. Pierce is the kind of man who needs a lady."

Ryan became very interested in the color of her drink. "Why do you say that?"

"Because he has class, always has. He needs a classy woman and one who's warm like he is."

"Is he warm, Bess?" Ryan's eyes came back up, searching. "Sometimes he seems so . . . distant."

"You know where he got that stupid cat?" Ryan shook her head at the question. "Somebody'd hit it and left it on the side of the road. Pierce was driving back after a week's run in San Francisco. He stopped and took it to the vet. Two o'clock in the morning, and he's waking up the vet and making him operate on some stray cat. Cost him three hundred dollars. Link told me." She pulled out another cigarette. "How many people you know who'd do that?"

Ryan looked at her steadily. "Pierce wouldn't like it if he knew you'd told me all this, would he?"

"No."

"Why have you?"

Bess flashed her a smile again. "It's a trick I learned from him over the years. You look dead in somebody's eyes and you know if you can trust them."

Ryan met the look and spoke seriously. "Thank you."

"And," Bess added casually as she downed more champagne, "you're in love with him."

The words Ryan had begun to say jammed in her throat. She began coughing fitfully.

"Drink up, sweetie. Nothing like love to make you choke. Here's to it." She clinked her glass against Ryan's. "And good luck to both of us."

"Luck?" Ryan said weakly.

"With men like those two, we need it."

This time Ryan signaled for another round.

Chapter 8

When Ryan walked through the casino with Bess, she was laughing. The wine had lifted her mood, but more, Bess's company had cheered her. Since she had returned from school, Ryan had given herself little time to develop friendships. Finding one so quickly took her higher than the champagne.

"Celebrating?"

Both of them looked up and spotted Pierce. In unison, their faces registered the abashed guilt of children caught with one hand in the cookie jar. Pierce's brow lifted. With a laugh, Bess leaned over and kissed him enthusiastically.

"Just a little girl talk, sweetie. Ryan and I found out we have a lot in common."

"Is that so?" He watched as Ryan pressed her fingers to her mouth to stifle a giggle. It was apparent they'd had more than talk.

"Isn't he terrific when he's all serious and dry?" Bess asked Ryan. "Nobody does it better than Pierce." She kissed him again. "I didn't get your lady drunk, just maybe a little looser than she's used to. Besides, she's a big girl." Still resting her hand on his shoulder, Bess looked around. "Where's Link?"

"Watching the keno board."

"See you later." She gave Ryan a wink and was off.

"She's crazy about him, you know," Ryan said confidentially.

"Yes, I know."

She took a step closer. "Is there anything you don't know, Mr. Atkins?" She watched his lips curve at her emphasis on his surname. "I wondered if you'd ever do that for me again."

"Do what?"

"Smile. You haven't smiled at me in days."

"Haven't I?" He couldn't stop the surge of tenderness but contented himself with brushing the hair back from her face.

"No. Not once. Are you sorry?"

"Yes." Pierce steadied her with a hand on her shoulder and wished she wouldn't look at him in quite that way. He had managed to back down on needs while sharing the same set of rooms with her. Now, surrounded by noise and people and lights, he felt the force of desire building. He removed his hand. "Would you like me to take you upstairs?"

"I'm going to play blackjack," she informed him grandly. "I've wanted to for days, but I kept remembering gambling was foolish. I've just forgotten that."

Pierce held her arm as she started to walk to the table. "How much money do you have on you?"

"Oh, I don't know." Ryan rummaged in her purse. "About seventy-five dollars."

"All right." If she lost, Pierce decided, seventy-five would put no great hole in her bank account. He went with her.

"I've been watching this for days," she whispered as she took a seat at a ten-dollar table. "I've got it all figured out."

"Doesn't everyone?" he muttered and stood beside her. "Give the lady twenty dollars worth of chips," he told the dealer.

"Fifty," Ryan corrected, counting out bills.

With a nod from Pierce, the dealer exchanged the bills for colored chips.

"Are you going to play?" Ryan asked him.

"I don't gamble."

She lifted her brows. "What do you call being nailed inside a packing crate?"

He gave her one of his slow smiles. "My profession."

She laughed and sent him a teasing grin. "Do you disapprove of gambling and other vices, Mr. Atkins?"

"No." He felt another leap of desire and controlled it. "But I like to figure my own odds." He nodded as the cards were dealt. "It's never easy to beat the house at its own game."

"I feel lucky tonight," she told him.

The man beside Ryan swirled a bourbon and signed his name on a sheet of paper. He had just dropped over two thousand dollars. Philosophically, he bought another five thousand dollars worth of chips. Ryan watched a diamond glitter on his pinky as the cards were dealt. A triple deck, she remembered and lifted the tips of her own cards carefully. She saw an eight and a five. A young blonde in a black Halston took a hit and busted on twenty-three. The man with the diamond held on eighteen. Ryan took a hit and was pleased with another five. She held, then waited patiently as two more players took cards.

The dealer turned over fourteen, flipped over his next card and hit twenty. The man with the diamond swore softly as he lost another five hundred dollars.

Ryan counted her next cards, watched the hits and lost again. Undaunted, she waited for her third deal. She drew seventeen. Before she could signal the dealer she would hold, Pierce nodded for the hit.

"Wait a minute," Ryan began.

"Take it," he said simply.

With a huff and a shrug, she did. She hit twenty. Eyes wide, she swiveled in her chair to stare at him, but he was watching the cards. The dealer held on nineteen and paid her off.

"I won!" she exclaimed, pleased with the stack of chips pushed at her. "How did you know?"

He only smiled at her and continued to watch the cards.

On the next hand she drew a ten and a six. She would have taken the hit, but Pierce touched her shoulder and shook his head. Swallowing her protest, Ryan stayed pat. The dealer broke on twenty-two.

She laughed, delighted, but looked over at him again. "How do you do that?" she demanded. "It's a triple deck. You can't possibly remember all the cards dealt or figure what's left." He said nothing, and her brow creased. "Can you?"

Pierce smiled again and shook his head simply. Then he steered Ryan to another win.

"Want to take a look at mine?" the man with the diamond demanded, pushing aside his cards in disgust.

Ryan leaned toward him. "He's a sorcerer, you know. I take him everywhere."

The young blonde tucked her hair behind her ear. "I could use a spell or two myself." She sent Pierce a slow invitation. Ryan caught her eye as the cards were dealt.

"Mine," she said coolly and didn't see Pierce's brow go up. The blonde went back to her cards.

For the next hour Ryan's luck—or Pierce's—held. When the pile of chips in front of her had grown considerably, he opened her purse and swept them inside.

"Oh, but wait. I'm just getting started!"

"The secret of winning is knowing when to stop," Pierce told her and helped her off the stool. "Cash them in, Ryan, before you take it into your head to lose them at baccarat."

"But I did want to play," she began, casting a glance behind her.

"Not tonight."

With a heavy sigh she dumped the contents of her purse at the cashier's booth. Along with the chips was a comb, a lipstick and a penny that had been flattened by the wheel of a train.

"That's for luck," she said when Pierce picked it up to examine it.

"Superstition, Miss Swan," he murmured. "You surprise me."

"It's not superstition," she insisted, stuffing bills in her purse as the cashier counted them out. "It's for luck."

"I stand corrected."

"I like you, Pierce." Ryan linked her arm with his. "I thought I should tell you."

"Do you?"

"Yes," she said definitely. She could tell him that, she thought as they moved to the elevators. That was safe and certainly true. She wouldn't tell him what Bess had said so casually. *Love him?* No, that was far from safe, and it wasn't necessarily true. Even though . . . even though she was becoming more and more afraid it was.

"Do you like me?" Ryan turned to him and smiled as the elevator doors clicked shut.

"Yes, Ryan." He ran his knuckles over her cheek. "I like you."

"I wasn't sure." She stepped closer to him, and he felt a tingle race along his skin. "You've been angry with me."

"No, I haven't been angry with you."

She was staring up at him. Pierce could feel the air grow thick, as it did when the lid closed on him in a box or a trunk. His heart rate speeded up, and with sheer mental determination, he leveled it. He wasn't going to touch her again.

Ryan saw something flicker in his eyes. A hunger. Hers grew as well, but more, she felt a need to touch, to soothe. To love. She knew him now, though he was unaware of it. She wanted to give him something. She reached up to touch his cheek, but Pierce caught her fingers in his as the door opened.

"You must be tired," he said roughly and drew her into the corridor.

"No." Ryan laughed with the new sense of power. He was just a little afraid of her. She sensed it. Something shot into her—a combination of wine and winning and knowledge. And she wanted him.

"Are you tired, Pierce?" she asked when he unlocked the door to the suite.

"It's late."

"No. No, it's never late in Las Vegas." She tossed her purse aside and stretched. "There's no time here, don't you know? No clocks." Lifting her hair, she let it fall slowly through her fingers. "How can it be late when you don't know what time it is?" She spotted his papers on the table and crossed to them, kicking off her shoes as she went. "You work too much, Mr. Atkins." Laughing, she turned back to him. "Miss Swan's like that, isn't she?"

Her hair had tumbled over her shoulders, and her cheeks were flushed. Her eyes were alive, dancing, alluring. In them he saw that his thoughts were no secret to her. Desire was a hammer thrust in his stomach. Pierce said nothing.

"But you like Miss Swan," she murmured. "I don't always. Come sit down. Explain this to me." Ryan dropped to the couch and picked up one of his papers. It was covered with drawings and notes that made absolutely no sense to her.

Pierce moved then, telling himself it was only to keep her from disturbing his work. "It's too complicated." He took the sheet from her hand and set it back down.

"I've a very quick mind." Ryan pulled his arm until he sat beside her. She looked at him and smiled. "Do you know, the first time I looked into your eyes I thought my heart stopped." She put her hand to his cheek. "The first time you kissed me I knew it did."

Pierce caught her hand again, knowing he was close to the edge. Her free one ran up his shirtfront to his throat. "Ryan, you should go to bed."

She could hear the desire in his voice. Under her fingertip the pulse in his throat throbbed quickly. Her own heart began to match the rhythm. "No one's ever kissed me like that before," she murmured and slipped her fingers to the first button of his shirt. She freed it, watching his eyes. "No one's ever made me feel like that before. Was it magic, Pierce?" She loosened the second and third buttons.

"No." He reached up to stop the questing fingers that were driving him mad.

"I think it was." Ryan shifted and caught his earlobe lightly between her teeth. "I know it was." The whispering breath went straight to the pit of his stomach to stoke the flames. They flared high and threatened to explode. Catching her by the shoulders, Pierce started to draw her away, but her hands were on his naked chest. Her mouth brushed his throat. His fingers tightened as the tug of war went on inside him.

"Ryan." Though he concentrated, he couldn't steady his pulse. "What are you trying to do?"

"I'm trying to seduce you," she murmured, trailing her lips down to follow her fingers. "Is it working?"

Her hands ran down his rib cage to play lightly over his stomach. She felt the quiver of response and grew bolder.

"Yes, it's working very well."

Ryan laughed, a throaty, almost mocking sound that made his blood pound. Though he didn't touch her, he was no longer able to stop her from touching him. Her hands were soft and teasing while her tongue flicked lightly at his ear.

"Are you sure?" she whispered as she slipped his shirt from his shoulders. "Maybe I'm doing something wrong." She trailed her mouth to his chin, then let her tongue run briefly over his lips. "Maybe you don't want me to touch you like this." She ran a fingertip down the center of his chest to the waist of his jeans. "Or like this." She nipped his bottom lip, still watching his eyes.

No, she'd been wrong. They were black—black, not gray. Needs drove her until she thought she would be swallowed by them. Could it be possible to want so much? So much that your whole body ached and pounded and threatened to shatter?

"I wanted you when you walked offstage tonight," she said huskily. "Right then, while I still half-believed you were a wizard and not a man. And now." She ran her hands up his chest to link them behind his neck. "Now, knowing you're a man, I want you more." She let her eyes lower to his mouth, then lifted them back to his. "But maybe you don't want me. Maybe I don't . . . arouse you."

"Ryan." He'd lost the ability to control his pulse, his thoughts, his concentration. He'd lost the will to try to find it again. "There won't be any turning back in a moment."

She laughed, giddy with excitement, driven by desire. She let her lips hover a breath from his. "Promise?"

Ryan exulted in the power of the kiss. His mouth was on hers fiercely, painfully. She was under him with such speed, she never felt the movement, only his hard body on hers. He was pulling at her blouse, impatient with buttons. Two flew off to land some-where on the carpet before his hand took her breast. Ryan moaned and arched against him, desperate to be touched. His tongue went deep to tangle with hers.

Desire was white-hot—flashes of heat, splashes of color. Her skin was searing wherever he touched. She was naked without knowing how she had become so, and his bare flesh was melded to hers. His teeth were on her breast, lightly at the edge of control, then his tongue swept across her nipple until she moaned and pressed closer.

Pierce could feel the hammer beat of her pulse, almost taste it as his mouth hurried to her other breast. Her moans and her urging hands were driving him beyond reason. He was trapped in a furnace, but there would be no escape this time. He knew his flesh would melt into hers until there was nothing left to keep him separate. The heat, her scent, her taste all whirled inside his head. Excitement? No, this was more than excitement. It was obsession.

He slipped his fingers inside her. She was so soft, so warm and moist, he had no more will left.

He entered her with a wildness that stunned them both. Then she was moving with him, frantic and strong. He felt the pain of impossible pleasure, knowing he had been the enchanted, not the enchanter. He was utterly hers.

Ryan felt his ragged breath against her neck. His heart was still racing. For me, she thought dreamily as she floated on the after-math of passion. *Mine*, she thought again and sighed. How had Bess known before she had? Ryan closed her eyes and let herself drift.

It must show on her face like a neon sign. Is it too soon to tell him? she wondered. Wait, she decided, touching his hair. She would let herself have time to get used to love before she proclaimed it. At that moment she felt she had all the time in the world.

She gave a murmured protest when Pierce took his weight from her. Slowly, she opened her eyes. He stared down at his hands. He was cursing himself steadily.

"Did I hurt you?" he demanded in a quick, rough burst.

"No," she said, surprised, then remembered Bess's story. "No, you didn't hurt me, Pierce. You couldn't. You're a very gentle man."

His eyes whipped back to hers, dark, anguished. There had been no gentleness in him when he had loved her. Only needs and desperation. "Not always," he said sharply and reached for his jeans.

"What are you doing?"

"I'll go down and get another room." He was dressing swiftly as she looked on. "I'm sorry this happened. I won't . . ." He stopped when he looked and saw tears welling in her eyes. Something ripped inside his stomach. "Ryan, I am sorry." Sitting beside her again, he brushed a tear away with his thumb. "I swore I wasn't going to touch you. I shouldn't have. You'd had too much to drink. I knew that and should've—"

"Damn you!" She slapped his hand away. "I was wrong. You *can* hurt me. Well, you don't have to get another room." She reached down for her blouse. "I'll get one myself. I won't stay here after you've turned something wonderful into a mistake."

She was up and tugging on her blouse, which was inside out.

"Ryan, I—"

"Oh, shut up!" Seeing the two middle buttons were missing, she tore the blouse off again and stood facing him, haughtily naked, eyes blazing. He nearly pulled her to the floor and took her again. "I knew exactly what I was doing, do you hear? Exactly! If you think it only takes a few drinks to make me throw myself at a man, then you're wrong. I wanted you, I thought you wanted me. So if it was a mistake, it was yours."

"It wasn't a mistake for me, Ryan." His voice had softened, but when he reached out to touch her, she jerked back. He let his hand drop to his side and chose his words carefully. "I wanted you; perhaps, I thought, too much. And I wasn't as gentle with you as I wanted to be. It's difficult for me to deal with knowing I couldn't stop myself from having you."

For a moment she studied him, then brushed tears away with the back of her hand. "Did you want to stop yourself?"

"The point is, I tried and couldn't. And I've never taken a woman with less . . ." He hesitated. "Care," he murmured. "You're very small, very fragile."

Fragile? she thought and lifted a brow. No one had ever called her that before. At another time she might have enjoyed it, but now she felt there was only one way to handle a man like Pierce. "Okay," she told him and took a deep breath. "You've got two choices."

Surprised, Pierce drew his brows together. "What are they?"

"You can get yourself another room or you can take me to bed and make love to me again." She took a step toward him. "Right now."

He met the challenge in her eyes and smiled. "Those are my only choices?"

"I suppose I could seduce you again if you want to be stubborn," she said with a shrug. "It's up to you."

He let his fingers dive into her hair as he drew her closer. "What if we combined two of those choices?"

She gave him a look of consideration. "Which two?"

He lowered his mouth to hers for a soft, lingering kiss. "How about I take you to bed and you seduce me?"

Ryan allowed him to lift her into his arms. "I'm a reasonable person," she agreed as he walked to the bedroom. "I'm willing to discuss a compromise as long as I get my own way."

"Miss Swan," Pierce murmured as he laid her gently on the bed. "I like your style."

Chapter 9

Ryan's body ached. Sighing, she snuggled deeper into the pillow. It was a pleasant discomfort. It reminded her of the night—the night that had lasted until dawn.

She hadn't known she had so much passion to give or so many needs to fill. Each time she had thought herself drained, body and mind, she had only to touch him again, or he her. Strength would flood back into her, and with it the unrelenting demands of desire.

Then they had slept, holding each other as the rosy tones of sunrise had slipped into the room. Drifting awake, clinging to sleep, Ryan shifted toward Pierce, wanting to hold him again.

She was alone.

Confusion had her eyes slowly opening. Sliding her hand over the sheets beside her, Ryan found them cold. *Gone?* she thought hazily. How long had she been sleeping alone? All of her dreamy pleasure died. Ryan touched the sheets again. No, she told herself and stretched, he's just in the other room. He wouldn't have left me alone.

The phone shrilled and jolted her completely awake.

"Yes, hello." She answered it on the first ring and pushed her hair from her face with her free hand. *Why was the suite so quiet?*

"Miss Swan?"

"Yes, this is Ryan Swan."

"Bennett Swan calling, please hold."

Ryan sat up, automatically pulling the sheets to her breast. Disoriented, she wondered what time it was. And where, she thought again, was Pierce?

"Ryan, give me an update."

An update? she repeated silently, hearing her father's voice. She struggled to put her thoughts into order.

"Ryan!"

"Yes, I'm sorry."

"I haven't got all day."

"I've watched Pierce's rehearsals daily," she began, wishing for a cup of coffee and a few moments to pull herself together. "I think you'll find he has the technical areas and his own crew well in hand." She glanced around the bedroom, looking for some sign of him. "He opened last night, flawlessly. We've already discussed some alterations for the special, but nothing's firmed up as yet. At this point whatever new routines he's worked out he's keeping to himself."

"I want some firm estimates on the set within two weeks," he told her. "We might have a change in the scheduling. You work it out with Atkins. I want a list of his proposed routines and the time allowance for each one."

"I've already discussed it with him," Ryan said coolly, annoyed that her father was infringing on her territory. "I am the producer, aren't I?"

"You are," he agreed. "I'll see you in my office when you get back."

Hearing the click, Ryan hung up with a sigh of exasperation. It had been a typical Bennett Swan conversation. She pushed the phone call from her mind and scrambled from the bed. Pierce's robe lay draped over a chair, and picking it up, Ryan slipped it on.

"Pierce?" Ryan hurried out into the living area of the suite but found it empty. "Pierce?" she called again, stepping on one of the lost buttons from her blouse. Absently, Ryan picked it up and dropped it in the pocket of the robe before she walked through the suite.

Empty. The pain started in her stomach and spread. He had left her alone. Shaking her head, Ryan searched the rooms again. He must have left her a note telling her why and where he'd gone. He wouldn't just wake up and leave her, not after last night.

But there was nothing. Ryan shivered, suddenly cold.

It was the pattern of her life, she decided. Moving to the window, she stared out at unlit neon. Whoever she cared for, whoever she gave love to, always went their own way. Yet somehow, she still expected it to be different.

When she had been small, it had been her mother, a young, glamour-loving woman jetting off to follow Bennett Swan all over the world. *You're a big girl, Ryan, and so self-sufficient. I'll be back in a few days.* Or a few weeks, Ryan remembered. There had always been a housekeeper and other servants to see that she was tended to. No, she had never been neglected or abused. Just forgotten.

Later it had been her father, dashing here and there at a moment's notice. But of course, he'd seen that she had had a solid, dependable nanny whom he had paid a very substantial salary. Then she'd been shipped off to Switzerland, the best boarding school available. *That daughter of mine has a head on her shoulders. Top ten percent of her class.*

There'd always been an expensive present on her birthday with a card from thousands of miles away telling her to keep up the good work. Of course, she had. She would never have risked disappointing him.

Nothing ever changes, Ryan thought as she turned to stare at herself in the mirror. Ryan's strong. Ryan's practical. Ryan doesn't need all the things other women do—hugs, gentleness, romance.

They're right, of course, she told herself. It's foolish to be hurt. We wanted each other. We spent the night together. Why romanticize it? I don't have any claim on Pierce. And he has none on me. She fingered the lapel of his robe, then quickly dropped her hand. Moving swiftly, Ryan stripped and went to shower.

Ryan kept the water almost unbearably hot, allowing it to beat full force against her skin. She wasn't going to think. She knew herself well. If she kept her mind a blank, when she opened it again, she'd know what she had to do.

The air in the bath was steamy and moist when she stepped out to towel herself. Her moves were brisk again. There was work to be done—notes to write on ideas and plans. Ryan Swan, Executive Producer. That's what she had to concentrate on. It was time to stop worrying about the people who couldn't—or wouldn't—give her what she wanted. She had a name to make for herself in the industry. That was all that really mattered.

As she dressed, she was perfectly calm. Dreams were for sleeping, and she was wide awake. There were dozens of details to be seen to. She had meetings to set up, department heads to deal with. Decisions had to be made. She had been in Las Vegas long enough. She knew Pierce's style as well as she ever would. And, more important to her at the moment, she knew precisely what she wanted in the finished product. Back in Los Angeles, Ryan could start putting her ideas into motion.

It was going to be her first production, but she'd be damned if it was going to be her last. This time she had places of her own to go to.

Ryan picked up her comb and ran it through her damp hair. The door opened behind her.

"So, you're awake." Pierce smiled and started to cross to her. The look in her eyes stopped him. Angry hurt—he could feel waves of it.

"Yes, I'm awake," she said easily and continued to comb her hair. "I've been up for some time. My father called earlier. He wanted a progress report."

"Oh?" Her emotions weren't directed toward her father, Pierce decided, watching her steadily. "Have you ordered anything from room service?"

"No."

"You'll want some breakfast," he said, taking another step toward her. He went no farther, feeling the wall she had thrown up between them.

"No, actually, I don't." Ryan took out her mascara and began to apply it with great care. "I'll get some coffee at the airport. I'm going back to L.A. this morning."

The cool, matter-of-fact tone had his stomach muscles tightening. Could he have been so wrong? Had the night they had shared meant so little to her? "This morning?" he repeated, matching her tone. "Why?"

"I think I have a fairly good handle on how you work and what you'll want for the special." She kept her eyes focused only on her own in the mirror. "I should start on the preliminary stages, then we can set up a meeting when you're back in California. I'll call your agent."

Pierce bit off the words he wanted to say. He never put chains on anyone but himself. "If that's what you want."

Ryan's fingers tightened on the tube of mascara before she set it down. "We both have our jobs to do. Mine's in L.A.; yours, for the moment, is here." She turned to go to the closet, but he laid a hand on her shoulder. Pierce dropped it immediately when she stiffened.

"Ryan, have I hurt you?"

"Hurt me?" she repeated and continued on to the closet. Her tone was like a shrug, but he couldn't see her eyes. "How could you have possibly hurt me?"

"I don't know." He spoke from directly behind her. Ryan pulled out an armful of clothes. "But I have." He turned her to face him. "I can see it in your eyes."

"Forget it," she told him. "I will." She started to walk away, but this time he kept his hands firm.

"I can't forget something unless I know what it is." Though he kept his hands light, annoyance had crept into his tone. "Ryan, tell me what's wrong."

"Drop it, Pierce."

"No."

Ryan tried to jerk away again, and again he held her still. She told herself to be calm. "You *left* me!" she exploded and tossed the clothes aside. The passion erupted from her so swiftly, it left him staring and speechless. "I woke up and you were gone, without a word. I'm not used to one-night stands."

His eyes kindled at that. "Ryan—"

"No, I don't want to hear it." She shook her head vigorously. "I expected something different from you. I was wrong. But that's all right. A woman like me doesn't need all the niceties. I'm an expert on surviving." She twisted but found herself held against him. "Don't! Let me go, I have to pack."

"Ryan." Even as she resisted, he held her closer. The hurt went deep, he thought, and hadn't started with him. "I'm sorry."

"I want you to let me go, Pierce."

"You won't listen to me if I do." He stroked a hand down her wet hair. "I need you to listen."

"There's nothing to say."

Her voice had thickened, and he felt a wicked stab of self-blame. How could he have been so stupid? How could he not have seen what would be important to her?

"Ryan, I know a lot about one-night stands." Pierce drew her away, just far enough so that he could see her eyes. "That isn't what last night was for me."

She shook her head fiercely, struggling for composure. "There's no need for you to say that."

"I told you once, I don't lie, Ryan." He slipped his hands up to her shoulders. "What we had together last night is very important to me."

"You were gone when I woke up." She swallowed and shut her eyes. "The bed was cold."

"I'm sorry. I went down to smooth out a few things before tonight's show."

"If you'd woken me—"

"I never thought to wake you, Ryan," he said quietly. "Just as I never thought how you might feel waking up alone. The sun was coming in when you fell asleep."

"You were up as long as I was." She tried to turn away again.

"Pierce, *please!*" Hearing the desperation in the word, she bit her lip. "Let me go."

He lowered his hands, then watched as she gathered her clothes again. "Ryan, I never sleep more than five or six hours. It's all I need." Was this panic he was feeling watching her fold a blouse into a suitcase? "I thought you'd still be sleeping when I got back."

"I reached for you," she said simply. "And you were gone."

"Ryan—"

"No, it doesn't matter." She pressed her hands to her temples a moment and let out a deep breath. "I'm sorry. I'm acting like a fool. You haven't done anything, Pierce. It's me. I always expect too much. I'm always floored when I don't get it." Quickly, she began to pack again. "I didn't mean to make a scene. Please forget it."

"It isn't something I want to forget," he murmured.

"I'd feel less foolish if I knew you would," she said, trying to make her voice light. "Just put it down to a lack of sleep and a bad disposition. I should be going back, though. I've a lot of work to do."

He had seen her needs from the first—her response to gentleness, her pleasure in the gift of a flower. She was an emotional, romantic woman who tried very hard not to be. Pierce cursed himself, thinking how she must have felt to find the bed empty after the night they had spent together.

"Ryan, don't go." That was difficult for him. It was something he never asked of anyone.

Her fingers hesitated at the locks of her suitcase. Clicking them shut, Ryan set it on the floor, then turned. "Pierce, I'm not angry, honestly. A little embarrassed, maybe." She managed a smile. "I really should go back and start things moving. There might be a change in the scheduling, and—"

"Stay," he interrupted, unable to stop himself. "Please."

Ryan remained silent a moment. Something she saw in his eyes had a block lodging in her throat. It was costing him something to ask. Just as it was going to cost her something to ask. "Why?"

"I need you." He took a breath after what was for him a staggering admission. "I don't want to lose you."

Ryan took a step toward him. "Does it matter?"

"Yes. Yes, it matters."

She waited for a moment but was unable to convince herself to walk out the door. "Show me," she told him.

Going to her, he gathered her close. Ryan shut her eyes. It was exactly what she had needed—to be held, just to be held. His chest was firm against her cheek, his arms strong around her. Yet she knew she was being held as if she were something precious. Fragile, he had called her. For the first time in her life, Ryan wanted to be.

"Oh, Pierce, I'm an idiot."

"No." He lifted her chin with a finger and kissed her. "You're very sweet." He smiled then and laid his forehead on hers. "Are you going to complain when I wake you up after five hours sleep?"

"Never." Laughing, she threw her arms around his neck. "Or maybe just a little."

She smiled at him, but his eyes were suddenly serious. Pierce slid a hand up to cup the back of her neck before his mouth lowered to hers.

It was like the first time—the gentleness, the feather-light pressure that turned her blood to flame. She was utterly helpless when he kissed her like this, unable to pull him closer, unable to demand. She could only let him take in his own time.

Pierce knew that this time the power was his alone. It made his hands move tenderly as they undressed her. He let her blouse slip slowly off her shoulders, down her back, to flutter to the floor. Her skin quivered as his hands passed over it.

Unhooking her trousers, he drew them down her hips, letting his fingers toy with the tiny swatch of silk and lace that rose high at her thighs. All the while his mouth nibbled at hers. Her breath caught, then she moaned as he trailed a finger inside the silk. But he didn't remove it. Instead, he slid his hand to her breast to stroke and tease until she began to tremble.

"I want you," she said shakily. "Do you know how much I want you?"

"Yes." He brushed soft, butterfly kisses over her face. "Yes."

"Make love to me," Ryan whispered. "Pierce, make love to me."

"I am," he murmured and pressed his mouth to the frantic pulse in her neck.

"Now," she demanded, too weak to pull him to her.

He laughed, deep in his throat, and lowered her to the bed. "You drove me mad last night, Miss Swan, touching me like this." Pierce trailed a finger down the center of her body, stopping to linger at the soft mound between her legs. Slowly, lazily, he took his mouth to follow the trail.

In the night a madness had been on him. He had known impatience, desperation. He had taken her again and again, passionately, but had been unable to savor. It was as though he had been starved, and greed had driven him. Now, though he wanted her no less, he could restrain the need. He could taste and sample and enjoy.

Ryan's limbs were heavy. She couldn't move them, could only let him touch and caress and kiss wherever he wished. The strength that had driven her the night before had been replaced by a honeyed weakness. She lay steeped in it.

His mouth loitered at her waist, his tongue circling lower while he ran his hands lightly over her, tracing the shape of her breasts, stroking her neck and shoulders. He teased rather than possessed, aroused rather than fulfilled.

He caught the waistband of the silk in his teeth and took it inches lower. Ryan arched and moaned. But it was the skin of her thigh he tasted, savoring until she knew madness was only a breath away. She heard herself sighing his name, a soft, urgent sound, but he made no answer. His mouth was busy doing wonderful things to the back of her knee.

Ryan felt the heated skin of his chest brush over her leg, though she had no idea how or when he had rid himself of his shirt. She had never been more aware of her own body. She learned of the drugging, heavenly pleasure that could come from the touch of a fingertip on the skin.

He was lifting her, Ryan thought mistily, though her back was pressed into the bed. He was levitating her, making her float. He was showing her magic, but this trance was no illusion.

They were both naked now, wrapped together as his mouth journeyed back to hers. He kissed her slowly, deeply, until she was limp. His nimble fingers aroused. She hadn't known passion could pull two ways at once—into searing fire and into the clouds.

Her breath was heaving, but still he waited. He would give her everything first, every dram of pleasure, every dark delight he knew. Her skin was like water in his hands, flowing, rippling. He nibbled and sucked gently on her swollen lips and waited for her final moan of surrender.

"Now, love?" he asked, spreading light, whispering kisses over her face. "Now?"

She couldn't answer. She was beyond words and reason. That was where he wanted her. Exhilarated, he laughed and pressed his mouth to her throat. "You're mine, Ryan. Tell me. Mine."

"Yes." It came out on a husky breath, barely audible. "Yours." But his mouth swallowed the words even as she said them. "Take me." She didn't hear herself say it. She thought the demand was only in her brain, but then he was inside her. Ryan gasped and arched to meet him. And still he moved with painful slowness.

The blood was roaring in her ears as he drew the ultimate pleasure to its fullest. His lips rubbed over hers, capturing each trembling breath.

Abruptly, he crushed his mouth on hers—no more gentleness, no more teasing. She cried out as he took her with a sudden, wild fury. The fire consumed them both, fusing skin and lips until Ryan thought they both had died.

Pierce lay on her, resting his head between her breasts. Under his ear he heard the thunder of her heartbeat. She had yet to stop trembling. Her arms were twined around him, with one hand still tangled in his hair. He didn't want to move. He wanted to keep her like this—alone, naked, his. The fierce desire for possession shook him. It wasn't his way. Had never been his way before Ryan. The drive was too strong to resist.

"Tell me again," he demanded, lifting his face to watch hers.

Ryan's eyes opened slowly. She was drugged with love, sated with pleasure. "Tell you what?"

His mouth came to hers again, seeking, then lingered to draw the last taste. When he lifted it, his eyes were dark and demanding. "Tell me that you're mine, Ryan."

"Yours," she murmured as her eyes closed again. She sighed into sleep. "For as long as you want me."

Pierce frowned at her answer and started to speak, but her breathing was slow and even. Shifting, he lay beside her and pulled her close.

This time he would wait until she woke.

Chapter 10

Ryan had never known time to pass so quickly. She should have been glad of it. When Pierce's Las Vegas engagement was over, they could begin work on the special. It was something she was eager to do, for herself and for him. She knew it could be the turning point of her career.

Yet she found herself wishing the hours wouldn't fly by. There was something fanciful about Vegas, with its lack of time synchronization, its honky-tonk streets and glittery casinos. There, with the touch of magic all around, it seemed natural to love him, to share the life he lived. Ryan wasn't certain it would be so simple once they returned to the practical world.

They were both taking each day one at a time. There was no talk of the future. Pierce's burst of possessiveness had never reoccurred, and Ryan wondered at it. She nearly believed she had dreamed those deep, insistent words—*You're mine. Tell me.*

He had never demanded again, nor had he given her any words of love. He was gentle, at times achingly so, with words or looks or gestures. But he was never completely free with her. Nor was Ryan ever completely free with him. Trusting came easily to neither of them.

On closing night Ryan dressed carefully. She wanted a special evening. Champagne, she decided as she slipped into a frothy dress in a rainbow of hues. She would order champagne to be sent up to the suite after the performance. They had one long, last night to spend together before the idyll ended.

Ryan studied herself critically in the mirror. The dress was sheer and much more daring, she noted, than her usual style. Pierce would say it was more Ryan than Miss Swan, she thought and laughed. He would be right, as always. At the moment she didn't feel at all like Miss Swan. Tomorrow would be soon enough for business suits.

She dabbed perfume on her wrists, then at the hollow between her breasts.

"Ryan, if you want dinner before the show, you'll have to hurry along. It's nearly . . ." Pierce broke off as he came into the room. He stopped to stare at her. The dress floated here, clung there, wisping enticingly over her breasts in colors that melded and ran like a painting left in the rain.

"You're so lovely," he murmured, feeling the familiar thrill along his skin. "Like something I might have dreamed."

When he spoke like that, he had her heart melting and her pulse racing at the same time. "A dream?" Ryan walked to him and slid her arms around his neck. "What sort of a dream would you like me to be?" She kissed one cheek, then the other. "Will you conjure a dream for me, Pierce?"

"You smell of jasmine." He buried his face in her neck. He thought he had never wanted anything—anyone—so much in his life. "It drives me mad."

"A woman's spell." Ryan tilted her head to give his mouth more freedom. "To enchant the enchanter."

"It works."

She gave a throaty laugh and pressed closer. "Wasn't it a woman's spell that was Merlin's undoing in the end?"

"Have you been researching?" he asked in her ear. "Careful, I've been in the business longer than you." Lifting his face, he touched his lips to hers. "It isn't wise to tangle with a magician, you know."

"I'm not in the least wise." She let her fingers run up the back of his neck, then through the thick mane of his hair. "Not in the least."

He felt a wave of power—and a wave of weakness. It was always the same when she was in his arms. Pierce pulled her close again just to hold her. Sensing some struggle, Ryan remained passive. He had so much to give, she thought, so much emotion he would offer or hold back. She could never be sure which he would choose to do. Yet wasn't it the same with her? she asked herself. She loved him but hadn't been able to say the words aloud. Even as the love grew, she still wasn't able to say them.

"Will you be in the wings tonight?" he asked her. "I like knowing you're there."

"Yes." Ryan tilted back her head and smiled. It was so rare for him to ask anything of her. "One of these days I'm going to spot something. Even *your* hand isn't always quicker than the eye."

"No?" He grinned, amused at her continued determination to catch him. "About dinner," he began and toyed with the zipper at the back of her dress. He was beginning to wonder what she wore under it. If he chose, he could have the dress on the floor at her feet before she could draw a breath.

"What about it?" she asked with a gleam of mischief in her eyes.

The knock at the door had him swearing.

"Why don't you turn whoever it is into a toad?" Ryan suggested. Then, sighing, she rested her head on his shoulder. "No, that would be rude, I suppose."

"I rather like the idea."

She laughed and drew back. "I'll answer it. I can't have that on my conscience." Toying with his top button, she lifted a brow. "You won't forget what you were thinking about while I'm sending them away?"

He smiled. "I have a very good memory." Pierce let her go and watched her walk away. Miss Swan hadn't picked out that dress, he decided, echoing Ryan's earlier thoughts.

"Package for you, Miss Swan."

Ryan accepted the small plainly wrapped box and the card from the messenger. "Thank you." After closing the door, she set down the package and opened the envelope. The note was brief and typewritten.

Ryan,
Your report in good order. Expect a thorough briefing on Atkins project on your return. First full meeting scheduled one week from today. Happy birthday.

Your Father

Ryan read it over twice, then glanced briefly at the package. He wouldn't miss my birthday, she thought as she scanned the typed words a third time. Bennett Swan always did his duty. Ryan felt a surge of disappointment, of anger, of futility. All the familiar emotions of Swan's only child.

Why? she demanded of herself. Why hadn't he waited and given her something in person? Why had he sent an impersonal note that read like a telegram and a proper token his secretary no doubt selected? Why couldn't he have just sent his love?

"Ryan?" Pierce watched her from the doorway of the bedroom. He had seen her read the note. He had seen the look of emptiness in her eyes. "Bad news?"

"No." Quickly, Ryan shook her head and slipped the note into her purse. "No, it's nothing. Let's go to dinner, Pierce. I'm starving."

She was smiling, reaching out her hand for his, but the hurt in her eyes was unmistakable. Saying nothing, Pierce took her hand. As they left the suite, he glanced at the package she had never opened.

As Pierce had requested, Ryan watched the show from the wings. She had blocked all thoughts of her father from her mind. It was her last night of complete freedom, and Ryan was determined to let nothing spoil it.

It's my birthday, she reminded herself. I'm going to have my own private celebration. She had said nothing to Pierce, initially because she had forgotten her birthday entirely until her father's note had arrived. Now, she decided, it would be foolish to mention it. She was twenty-seven, after all, too old to be sentimental about the passing of a year.

"You were wonderful, as always," she told Pierce as he walked off-stage, applause thundering after him. "When are you going to tell me how you do that last illusion?"

"Magic, Miss Swan, has no explanation."

She narrowed her eyes at him. "I happen to know that Bess is in her dressing room right now, and that the panther—"

"Explanations disappoint," he interrupted. He took her hand to lead her into his own dressing room. "The mind's a paradox, Miss Swan."

"Do tell," she said dryly, knowing full well he was going to explain nothing.

He managed to keep his face seriously composed as he stripped off his shirt. "The mind wants to believe the impossible," he continued as he went into the bath to wash. "Yet it doesn't. Therein lies the fascination. If the impossible is *not* possible, then how was it done before your eyes and under your nose?"

"That's what I want to know," Ryan complained over the sound of running water. When he came back in, a towel slung over his shoulder, she shot him a straight, uncompromising look. "As your producer in this special, I should—"

"Produce," he finished and pulled on a fresh shirt. "I'll do the impossible."

"It's maddening not to know," she said darkly but did up the buttons of his shirt herself.

"Yes." Pierce only smiled when she glared at him.

"It's just a trick," Ryan said with a shrug, hoping to annoy him.

"Is it?" His smile remained infuriatingly amiable.

Knowing defeat when faced with it, Ryan sighed. "I suppose you'd suffer all sorts of torture and never breathe a word."

"Did you have some in mind?"

She laughed then and pressed her mouth to his. "That's just

the beginning," she promised dangerously. "I'm going to take you upstairs and drive you crazy until you talk."

"Interesting." Pierce slipped an arm around her shoulders and led her into the corridor. "It could take quite a bit of time."

"I'm in no hurry," she said blithely.

They rode to the top floor, but when Pierce started to slip the key into the lock of the suite, Ryan laid her hand on his. "This is your last chance before I get tough," she warned. "I'm going to make you talk."

He only smiled at her and pushed the door open.

"Happy birthday!"

Ryan's eyes widened in surprise, Bess, still in costume, opened a bottle of champagne while Link did his best to catch the spurt of wine in a glass. Speechless, Ryan stared at them.

"Happy birthday, Ryan." Pierce kissed her lightly.

"But how . . ." She broke off to look up at him. "How did you know?"

"Here you go." Bess stuck a glass of champagne in Ryan's hand, then gave her a quick squeeze. "Drink up, sweetie. You only get one birthday a year. Thank God. The champagne's from me—a bottle for now and one for later." She winked at Pierce.

"Thank you." Ryan looked helplessly into her glass. "I don't know what to say."

"Link's got something for you, too," Bess told her.

The big man shifted uncomfortably as all eyes turned to him. "I got you a cake," he mumbled, then cleared his throat. "You have to have a birthday cake."

Ryan walked over to see a sheet cake decorated in delicate pinks and yellows. "Oh, Link! It's lovely."

"You have to cut the first piece," he instructed.

"Yes, I will in a minute." Reaching up, Ryan drew his head down until she could reach it on tiptoe. She pressed a kiss on his mouth. "Thank you, Link."

He turned pink, grinned, then sent Bess an agonized look. "Welcome."

"I have something for you." Still smiling, Ryan turned to Pierce. "Will you kiss me, too?" he demanded.

"After I get my present."

"Greedy," he decided and handed her a small wooden box. It was old and carved. Ryan ran her finger over it to feel the places that had worn smooth with age and handling. "It's beautiful," she murmured. She opened it and saw a tiny silver symbol on a chain. "Oh!"

"An ankh," Pierce told her, slipping it out to fasten it around her neck. "An Egyptian symbol of life. Not a superstition," he said gravely. "It's for luck."

"Pierce." Remembering her flattened penny, Ryan laughed and threw her arms around him. "Don't you ever forget anything?"

"No. Now you owe me a kiss."

Ryan complied, then forgot there were eyes on them.

"Hey, look, we want some of this cake. Don't we, Link?" Bess slipped an arm around his thick waist and grinned as Ryan surfaced.

"Will it taste as good as it looks?" Ryan wondered aloud as she picked up the knife and sliced through it. "I don't know how long it's been since I've eaten birthday cake. Here, Link, you have the first piece." Ryan licked icing from her finger as he took it. "Terrific," she judged, then began to cut another slice. "I don't know how you found out. I'd forgotten myself until . . ." Ryan stopped cutting and straightened. "You read my note!" she accused Pierce. He looked convincingly blank.

"What note?"

She let out an impatient breath, not noticing that Bess had taken the knife and was slicing the cake herself. "You went in my purse and read that note."

"Went in your purse?" Pierce repeated, lifting a brow. "Really, Ryan, would I do something so crude?"

She thought about that for a moment. "Yes, you would."

Bess snickered, but he only sent her a mild glance. He accepted a piece of cake. "A magician doesn't need to stoop to picking pockets to gather information."

Link laughed, a deep rumbling sound that caught Ryan by surprise. "Like the time you lifted that guy's keys in Detroit?" he reminded Pierce.

"Or the earrings from the lady in Flatbush," Bess put in. "Nobody's got a smoother touch than you, Pierce."

"Really?" Ryan drew out the word as she looked back at him. Pierce bit into a piece of cake and said nothing.

"He always gives them back at the end of the show," Bess went on. "Good thing Pierce didn't decide on a life of crime. Think of what would happen if he started cracking safes from the outside instead of the inside."

"Fascinating," Ryan agreed, narrowing her eyes at him. "I'd love to hear more about it."

"How about the time you broke out of that little jail in Wichita, Pierce?" Bess continued obligingly. "You know when they locked you up for—"

"Have some more champagne, Bess," Pierce suggested, lifting the bottle and tilting it into her glass.

Link let out another rumbling laugh. "Sure would liked to've seen that sheriff's face when he looked in and saw an empty cell, all locked up and tidy."

"Jail-breaking," Ryan mused, fascinated.

"Houdini did it routinely." Pierce handed her a glass of champagne.

"Yeah, but he worked it out with the cops first." Bess chuckled at the look Pierce sent her and cut Link another piece of cake.

"Picking pockets, breaking jail." Ryan enjoyed the faint discomfort she saw in Pierce's eyes. It wasn't often she had him at a disadvantage. "Are there any other things I should know about?"

"It would seem you know too much already," he commented.

"Yes," She kissed him soundly. "And it's the best birthday present I've ever had."

"Come on, Link." Bess lifted the half-empty bottle of champagne. "Let's go finish this and your cake. We'll leave Pierce to work his way out of this one. You ought to tell her the one about that salesman in Salt Lake City."

"Good night, Bess," Pierce said blandly and earned another chuckle.

"Happy birthday, Ryan." Bess gave Pierce a flashing grin as she pulled Link out of the room.

"Thank you, Bess. Thank you, Link." Ryan waited until the door shut before she looked back at Pierce. "Before we discuss the salesman in Salt Lake City, why were you in a little cell in Wichita?" Her eyes laughed at him over the rim of her glass.

"A misunderstanding."

"That's what they all say." Her brow arched. "A jealous husband, perhaps?"

"No, an annoyed deputy who found himself locked to a bar stool with his own handcuffs." Pierce shrugged. "He wasn't appreciative when I let him go."

Ryan smothered a laugh. "No, I imagine he wasn't."

"A small wager," Pierce added. "He lost."

"Then instead of paying off," Ryan concluded, "he tossed you in jail."

"Something like that."

"A desperate criminal." Ryan heaved a sigh. "I suppose I'm at your mercy." Setting down her glass, she went to him. "It was very sweet of you to do this for me. Thank you."

Pierce brushed back her hair. "Such a serious face," he murmured and kissed her eyes shut. He thought of the hurt he had seen in them when she had read her father's letter. "Aren't you going to open the present from your father, Ryan?"

She shook her head, then laid her cheek on his shoulder. "No, not tonight. Tomorrow. I've been given the presents that matter already."

"He didn't forget you, Ryan."

"No, he wouldn't forget. It would be marked on his calendar. Oh, I'm sorry." She shook her head again, drawing away. "That was petty. I've always wanted too much. He does love me—in his own way."

Pierce took her hands in his. "He only knows his own way."

Ryan looked back up at him. Her frown cleared into an expression of understanding. "Yes, you're right. I've never thought about it that way. I keep struggling to please him so he'll turn to me one day and say, 'Ryan, I love you. I'm proud to be your father.' It's silly." She sighed. "I'm a grown woman, but I keep waiting."

"We don't ever stop wanting that from our parents." Pierce drew her close again.

Ryan thought of his childhood while he wondered about hers.

"We'd be different people, wouldn't we, if our parents had acted differently?"

"Yes," he answered. "We would."

Ryan tilted her head back. "I wouldn't want you to be any different, Pierce. You're exactly what I want." Hungrily, she pressed her mouth to his. "Take me to bed," she whispered. "Tell me what you were thinking all those hours ago before we were interrupted."

Pierce swept her up, and she clung, delighting in the strength of his arms. "Actually," he began, crossing to the bedroom, "I was wondering what you had on under that dress."

Ryan laughed and pressed her mouth to his throat. "Well, there's hardly anything there to wonder about at all."

The bedroom was dark and quiet as Ryan lay curled up at Pierce's side. His fingers played absently with her hair. He thought she was sleeping; she was very still. He didn't mind his own wakefulness. It allowed him to enjoy the feel of her skin against his, the silken texture of her hair. While she slept, he could touch her without arousing her, only to comfort himself that she was there. He didn't like knowing she wouldn't be in his bed the following night.

"What are you thinking about?" she murmured and startled him.

"About you." He drew her closer. "I thought you were sleeping."

"No." He felt the brush of her lashes on his shoulder as she opened her eyes. "I was thinking about you." Lifting her finger, she traced it along his jawline. "Where did you get this scar?"

He didn't answer immediately. Ryan realized she'd unwittingly probed into his past. "I suppose it was in a battle with a sorceress," she said lightly, wishing she could take the question back.

"Not quite so romantic. I fell down some stairs when I was a kid."

She held her breath a moment. She hadn't expected him to volunteer anything on his past, even so small a detail. Shifting, she rested her head on his chest. "I tripped over a stool once and loosened a tooth. My father was furious when he found out. I was terrified it would fall out and he'd disown me."

"Did he frighten you so much?"

"His disapproval, yes. I suppose it was foolish."

"No." Staring up at the dark ceiling, Pierce continued to stroke her hair. "We're all afraid of something."

"Even you?" she asked with a half-laugh. "I don't believe you're afraid of anything."

"Of not being able to get out once I'm in," he murmured.

Surprised, Ryan looked up and caught the gleam of his eyes in the darkness. "Do you mean in one of your escapes?"

"What?" He brought his thoughts back to her. He hadn't realized he had spoken aloud.

"Why do you do the escapes if you feel that way?"

"Do you think that if you ignore a fear it goes away?" he asked her. "When I was small," he said calmly, "it was a closet, and I couldn't get out. Now it's a steamer trunk or a vault, and I can escape."

"Oh, Pierce." Ryan turned her face into his chest. "I'm sorry. You don't have to talk about it."

But he was compelled to. For the first time since his childhood, Pierce heard himself speak of it. "Do you know, I think that the memory of scent stays with you longer than anything else. I could always remember the scent of my father so clearly. It wasn't until ten years after I last saw him that I learned what it was. He smelled of gin. I couldn't have told you what he looked like, but I remembered that smell."

He continued to stare up at the ceiling as he spoke. Ryan knew he had forgotten her as he went back into his own past. "One night when I was about fifteen, I was down in the cellar. I used to like to explore down there when everyone was in bed. I came across the janitor passed out in a corner with a bottle of gin. That smell—I remember being terrified for a moment without having any idea why. But I went over and picked up the bottle, and then I knew. I stopped being afraid."

Pierce was silent for a long time, and Ryan said nothing. She waited, wanting him to continue yet knowing she couldn't ask him to. The room was quiet but for the sound of his heart beating under her ear.

"He was a very cruel, very sick man," Pierce murmured, and she knew he spoke again of his father. "For years I was certain that meant I had the same sickness."

Gripping him tighter, Ryan shook her head. "There's nothing cruel in you," she whispered. "Nothing."

"Would you think so if I told you where I came from?" he wondered. "Would you be willing to let me touch you then?"

Ryan lifted her head and swallowed tears. "Bess told me a week ago," she said steadily. "And I'm here." He said nothing, but she felt his hand fall away from her hair. "You have no right to be angry with her. She's the most loyal, the most loving woman I've ever met. She told me because she knew I cared, knew I needed to understand you."

He was very still. "When?"

"The night . . ." Ryan hesitated and took a breath. "Opening night." She wished she could see his expression, but the darkness cloaked it. "You said we'd be lovers when I knew you," she reminded him. "You were right." Because her voice trembled, she swallowed. "Are you sorry?"

It seemed to her an eternity before he answered. "No." Pierce drew her down to him again. "No." He kissed her temple. "How could I be sorry to be your lover?"

"Then don't be sorry that I know you. You're the most magnificent man I've ever met."

He laughed at that, half amused, half moved. And relieved, he discovered. The relief was tremendous. It made him laugh again. "Ryan, what an incredible thing to say."

She tilted up her chin. There would be no tears for him. "It's very true, but I won't tell you again. You'll get conceited." She lifted her palm to his cheek. "But just for tonight I'll let you enjoy it. And besides," she added, pulling his ear. "I like the way your eyebrows sweep up at the ends." She kissed his mouth, then let her lips roam his face. "And the way you write your name."

"The way I what?" he asked.

"On the contracts," Ryan elaborated, still planting light kisses all over his face. "It's very dashing." She felt the smile move his cheeks. "What do you like about me?" she demanded.

"Your taste," he said instantly. "It's impeccable."

Ryan bit his bottom lip, but he only rolled her over and turned the punishment into a very satisfying kiss. "I knew it would make you conceited," "she said disgustedly. "I'm going to sleep."

"I don't think so," Pierce corrected, then lowered his mouth.

He was right again.

Chapter 11

Saying goodbye to Pierce was one of the most difficult things Ryan had ever done. She had been tempted to forget every obligation, all of her ambitions, and ask him to take her with him. What were ambitions but empty goals if she was without him? She would tell him that she loved him, that nothing mattered but that they be together.

But when they had parted at the airport, she made herself smile, kiss him goodbye, and let go. She had to drive into Los Angeles, and he had to drive up the coast. The work that had brought them together would also keep them apart.

There had still been no talk of the future. Ryan had come to learn that Pierce didn't speak of tomorrows. That he had spoken to her of his past, however briefly, reassured her. It was a step, perhaps a bigger one than either of them realized.

Time, Ryan thought, would tell if what had been between them in Las Vegas would strengthen or fade. This was the period of waiting. She knew that if he had regrets they would surface now while they were apart. Absence didn't always make the heart grow fonder. It also allowed the blood and the brain to cool. Doubts had a habit of forming when there was time to think. When he came to L.A. for the first meetings, she would have her answer.

When Ryan entered her office, she glanced at her watch and ruefully realized that time and schedules were part of her world again. She had left Pierce only an hour before and missed him unbearably already. Was he thinking of her—right now, at this moment? If she concentrated hard enough, would he know that she thought of him? With a sigh Ryan sat behind her desk. Since she had become involved with Pierce, she'd become freer with her imagination. There were times, she had to admit, that she believed in magic.

What's happened to you, Miss Swan? she asked herself. Your feet aren't on the ground, where they belong. Love, she mused and cupped her chin on her hands. When you're in love, nothing's impossible.

Who could say why her father had taken ill and sent her to Pierce? What force had guided her hand to choose that fateful card from the Tarot deck? Why had the cat picked her window in the storm? Certainly there were logical explanations for each step that had taken her closer to where she was at that moment. But a woman in love doesn't want logic.

It *had* been magic, Ryan thought with a smile. From the first moment their eyes had met, she had felt it. It had simply taken her time to accept it. Now that she did, her only choice was to wait and see if it lasted. No, she corrected, this wasn't a time for choices. She was going to make it last. If it took patience, then she'd be patient. If it took action, then she would act. But she was going to make it work, even if it meant trying her own hand at enchantment.

Shaking her head, she sat back in her chair. Nothing could be done until he was back in her life again. That would take a week. For now, there was still work to do. She couldn't wave a wand and brush the days away until he came back. She had to fill them. Flipping open her notes on Pierce Atkins, Ryan began to transcribe them. Less than thirty minutes later her buzzer sounded.

"Yes, Barbara."

"The boss wants you."

Ryan frowned at the litter of papers on her desk. "Now?"

"Now."

"All right, thanks." Swearing under her breath, Ryan stacked her papers, then separated what was in order to take with her. He might have given her a few hours to get organized, she thought. But the fact remained that he was going to be looking over her shoulder on this project. She was a long way from proving her worth to Bennett Swan. Knowing this, Ryan slipped papers into a folder and went to see her father.

"Good morning, Miss Swan." Bennett Swan's secretary glanced up as Ryan entered. "How was your trip?"

"It went very well, thank you." Ryan watched the woman's eyes shift briefly to the discreet, expensive pearl clusters at her ears. Ryan had worn her father's birthday gift knowing he would want to see them to assure himself they were correct and appreciated.

"Mr. Swan had to step out for a moment, but he'll be right with you. He'd like you to wait in his office. Mr. Ross is already inside."

"Welcome back, Ryan." Ned rose as she shut the door behind her. The coffee he held in his hand was steaming.

"Hello, Ned. Are you in on this meeting?"

"Mr. Swan wants me to work with you on this." He gave her a charming, half-apologetic smile. "Hope you don't mind."

"Of course not," she said flatly. Setting down the folder, she accepted the coffee Ned offered her. "In what capacity?"

"I'll be production coordinator," he told her. "It's still your baby, Ryan."

"Yes." With you as my proctor, she thought bitterly. Swan would still be calling the shots.

"How was Vegas?"

"Unique," Ryan told him as she wandered to the window.

"I hope you found some time to try your luck. You work too hard, Ryan."

She fingered the ankh at her neck and smiled. "I played some blackjack. I won."

"No kidding! Good for you."

After sipping at the coffee, she set the cup aside. "I think I have a firm basis for what will suit Pierce, Swan Productions and the network," she went on. "He doesn't need names to draw ratings. I think more than one guest star would crowd him. As for the set, I'll need to talk to the designers, but I have something fairly definite in mind already. As to the sponsors—"

"We can talk shop later," Ned interrupted. He moved to her and twined the ends of her hair around his fingers. Ryan stayed still and stared out of the window. "I've missed you, Ryan," Ned said softly. "It seemed as though you were gone for months."

"Strange," she murmured watching a plane cruise across the sky. "I've never known a week to pass so quickly."

"Darling, how long are you going to punish me?" He kissed the top of her head. Ryan felt no resentment. She felt nothing at all. Oddly, Ned had found himself more attracted to her since she had rejected him. There was something different about her now, which he couldn't quite put his finger on. "If you'd just give me a chance, I could make it up to you."

"I'm not punishing you, Ned." Ryan turned to face him. "I'm sorry if it seems that way."

"You're still angry with me."

"No, I told you before that I wasn't." She sighed, deciding it would be better to clear the air between them. "I was angry and hurt, but it didn't last. I was never in love with you, Ned."

He didn't like the faint apology in her voice. It put him on the defensive. "We were just getting to know each other." When he started to take her hands, she shook her head.

"No, I don't think you know me at all. And," she added without rancor, "if we're going to be honest, that wasn't what you were after."

"Ryan, how many times do I have to apologize for that stupid suggestion?" There was a combination of hurt and regret in his voice.

"I'm not asking for an apology, Ned, I'm trying to make myself clear. You made a mistake assuming I could influence my father. You have more influence with him than I have."

"Ryan—"

"No, hear me out," she insisted. "You thought because I'm Bennett Swan's daughter I have his ear. That's just not true and never has been. His business associates have more input with him than I do. You wasted your time cultivating me to get to him. And, leaving that aside," she continued, "I'm not interested in a man who wants to use me as a springboard. I'm sure we'll work together very well, but I have no desire to see you outside of the office."

They both jolted when they heard the office door shut.

"Ryan . . . Ross." Bennett Swan walked over to his desk and sat down.

"Good morning." Ryan fumbled a bit over the greeting before she took a chair. How much had he heard? she wondered. His face revealed nothing, so Ryan reached for the folder. "I've outlined my thoughts and ideas on Atkins," she began, "though I haven't had time to complete a full report."

"Give me what you have." He waved Ned to a chair, then lit a cigar.

"He has a very tight club act." Ryan laced her fingers together to keep them still. "You've seen the tapes yourself, so you know that his act ranges from sleight of hand to large, complicated illusions to escapes that take two or three minutes. The escapes will keep him off camera for that amount of time, but the public expects that." She paused to cross her legs. "Of course, we know there'll have to be modifications for television, but I see no problem. He's an extraordinarily creative man."

Swan gave a grunt that might have been agreement and held out his hand for Ryan's report. Rising, she handed it to him, then took her seat again. He wasn't in one of his better moods, she noted. Someone had displeased him. She could only be grateful she hadn't been that someone.

"This is pretty slim," he commented, scowling at the folder.

"It won't be by the end of the day."

"I'll talk to Atkins myself next week," Swan stated as he skimmed through the papers. "Coogar's going to direct."

"Good, I'd like to work with him. I want Bloomfield on the set design," she said casually, then held her breath.

Swan glanced up and stared at her. Bloomfield had been his

own choice. He'd decided on him less than an hour before. Ryan met the hard look unwaveringly. Swan wasn't altogether certain if he was pleased or annoyed that his daughter was one step ahead of him. "I'll consider it," he said and went back to her report. Quietly, Ryan let out her breath.

"He'll bring his own music director," she went on, thinking of Link. "And his own crew and gimmicks. If we have a problem, I'd say it'll be getting him to cooperate with our people in preproduction and on the set. He has his own way of doing things."

"That can be dealt with," Swan muttered. "Ross will be your production coordinator." Lifting his eyes, he met Ryan's.

"So I understand." Ryan met the look equally. "I can't argue with your choice, but I do feel that if I'm the producer on this project, I should pick my own team."

"You don't want to work with Ross?" Swan demanded as if Ned hadn't been sitting beside her.

"I think Ned and I will deal very well together," she said mildly. "And I'm sure Coogar knows the camera people he wants. It would be ridiculous to interfere with him. However," she added with a hint of steel in her voice, "I also know who *I* want working on this project."

Swan sat back and puffed for a moment on his cigar. The flush of color in his cheeks warned of temper. "What the hell do you know about producing?" he demanded.

"Enough to produce this special and make it a success," she replied. "Just as you told me to do a few weeks ago."

Swan had had time to regret the impulse that had made him agree to Pierce's terms. "You're the producer on record," he told her shortly. "Your name will be on the credits. Just do as you're told."

Ryan felt the tremor in her stomach but kept her eyes level. "If you feel that way, pull me now." She rose slowly. "But if I stay, I'm going to do more than watch my name roll on the credits. I know how this man works, and I know television. If that isn't enough for you, get someone else."

"Sit down!" he shouted at her. Ned sank a bit deeper in his own chair, but Ryan remained standing. "Don't give me ultimatums. I've been in this business for forty years." He banged his palm on the desk. "*Forty years!* So you know television," he said scornfully. "Pulling off a live show isn't like changing a damn contract. I can't have some hysterical little girl come running to me five minutes before air time telling me there's an equipment failure."

Ryan swallowed raw rage and answered coldly. "I'm not a hysterical little girl, and I've never come running to you for anything."

Completely stunned, he stared at her. The twinge of guilt made his anger all the more explosive. "You're just getting your feet wet," he snapped as he flipped the folder shut. "And you're getting them wet because I say so. You're going to take my advice when I give it to you."

"Your advice?" Ryan countered. Her eyes glistened with conflicting emotions, but her voice was very firm. "I've always respected your advice, but I haven't heard any here today. Just orders. I don't want any favors from you." She turned and headed for the door.

"Ryan!" There was absolute fury in the word. No one but no one walked out on Bennett Swan. "Come back here and sit down. *Young lady!*" he bellowed when she ignored the command.

"I'm not your young lady," she returned, spinning back. "I'm your employee."

Taken aback, he stared at her. What answer could he make to that? He waved his hand at a chair impatiently. "Sit down," he said again, but she stayed at the door. "Sit, sit," he repeated with more exasperation than temper.

Ryan came back and calmly took her place.

"Take Ryan's notes and start working on a budget," he told Ned.

"Yes, sir." Grateful for the dismissal, Ned took the folder and retreated. Swan waited for the door to close before he looked back at his daughter.

"What do you want?" he asked her for the first time in his life. The fact occurred to them both at the same moment.

Ryan took time to separate her personal and professional feelings. "The same respect you'd show any other producer."

"You haven't got any track record," he pointed out.

"No," she agreed. "And I never will if you tie my hands."

Swan let out a sigh, saw his cigar was dead and dropped it into an ashtray. "The network has a tentative slot, the third Sunday in May, nine to ten east coast time."

"That only gives us two months."

He nodded. "They want it before the summer season. How fast can you work?"

Ryan lifted a brow and smiled. "Fast enough. I want Elaine Fisher to guest star."

Swan narrowed his eyes at her. "Is that all?" he asked dryly.

"No, but it's a start. She's talented, beautiful and as popular with women as she is with men. Plus, she's had experience at working clubs and live theater," she pointed out as Swan frowned and said nothing. "That guileless, wide-eyed look of hers is the perfect contrast for Pierce."

"She's shooting in Chicago."

"That film wraps next week." Ryan sent him a calm smile. "And she's under contract with Swan. If the film goes a week or two over schedule, it won't matter," she added as he remained silent. "We won't need her in California for more than a few days. Pierce carries the show."

"She has other commitments," Swan pointed out.

"She'll fit it in."

"Call her agent."

"I will." Ryan rose again. "I'll set up a meeting with Coogar and get back to you." She paused a moment, then on impulse walked around his desk to stand beside his chair. "I've watched you work for years," she began. "I don't expect you to have the confidence in me you have in yourself or someone with experience. And if I make mistakes, I wouldn't want them to be overlooked. But if I do a good job, and I'm going to, I want to be sure *I* did it, not that I just got the credit for it."

"Your show," he said simply.

"Yes." Ryan nodded. "Exactly. There are a lot of reasons why this project is particularly important to me. I can't promise not to make mistakes, but I can promise you there's no one else who'll work harder on it."

"Don't let Coogar push you around," he muttered after a moment. "He likes to drive producers crazy."

Ryan smiled. "I've heard the stories, don't worry." She started to leave again, then remembered. After a brief hesitation, she leaned down to brush his cheek with her lips. "Thank you for the earrings. They're lovely."

Swan glanced at them. The jeweler had assured his secretary they were an appropriate gift and a good investment. What had he said in the note he had sent with them? he wondered. Chagrined that he couldn't remember, he decided to ask his secretary for a copy of it.

"Ryan." Swan took her hand. Seeing her blink in surprise at the gesture, he stared down at his own fingers. He had heard all of her conversation with Ned before he had come into the office. It had angered him, disturbed him, and now, when he saw his daughter stunned that he took her hand, it left him frustrated.

"Did you have a good time in Vegas?" he asked, not knowing what else to say.

"Yes." Uncertain what to do next, Ryan went back to business. "I think it was a smart move. Watching Pierce work up close gave me a good perspective. It's a much more overall view than a tape. And I got to know the people who work with him. That won't hurt when they have to work with me." She gave their joined hands another confused look. Could he be ill? she wondered and glanced quickly at his face. "I'll—I'll have a much more concise report for you by tomorrow."

Swan waited until she was finished. "Ryan, how old were you yesterday?" He watched her closely. Her eyes went from bewildered to bleak.

"Twenty-seven," she told him flatly.

Twenty-seven! On a long breath, Swan released her hand. "I've lost some years somewhere," he mumbled. "Go set up with

Coogar," he told her and shuffled through the papers on his desk. "Send me a memo after you contact Fisher's agent."

"All right."

Over the top of the papers, Swan watched her walk to the door. When she had left him, he sat back in his chair. He found it staggering to realize he was getting old.

Chapter 12

Producing, Ryan found, kept her as effectively buried in paper-work as contracts had. She spent her days behind her desk, on the phone or in someone else's office. It was hard, grueling work with little glamour. The hours were long, the problems endless. Yet she found she had a taste for it. She was, after all, her father's daughter.

Swan hadn't given her a free hand, but their confrontation on the morning of her return to L.A. had had its benefits. He was lis-tening to her. For the most part she found him surprisingly agree-able to her proposals. He didn't veto arbitrarily as she had feared he would but altered from time to time. Swan knew the business from every angle. Ryan listened and learned.

Her days were full and chaotic. Her nights were empty. Ryan had known Pierce wouldn't phone her. It wasn't his way. He would be down in his workroom, planning, practicing, perfecting. She doubted he would even notice the passing of time.

Of course, she could phone him, Ryan thought as she wandered around her empty apartment. She could invent any number of vi-able excuses for calling him. There was the change in the taping schedule. That was a valid reason, though she knew he'd already been informed through his agent. And there were at least a dozen minor points they could go over before the meeting the following week.

Ryan glanced thoughtfully at the phone, then shook her head.

It wasn't business that she wanted to discuss with him, and she wouldn't use it as a smoke screen. Going into the kitchen, she began to prepare herself a light supper.

Pierce ran through the water illusion for a third time. It was nearly perfect. But nearly was never good enough. He thought, not for the first time, that the camera's eye would be infinitely sharper than the human eye. Every time he had watched himself on tape, he had found flaws. It didn't matter to Pierce that only he knew where to look for them. It only mattered that they were there. He ran through the illusion again.

His workroom was quiet. Though he knew Link was upstairs at the piano, the sound didn't carry down to him. But he wouldn't have heard it if they had been in the same room. Critically, he watched himself in a long mirror as water seemed to shimmer in an unsupported tube. The mirror showed him holding it, top and bottom, while it flowed from palm to palm. Water. It was only one of the four elements he intended to command for Ryan's special.

He thought of the special as hers more than his own. He thought of her when he should have been thinking of his work. With a graceful movement of his hands, Pierce had the water pouring back into a glass pitcher.

He had almost phoned her a dozen times. Once, at three o'clock in the morning, his hand had been on the dial. Just her voice—he had only wanted to hear her voice. He hadn't completed the call, reminding himself of his vow never to put obligations on anyone. If he phoned, it meant he expected her to be there to answer. Ryan was free to do as she pleased; he had no claim on her. Or on anyone. Even the bird he kept had its cage door open at all times.

There had been no one in his life whom he had belonged to. Social workers had brought rules and compassion, but ultimately he had been just one more name in the file. The law had seen to it that he was properly placed and properly cared for. And the law had kept him bound to two people who didn't want him but wouldn't set him free.

Even when he loved—as with Link and Bess—he accepted but demanded no bonds. Perhaps that was why he continued to devise more complicated escapes. Each time he succeeded, it proved no one could be held forever.

Yet he thought of Ryan when he should have been working.

Picking up the handcuffs, Pierce studied them. They had fit cleanly over her wrist. He had held her then. Idly, he snapped one half over his right wrist and toyed with the other, imagining Ryan's hand locked to his.

Was that what he wanted? he wondered. To lock her to him? He remembered how warm she was, how steeped in her he would become after one touch. Who would be locked to whom? Annoyed, Pierce released himself as swiftly as he had snapped on the cuff.

"Double, double, toil and trouble," Merlin croaked from his perch.

Amused, Pierce glanced over. "I think you're quite right," he murmured, jiggling the cuffs in his hand a moment. "But then, you couldn't resist her either, could you?"

"Abracadabra."

"Abracadabra indeed," Pierce agreed absently. "But who's bewitched whom?"

Ryan was just about to step into the tub when she heard the knock on the door. "Damn!" Irritated by the interruption, she slipped back into her robe and went to answer. Even as she pulled the door open, she was calculating how to get rid of the visitor before her bath water chilled.

"Pierce!"

He saw her eyes widen in surprise. Then, with a mixture of relief and pleasure, he saw the joy. Ryan launched herself into his arms.

"Are you real?" she demanded before her mouth fastened on his. Her hunger shot through him, matching his own. "Five days," Ryan murmured and clung to him. "Do you know how many hours there are in five days?"

"A hundred and twenty." Pierce drew her away to smile at her.

"We'd better go inside. Your neighbors are finding this very entertaining."

Ryan pulled him in and shut the door by pressing him back against it. "Kiss me," she demanded. "Hard. Hard enough for a hundred and twenty hours."

His mouth came down on hers. She felt the scrape of his teeth against her lips as he groaned and crushed her to him. Pierce struggled to remember his strength and her fragility, but her tongue was probing, her hands were seeking. She was laughing that husky, aroused laugh that drove him wild.

"Oh, you're real." Ryan sighed and rested her head on his shoulder. "You're real."

But are you? he wondered, a little dazed by the kiss.

After one last hug she pulled out of his arms. "What are you doing here, Pierce? I didn't expect you until Monday or Tuesday."

"I wanted to see you," he said simply and lifted his palm to her cheek. "To touch you."

Ryan caught his hand and pressed the palm to her lips. A fire kindled in the pit of his stomach. "I've missed you," she murmured as her eyes clung to his. "So much. If I had known wishing you here would bring you, I'd have wished harder."

"I wasn't certain you'd be free."

"Pierce," she said softly and laid her hands on his chest. "Do you really think I want to be with anyone else?"

He stared down at her without speaking, but she felt the increased rate of his heartbeat under her hand. "You interfere with my work," he said at length.

Puzzled, Ryan tilted her head. "I do? How?"

"You're in my mind when you shouldn't be."

"I'm sorry." But she smiled, clearly showing she wasn't. "I've been breaking your concentration?"

"Yes."

She slid her hands up to his neck. "That's too bad." Her voice was mocking and seductive. "What are you going to do about it?"

For an answer, Pierce dragged her to the floor. The movement was so swift, so unexpected, Ryan gasped but the sound was swallowed by his mouth. The robe was whipped from her before she could draw a breath. Pierce took her to the summit so quickly, she was powerless to do anything but answer the desperate mutual need.

His clothes were gone with more speed than was reasonable, but he gave her no time to explore him. In one move Pierce rolled her on top of him, then, lifting her as though she were weightless, he set her down to plunge fully inside her.

Ryan cried out, stunned, exhilarated. The speed had her mind spinning. The heat had her skin drenched. Her eyes grew wide as pleasure went beyond all possibilities. She could see Pierce's face, damp with passion, eyes closed. She could hear each tearing breath as he dug his long fingers into her hips to keep her moving with him. Then a film was over her eyes—a white, misty film that hazed her vision. She pressed her hands to his chest to keep from falling. But she was falling, slowly, slowly, drained of everything.

When the mist cleared, Ryan found she was in his arms with his face buried in her hair. Their damp bodies were fused together.

"Now I know you're real, too," Pierce murmured and helped himself to her mouth. "How do you feel?"

"Dazed," Ryan answered breathlessly. "Wonderful."

Pierce laughed. Rising, he lifted her into his arms. "I'm going to take you to bed and love you again before you recover."

"*Mmm*, yes." Ryan nuzzled his neck. "I should let the water out of the tub first."

Pierce lifted a brow, then smiled. With Ryan half-dozing in his arms, he wandered the apartment until he found the bath. "Were you in the tub when I knocked?"

"Almost." Ryan sighed and snuggled against him. "I was going to get rid of whoever had interrupted me. I was very annoyed."

With a flick of his wrist, Pierce turned the hot water on full. "I didn't notice."

"Couldn't you see how I was trying to get rid of you?"

"I have very thick skin at times," he confessed. "I suppose the water's cooled off a bit by now."

"Probably," she agreed.

"You use a free hand with the bubbles."

"*Mmm-hmm.* Oh!" Ryan's eyes shot open as she found herself lowered into the tub.

"Cold?" He grinned at her.

"No." Ryan reached up and turned off the water that steamed hot into the tub. For a moment she allowed her eyes to feast on him—the long, lean body, the wiry muscles and narrow hips. She tilted her head and twirled a finger in the bubbles. "Would you like to join me?" she invited politely.

"The thought had crossed my mind."

"Please." She gestured with her hand. "Be my guest. I've been very rude. I didn't even offer you a drink." She gave him a sassy grin.

The water rose when Pierce lowered himself into it. He sat at the foot of the tub, facing her. "I don't often drink," he reminded her.

"Yes, I know." She gave him a sober nod. "You don't smoke, rarely drink, hardly ever swear. You're a paragon of virtue, Mr. Atkins."

He threw a handful of bubbles at her.

"In any case," Ryan continued, brushing them from her cheek, "I did want to discuss the sketches for the set design with you. Would you like the soap?"

"Thank you, Miss Swan." He took it from her. "You were going to tell me about the set?"

"Oh, yes, I think you'll approve the sketches, though you might want some minor changes." She shifted, sighing a little as her legs brushed against his. "I told Bloomfield I wanted something a little fanciful, medieval, but not too cluttered."

"No suits of armor?"

"No, just atmosphere. Something moody, like . . ." She broke off when he took her foot in his hand and began to soap it.

"Yes?" he prompted.

"A tone," she said as gentle pulses of pleasure ran up her leg. "Muted colors. The sort you have in your parlor."

Pierce began to massage her calf. "Only one set?"

Ryan trembled in the steamy water as he slid soapy fingers up her leg. "Yes, I thought—*mmm*—I thought the basic mood . . ." He moved his hands slowly up and down her legs as he watched her face.

"What mood?" He lifted a hand to soap her breast in circles while using his other to massage the top of her thigh.

"Sex," Ryan breathed. "You're very sexy onstage."

"Am I?" Through drugging ripples of sensation, she heard the amusement in the question.

"Yes, dramatic and rather coolly sexy. When I watch you perform . . ." She trailed off, struggling for breath. The heady scent of the bath salts rose around her. She felt the water lap under her breasts, just below Pierce's clever hand. "Your hands," she managed, steeped in hot, tortured pleasure.

"What about them?" he asked as he slipped a finger inside her.

"Magic." The word trembled out. "Pierce, I can't talk when you're doing things to me."

"Shall I stop?" She was no longer looking at him. Her eyes were closed, but he watched her face, using fingertips only to arouse her.

"No." Ryan found his hand under the water and pressed it against herself.

"You're so beautiful, Ryan." The water swayed as he moved to nibble at her breast, then at her mouth. "So soft. I could see you when I was alone in the middle of the night. I could imagine touching you like this. I couldn't stay away."

"Don't." Her hands were in his hair, pulling his mouth more firmly to hers. "Don't stay away. I've waited so long already."

"Five days," he murmured as he urged her legs apart.

"All my life."

At her words something coursed through him which passion wouldn't permit him to explore. He had to have her, that was all.

"Pierce," Ryan murmured hazily. "We're going to sink."

"Hold your breath," he suggested and took her.

"I'm sure my father will want to see you," Ryan told Pierce the next morning as he pulled into her space in the parking complex of Swan Productions. "And I imagine you'd like to see Coogar."

"Since I'm here," Pierce agreed and shut off the ignition. "But I came to see you."

With a smile Ryan leaned over and kissed him. "I'm so glad you did. Can you stay over the weekend, or do you have to get back?"

He tucked a lock of hair behind her ear. "We'll see."

She slid from the car. She could hope for no better answer.

"Of course, the first full meeting isn't scheduled until next week, but I imagine they'll accommodate you." They walked into the building. "I can make the calls from my office."

Ryan led him down the corridors briskly, nodding or answering now and again when someone greeted her. She was all business, he noted, the moment she stepped through the front doors.

"I don't know where Bloomfield is today," she continued as she pushed the button in the elevator for her floor. "But if he's unavailable, I can get the sketches and go over them with you myself." They stepped inside as she began to outline her day's schedule, balancing and altering to allow for Pierce's presence. "You and I might go over the timing, too," she continued. "We have fifty-two minutes to fill. And . . . "

"Will you have dinner with me tonight, Miss Swan?"

Ryan broke off what she was saying and found him smiling at her. The look in his eyes made it difficult for her to recall her plans for the day. She could only remember what had passed in the night. "I think I might fit that into my schedule, Mr. Atkins," she murmured as the elevator doors opened.

"You'll check your calendar?" he asked and kissed her hand.

"Yes." Ryan had to stop the doors from closing again. "And don't look at me like that today," she said breathlessly. "I'll never be able to function."

"Is that so?" Pierce let her pull him into the corridor. "I might consider it suitable revenge for all the times you've made it impossible for me to do my work."

Unnerved, Ryan led him into her office. "If we're going to manage to pull off this show . . ." she began.

"Oh, I have complete faith in the very organized, very dependable

Miss Swan," Pierce said easily. He took a chair and waited for her to
sit behind her desk.

"You're going to be difficult to work with, aren't you?" she asked.

"Most likely."

Wrinkling her nose at him, Ryan picked up the phone and
pushed a series of buttons. "Ryan Swan," she announced, deliberately keeping her eyes away from Pierce.

"Is he free?"

"Please hold, Miss Swan."

In a moment she heard her father's voice answer impatiently.
"Make it fast, I'm busy."

"I'm sorry to disturb you," she said automatically. "I have Pierce
Atkins in my office. I thought you might like to see him."

"What's he doing here?" Swan demanded, then continued before Ryan could answer. "Bring him up." He hung up without
waiting for her agreement.

"He'd like to see you now," Ryan said as she replaced the receiver.

Pierce nodded, rising as she did. The brevity of the phone conversation had told him a great deal. Minutes later, after entering
Swan's office, he learned a great deal more.

"Mr. Atkins" Swan rose to come around his massive desk with
his hand extended. "What a pleasant surprise. I didn't expect to
meet you personally until next week."

"Mr. Swan." Pierce accepted the offered hand and noted Swan
had no greeting for his daughter.

"Please sit down," he suggested with a wide sweep of his hand.
"What can I get for you? Coffee?"

"No, nothing."

"Swan Productions is very pleased to have your talents, Mr. Atkins." Swan settled behind his desk again. "We're going to put a
lot of energy into this special. Promotion and press have already
been set into motion."

"So I understand. Ryan keeps me informed."

"Of course." Swan sent her a quick nod. "We'll shoot in studio
twenty-five. Ryan can arrange for you to see it today if you'd like.

And anything else you'd like to see while you're here." He sent her another look.

"Yes, of course," she answered. "I thought Mr. Atkins might like to see Coogar and Bloomfield if they're available."

"Set it up," he ordered, dismissing her. "Now, Mr. Atkins, I have a letter from your representative. There are a few points we might go over before you meet the more artistic members of the company."

Pierce waited until Ryan had shut the door behind her. "I intend to work with Ryan, Mr. Swan. I contracted with you with that stipulation."

"Naturally," Swan answered, thrown off balance. As a rule talent was flattered to receive his personal attention. "I can assure you she's been hard at work on your behalf."

"I don't doubt it."

Swan met the measuring gray eyes levelly. "Ryan is producing your special at your request."

"Your daughter is a very interesting woman, Mr. Swan." Pierce waited a moment, watching Swan's eyes narrow. "On a professional level," he continued smoothly. "I have complete faith in her abilities. She's sharp and observant and very serious about her business."

"I'm delighted you're satisfied with her," Swan replied, not certain what lay beyond Pierce's words.

"It would be a remarkably stupid man who wasn't satisfied with her," Pierce countered, then continued before Swan could react. "Don't you find talent and professionalism pleasing, Mr. Swan?"

Swan studied Pierce a moment, then leaned back in his chair. "I wouldn't be the head of Swan Productions if I didn't," he said wryly.

"Then we understand each other," Pierce said mildly. "Just what are the points you would like to clear up?"

It was five-fifteen before Ryan was able to wind up the meeting with Bloomfield and Pierce. She'd been on the run all day, arranging spur-of-the-moment conferences and covering her scheduled work.

There had been no moment to spare for a *tête-à-tête* with Pierce. Now, as they walked down the corridor together from Bloomfield's office, she let out a long breath.

"Well, that seems to be about it. Nothing like the unexpected appearance of a magician to throw everybody into a dither. As seasoned as Bloomfield is, I think he was just waiting for you to pull a rabbit out of your hat."

"I didn't have a hat," Pierce pointed out.

"Would that stop you?" Ryan laughed and checked her watch. "I'll have to stop by my office and clear up a couple of things, touch base with my father and let him know the talent was properly fussed over, then . . ."

"No."

"No?" Ryan looked up in surprise. "Is there something else you wanted to see? Was there something wrong with the sketches?"

"No," Pierce said again, "You're not going back to your office to clear up a couple of things or to touch base with your father."

Ryan laughed again and continued to walk. "It won't take long, twenty minutes."

"You agreed to have dinner with me, Miss Swan," he reminded her.

"As soon as I clear my desk."

"You can clear your desk Monday morning. Is there something urgent?"

"Well, no, but . . ." She trailed off when she felt something on her wrist, then stared down at the handcuff. "Pierce, what are you doing?" Ryan tugged her arm but found it firmly chained to his.

"Taking you to dinner."

"Pierce, take this thing off," she ordered with amused exasperation. "It's ridiculous."

"Later," he promised before he pulled her to the elevator. He waited calmly for it to reach their floor as two secretaries eyed him, the cuffs and Ryan.

"Pierce," she said in undertones. "Take these off right now. They're staring at us."

"Who?"

"Pierce, I mean it!" She let out a frustrated moan as the doors opened and revealed several other members of Swan Productions' staff. Pierce stepped inside the car, leaving her no choice but to follow. "You're going to pay for this," she muttered, trying to ignore speculative stares.

"Tell me, Miss Swan," Pierce said in a friendly, carrying voice, "is it always so difficult to persuade you to keep a dinner engagement?"

After an unintelligible mutter, Ryan stared straight ahead.

Still handcuffed to Pierce, Ryan walked across the parking lot. "All right, joke's over," she insisted. "Take these off. I've never been so embarrassed in my life! Do you have any idea how—"

But her heated lecture was cut off by his mouth. "I've wanted to do that all day," Pierce told her, then kissed her again before she could retort.

Ryan tried her best to hang on to her annoyance. His mouth was so soft. His hand, as it pressed into the small of her back, was so gentle. She drew closer to him, but when she started to lift her arms around his neck, the handcuff prevented her. "No," she said firmly, remembering. "You're not going to sneak out of this one." Ryan pulled away, ready to rage at him. He smiled at her. "Damn you, Pierce," she said on a sigh. "Kiss me again."

He kissed her softly. "You're very exciting when you're angry, Miss Swan," he whispered.

"I *was* angry," she muttered, kissing him back. "I *am* angry."

"And exciting." He drew her over to the car.

"Well?" Holding their joined wrists aloft, she sent him an inquiring glance. Pierce opened the car door and gestured her inside. "Pierce!" Exasperated, Ryan jiggled her arm. "Take these off. You can't drive this way."

"Of course I can. You'll have to climb over," he instructed, nudging her into the car.

Ryan sat in the driver's seat a moment and glared at him. "This is absurd."

326 • Nora Roberts

"Yes," he agreed. "And I'm enjoying it. Move over."

Ryan considered refusing but decided he would simply lift her into the passenger seat bodily. With little trouble and less grace, she managed it. Pierce gave her another smile as he switched on the ignition.

"Put your hand on the gearshift and we'll do very well."

Ryan obeyed. His palm rested on the back of her hand as he put the car in reverse. "Just how long are you going to leave these on?"

"Interesting question. I haven't decided." He pulled out of the parking lot and headed north.

Ryan shook her head, then laughed in spite of herself. "If you'd told me you were this hungry, I'd have come along peacefully."

"I'm not hungry," he said easily. "I thought we'd stop and eat on the way."

"On the way?" Ryan repeated. "On the way where?"

"Home."

"Home?" A glance out the window showed her he was heading out of L.A. in the opposite direction of her apartment. "*Your* home?" she asked incredulously. "Pierce, that's a hundred and fifty miles from here."

"More or less," he agreed. "You're not needed in L.A. until Monday."

"Monday! Do you mean we're going there for the weekend? But I can't." She hadn't thought she could be any more exasperated than she already was. "I can't just pop in the car and go off for a weekend."

"Why not?"

"Well, I . . ." He made it sound so reasonable, she had to search for the flaw. "Because I can't. I don't have any clothes, for one thing, and—"

"You won't need them."

That stopped her. Ryan stared at him while a strange mixture of excitement and panic ran through her. "I think you're kidnapping me."

"Exactly."

"Oh."

"Any objections?" he asked, giving her a brief glance. "I'll let you know Monday," she told him and settled back in the seat, prepared to enjoy her abduction.

Chapter 13

Ryan awoke in Pierce's bed. She opened her eyes to streaming sunlight. It had barely been dawn when Pierce had awakened her to murmur that he was going down to work. Ryan reached for his pillow, drew it closer and lingered a few minutes longer in bed.

What a surprising man he was, she mused. She would never have thought he would do anything as outrageous as handcuffing her to him and bundling her off for a weekend with nothing more than the clothes on her back. She should have been angry, indignant.

Ryan buried her face in his pillow. How could she be? Could you be angry with a man for showing you—with a look, with a touch—that you were needed and desired? Could you be indignant when a man wanted you enough to spirit you off to make love to you as though you were the most precious creature on earth?

Ryan stretched luxuriously, then picked up her watch from the nightstand. Nine-thirty! she thought with a jolt. How could it be so late? It seemed only moments ago that Pierce had left her. Jumping from the bed, she raced to the shower. They only had two days together; she wasn't going to waste them sleeping.

When she came back into the bedroom with a towel wrapped around her, Ryan studied her clothes dubiously. There was something to be said for being kidnapped by a dashing magician, she admitted, but it was really too bad he hadn't let her pack something first. Philosophically, she began to dress in the suit she had worn the day before. He'd simply have to find her something else to wear, she decided, but for now she'd make do.

With some consternation Ryan realized she didn't even have her purse with her. It was still in the bottom drawer of her desk. She wrinkled her nose at the reflection in the mirror. Her hair was tumbled, her face naked of cosmetics. Not even a comb and a lipstick, she thought and sighed. Pierce was going to have to conjure up something. With this in mind she went downstairs to look for him.

When she came to the foot of the stairs, she saw Link getting ready to leave. "Good morning." Ryan hesitated, unsure what to say to him. He'd been nowhere to be seen when they had arrived the night before.

"Hi." He grinned at her. "Pierce said you were here."

"Yes, I—he invited me for the weekend." It seemed the simplest way to put it.

"I'm glad you came. He missed you."

Her eyes lit up at that. "I missed him, too. Is he here?"

"In the library. He's on the phone." He hesitated, and Ryan saw the faint pink flush in his cheeks.

Smiling, she came down the last step. "What is it, Link?"

"I—uh—I finished writing that song you liked."

"That's wonderful. I'd love to hear it."

"It's on the piano." Excruciatingly embarrassed, he lowered his eyes to his shoes. "You can play it later if you want to."

"Won't you be here?" She wanted to take his hand as she would a little boy's but felt it would only embarrass him more. "I've never heard you play."

"No, I'm . . ." His color deepened, and he sent her a quick look. "Bess and I . . . well, she wanted to drive to San Francisco." He cleared his throat. "She likes to ride the streetcars."

"That's nice, Link." On impulse, Ryan decided to see if she could give Bess a hand. "She's a very special lady, isn't she?"

"Oh, sure. There's nobody else like Bess," he agreed readily, then stared at his shoes again.

"She feels just the same way about you."

His eyes darted to her face, then over her shoulder. "You think so?"

"Oh, yes." Though she wanted badly to smile, Ryan kept her voice serious. "She told me how she first met you. I thought it was terribly romantic."

Link gave a nervous little laugh. "She was awful pretty. Lots of guys hang around her when we go on the road."

"I imagine so," Ryan agreed and gave him a mental shove. "But I think she has a taste for musicians. Piano players," she added when he looked back at her. "The kind who know how to write beautifully romantic songs. Time's wasting, don't you think?"

Link was staring at her as though trying to sort out her words. "Huh? Oh, yeah." He wrinkled his brow, then nodded. "Yeah, I guess so. I should go get her now."

"I think that's a very good idea." She did take his hand now, giving it a quick squeeze. "Have a good time."

"Okay." He smiled and turned for the door. With his hand on the knob, he stopped to look over his shoulder. "Ryan, does she really like piano players?"

"Yes, Link, she really does."

He grinned again and opened the door. "Bye."

"Goodbye, Link. Give Bess my love."

When the door shut, Ryan remained where she was a moment. What a sweet man, she thought, then crossed her fingers for Bess. They would be wonderful together if they could just get over the obstacle of his shyness. Well, Ryan thought with a pleased smile, she had certainly done all she could in her first attempt at matchmaking. The rest was up to the two of them.

Turning down the hall, she went to the library. The door was open, and she could hear Pierce's low-pitched voice as it carried to her. Even the sound of it had something stirring inside her. He was here with her, and they were alone. When she stood in the doorway, his eyes met hers.

Pierce smiled, and continued his conversation, gestured her inside. "I'll send you the exact specifications in writing," he said, watching Ryan enter and wander to a bookshelf. Why was it, he wondered, that the sight of her in one of those prim business suits never failed to excite him? "No, I'll need it completed in three weeks. I can't give you any more time than that," he continued with his eyes fixed on Ryan's back. "I need time to work with it before I can be sure I can use it."

Ryan turned around, then, perching on the arm of a chair, she watched him. He wore jeans with a short-sleeved sweatshirt, and his hair was disheveled, as though he had run his hands through it. She thought he had never looked more attractive, sunk back in an overstuffed chair, more relaxed than usual. The energy was still there, the live-wire energy that seemed to spark from him onstage or off. But it was on hold, she mused. He was more at ease in this house than he was anywhere else.

He continued to give instructions to whomever it was he spoke to, but Ryan watched his eyes skim her briefly. Something impish shot through her. Perhaps she could ruffle that calm of his.

Rising idly, she began to wander the room again, stepping out of her shoes as she did so. She took a book from the shelf, skimmed through it, then replaced it.

"I'll need the entire list delivered here," Pierce stated and watched Ryan slip out of her suit jacket. She draped it over the back of a chair. "Yes, that's exactly what I want. If you'll—" He broke off as she began to unbutton her blouse. She looked up when he stopped speaking and smiled at him. "If you'll contact me when you have . . ." The blouse slid to the floor before she casually unzipped her skirt. "When you have . . ." Pierce went on, struggling to remember what he had been saying, "the—ah—all the items, I'll arrange for the freight."

Bending over after she stepped out of her skirt, Ryan began to unhook her stockings. "No, that won't—it won't be necessary." She tossed her hair behind her shoulder and sent Pierce another smile. The look held for several pulsing seconds. "Yes," Pierce mumbled into the phone. "Yes, that's fine."

Leaving the pool of nylons on the discarded skirt, she straightened. Her chemise laced up the front. With one finger Ryan pulled at the small bow between her breasts until it loosened. She kept her eyes on his, smiling again when she watched them lower to where her fingers worked slowly with the laces.

"What?" Pierce shook his head. The man's voice had been nothing but an unintelligible buzz in his ear. "What?" he said again as the silk parted. Very slowly, Ryan drew it off. "I'll get back to you." Pierce dropped the receiver back on the hook.

"All finished?" she asked as she walked to him. "I wanted to talk to you about my wardrobe."

"I like what you have on." He pulled her into the chair with him and found her mouth. Tasting the wild need, she let herself go limp.

"Was that an important call?" she asked when his lips moved to her neck. "I didn't want to disturb you."

"The hell you didn't." He reached for her breast, groaning when he took possession. "God, you drive me crazy! Ryan . . ." His voice was rough with urgency as he slid her to the floor. "Now."

"Yes," she murmured even as he entered her.

He trembled as he lay on top of her. His breath was ragged. No one, he thought, no one had ever been able to destroy his control this way. It was terrifying. Part of him wanted to stand up and walk away—to prove he could still walk away. But he stayed where he was.

"Dangerous," he murmured in her ear just before he let the tip of his tongue trace it. He heard her sigh. "You're a dangerous woman."

"*Mmm*, how so?"

"You know my weaknesses, Ryan Swan. Maybe you are my weakness."

"Is that bad?" she murmured.

"I don't know." He lifted his head and stared down at her. "I don't know."

Ryan lifted a hand to tenderly brush the hair from his forehead. "It doesn't matter today. Today there's only the two of us."

The look he gave her was long and deep, as intense as the first time their eyes had met. "The more I'm with you, the more there are only the two of us."

She smiled, then pulled him back to cradle him in her arms. "The first time you kissed me, the whole world dropped away. I tried to tell myself you had hypnotized me."

Pierce laughed and reached up to fondle her breast. The nipple was still taut, and she quivered at his touch. "Do you have any idea how badly I wanted to take you to bed that night?" He ran his thumb lazily back and forth over the point of her breast, listening to her quickening breathing as he spoke. "I couldn't work, I couldn't sleep. I lay there thinking about how you'd looked in that little bit of silk and lace."

"I wanted you," Ryan said huskily as fresh passion kindled. "I was shocked that I'd only known you for a few hours and I wanted you."

"I would have made love to you like this that night." Pierce touched his mouth to hers. He kissed her, using his lips only until hers were hot and soft and hungry. Both of his hands were in her hair now, drawing it back from her face as his tongue gently plundered.

It seemed he would kiss her endlessly. There were soft, murmuring sounds as their lips parted and met again, then again. Hot, heady, unbearably sweet. He stroked her shoulders, lingering at the slope while the kiss went on and on. She knew the world centered on his lips.

No matter where else he touched, his mouth remained on hers. He might run his hands wherever he chose, but his kiss alone kept her prisoner. He seemed to crave her taste more than he craved breath. She gripped his shoulders, digging her nails into his flesh and totally unaware of it. Her only thought was that the kiss go on forever.

He knew her body was totally his and touched where it gave them both the most pleasure. At the slightest urging, her legs parted for him. He traced a fingertip up and down the inside of her thigh, delighting in its silken texture and in her trembling response. He passed over the center of her only briefly on the journey to her other thigh, all the while toying with her lips.

He used his teeth and his tongue, then his lips only. Her delirious murmuring of his name sent fresh thrills racing along his skin. There was the subtle sweep of her hips to trace, the curve of her waist. Her arms were satin smooth. He could find endless delight in touching only them. She was his—he thought it again and had to control an explosive urge to take her quickly. Instead, he let the kiss speak for him. It spoke of dark, driving needs and infinite tenderness.

Even when he slipped inside her, Pierce continued to savor the taste of her mouth. He took her slowly, waiting for her needs to build, forcing back his own passion until it was no longer possible to deny it.

His mouth was still crushed to hers when she cried out with the final flash of pleasure.

No one but her, he thought dizzily as he breathed in the scent of her hair. No one but her. Ryan's arms came around him to keep him close. He knew he was trapped.

Hours later Ryan slid two steaks under the broiler. She was dressed now in a pair of Pierce's jeans, cinched at the waist with a belt, with the legs rolled up several times to adjust for their difference in height. The sweatshirt bagged over her hips. Ryan pushed the sleeves up past the elbow while she helped him prepare dinner.

"Do you cook as well as Link?" she demanded, turning to watch him add croutons to the salad he was making.

"No. When you're kidnapped, Miss Swan, you can't expect gourmet meals."

Ryan went to stand behind him, then slipped her arms around his waist. "Are you going to demand a ransom?" With a sigh she rested her cheek on his back. She had never been happier in her life.

"Perhaps. When I'm through with you."

She pinched him hard, but he didn't even flinch. "Louse," she said lovingly, then slipped her hands under his shirt to trail her fingers up his chest. This time she felt him quiver.

"You distract me, Ryan."

"I was hoping to. It isn't the simplest thing to do, you know."

"You've been having a remarkable streak of success," he commented as she ran her hands over his shoulders.

"Can you really dislocate your shoulders to get out of a straight-jacket?" she wondered aloud as she felt the strength of their solidity.

Amused, he continued to cube cheese for the salad. "Where did you hear that?"

"Oh, somewhere," she said vaguely, not willing to admit she had devoured every write-up she could find on him. "I also heard you have complete control over your muscles." They rippled under her curious fingers. She pressed into his back, enjoying the faint forest scent that clung to him.

"Do you also hear that I only eat certain herbs and roots that I gather under a full moon?" He popped a morsel of cheese in his mouth before he turned to gather her into his arms. "Or that I studied the magic arts in Tibet when I was twelve?"

"I read that you were tutored by Houdini's ghost," she countered.

"Really? I must have missed that one. Very flattering."

"You really enjoy the ridiculous things they print about you, don't you?"

"Of course." He kissed her nose. "I'd have a sorry sense of humor if I didn't."

"And of course," she added, "if the fact and fantasy are so mixed, nobody ever knows which is which or who you are."

"There's that, too." He twined a lock of her hair around his finger. "The more they print about me, Ryan, the more actual privacy I have."

"And your privacy is important to you."

"When you grow up the way I did, you learn to value it."

Pressing her face to his chest, Ryan clung to him. Pierce put his hand under her chin and lifted it. Her eyes were already glistening with tears.

"Ryan," he said carefully, "there's no need for you to feel sorry for me."

"No." She shook her head, understanding his reluctance to accept sympathy. It had been the same with Bess. "I know that, but it's difficult not to feel sorry for a small boy."

He smiled, brushing a finger over her lips. "He was very resilient." He set her away from him. "You'd better turn those steaks."

Ryan busied herself with the steaks, knowing he wanted the subject dropped. How could she explain she was hungry for any detail of his life, anything that would bring him closer to her? And perhaps she was wrong, she thought, to touch on the past when she was afraid to touch on the future.

"How do you like them cooked?" she asked as she bent down to the broiler.

"*Mmm*, medium rare." He was more interested in the view she provided as she leaned over. "Link has his own dressing made up for the salad. It's quite good."

"Where did he learn to cook?" she asked as she turned the second steak.

"It was a matter of necessity," Pierce told her. "He likes to eat. Things were lean in the early days when we were on the road. It turned out he was a lot more handy with a can of soup than Bess or me."

Ryan turned and sent him a smile. "You know, they were going to San Francisco today."

"Yes." He quirked a brow. "So?"

"He's just as crazy about her as she is about him."

"I know that, too."

"You might have done something to move things along after all these years," she stated, gesturing with the kitchen fork. "After all, they're your friends."

"Which is exactly why I don't interfere," he said mildly. "What did you do?"

"Well, I didn't interfere," she said with a sniff. "I merely gave him a very gentle shove in the right direction. I mentioned that Bess has a preference for piano players."

"I see."

"He's so shy," she said in exasperation. "He'll be ready for social security before he works up the nerve to—to . . ."

"To what?" Pierce asked, grinning.

"To anything," Ryan stated. "And stop leering at me."

"Was I?"

"You know very well you were. And anyway—" She gasped and dropped the kitchen fork with a clatter when something brushed past her ankles.

"It's just Circe," Pierce pointed out, then grinned as Ryan sighed. "She smells the meat." He picked up the fork to rinse it off while the cat rubbed against Ryan's legs and purred lovingly. "She'll do her best to convince you she deserves some for herself."

"Your pets have a habit of catching me off guard."

"Sorry." But he smiled, not looking sorry at all.

Ryan put her hands on her hips. "You like to see me rattled, don't you?"

"I like to see you," he answered simply. He laughed and caught her up in his arms. "Though I have to admit, there's something appealing about seeing you wear my clothes while you putter around the kitchen in your bare feet."

"Oh," she said knowingly. "The caveman syndrome."

"Oh, no, Miss Swan." He nuzzled her neck. "I'm your slave."

"Really?" Ryan considered the interesting possibilities of the statement. "Then set the table," she told him. "I'm starving."

They ate by candlelight. Ryan never tasted a mouthful of the meal. She was too full of Pierce. There was wine—something smooth and mellow, but it might have been water, for all it mattered. In the baggy sweatshirt and jeans, she had never felt more like a woman. His eyes told her constantly that she was beautiful, interesting, desirable. It seemed as though they had never been lovers, never been intimate. He was wooing her.

338 • Nora Roberts

He made her glow with a look, with a soft word or the touch of his hand on hers. It never ceased to please her, even overwhelm her, that he had so much romance in him. He had to know that she would be with him under any circumstances, yet he courted her. Flowers and candlelight and the words of a man captivated. Ryan fell in love again.

Long after both of them had lost any interest in the meal, they lingered. The wine grew warm, the candles low. He was content to watch her in the flickering light, to let her quiet voice flow over him. Whatever needs built inside him could be soothed by merely running his fingers over the back of her hand. He wanted nothing more than to be with her.

Passion would come later, he knew. In the night, in the dark when she lay beside him. But for now it was enough to see her smile.

"Will you wait for me in the parlor?" he murmured and kissed her fingers one at a time. Shivery delight shot up her arm.

"I'll help with the dishes." But her thoughts were far, far away from practical matters.

"No, I'll see to it." Pierce turned her hand over and pressed his lips to her palm. "Wait for me."

Her knees trembled, but she rose when he drew her to her feet. She couldn't take her eyes from his. "You won't be long?"

"No." He slid his hands down her arms. "I won't be long, love." Gently, he kissed her.

Ryan walked to the parlor in a daze. It hadn't been the kiss but the one simple word of endearment that had her heart pounding. It seemed impossible, after what they had been to each other, that a casual word would send her pulses racing. But Pierce was careful with words.

And it was a night for enchantment, she thought as she entered the parlor. A night made for love and romance. She walked to the window to look out at the sky. Even the moon was full, as if it knew it had to be. It was quiet enough that she could just hear the sound of waves against rock.

They were on an island, Ryan imagined. It was a small, wind-swept island in some dark sea. And the nights were long. There was no phone, no electricity. On impulse, she turned from the window and began to light the candles that were scattered around the room. The fire was laid, and she set a match to the kindling. The dry wood caught with a crackle.

Rising, she looked around the room. The light was just as she wanted it—insubstantial with shadows shifting. It added just a touch of mystery and seemed to reflect her own feelings toward Pierce.

Ryan glanced down at herself and brushed at the sweatshirt. If only she had something lovely to wear, something white and filmy. But perhaps Pierce's imagination would be as active as hers.

Music, she thought suddenly and looked around. Surely he had a stereo, but she wouldn't have any idea where to look for it. Inspired, she went to the piano.

Link's staff paper was waiting. Between the glow from the fire behind her and the candles on the piano, Ryan could see the notes clearly enough. Sitting down, she began to play. It took only moments for her to be caught up in the melody.

Pierce stood in the doorway and watched her. Although her eyes were fixed on the paper in front of her, they seemed to be dreaming. He'd never seen her quite like this—so caught up in her own thoughts. Unwilling to break her mood, he stood where he was. He could have watched her forever.

In the candlelight her hair was only a mist falling over her shoulders. Her skin was pale. Only her eyes were dark, moved by the music she played. He caught the faint whiff of wood smoke and melting wax. It was a moment he knew he would remember for the rest of his life. Years and years could pass, and he would be able to close his eyes and see her just like this, hear the music drifting, smell the candles burning.

"Ryan." He hadn't meant to speak aloud, indeed had only whispered her name, but her eyes lifted to his.

She smiled, but the flickering light caught the glistening tears. "It's so beautiful."

"Yes." Pierce could hardly trust himself to speak. A word, a wrong move might shatter the mood. What he saw, what he felt might be an illusion after all. "Please, play it again."

Even after she had begun, he came no closer. He wanted the picture to remain exactly as it was. Her lips were just parted. He could taste them as he stood there. He knew how her cheek would feel if he laid his hand on it. She would look up at him and smile with that special warmth in her eyes. But he wouldn't touch her, only absorb all she was in this one special moment out of time.

The flames of the candles burned straight. A log shifted quietly in the grate. And then she was finished.

Her eyes lifted to his. Pierce went to her.

"I've never wanted you more," he said in a low, almost whispering voice. "Or been more afraid to touch you."

"Afraid?" Her fingers stayed lightly on the keys. "Why?"

"If I were to touch you, my hand might pass through you. You might only be a dream after all."

Ryan took his hand and pressed it to her cheek. "It's no dream," she murmured. "Not for either of us."

Her skin was warm and real under his fingers. He was struck by a wave of incredible tenderness. Pierce lifted her other hand, holding it as though it were made of porcelain. "If you had one wish, Ryan, only one, what would it be?"

"That tonight, just tonight, you'd think of nothing and no one but me."

Her eyes were brilliant in the dim, shifting light. Pierce drew her to her feet, then cupped her face in his hand. "You waste your wishes, Ryan, asking for something that already is." He kissed her temples, then her cheeks, leaving her mouth trembling for the taste of his.

"I want to fill your mind," she told him, her voice wavering, "so there's no room for anything else. Tonight I want there to be only me. And tomorrow—"

"Shh." He kissed her mouth to silence her, but so lightly she was left with only a promise of what was to come. "There's no one but you, Ryan." Her eyes were closed, and he brushed his lips delicately over the lids. "Come to bed," he murmured. "Let me show you."

Taking her hand, he walked through the room, putting out the candles. He lifted one, letting its quivering light show them the way.

Chapter 14

They had to be separated again. Ryan knew it was necessary in the course of preparing the special. When she was lonely for him, she had only to remember that last magic night they had spent together. It would be enough to hold her until she could see him again.

Though she saw him off and on during the next weeks, it was only professionally. He came to her for meetings or to oversee certain points of his own business. He kept to himself on these. Ryan still knew nothing about the construction of the props and gags he would use. He would give her a detailed list of the illusions he would perform, their time sequence and only the barest explanation of their mechanics.

Ryan found this frustrating, but she had little else to complain about. The set was forming along the lines she, Bloomfield and Pierce had ultimately agreed on. Elaine Fisher was signed for a guest appearance. Ryan had managed to hold her own through the series of tough, emotional meetings. And so, she recalled with amusement, had Pierce.

He could say more with his long silences and one or two calm words than a dozen frantic, bickering department heads. He sat through their demands and complaints with complete amiability and always came out on top.

He wouldn't agree to use a professional script for the show. It was as simple as that. He said no. And he had stuck to it—because he knew he was right. He had his own music, his own director, his own prop crew. Nothing would sway him from using his own people on key posts. He turned down six costume sketches with a careless shake of the head.

Pierce did things his own way and bent only when it suited him to bend. Yet Ryan saw that the creative staff, as temperamental as they came, offered little complaint about him. He charmed them, she noted. He had a way with people. He would warm you or freeze you—it only took a look.

Bess was to have the final say on her own wardrobe. Pierce simply stated that she knew best what suited her. He refused to rehearse unless the set was closed. Then he entertained the stage-hands with sleight of hand and card tricks. He knew how to keep control without rippling the waters.

Ryan, however, found it difficult to function around the restrictions he put on her and her staff. She tried reasoning, arguing, pleading. She got nowhere.

"Pierce." Ryan cornered him on the set during a break in rehearsal. "I have to talk to you."

"*Hmm?*" He watched his crew set up the torches for the next segment. "Exactly eight inches apart," he told them.

"Pierce, this is important."

"Yes, I'm listening."

"You can't bar Ned from the set during rehearsal," she said and tugged on his arm to get his full attention.

"Yes, I can. I did. Didn't he tell you?"

"Yes, he told me." She let out a sigh of exasperation. "Pierce, as production coordinator, he has a perfectly legitimate reason to be here."

"He gets in the way. Make sure there's a foot between the rows, please."

"Pierce!"

"What?" he said pleasantly and turned back to her. "Have I told you that you look lovely today, Miss Swan?" He ran the lapel of her jacket between his thumb and forefinger. "That's a very nice suit."

"Listen, Pierce, you've got to give my people a little more room." She tried to ignore the smile in his eyes and continued. "Your crew is very efficient, but on a production of this size we need more hands. Your people know your work, but they don't know television."

"I can't have your people poking into my props, Ryan. Or wandering around when I'm setting up."

"Good grief, do you want them to sign a blood oath not to reveal your secrets?" she demanded, waving her clipboard. "We could set it up for the next full moon."

"A good idea, but I don't know how many of your people would go along with it. Not your production coordinator, at any rate," he added with a grin. "I don't think he'd care for the sight of his own blood."

Ryan lifted a brow. "Are you jealous?"

He laughed with such great enjoyment she wanted to hit him. "Don't be absurd. He's hardly a threat."

"That's not the point," she muttered, miffed. "He's very good at his job, but he can hardly do it if you won't be reasonable."

"Ryan," he said, looking convincingly surprised, "I'm always reasonable. What would you like me to do?"

"I'd like you to let Ned do what he has to do. And I'd like you to let my people in the studio."

"Certainly," he agreed. "But not when I'm rehearsing."

"Pierce," she said dangerously. "You're tying my hands. You have to make certain concessions for television."

"I'm aware of that, Ryan, and I will." He kissed her brow. "When I'm ready. No," he continued before she could speak again, "you have to let me work with my own crew until I'm sure it's smooth."

"And how long is that going to take?" She knew he was winning her over as he had everyone from Coogar down.

"A few more days." He took her free hand. "Your key people are here, in any case."

"All right," she said with a sigh. "But by the end of the week the lighting crew will have to be in on rehearsals. That's essential."

"Agreed." He gave her hand a solemn shake. "Anything else?"

"Yes." Ryan straightened her shoulders and shot him a level look. "The time for the first segment runs over by ten seconds. You're going to have to alter it to fit the scheduled run of the commercials."

"No, you'll have to alter the scheduled run of commercials." He gave her a light kiss before he walked away.

Before she could shout at him, Ryan found there was a rosebud pinned to her lapel. Pleasure mixed with fury until it was too late to act.

"He's something, isn't he?"

Ryan turned her head to see Elaine Fisher. "Something," she agreed. "I hope you're satisfied with everything, Miss Fisher," she continued, then smiled at the petite, kittenlike blonde. "Your dressing room's agreeable?"

"It's fine." Elaine flashed her winning, toothy smile. "There's a bulb burned out on my mirror, though."

"I'll see to it."

Elaine watched Pierce and gave her quick, bubbling laugh. "I've got to tell you, I wouldn't mind finding him in my dressing room."

"I don't think I can arrange that for you, Miss Fisher," Ryan returned primly.

"Oh, honey, I could arrange it for myself if it weren't for the way he looks at you." She sent Ryan a friendly wink. "Of course, if you're not interested, I could try to console him."

The actress's charm wasn't easy to resist. "That won't be necessary," Ryan told her with a smile. "It's a producer's job to keep the talent happy, you know."

"Why don't you see if you could come up with a clone for me?" Leaving Ryan, she walked to Pierce. "Ready for me?"

Watching them work together, Ryan saw that her instincts had been on the mark. They were perfectly suited. Elaine's frothy blond beauty and ingenue charm masked a sharp talent and flair for comedy. It was the exact balance Ryan had hoped for.

Ryan waited, holding her breath as the torches were lit. It was the first time she had seen the illusion all the way through. The flames burned high for a moment, sending out an almost blinding light before Pierce spread his hands and calmed them. Then he turned to Elaine.

"Don't burn the dress," she cracked. "It's rented."

Ryan scribbled down a note to keep in the ad lib even as he began to levitate Elaine. In moments she was floating just above the flames.

"It's going well."

Glancing up, Ryan smiled at Bess. "Yes, for all the problems he causes, Pierce makes it impossible for it to go otherwise. He's relentless."

"Tell me about it." They watched him in silence a moment, then Bess squeezed Ryan's arm. "I can't stand it," she said in undertones to keep from disturbing the rehearsal. "I have to tell you."

"Tell me what?"

"I wanted to tell Pierce first, but . . ." She grinned from ear to ear. "Link and I—"

"Oh, congratulations!" Ryan interrupted and hugged her. Bess laughed. "You didn't let me finish."

"You were going to tell me you're getting married."

"Well, yeah, but—"

"Congratulations," Ryan said again. "When did it happen?"

"Just now, practically." Looking a little dazed, Bess scratched her head. "I was in my dressing room getting ready when he knocked on the door. He wouldn't come in, he just stood there in the doorway sort of shuffling his feet, you know? Then all of a sudden he asked me if I wanted to get married." Bess shook her head and laughed again. "I was so surprised, I asked him to whom."

"Oh, Bess, you didn't!"

"Yeah, I did. Well, you just don't expect that sort of question after twenty years."

"Poor Link," Ryan murmured with a smile. "What did he say?"

"He just stood there for a minute, staring at me and turning colors, then he said, 'Well, to me, I guess.'" She gave a low chuckle. "It was real romantic."

"I think it was lovely," Ryan told her. "I'm so happy for you."

"Thanks." After a breathy sigh, she looked over at Pierce again. "Don't say anything to Pierce, okay? I think I'll let Link tell him."

"I won't say anything," she promised. "Will you be married soon?"

Bess sent her a lopsided grin. "Sweetie, you better believe it. As far as I can see, we've already been engaged for twenty years, and that's long enough." She pleated the hem of her sweatshirt between her fingers. "I guess we'll just wait until after the special airs, then make the jump."

"Will you stay with Pierce?"

"Sure." She looked at Ryan quizzically. "We're a team. 'Course, Link and I will live at my place, but we wouldn't break up the act."

"Bess," Ryan began slowly. "There's something I've been wanting to ask you. It's about the final illusion." She sent Pierce a worried frown as he continued to work with Elaine. "He's so secretive about it. All he'll say so far is that it's an escape and he'll need four minutes and ten seconds from intro to finish. What do you know about it?"

Bess shrugged restlessly. "He's keeping that one close because he hasn't worked out all the bugs."

"What sort of bugs?" Ryan persisted.

"I don't know, really, except . . ." She hesitated, torn between her own doubts and her loyalty. "Except Link doesn't like it."

"Why?" Ryan put a hand on Bess's arm. "Is it dangerous? Really dangerous?"

"Look, Ryan, all the escapes can be dangerous, unless you're talking a straightjacket and handcuffs. But he's the best." She watched Pierce lower Elaine to the floor. "He's going to need me in a minute."

"Bess." She kept her hand firm on the redhead's arm. "Tell me what you know."

"Ryan." Bess sighed as she looked down at her. "I know how you feel about him, but I can't. Pierce's work is Pierce's work."

"I'm not asking you to break the magician's code of ethics," Ryan said impatiently. "He'll have to tell me what the illusion is, anyway."

"Then he'll tell you." Bess patted her hand but moved away.

The rehearsals ran over, as Pierce's rehearsals had a habit of doing. After attending a late afternoon production meeting, Ryan decided to wait for him in his dressing room. The problem of the final illusion had nagged at her throughout the day. She hadn't liked the worried look in Bess's eyes.

Pierce's dressing room was spacious and plush. The carpeting was thick, the sofa plump and wide enough to double as a bed. There was a large-screen television, a complex stereo system and a fully stocked bar that she knew Pierce never used. On the wall were a pair of very good lithographs. It was the sort of dressing room Swan reserved for their special performers. Ryan doubted that Pierce spent more than thirty minutes a day within its walls when he was in L.A.

Ryan poked in the refrigerator, found a quart of orange juice and fixed herself a cold drink before sinking down on the sofa. Idly, she picked up a book from the table. It was one of Pierce's, she noted, another work on Houdini. With absent interest she thumbed through the pages.

When Pierce entered, he found her curled up on the sofa, halfway through the volume.

"Research?"

Ryan's head shot up. "Could he really do all these things?" she demanded. "I mean this business about swallowing needles and a ball of thread, then pulling them out threaded. He didn't really do that, did he?"

"Yes." He stripped out of his shirt.

Ryan gave him a narrowed look. "Can you?"

He only smiled. "I don't make a habit of copying illusions. How was your day?"

"Fine. It says in here that some people thought he had a pocket in his skin."

This time he laughed. "Don't you think you'd have found mine by now if I had one?"

Ryan set the book aside and rose. "I want to talk to you."

"All right." Pierce pulled her into his arms and began to roam her face with kisses. "In a few minutes. It's been a long three days without you."

"You were the one who went away," she reminded him, then halted his wandering mouth with her own.

"I had a few details to smooth out. I can't work seriously here."

"That's what your dungeon's for," she murmured and found his mouth again.

"Exactly. We'll go to dinner tonight. Some place with candles and dark corners."

"My apartment has candles and dark corners," she said against his lips. "We can be alone there."

"You'll try to seduce me again."

Ryan laughed and forgot what she had wanted to talk to him about. "I *will* seduce you again."

"You've gotten cocky, Miss Swan." He drew her away.

"I'm not always so easy."

"I like challenges."

He rubbed his nose against hers. "Did you like your flower?"

"Yes, thank you." She circled his neck with her arms. "It kept me from harassing you."

"I know. You find me difficult to work with, don't you?"

"Extremely. And if you let anyone else produce your next special, I'll sabotage every one of your illusions."

"Well, then, I'll have to keep you and protect myself."

He touched his lips to hers gently, and the wave of love hit her with such force, such suddenness, Ryan clutched at him.

"Pierce." She wanted to speak quickly before the old fear prevented her. "Pierce, read my mind." With her eyes tightly shut, she buried her face against his shoulder. "Can you read my mind?"

Puzzled by the urgency in her tone, he drew her away to study her. She opened her eyes wide, and in them he saw that she was a little frightened, a little dazed. And he saw something else that had his heart taking an erratic beat.

"Ryan?" Pierce lifted a hand to her cheek, afraid he was seeing something only he needed to see. Afraid, too, that it was real.

"I'm terrified," she whispered. "The words won't come. Can you see them?" Her voice was jerky. She bit her lip to steady it. "If you can't, I'll understand. It doesn't have to change anything."

Yes, he saw them, but she was wrong. Once they were said, they changed everything. He hadn't wanted it to happen, yet he had known, somehow, they would come to this. He had known the moment he had seen her walk down the steps to his workroom. She was the woman who would change everything. Whatever power he had would become partially hers once he said three words. It was the only real incantation in a world of illusion.

"Ryan." He hesitated a moment but knew there was no stopping what already was. "I love you."

Her breath came out in a rush of relief. "Oh, Pierce, I was so afraid you wouldn't want to see." They drew together and clung. "I love you so much. So very much." Her sigh was shaky. "It's good, isn't it?"

"Yes." He felt her heartbeat match his own. "Yes, it's good."

"I didn't know I could be so happy. I wanted to tell you before," she murmured against his throat. "But I was so afraid. It seems silly now."

"We were both afraid." He drew her closer, but it still wasn't enough. "We've wasted time."

"But you love me," she whispered, only wanting to hear the words again.

"Yes, Ryan, I love you."

"Let's go home, Pierce." She ran her lips along his jaw. "Let's go home. I want you."

"Uh-uh. Now."

Ryan threw her head back and laughed. "Now? Here?"

"Here and now," he agreed, enjoying the flash of devilment in her eyes.

"Somebody might come in," she said and drew away from him.

Saying nothing, Pierce turned to the door and flicked the lock. "I don't think so."

"Oh." Ryan bit her lip, trying not to smile. "It looks like I'm going to be ravished."

"You could call for help," he suggested as he pushed the jacket from her shoulders.

"Help," she said quietly while he unbuttoned her blouse. "I don't think anyone heard me."

"Then it looks like you're going to be ravished."

"Oh, good," Ryan whispered. Her blouse slid to the floor.

They touched each other and laughed with the sheer joy of being in love. They kissed and clung as though there were no tomorrow. They murmured soft words and sighed with pleasure. Even when the lovemaking intensified and passion began to rule, there was an underlying joy that remained innocent.

He loves me, Ryan thought and ran her hands up his strong back. *He belongs to me.* She answered his kiss with fervor.

She loves me, Pierce thought and felt her skin heat under his fingers. *She belongs to me.* He sought her mouth and savored it.

They gave to each other, took from each other until they were more one than two. There was rising passion, an infinite tenderness and a new freedom. When the loving was over, they could still laugh, dizzy with the knowledge that for them it was only the beginning.

"You know," Ryan murmured, "I thought it was the producer who lured the talent to the couch."

"Didn't you?" Pierce let her hair run through his fingers.

With a chuckle Ryan kissed him between the eyes. "You were supposed to think it was all your idea." Sitting up, she reached for her blouse.

Pierce sat up behind her and ran a fingertip up her spine. "Going somewhere?"

"Look, Atkins, you'll get your screen test." She squealed when he bit her shoulder. "Don't try to change my mind," she said before she slipped out of reach. "I'm finished with you."

"Oh?" Pierce leaned back on his elbow to watch her dress.

"Until we get home." Ryan wriggled into her teddy, then began to hook her stockings. She eyed his nakedness. "You'd better get dressed before I change my mind. We'll end up locked in the building for the night."

"I could get us out when we wanted to go."

"There are alarms."

He laughed. "Ryan, really."

She shot him a look. "I suppose it is a good thing you decided not to be a criminal."

"It's simpler to charge for picking locks. People will always find a fascination in paying to see if it can be done." He grinned as he sat up. "They don't appreciate it if you do it for free."

Curious, she tilted her head. "Have you ever come across a lock you can't beat?"

"Given enough time," Pierce said as he reached for his clothes, "any lock can be opened."

"Without tools?"

He lifted a brow. "There are tools, and there are tools."

Ryan frowned at him. "I'm going to have to check for that pocket in your skin again."

"Anytime," he agreed obligingly.

"You could be nice and teach me just one thing, like how to get out of those handcuffs."

"Uh-uh." He shook his head as he slipped into his jeans. "They might come in handy again."

Ryan shrugged as if she didn't care anyway and began to button her blouse. "Oh, I forgot. I wanted to talk to you about the finale."

Pierce pulled a fresh shirt out of the closet. "What about it?"

"That's precisely what I want to know," Ryan told him. "What exactly do you have planned?"

"It's an escape, I told you." He drew on the shirt.

"I need more than that, Pierce. The show goes on in ten days."

"I'm working it out."

Recognizing the tone, Ryan stepped to him. "No, this isn't a solo production. I'm the producer, Pierce; you wanted it that way. Now, I can go along with some of your oddities about the staff." She ignored his indignant expression. "But I have to know exactly what's going to be aired. You can't keep me in the dark with less than two weeks to go until taping."

"I'm going to break out of a safe," he said simply and handed Ryan her shoe.

"Break out of a safe." She took it, watching him. "There's more to it than that, Pierce. I'm not a fool."

"I'll have my hands and feet manacled first."

Ryan stooped to retrieve her other shoe. His continued reluctance to elaborate brought on a very real fear. Wanting her voice to be steady, she waited a moment. "What else, Pierce?"

He said nothing until he had buttoned his shirt. "It's a play on a box within a box within a box. An old gimmick."

The fear grew. "Three safes? One within the other?"

"That's right. Each one's larger than the last."

"Are the safes airtight?"

"Yes."

Ryan's skin grew cold. "I don't like it."

He gave her a calm measuring look. "You don't have to like it, Ryan, but you don't have to worry, either."

She swallowed, knowing it was important to keep her head. "There's more, too, isn't there? I know there is, tell me."

"The last safe has a time lock," he said flatly. "I've done it before."

"A time lock?" Ice ran down her back. "No, you can't. It's just foolish."

"Hardly foolish," Pierce returned. "It's taken me months to work out the mechanics and timing."

"Timing?"

"I have three minutes of air."

Three minutes! she thought and struggled not to lose control. "And how long does the escape take?"

"At the moment, just over three minutes."

"Just over," Ryan repeated numbly. "Just over. What if something goes wrong?"

"I don't intend for anything to go wrong. I've been over and over it, Ryan."

She spun away, then whirled back to him. "I'm not going to

354 • Nora Roberts

allow this. It's out of the question. Use the panther business for the finale, but not this."

"I'm using the escape, Ryan." His voice was very calm and very final.

"No!" Panicked, she grabbed his arms. "I'm cutting it. It's out, Pierce. You can use one of your other illusions or come up with a new one, but this is out."

"You can't cut it." His tone never altered as he looked down at her. "I have final say; read the contract."

She paled and stepped back from him. "Damn you, I don't care about the contract. I know what it says. I wrote it!"

"Then you know you can't cut the escape," he said quietly.

"I won't let you do this." Tears had sprung to her eyes, but she blinked them away. "You can't do it."

"I'm sorry, Ryan."

"I'll find a way to scrub the show." Her breath was heaving with anger and fear and hopelessness. "I can find a way to break the contract."

"Maybe." He laid his hands on her shoulders. "I'll still do the escape, Ryan, next month in New York."

"Pierce, God!" Desperately, she clung to his arms. "You could die in there. It's not worth it. Why do you have to try something like this?"

"Because I can do it. Ryan, understand that this is my work."

"I understand that I love you. Doesn't that matter?"

"You know that it does," he said roughly. "You know how much."

"No, I don't know how much." Frantically, she pushed away from him. "I only know that you're going to do this no matter how much I beg you not to. You'll expect me to stand by and watch you risk your life for some applause and a write-up."

"It has nothing to do with applause or write-ups." The first hint of anger shot into his eyes. "You should know me better than that."

"No, no, I don't know you," she said desperately. "How can I understand why you insist on doing something like this? It's not necessary to the show, to your career!"

He struggled to hold his temper in check and answered calmly. "It's necessary to me."

"Why?" she demanded furiously. "Why is it necessary to risk your life?"

"That's your viewpoint, Ryan, not mine. This is part of my work and part of what I am." He paused but didn't go to her. "You'll have to accept that if you accept me."

"That's not fair."

"Maybe not," he agreed. "I'm sorry."

Ryan swallowed, fighting back tears. "Where does that leave us?"

He kept his eyes on hers. "That's up to you."

"I won't watch." She backed to the door. "I won't! I won't spend my life waiting for the time you go too far. I can't." She fumbled for the lock with trembling fingers. "Damn your magic," she sobbed as she darted through the door.

Chapter 15

After leaving Pierce, Ryan went straight to her father's office. For the first time in her life she entered without knocking. Annoyed at the interruption, Swan bit off what he was saying into the phone and scowled up at her. For a moment he stared at her. He'd never seen Ryan like this: pale, trembling, her eyes wide and brilliant with suppressed tears.

"I'll get back to you," he muttered and hung up. She still stood by the door, and Swan found himself in the unusual position of not knowing what to say. "What is it?" he demanded, then cleared his throat.

Ryan supported herself against the door until she was sure her legs were steady enough to walk. Struggling for composure, she crossed to her father's desk. "I need—I want you to cancel the Atkins special."

"What!" He sprang to his feet and glared at her. "What the hell is this? If you've decided to fall apart under the pressure, I'll get a replacement. Ross can take over. Damn it!" He slammed his hand on the desk. "I should have known better than to put you in charge in the first place." He was already reaching for the phone.

"Please." Ryan's quiet voice stopped him. "I'm asking you to pay off the contract and scrub the show."

Swan started to swear at her again, took another careful study of her face, then walked to the bar. Saying nothing, he poured a healthy dose of French brandy into a snifter. Blast the girl for making him feel like a clumsy ox. "Here," he said gruffly as he pushed the snifter into her hands. "Sit down and drink this." Not certain what to do with a daughter who looked shattered and helpless, he awkwardly patted her shoulder before he went back behind his desk.

"Now." Settled again, he felt more in control of the situation. "Tell me what this is all about. Trouble at rehearsals?" He gave her what he hoped was an understanding smile. "Now, you've been around the business long enough to know that's part of the game."

Ryan took a deep breath, then swallowed the brandy. She let it burn through the layers of fear and misery. Her next breath was steadier. She looked at her father again. "Pierce is planning an escape for the finale."

"I know that," he said impatiently. "I've seen the script."

"It's too dangerous."

"Dangerous?" Swan folded his hands on the desk. This he could handle, he decided. "Ryan, the man's a pro. He knows what he's doing." Swan tilted his wrist slightly so he could see his watch. He could give her about five minutes.

"This is different," she insisted. To keep from screaming, she gripped the bowl of the snifter tightly. Swan would never listen to hysterics. "Even his own people don't like it."

"All right, what's he planning?"

Unable to form the words, Ryan took another swallow of brandy. "Three safes," she began. "One within the other. The last one . . ." She paused for a moment to keep her voice even. "The last one has a time lock. He'll only have three minutes of air once he's closed inside the first safe. He's just—he's just told me that the routine takes more time than that."

"Three safes," Swan mused, pursing his lips. "A real show-stopper."

Ryan slammed down her glass. "Especially if he suffocates. Think what that will do for the ratings! They can give him his Emmy posthumously."

Swan lowered his brows dangerously. "Calm down, Ryan."

"I will not calm down." She sprang up from her chair. "He can't be allowed to do this. We have to cancel the contract."

"Can't do it." Swan lifted his shoulders to brush off the notion.

"Won't do it," Ryan corrected furiously.

"Won't do it," Swan agreed, matching her tone. "There's too much at stake."

"*Everything's* at stake!" Ryan shouted at him. "I'm in love with him."

He had started to stand and shout back at her, but her words took him by surprise. Swan stared at her. There were tears of desperation in her eyes now. Again he was at a loss. "Ryan." He sighed and reached for a cigar. "Sit down."

"No!" She snatched the cigar from his fingers and flung it across the room. "I will not sit down, I will not calm down. I'm asking for your help. Why won't you look at me?" she demanded in angry despair. "Really look at me!"

"I am looking at you!" he bellowed in defense. "And I can tell you I'm not pleased. Now you sit down and listen to me."

"No, I'm through listening to you, trying to please you. I've done everything you've ever wanted me to do, but it's never been enough. I can't be your son, I can't change that." She covered her face with her hands and broke down completely. "I'm only your daughter, and I need you to help me."

The words left him speechless. The tears unmanned him. He couldn't remember if he had ever seen her cry before; certainly she'd never done it this passionately. Getting awkwardly to his feet, he fumbled for his handkerchief. "Here, here now." He pushed the handkerchief into her hands and wondered what to do next. "I've always . . ." He cleared his throat and looked helplessly around the room. "I've always been proud of you, Ryan." When she responded by weeping more desperately, he stuck his hands in his pockets and lapsed into silence.

"It doesn't matter." Her voice was muffled behind the handkerchief. She felt a wave of shame for the words and the tears. "It doesn't matter anymore."

"I'd help you if I could," he muttered at length. "I can't stop him. Even if I could scrub the show and deal with the suits the network and Atkins would bring against Swan Productions, he'd do the damn thing anyway."

Faced with the bald truth, Ryan turned away from him. "There must be something . . ."

Swan shifted uncomfortably. "Is he in love with you?"

Ryan let out an unsteady breath and dashed the tears away. "It doesn't matter how he feels about me. I can't stop him."

"I'll talk to him."

Wearily, she shook her head. "No, it wouldn't do any good. I'm sorry." She turned back to her father. "I shouldn't have come here like this. I wasn't thinking straight." Looking down, she crumpled the handkerchief into a ball. "I'm sorry I made a scene."

"Ryan, I'm your father."

She looked up at him then, but her eyes were expressionless. "Yes."

He cleared his throat and found he didn't know what to do with his hands. "I don't want you to apologize for coming to see me." She only continued to look at him with eyes devoid of emotion. Tentatively, he reached out to touch her arm. "I'll do what I can to persuade Atkins to drop the routine, if that's what you want."

Ryan let out a long sigh before she sat down. "Thank you, but you were right. He'll do it another time, anyway. He told me so himself. I'm just not able to deal with it."

"Do you want Ross to take over?"

She pressed her fingers to her eyes. "No," she said with a shake of her head. "No, I'll finish what I started. Hiding won't change anything, either."

"Good girl," he said with a pleased nod. "Now, ah . . ." He hesitated while he sought the correct words. "About you and the magician." He coughed and fiddled with his tie. "Are you planning—that is, should I talk to him about his intentions?"

Ryan hadn't thought she could smile. "No, that won't be necessary." She saw relief in Swan's eyes and rose. "I'd appreciate some time off after the taping."

"Of course, you've earned it."

"I won't keep you any longer." She started to turn away, but he put a hand on her shoulder. Ryan glanced at him in surprise.

"Ryan . . ." He couldn't get a clear hold on what he wanted to say to her. Instead, he squeezed her shoulder. "Come on, I'll take you to dinner."

Ryan stared at him. When was the last time, she wondered, she had gone to dinner with her father? An awards banquet? A business party? "Dinner?" she said blankly.

"Yes." Swan's voice sharpened as his thoughts followed the same path Ryan's had. "A man can take his daughter to dinner, can't he?" He slipped his arm around her waist and led her to the door. How small she was! he realized with a jolt. "Go wash your face," he muttered. "I'll wait for you."

At ten o'clock the next morning Swan finished reading the Atkins contract a second time. A tricky business, he thought. It wouldn't be easy to break. But he had no intention of breaking it. That would not only be poor business sense but a useless gesture. He'd just have to deal with Atkins himself. When his buzzer sounded, he turned the contract facedown.

"Mr. Atkins is here, Mr. Swan."

"Send him in."

Swan rose as Pierce entered, and as he had done the first time, he walked across the room with his hand extended. "Pierce," he said jovially. "Thanks for coming up."

"Mr. Swan."

"Bennett, please," he said as he drew Pierce to a chair.

"Bennett," Pierce agreed, taking a seat.

Swan sat in the chair opposite him and leaned back. "Well, now, are you satisfied with how everything's going?"

Pierce lifted a brow. "Yes."

Swan took out a cigar. The man's too cool, he thought grudgingly. He doesn't give anything away. Swan decided to approach the subject from the side door. "Coogar tells me the rehearsals are smooth as silk. Worries him." Swan grinned. "He's a superstitious bastard, likes plenty of trouble before a taping. He tells me you could almost run the show yourself."

"He's a fine director," Pierce said easily, watching Swan light his cigar.

"The best," Swan agreed heartily. "We are a bit concerned about your plans for the finale."

"Oh?"

"This is television, you know," Swan reminded him with an expansive smile. "Four-ten is a bit long for one routine."

"It's necessary." Pierce let his hands rest on the arms of the chair. "I'm sure Ryan's told you."

Swan's eyes met the direct stare. "Yes, Ryan's told me. She came up here last night. She was frantic."

Pierce's fingers tensed slightly, but he kept his eyes level. "I know. I'm sorry."

"Look, Pierce, we're reasonable men." Swan leaned toward him, poking with his cigar. "This routine of yours sounds like a beauty. The time lock business is a real inspiration, but with a little modification—"

"I don't modify my illusions."

The cool dismissal had Swan blustering. "No contract's carved in stone," he said dangerously.

"You can try to break it," Pierce agreed. "It'll be a great deal more trouble for you than for me. And in the end it won't change anything."

"Damn it, man, the girl's beside herself!" Banging his thigh with his fist, Swan flopped back in the chair. "She says she's in love with you."

"She is in love with me," Pierce returned quietly and ignored the twist in his stomach.

"What the hell do you mean to do about it?"

"Are you asking me as her father or as Swan Productions?"

Swan drew his brows together and muttered for a moment. "As her father," he decided.

"I'm in love with Ryan." Pierce met Swan's stare calmly. "If she's willing to have me, I'll spend my life with her."

"And if she's not?" Swan retorted.

Pierce's eyes darkened, something flickered, but he said nothing. That was something he'd yet to deal with. In the brief passage of seconds Swan saw what he wanted to know. He pressed his advantage.

"A woman in love isn't always reasonable," he said with an avuncular smile. "A man has to make certain adjustments."

"There's very little I wouldn't do for Ryan," Pierce returned. "But it isn't possible for me to change what I am."

"We're talking about a routine," Swan tossed back, losing patience.

"No, we're talking about my way of life. I could drop this escape," he continued while Swan frowned at him, "but there'd be another one and still another. If Ryan can't accept this one now, how can she accept one later?"

"You'll lose her," Swan warned.

Pierce rose at that, unable to sit any longer. "Perhaps I've never had her." He could deal with the pain, he told himself. He knew how to deal with pain. His voice was even when he continued. "Ryan has to make her own choices. I have to accept them."

Swan rose to his feet and glared. "Damn if you sound like a man in love to me."

Pierce gave him a long, cold stare that had Swan swallowing. "In a lifetime of illusions," he said roughly, "she's the only thing that's real." Turning, he strode from the room.

Chapter 16

They would tape at six o'clock west coast time. By 4:00 p.m. Ryan had dealt with everything from an irate property manager to a frazzled hairstylist. There was nothing like a live broadcast to throw even the most seasoned veterans into a state of madness. As it was put to her by a fatalistic stagehand, "Whatever could go wrong, would." It wasn't what Ryan wanted to hear.

But the problems, the demands, the touch of insanity kept her from crawling into a convenient corner to weep. She was needed and had no choice but to be dependable. If her career was all she was going to have left, Ryan knew she had to give it her best shot.

She had avoided Pierce for ten days by keeping an emotional distance. They had no choice but to come together time and again, but only as producer and star. He made no attempt to close the gap between them.

Ryan hurt. At times it still amazed her how much. Still, she welcomed it. The hurt helped smother the fear. The three safes had been delivered. When she had forced herself to examine them, she had seen that the smallest was no more than three feet high and two feet across. The thought of Pierce folding himself into the small black box had her stomach rolling.

She had stood studying the largest safe with its thick door and complex time lock when she had sensed him behind her. When she had turned, they had looked at each other in silence. Ryan had felt the need, the love, the hopelessness before she had walked away from him. Neither by word nor gesture had he asked her to stay.

From then on Ryan had kept away from the safes, concentrating instead on the checking and rechecking of all the minute details of production.

Wardrobe had to be supervised. A broken spotlight needed repair at the eleventh hour. A sick technician had to be replaced. And timing, the most crucial element of all, had to be worked out to the last second.

There seemed to be no end to the last-minute problems, and she could only be grateful when each new one cropped up. There was no time for thinking, right up to the moment when the studio audience began to file in.

With her stomach in knots, her face composed, Ryan waited in the control booth as the floor director gave the final countdown.

It began.

Pierce was onstage, cool and competent. The set was perfect: clean, uncluttered and faintly mysterious with the understated lighting. In unrelieved black, he was a twentieth-century sorcerer with no need for magic wands or pointed hats.

Water flowed between his palms, fire shot from his fingertips. Ryan watched as he balanced Bess on the point of a saber, making her spin like a top, then drawing the sword out with a flourish until she spun on nothing at all.

Elaine floated on the torch flames while the audience held their breath. Pierce enclosed her in a clear glass bubble, covered it with red silk and sent it floating ten feet above the stage. It swayed gently to Link's music. When Pierce brought it down and whipped off the silk, Elaine was a white swan.

He varied his illusions—dashing, spectacular and simply beautiful. He controlled the elements, defied nature and baffled all.

"Going like a dream," Ryan heard someone say excitedly. "See if we don't cop a couple of Emmys for this one. Thirty seconds, camera two. God, is this guy good!"

Ryan left the control booth and went down to the wings. She

told herself she was cold because the air-conditioning in the booth was turned up so high. It would be warmer near the stage. The lights there shone hotly, but her skin stayed chilled. She watched while he did a variation on the transportation illusion he had used in Vegas.

He never glanced in her direction, but Ryan sensed he knew she was there. He had to know, because her thoughts were so completely centered on him.

"It's going good, isn't it?"

Looking up, Ryan saw Link beside her. "Yes, perfect so far."

"I liked the swan. It's pretty."

"Yes."

"Maybe you should go into Bess's dressing room and sit down," he suggested, wishing she didn't look so pale and cold. "You could watch on the TV in there."

"No. No, I'll stay."

Pierce had a tiger onstage, a lean, pacing cat in a gilt cage. He covered it with the same silk he had used on the bubble. When he removed it, Elaine was caged and the tiger had vanished. Knowing it was the last illusion before the final escape, Ryan took a deep breath.

"Link." She reached for his hand, needing something to hold on to.

"He'll be all right, Ryan." He gave her fingers a squeeze. "Pierce is the best."

The smallest safe was brought out, its door open wide as it was turned around and around to show its solidity. Ryan tasted the iron tang of fear. She didn't hear Pierce's explanation to the audience as he was manacled hand and foot by a captain of the Los Angeles Police Department. Her eyes were glued to his face. She knew the deepest part of his mind was already locked inside the vault. Already, he was working his way out. That's what she held on to as firmly as Link's hand.

He barely fit inside the first safe. His shoulders brushed the sides. He won't be able to move in there, she thought on a stab of panic. As the door was shut, she took a step toward the stage. Link held her by the shoulders.

"You can't, Ryan."

"But, God, he can't move. He can't breathe!" She watched with mounting horror as the second safe was brought out.

"He's already out of the cuffs," Link said soothingly, though he didn't like watching the safe that held Pierce lifted and locked inside the second one. "He'll be opening the first door now," he said to comfort himself as much as Ryan. "He works fast. You know, you've seen him."

"Oh, no." The third safe had the fear rocketing almost beyond her control. She felt a bright dizziness and would have swayed if Link's hands hadn't held her upright. The largest safe swallowed the two others and the man inside. It was shut, bolted. The time lock was set for midnight. There was no way in from the outside now.

"How long?" she whispered. Her eyes were glued to the safe, on the shiny, complicated timer. "How long since he's been in?"

"Two and a half minutes." Link felt a bead of sweat run down his back. "He's got plenty of time."

He knew the safes fit together so snugly that the doors could only be pushed open far enough for a child to crawl through. He never understood how Pierce could twist and fold his body the way he did. But he'd seen him do it. Unlike Ryan, Link had watched Pierce rehearse the escape countless times. The sweat continued to roll down his back.

The air was thin, Ryan could barely draw it into her lungs. That was how it was inside the safe, she thought numbly. No air, no light. "Time, Link!" She was shaking like a leaf now. The big man stopped praying to answer.

"Two-fifty. It's almost over. He's working on the last one now."

Gripping her hands together, Ryan began to count off the seconds in her head. The roaring in her ears had her biting down hard on her lip. She had never fainted in her life, but she knew she was perilously close to doing so now. When her vision blurred, she squeezed her eyes tight to clear it. But she couldn't breathe.

Pierce had no air now and neither did she. On a bubble of hysteria, she thought she would suffocate standing there as surely as Pierce would inside the trio of safes.

Then she saw the door opening, heard the unified gasp of relief from the audience before the burst of applause. He stood on the stage, damp with sweat and drawing in air.

Ryan swooned back against Link as darkness blocked out the spotlights. She lost consciousness for no more than seconds, coming back when she heard Link calling her.

"Ryan, Ryan, it's all right. He's out. He's okay."

Bracing herself against Link, she shook her head to clear it. "Yes, he's out." For one last second she watched him, then turning, she walked away.

The moment the cameras shut off, Pierce walked offstage. "Where's Ryan?" he demanded of Link.

"She left." He watched a trickle of sweat run down Pierce's face. "She was pretty upset." He offered Pierce the towel he'd been holding for him. "I think maybe she fainted for a minute."

Pierce didn't brush away the sweat, he didn't grin as he always did when an escape was completed. "Where did she go?"

"I don't know. She just left."

Without a word, Pierce went to look for her.

Ryan lay baking in the strong sun. There was an itch in the center of her back, but she didn't move to scratch it. She lay still and let the heat soak into her skin.

She had spent a week on board her father's yacht off the coast of St. Croix. Swan had let her go alone, as she requested, asking no questions when she had arrived at his house and asked for the favor. He'd made the arrangements for her and had taken her to the airport himself. Ryan was to think later that it was the first time he hadn't put her in a limo with a driver and sent her off to catch a plane by herself.

For days now she had lain in the sun, swam and kept her mind a blank. She hadn't even gone back to her apartment after the taping. She had arrived in St. Croix with the clothes on her back. Whatever she needed she bought on the island. She spoke to no one but the crew and sent no messages back to the States. For a week she simply slipped off the face of the earth.

Ryan rolled over on her back and dropped the sunglasses over her eyes. She knew that if she didn't force herself to think, the answer she needed would come to her in time. When it came, it would be right, and she would act on it. Until then, she waited.

In his workroom, Pierce shuffled and cut the Tarot cards. He needed to relax. The tension was eating at him.

After the taping he had searched the entire building for Ryan. When she was nowhere to be found, he had broken one of his own cardinal rules and had picked the lock on her apartment. He had waited for her through the next morning. She had never come home. It had driven him wild, furious. He'd let the rage take him, blocking out the pain. Anger, the undisciplined anger he never allowed himself, came in full force. Link had borne the brunt of his temper in silence.

It had taken Pierce days to regain his control. Ryan was gone, and he had to accept it. His own set of rules left him no choice. Even if he'd known where to find her, he couldn't bring her back.

In the week that had passed he had done no work. He had no power. Whenever he tried to focus his concentration, he saw only Ryan—felt her, tasted her. It was all he could conjure. He had to work his way back. Pierce knew if he didn't find his rhythm again soon he would be finished.

He was alone now, with Link and Bess honeymooning in the mountains. When he had regained some of his control, he had insisted they keep to their plans. He had sent them on their way, struggling to give them happiness while his own life loomed empty ahead of him.

It was time to go back to the only thing he had left. And even that brought a small trickle of fear. He was no longer sure he had any magic.

Setting the cards aside, Pierce rose to set up one of his more complicated illusions. He wouldn't test himself on anything simplistic. Even as he began to train his concentration, flex his hands, he looked up and saw her.

Pierce stared hard at the image. She had never come this clearly to him before. He could even hear her footsteps as she crossed the room to the stage. Her scent reached him first and had his blood humming. He wondered, almost dispassionately, if he were going mad.

"Hello, Pierce."

Ryan saw him jolt as if she had startled him out of a dream, "Ryan?" Her name on his lips was soft, questioning.

"Your front door wasn't locked, so I came in. I hope you don't mind."

He continued to stare at her and said nothing. She mounted the steps of the stage.

"I've interrupted your work."

Following her gaze, Pierce looked down at the glass vial in his hand and the colored cubes on the table.

"Work? It—no, it's all right." He set the vial down. He couldn't have managed the most basic illusion.

"This won't take long," Ryan told him with a smile. She had never seen him rattled and was all but certain she would never see him so again. "There's a new contract we need to discuss."

"Contract?" he repeated, unable to take his eyes from hers.

"Yes, that's why I've come."

"I see." He wanted to touch her but kept his hands on the table. He wouldn't touch what was no longer his. "You look well," he managed and started to offer her a chair. "Where have you been?" It was out before he could stop it; it was perilously close to an accusation. Ryan only smiled again.

"I've been away," she said simply, then took a step closer. "Have you thought of me?"

It was he who stepped back. "Yes, I've thought of you."

"Often?" The word was quiet as she moved toward him again.

"Don't, Ryan!" His voice was defensively sharp as he moved back.

"I've thought of you often," she continued as if he hadn't spoken. "Constantly, though I tried not to. Do you dabble in love potions, Pierce? Is that what you did to me?" She took another step toward him. "I tried very hard to hate you and harder still to forget you. Your magic's too strong."

Her scent whirled through his senses until they were all clouded with her. "Ryan, I'm only a man, and you're my weakness. Don't do this." Pierce shook his head and called on the last of his control. "I have work to do."

Ryan glanced at the table, then toyed with one of the colored cubes. "It'll have to wait. Do you know how many hours there are in a week?" she asked and smiled at him.

"No. Stop this, Ryan." The blood was pounding in his head. The need was growing unmanageable.

"A hundred and sixty-eight," she whispered. "A lot to make up for."

"If I touch you, I won't let you go again."

"And if I touch you?" She laid her hand on his chest.

"Don't," he warned quickly. "You should leave while you still can."

"You'll do that escape again, won't you?"

"Yes. Yes, damn it." His fingertips were tingling, demanding that he reach for her. "Ryan, for God's sake, go."

"You'll do it again," she went on. "And others, probably more dangerous, or at least more frightening, because that's who you are. Isn't that what you told me?"

"Ryan—"

"That's who I fell in love with," she said calmly. "I don't know why I thought I could or should try to change that. I told you once you were exactly what I wanted, that was the truth. But I suppose I had to learn what that meant. Do you still want me, Pierce?"

He didn't answer, but she saw his eyes darken, felt his heart speed under her hand. "I can leave and have a very calm, undemanding life." Ryan took the last step to him. "Is that what you want for me? Have I hurt you so much you wish me a life of unbearable boredom? Please, Pierce," she murmured, "won't you forgive me?"

"There's nothing to forgive." He was drowning in her eyes no matter how he struggled not to. "Ryan, for the love of God!" Desperate, he pushed her hand from his chest. "Can't you see what you're doing to me?"

"Yes, and I'm so glad. I was afraid you could really shut me out." She let out a quiet sigh of relief. "I'm staying, Pierce. There's nothing you can do about it." She had her arms around his neck and her mouth a breath away from his. "Tell me again that you want me to go."

"No." He dragged her against him. "I can't." His mouth was devouring hers. Power flowed into him again, hot and painful. He pressed her closer and felt her mouth respond to the savageness of his. "It's too late," he murmured. "Much too late." Excitement was burning through him. He couldn't hold her near enough. "I won't be able to leave the door open for you now, Ryan. Do you understand?"

"Yes. Yes, I understand." She drew her head back, wanting to see his eyes. "But it'll be closed for you, too. I'm going to see to it this is one lock you can't beat."

"No escape, Ryan. For either of us." And his mouth was on hers again, hot, desperate. He felt her give against him as he crushed her to him, but her hands were strong and sure on his body. "I love you, Ryan," he told her again as he roamed her face and neck with kisses. "I love you. I lost everything when you left me."

"I won't leave you again." She took his face in her hands to stop his wandering lips. "I was wrong to ask you what I did. I was wrong to run away. I didn't trust enough."

"And now?"

"I love you, Pierce, exactly as you are."

He pulled her close again and pressed his mouth to her throat. "Beautiful Ryan, so small, so soft. God, how I want you. Come upstairs, come to bed. Let me love you properly."

373 • Nora Roberts

Her pulses hammered at the quiet, rough words he spoke against her throat. Ryan took a deep breath, then, putting her hands on his shoulders, she pulled away. "There's the matter of a contract."

"The hell with contracts," he mumbled and tried to pull her back.

"Oh, no." Ryan stepped away from him. "I want this settled."

"I've already signed your contract," he reminded her impatiently. "Come here."

"This is a new one," she stated, ignoring him. "An exclusive life term."

He frowned. "Ryan, I'm not going to tie myself to Swan Productions for the rest of my life."

"Not Swan Productions," she countered. "Ryan Swan."

The annoyed retort on the tip of his tongue never materialized. She saw his eyes change, become intense. "What sort of contract?"

"A one-to-one, with an exclusivity clause and a lifetime term." Ryan swallowed, losing some of the confidence that had carried her this far.

"Go on."

"It's to begin immediately, with the provision of a legally binding ceremony to follow at the first reasonable opportunity." She laced her fingers together. "With a proviso for the probability of offspring." She saw Pierce's brow lift, but he said nothing. "The number of which is negotiable."

"I see," he said after a moment. "Is there a penalty clause?"

"Yes. If you try to break the terms, I'm allowed to murder you."

"Very reasonable. Your contract's very tempting, Miss Swan. What are my benefits?"

"Me."

"Where do I sign?" he asked, taking her in his arms again.

"Right here." She let out a sigh as she lifted her mouth. The kiss was gentle, promising. With a moan, Ryan drew closer.

"This ceremony, Miss Swan." Pierce nibbled at her lip as his hands began to roam. "What do you consider the first reasonable opportunity?"

"Tomorrow afternoon." She laughed and again pulled out of

his arms. "You don't think I'm going to give you time to find an escape hatch, do you?"

"I've met my match, I see."

"Absolutely," she agreed with a nod. "I have a few tricks up my sleeve." Lifting the Tarot cards, she surprised Pierce by fanning them with some success. She'd been practicing for months.

"Very good." He grinned and went to her. "I'm impressed."

"You haven't seen anything yet," she promised. "Pick a card," she told him, her eyes laughing. "Any card."

Bruce Wilder

Nora Roberts is the #1 *New York Times* bestselling author of more than 230 novels, including *Legacy, The Awakening, Hideaway, Under Currents,* The Chronicles of The One trilogy, and many more. She is also the author of the bestselling In Death series written under the pen name J. D. Robb. There are more than 500 million copies of her books in print.